────────●────────

This, for the memory of
PADRAIC PEARSE
patriot and martyr
for the cause of individual liberty
and equal justice in law
1916

The
Scalpel
and the
Sword

The Scalpel and the Sword

Dell Shannon

WILLIAM MORROW AND COMPANY, INC. · NEW YORK

C.2

———•———————•———

Library of Congress Cataloging-in-Publication Data

Shannon, Dell, 1921–
    The scalpel and the sword.
    1. Napoleonic Wars, 1800–1814—Fiction.   2. Ireland—History—1800–1837—Fiction.   I. Title.
PS3562.I515S32   1987   813'.54   86-31218
ISBN 0-688-07216-X

Printed in the United States of America

First Edition

1   2   3   4   5   6   7   8   9   10

BOOK DESIGN BY BARBARA MARKS

*Variable, and therfor miserable
condition of Man; this minute I was well, and am ill, this minute. I am surpriz'd by a sodaine change ... Is this the honour
which Man hath by being a little world, That he hath these
earthquakes in him selfe, sodaine shakings; these lightnings, sodaine flashes; these thunders ... Though you have by physike
and diet raked up the embers of your disease, still there is a feare
of a relapse.... It adds to the affliction that relapses are ... im-
puted to ourselves, as occasioned by some disorder in us; and so
we are not onely passive, but active, in our owne ruin; we doe
not onely stand under a falling house, but pull it downe upon
us; and we are not onely executed ... but we are execution-
ers.... For this life ... is a business, and a perplext business, a
warfare, and a bloody warfare, a voyage, and a tempestuous
voyage.*

—JOHN DONNE, *Devotions*

In the year 1798 the motley force of the United Irish Brotherhood mounted the largest and most ambitious rebellion in Ireland against British rule since Patrick Sarsfield and his army had laid down their arms in 1691, under promise of amnesty in a treaty immediately dishonored by England. The chief leader of the rebellion, Wolfe Tone, was in negotiation with France for arms and financial support, but this was largely intercepted by the British navy, and little came through to the United Irishmen. The insurrection was short-lived, and the fighting savage.

In the north the Protestant leader Henry McCracken, like others remaining alive, was hanged without trial along with many of his supporters. In the south and west of Ireland several of the leaders of the rebellion were militant Catholic priests; those who were captured and executed without trial were tortured on the rack and their bodies burned. There was no amnesty for any who had joined the United forces, and even years later, if their participation was proven, they were liable to hanging for treason.

Among the British army forces sent against the rebels were several Hessian regiments. These had been formed nearly thirty years before of the mercenary soldiers hired from Germany by George III prior to the American War of Independence. Some of the Hessians defected to the American cause during that war, and twenty-five years later, at the time of the 1798 rebellion, though these troops still bore the name, they were made up of regular British soldiers. At the battlefields of Vinegar Hill and Enniscorthy, two of the most savagely fought engagements of the rebellion, the Hessian companies ran berserk after the rebels' defeat, butchering and mutilating the wounded left on the field.

Five years later, in the summer of 1803, a new rebellion was being planned by the new patriot leader Robert Emmet and the cohorts remaining of the United Brotherhood. That rebellion never happened. Emmet, who was engaged to be married to Sarah, the daughter of the great Irish lawyer John Curran, came secretly to Dublin for a last meeting with her and was either betrayed or accidentally apprehended by the British authorities. He was hanged shortly afterward.

While awaiting his death, Emmet wrote a will in which he asked that no epitaph be written for him until his entire country should be released from foreign occupation and domination and could take her place among the roll of free nations.

That epitaph has never been written.

This story begins on the night of that hanging.

The Scalpel and the Sword

1

It was a small, shabby, separate house hid away in a narrow back street, and he'd not have known it was a tavern if he hadn't been told. No, Matthew wouldn't have brought him here before. The door stood ajar; he went into a dark little passage, and there was light under a door to his left, so he opened that and came into a largish room where twenty or thirty men sat about. There was a long counter at the end, with an elderly man behind it.

McDonagh walked up to that, aware of eyes on him. "Whiskey," he said.

The landlord poured it silently. There was no sudden cessation of talk, but that sort of feeling in the place. McDonagh swallowed half the whiskey and turned a leisurely survey around the room. "Has O'Breslin been in?" he asked the landlord.

"I'm not just sure I know the fellow y' mean—sir," said the man politely.

"Cathal O'Breslin," said McDonagh, and added in Gaelic, "I have a message for him."

There was a weedy young man, hollow chest, pale face, general effect of boniness and ill health—*rickets,* said McDonagh's mind, and the usual malformation—with a fiddle, sitting alongside the hearth, with a couple of other men. He scraped his bow thoughtfully on the strings, tightened a peg, loosened a peg. Several men turned from covert study of the newcomer to their glasses again. "Well, let me think," said the landlord slowly.

McDonagh wanted to swear at him. All this damn stupid caution and suspicion! Matthew so damned confident, you just go there and find O'Breslin, they'll know you're safe because you know the house, none other does. And for how long?—every minute these fellows would be expecting betrayal, and with reason. None of them was going to produce O'Breslin for a stranger's asking.

And by the same token, he wasn't going to risk giving Matt away until he was sure. Conal McDonagh wasn't exactly a public figure in Dublin, but plenty of people knew who he was and that he was connected with one Matthew DeLancey, who was valued at twenty pounds by the military justices. He turned an impatient stare on the landlord and then laughed. By God, if it came to that, if there were traitors about, he'd stepped into trouble already by being here.

"A friend of mine by the name of Matthew was wanting to see him," he said.

"Well, indeed," said the landlord noncommittally. "A common name it is. Maybe some of my regular patrons'd know him—either one, that's to say."

"Very likely," said McDonagh, and finished his whiskey, and shoved the glass back for refilling. The landlord looked at the empty glass interestedly, and McDonagh put a shilling on the counter. The landlord refilled the glass. "I wouldn't doubt it at all."

The man with the fiddle tucked it under his chin and began to play, very soft and slow. The tune was *The Croppy Boy.* McDonagh looked at the landlord, and the landlord met his gaze impersonally, blankly. Very probably, of course, there was at least one man in the place with a price on his head too, maybe more. "Well?" said McDonagh.

"I'm sorry, sir, I can't help you at all, not knowing either of the names," said the landlord.

"That's strange," said McDonagh gently. "I'd think the name of Matthew DeLancey might be known in Dublin, seeing it's posted up here and there—among others." You'd get nowhere swearing at the fellow. But all this playacting at secrecy, all this dark suspicion, these damned desperate fools!

"Ah, now, indeed," said the landlord, "that's a bad thing, isn't it." It was not a question. "I hear as that young fellow's father's a well-respected man, something in the medical way. A shock it must be to him." He shook his head.

McDonagh drank whiskey to keep from throwing it in the man's bland face. He said, "Not all so much of a shock, seeing as Matt was out five years back too. Seeing that Mr. DeLancey dug the musket ball out of Matt's leg—a bad job, a fortnight in as it was, and he'll go lame all his life. The left leg, midway between hip and knee. He took the ball at Enniscorthy—but there, I daresay that's only a name to you, good man."

The landlord dropped his eyes before McDonagh's somewhat ferocious grin, but before he could answer another man spoke. "Damn me eternally! I was trying to think where I'd see that pair o' shoulders afore, and Enniscorthy jogs my mind. A minute and I'll have the name now. You've growed a bit since—just a young 'un you were—"

"Sixteen," said McDonagh, looking down at a broken nose, a long jaw, and one sightless eye filmed, above a scraggy middle-aged body in laborers' garments.

"Aye, about, but you'd near your full growth. Nothing of a marksman you were, and the officer took the gun away from you, but a very pretty nasty hand with the knife you had—for all you're educated. McDonagh," said the man triumphantly. "A black Protestant out of Ulster, and you'd shirked classes at the college school in Dublin to come out with us."

"I couldn't call your name, but I know your face—what's left of it."

The man grinned. "Brian Fitzroy, and pleased to see you again. All right, Jem"—to the landlord. "I'll vouch for him—he knows Matt DeLancey safe enough, they came out together."

"An old United man," said McDonagh sardonically. "How many of them have taken English money since?"

"A few," said Fitzroy briefly. "You bringing it up, I don't reckon you're one of them." He jerked his head. "Come and sit down private and we'll have a talk."

The fiddler changed over to *The Rising of the Moon* and a little, faintly relieved mutter of conversation rose. McDonagh followed Fitzroy across to the other corner of the hearth, to a tall settle, and they sat down. For a while the other man was silent. Then he said, "A lucky thing I was here. Jem can be close-mouthed."

"That I gathered. Damn and blast Matt DeLancey!" said McDonagh.

"Always an optimist he is. He used to come here once or twice a month. I can't call to mind you've ever been with him."

"And I would not be here now except for a reason you can guess."

One of the men sitting with the fiddler began to sing in a surprising clear tenor voice. He was halfway drunk, but not in his voice; or maybe liquor improved it. "Indeed, is that the way of it," said Fitzroy.

"I came along Green Street this afternoon."

"And saw a man hanging on a gallows, you would. It was about high noon they hanged him there, and I saw it, I saw him. His name is Robert Emmet, and he came to say good-bye to his sweetheart afore he escaped into France—just as the soldiers reckoned he would."

"Or just as a traitor told them. I may live next a racetrack," said McDonagh, "but I don't gamble against odds when every race is fixed beforehand by the judges."

Fitzroy swallowed beer and said, "I mind Matt's said how a fella with him at Enniscorthy fetched him home safe, against odds. Would that've been yourself?" He glanced sidewise at McDonagh.

"Five years back," said McDonagh with a shrug. "Let's talk about now."

"Ah," said Fitzroy, "just so ... Sean sings the better with more drink in him."

"Matt's a trade to practice, but he can't use it here and now."

"Ah, yes," said Fitzroy. "Sure enough, a bone sawer he is, like his father afore, isn't it? And maybe yourself?"

"And maybe myself. Tonight I am interested in live men, not dead ones."

"Why, damn, do we look like a crew of dirty corpse snatchers? Only decent respectable men come here."

"Oh, I know, I know!" said McDonagh. "Old United men! Well?"

The fiddler passed into some aimless fancy scales and runs, and several voices urged Sean to sing more. Fitzroy swallowed beer and said, "Matt is wanting to get out of Dublin, I daresay."

"And out of Ireland. With his name known, he can't practice here." One of the reaons Matt was a damned fool, but McDonagh didn't say so to Fitzroy. "He's thinking of going to America."

"Oh, yes, another one going off," said Fitzroy. "A man's got to live, and if he's a skilled trade and reputation, he needs to use it, sure. What else can he do but go off from home? But it's a bad thing for the country, McDonagh, so it is. So many of the best of us going other places. The ones with the guts and the brains and the ambition."

"There's nothing here," said McDonagh savagely. Nothing but unorganized hordes of damned fool idealists, throwing fixed dice with a gang of thieves and never learning that the thieves were bound to keep the upper hand, having all the money in the pot and knowing how the dice would fall.

"There will never be," said Fitzroy equably, "if all of us with the spirit left to us are run out away. Enough of them are dead. There has got to be some faith in God about it, boy. I'm not blaming Matt, mind you—I see how he's situated. But some of us have got to stay and carry on the good work."

"Now let's see," said McDonagh, "it's getting on to six hundred years' worth of work, isn't it?"

"And it might be a thousand afore we're done," said Fitzroy indifferently. "There's a saying about the mills of God."

The man called Sean began to sing again; he leaned on the mantelpiece casual and unsteady, with a blank, rapt look, and his sweet tenor rose clear on the inexpressibly sorrowful melody.

> *'Twas on the Belfast mountains I heard a maid*
>   *complain,*
> *And she vexed the sweet June evening with her*
>   *heartbroken strain,*
> *Saying, Woe is me, life's anguish is more than*
>   *I can dree—*

"O'Breslin," said Fitzroy, "has an uncle that runs a fishing boat along the channel."

> *Since Henry Joy McCracken died on the*
>   *gallows tree.*

"Matt is thinking to get to Plymouth or Liverpool and join some merchant ship there, desert in New York."
"So I reckoned."

> *When news came from Greencastle of a good ship*
>   *anchored nigh,*
> *'Twas down by yon green mountain-glen we met to*
>   *say good-bye.*

"Well, for God's sake . . ." began McDonagh angrily. All this cross talk! He wanted it done and arranged. The terrible sweet melancholy of the song pierced him like a knife, and that was another damned stupid thing.
"In a minute we'll see," said Fitzroy absently. "I never knew McCracken. They say he was a good man—some very pretty fighting he did at Antrim—the while we was busy in Wexford."

> *That night I climbed the Cavehill and watched*
>   *till morning blazed,*
> *And when its fires had kindled, across the*
>   *loch I gazed—*
> *I saw an English tender at anchor off Garmoyle,*
> *But alas, no ship to bear him away to France's soil.*

"Let's try to forget Wexford, in God's name," said McDonagh violently. He never would. The men maimed, the men dead. Thousands of them. The beautiful intricate cunning bodies, still hiding so many puzzles from science, all broken and spoiled. *A very pretty nasty hand with the knife.* Yes, you destroyed too, in fear of your own life and possessed by the fine blaze of violence, and afterward—afterward . . .

> *And twice that night a tramping came up the old*
> *shore road,*
> *'Twas Ellis and his yeomen, false Niblock with them*
> *strode—*
> *My father home returning the doleful story told—*

"Oh, a good fight's a cheerful thing to remember," said Fitzroy.

> *Oh, alas, says he, young Harry Joy for fifty pounds*
> *is sold!*

"I want to talk with this O'Breslin," said McDonagh, hanging on to his temper, "to arrange for getting Matt away."

"I had collected that," said Fitzroy. The singer ended his ballad and sat down to drink. "O'Breslin—step over a minute, would you?"

The weedy young fiddler put down his instrument, picked up his glass, and strolled across to them. "The name is McDonagh," said Fitzroy. "A friend of Matt DeLancey as you heard."

O'Breslin nodded. He had a hollow chest and a bad cough. There might be some congenital trouble there, but it was mostly the kind of thing you saw when there had been malnutrition in childhood. The bones would be mildly interesting to an anatomist, and it might not be too long before an anatomist saw them. Twenty-eight or thirty, O'Breslin might be, and he was a good fiddler. "Matt's thinking of getting away by my uncle's boat," he guessed casually. "Is he nearby enough to leave tomorrow night?" Politely he did not ask exactly where Matt was.

"Yes, he could."

"That's lucky," said the fiddler. "Uncle's off on tomorrow's late tide, and he can make for Plymouth as easy as anywhere else, and attend to fishing afterward. You tell Matt to meet me here round about ten tomorrow night. I'll take him to the right wharf and fix it up with Uncle meanwhile."

"Good enough," said McDonagh. "How much would it cost? Matt said he wouldn't put the man out for nothing."

O'Breslin smiled faintly. "This is very ill luck for Matthew, Mr. McDonagh. For all the men who were in on Mr. Emmet's plans, but maybe more on Matthew. He can't use his right name or work here anymore, and then too this will be a great grief to his father—even though he knew, and kept hands off Matthew's affairs."

"Mr. DeLancey is dead," said McDonagh, sharp and bitter. "Ten days ago."

"I'm sorry to hear that indeed. I hear he was a fine man. So Matt's really nothing to hold him, and he's best away. There've been eighteen too many hangings here the last while." The slight smile was fixed. "Matthew'll need what money he has when he gets to where he's going, Mr. McDonagh. Uncle will take him over to England. Tell him to be here tomorrow night at ten."

McDonagh said stiffly, "He'll thank you himself, but I'm grateful too. I'll tell him."

O'Breslin nodded and went back to his fiddle. McDonagh stood up abruptly. "Well, that's that. Thanks, Fitzroy."

"Could I buy you a drink?"

"Thanks, no. I'll get back and tell Matt." He was glad to be out in the cold dark again, away from the piercing sad music and the shabby, odorous room and the miasma of accepted tragedy over the men in it. This was a day they'd seen again the end of something, again a leader taken from them and killed, to add another name to the list of names they preserved as martyrs. The fiddler and the singer would be making a new mournful ballad about that man. Men would go on singing it for a long time, and making more desperate, grim little plans, and hiding weapons; and the spies would go on destroying, and the fools being fools, and there would be more men hanging on the gallows tree. All for nothing, damn all.

Except to save the anatomy teachers a little money. The price of corpses, to professional resurrection men, was always low in Dublin; there were so many legal sources and always so many corpses. Off the gallows, out of the workhouses and orphanages. Good fresh corpses, in prime state to be laid open and have the dyed liquid wax pumped into vein and artery—to teach students the intricacies of bone and muscle, so that they could better repair the damage brought to them when live men had shot and knifed and mauled each other later on, all over again. There was a saying about an ill wind.

McDonagh strode fast down the dark streets, against a cold wind. He did not think he had been followed; they weren't that patient or interested in one man. They had come and searched the house three weeks back, when they'd had Matt's name from one of those they caught, and doubtless they'd kept an eye on Mr. William DeLancey and his household; but when nothing came of it, they'd have left off. They didn't know about the little blocked-off wine cellar in the basement room. He would feel easier when Matt was safely away; but it wasn't his business, and he'd been a damned fool to involve himself this far. Only he owed something to Mr. DeLancey, even if he and Matt had not been friends.

He went straight back to the old house in Duke William Street, unlocked the front door and stepped into a dark entry. He thought, Safely away. Another one going off. God, this dirty, drab, grim country washed over with the color of tragedy and poverty and violence! He would not delay long after Matt; there was nothing here for any man. The house was empty of servants now; he had got rid of them last week. It was all finished here now, for him and Matt. Ten to one Matt was roaming around in the dark, waiting.

"Con?"

"Suppose I'd been an officer? You can't see me, you fool. Embroil both of us and ruin two careers instead of one." He tripped over a chair and swore and found the candles on the table.

"Where's the British officer could get the key off Con McDonagh?" Matt laughed. "I heard no explosions in the city, so I surmised you'd not been stopped or put to any trouble." He grinned at McDonagh amiably in the growing candlelight, a fair, blunt-featured man a couple of years the senior.

"I do not," said McDonagh distinctly, "lose my temper oftener than any man."

"Maybe it just seems that way, on account of your having more temper to lose?" Matt DeLancey sat down in the desk chair and commenced to fill his pipe, looking up at McDonagh affectionately, amusedly. "Every other big bruiser I ever met was slow to rouse—they get in the way of it, hold back the power in them for fear of hurting somebody unintentional, y' know—but you fight back at everything. Damn me if you don't need to get fighting mad at a fracture before you can set it, or a starched shirt before you can get it on straight, eh? Kill yourself with an aneurysm you will one day, you great black bastard." He offered his tobacco pouch.

McDonagh slammed open the cupboard in the corner and brought out whiskey, poured two glasses. He looked at Matt between anger and exasperation, hooked the other chair from under the desk with his foot and sat down. "So I'm a damned fool too? Never so goddamned a fool as Matt DeLancey! It's all arranged—you're to meet O'Breslin tomorrow night at ten, and his uncle will ferry you over. You can then spoil your hands at common sailor's work across the Atlantic to your new spiritual home."

"Good. Why spiritual?"

"These Christ-damned idealistic patriots!" said McDonagh, and drank. "Judging from hearsay, America's nearly as full of the breed as Ireland. Granted, they made a better job of fighting clear of Mother England, but you won't find their bold new world much different from the old one."

"I wonder," said Matt placidly. "They've founded it on some grand precepts anyway."

"Oh, the best thing politicians do is talk. And I'll be damned if I argue politics with you this time of night—or any other time." He added abruptly, "I'm sorry for it to end like this, Matt."

"I'm almost relieved Father's gone," said the other quietly, nodding. "He didn't see eye to eye with me over politics, but he never interfered, did he? Even when I persuaded you into the rebel army in '98. We had the rough side of his tongue, that's all. And shall I say I was very damn lucky you were there—and the stubborn son of a hound you are—and very damn lucky to get home five years back. You've said it often enough: once bit, twice shy. But somebody has to fight for the truth, my boyo, and go on fighting, damn the odds. If it's only out of stubbornness. I was sorry all this had to break when Father was ill, but at least I'll not be worrying about him now."

"There is that."

"Made up your mind what to do for yourself?"

"Yes, I've made up my mind," said McDonagh hardly. "I've got to get out of this damned country, I can't stay here." He massaged his temples, where a dull ache pounded. "This damned place," he said in a half whisper. "Half the people mourning and the other half plotting! Goddamned stupid romantics." Matt went on smoking quietly, looking at him.

It was all finished, this part of his life. He had come to Dublin from Belfast six years ago, through the offices of a surgeon friend of his father's, to train under William DeLancey. He'd had the best training that way, too. Not only the standard lectures at Trinity, but practical work at Queens' Hospital and apprenticeship in the old style to a working surgeon.... He was only a youngster five years ago, Matt filling him up with his own brand of windy patriotism; he should have had more sense than to listen; but all experience was grist to the mill, let it go, and he'd never be caught again by that particular emotionalism.

He didn't remember his mother—she was eight years dead when he came to Dublin—and his father fell at Antrim with McCracken's rebel forces. He had respected William DeLancey as a surgeon; like Matt, he could feel curious relief that the old man had died peacefully. He had lived here for six years with them; since six months ago he was an accredited surgeon, in practice here with Matt. He could stay and starve, trying to build a practice on his own, but even if the auspices had been favorable, he would not; he wanted violently to get out of Ireland.

More training and experience never came amiss. He'd learned more from Mr. DeLancy than from the classes at Trinity or staff work at Queens'; Dublin was scarcely reckoned one of the centers of medical teaching. Postgraduate work at a London hospital, that was something to think of for the future. And there was no big money here, not even the smell of a reasonable living, and he meant to make money and a name for himself. He would, by God. Not for just the one reason, but that was part of it, so that one day that pompous bastard Amison might regret he hadn't let his daughter marry Conal McDonagh, on the excuse that he'd nothing to offer her. Damn it, he had Conal McDonagh to offer her!

Lauretta. She had sailed for England two months ago, with a retinue of relatives, to marry the respectable snob Amison had picked for her, FitzEustace. Damn the lot of them, taking advantage of her right and left—damn his father for not bearing a high-sounding English name—damn everything.

"Well?" said Matt. "I might drop you a letter now and again if I knew where you were."

"I'm going to London," said McDonagh. "There's money to be had in England." He felt a sudden sharp and pressing need, irrelevant at this moment, for a woman.

"What are you thinking of in particular?"

"A woman," said McDonagh absently, and Matt laughed.

"When aren't you? But I was going to say, robbing the Bank of England?"

"Not immediately," said McDonagh. He would not go out tonight after a harlot, Matt's last night in Dublin. He stretched out his legs and contemplated his boots. "I don't fancy trying to build up a practice here. England's just gone to war with France again, and they'll be recommissioning navy ships and outfitting regiments hand over fist. There'll be jobs for surgeons in the service, easy had. I don't know what the pay might be, but it'd likely be more than I'd make here starting new, and there's always a chance of plunder in war."

"That's so."

"I'll need to present my credentials at the Royal College, and you might write me there—I daresay they'd pass on a letter."

"On second thought, better not maybe—do you no good to be linked with a renegade."

"Don't be a damn fool," said McDonagh. "They've got better things to do than pry into private letters. Get in touch that way at least."

"All right," said Matt amiably. "Con, I'd like for you to take Father's instruments. Mine are newer, and someone might as well have the set. I know you've not afforded to buy some of what you want."

"Well, I won't take the lot—we'll divide. Thanks, Matt, I'll be glad of that."

They smoked in silence for a while. "You'll maybe get more patients than you bargain for, as a military surgeon. Interesting."

"I don't doubt it. While you starve to death waiting for farmers to get trodden on by oxen."

"Oh, I don't know. There are some good-sized towns in the American states," said Matt. "If I give you a piece of advice, will you hold your temper?" He grinned at McDonagh. "Just take it easy, Con, wherever you end. You can't do everything at once, you know. If you get a place, don't go throwing your weight around with superior ranks, see, or lecturing the senior surgeon on compound fractures."

"And when do I ever—"

"Every time you open your mouth," said Matt.

"I've some common sense," said McDonagh mildly.

Matt poured himself more whiskey thoughtfully. "I expect you're right about the rearming. They're running a fever over Bonaparte, and I wouldn't say they're wrong. I do wonder if England might come out holding the dirty end of the stick this time."

McDonagh laughed abruptly. "Don't you know there's a rule about that? Mother England never comes out the wrong end of things. Never happened nor never will happen—the devil looks after his own."

"I am just superstitious enough," said Matt wryly, "almost to believe that."

"I don't give a damn about it this way or that way," said

McDonagh. "Patriotism is the panacea of fools." He contemplated this statement with a grin, partly at his own pompousness. "The politicians sell it to the lower orders to keep them satisfied with the state in which Providence sees fit to place 'em. My God in heaven, who says it's Providence's notion?—the politicians! They sell it to everybody for their own crooked personal advantage—fine words that mean just damn all. And to keep 'em convinced of their superiority to foreigners—which is to say suspicious of foreigners—because every now and then the big fellows've got to promote a war, you know, to keep things running smooth at home. Business falling off a bit, too many out of work, ungrateful lower classes grumbling about reform— shorter hours and privileges—hey, presto, like the street conjurers—blow up a war and take their minds off. Make 'em believe they're the greatest folk in the world, account of being Britishers—or Irish—or French—or Russian—and they'll put up with any hellish treatment from their own leaders. Go out and fight like demons for a country that keeps them living like animals and starving in the gutter—and count it a sacred privilege, account of all the windy patriotism they've had pumped into them. Oh, it's a damned good lay—for the politicians and upper classes!"

"You think all the rest are fools," said Matt a little sadly.

"Yes, they're fools, but it's not all their own blame, poor devils. And you know, if you've been shoved into an army willy-nilly and sent out to fight and maybe die in any of a thousand messy ways, it's some kind of comfort to believe you're dying for something—if it's only the principle of British superiority—or French—or Russian—let alone all the politicians' talk about truth and right and freedom."

"Well," said Matt. He prodded at his pipe a moment and then said without looking up, "It's like old Canning, seems to me. Such a cautious old fellow, way out o' date, of course, never changed any of his ideas since he was apprenticed to a barber-surgeon forty years back—remember how Father used to say, take Canning's lectures with a liberal helping o' salt? That demonstration lecture of his on amputation, must've given it a thousand times. I believe the old fellow could do it in his sleep—how did that part go?" He drew in his chin and dropped his voice to pomposity. " 'The greatest care must be taken, gentlemen, to cut well above the wound, through sound flesh and bone, in order to ensure uncomplicated recovery of the patient.' That bit always got Father's back up, didn't it? He used to say, doubtless in Canning's day you got a shattered anklebone and amputated above the knee. I reckon—like that—when you talk about patriotism, Con—you're cutting off a bit too much. Some truth in what you say, but less than you make out."

"I said I wouldn't argue politics with you," said McDonagh, shrugging. "Let's sort out those instruments. What about the house?"

"Nothing about the house. The lease is up for renewal in two years—let it go—I won't be here for the owner to sue. I take it you won't be delaying long after me."

"You take it right. I'll try to get off on Wednesday's packet to Liverpool."

2

When the mail-packet left on the late tide, McDonagh was on her foredeck, looking out to sea past the great shadowy hump of the Sugar Loaf. It was symbolic, he scoffed at himself; nothing to see in the dark anyway, but he would not look back. He was done with his own country. He'd known some good men and good times there; it was not all bitterness behind him. But there was enough that it seemed to him the whole land lay under a thin fog of fear and despair. He was glad to leave it; the good and the bad he would remember, but put away as catalogued past.

Matt had got away two nights ago, and maybe with luck was now in some merchant bound for New York. Good luck to him; they had been friends, and would not likely meet again. Little had remained for McDonagh to do in Dublin: shut the house, leave the key with a neighbor. He'd no private farewells to make. There was nothing left for him in Ireland. His father's law-office had been rented; the house he had owned in Belfast, whatever money he had had, had been confiscated after the '98 rebellion. McDonagh had twenty-two pounds twelve shillings on him, a small wardrobe, his surgeon's certificate and case of instruments.

He looked to sea, but he thought, briefly, of his father's house in Belfast, of the look of the green steep country about, dotted with lakes; of gray, busy, raffish Dublin and his years there. The chilly gloom of the lecture room and the dissecting hall; the degree examinations; his first live patients—by courtesy, he a bit nervous under Mr. DeLancey's kindly eye and absurdly pleased with small praise afterward. The little warlock's cave of an apothecary shop where he had worked in spare time, making up odd prescriptions, to earn his tuition fees and money for books. The first girl he had had in Dublin, and the last one. And going out with the great rebel army five years ago—that savage fiasco, ten thousand men dead and their war lost all because the French support came too late, or not at all.

He thought of all that and took his mind from it to think about the future. The hell with any homesickness, he told himself with a wry smile; he'd nothing to be homesick for. When the packet had cleared the Sugar Loaf and stood out in the channel, he went below out of the night wind to the tiny cabin and slept sound.

He was lucky in Liverpool and caught a stage just leaving for London. It decanted him in the courtyard of a busy tavern at midday two days later; he judged the inn too expensive, and set off to locate lodgings. Eventually he hired a room in White Cross Street, at eight shillings the week; it was a middle-class lodging house, quiet and reasonably clean.

Not being interested in gawking about at London like any raw sightseer—a dirty city, what he'd seen of it—he left his bags locked in his room, came out to find a tavern, had a scratch meal, and asked directions for the Royal College of Surgeons. After meeting several blank looks, he was directed to the Old Bailey, and wandered two miles out of his way in this damned rabbit warren of a town before finding the street half a mile from where he'd been.

The middle-aged clerk on duty in the foyer was vague. "I expect you'd best see Mr. Dane, sir. 'E'll know all about it, I daresay. I really don't know the procedure, sir, but my cousin's a clerk at the War Office, and I do know, it's what you might call fatal, sir, to start off on the wrong foot, as you might say, there. Great ones for 'avin' everything all haccording to regulations, if you see what I mean, sir."

"I don't doubt it," said McDonagh. "Could I see Mr. Dane now?"

" 'E ort to be in very shortly, sir, 'e's a class at St. Bartholomew's afternoons, but 'e did say 'e'd drop back later." A uniformed attendant entered, and the clerk beckoned him, beaming sympathetically at McDonagh. "Tell you what, sir, suppose you 'as a nice look rahnd our museum—I make sure you 'eard of our museum, all sorts o' things to interest surgical gentlemen in it—Will 'ere 'e'll show you rahnd, and I'll tell Mr. Dane when 'e comes in."

"Oh, very well." McDonagh was not much interested in the museum, but he did not want to waste time; he could not afford to. "Thanks very much."

"Not at all, sir. Will, you take an' show the gentleman O'Brien. He'll want to see O'Brien."

"Ow, yes," said Will enthusiastically, "everybody allus wants to see O'Brien."

"And you being an Irishman yerself," added the clerk, "you'll be the more interested maybe."

"Really," said McDonagh.

" 'E's the first thing," went on Will, holding the inner door for him politely, "as every visitor allus hasks for, sir. We've come to think of O'Brien as a kind of mascot, hif you hunnerstand me, sir. Hespecially as so many surgical gentlemen was so 'ot after 'im, you see. Prestige, that's what O'Brien gives our museum, as you can unnerstand."

"And who the hell is O'Brien?" asked McDonagh, annoyed at this assumption of knowledge.

Will gave him an astonished look. "You never 'eard of O'Brien, sir? Well—well, 'ere 'e is." They had come into a long, dim, vaulted hall, with glass cases and wall shelves about; the attendant gestured.

"Good God in heaven!" said McDonagh. He looked at O'Brien, fascinated. It was an enormous articulated skeleton; it must be over seven feet high, and it was mounted on a pedestal for further impressiveness.

"Yes, sir," said Will, gratified. "You may well say so, sir. Seven feet seven inches, sir. There's many a medical gentleman as well as surgeons come 'undreds o' miles to see 'im."

"No wonder. Where did the college locate him?" McDonagh went around to look at O'Brien from behind.

"Ah, that's quite a story, sir. Owe it all to Mr. John Hunter, we do. You'll know of Mr. Hunter, sir—"

"Every surgeon knows of Mr. Hunter."

"Yes, sir, a fine man 'e were. Peppery, I don't deny, an' 'e 'ad 'is queernesses, but a very deep-thinking gentleman. Mr. Hunter, 'e saw O'Brien at a fair, you see—that is, while the poor fella was alive—and 'e were just set on 'aving the skeleton, see. He knowed, as I daresay I needn't hexplain to you, as these freaks like, they don't general live very long, and so to get in afore anyun else, he tries for a deal with O'Brien, to leave 'isself to the college when 'e goes. Well, they do say as poor O'Brien were just terrified, sir, of Mr. Hunter's getting 'ands on 'is bones, and 'e led Mr. Hunter a merry chase hall over England, an' tried to fix things so as he'd be buried decent in one piece. But Mr. Hunter, sir, 'e were a Scotchman, you know, and to say no to 'im, well, it were just about like prodding a bull with a stick. And o' course, every hospital and most anatomists in England, they was after O'Brien, too. Come to think, the poor fella didn't 'ave a very 'appy last few years."

McDonagh grinned. "I don't suppose so."

"But Mr. Hunter diddled them all. 'E 'ad a man follerin' O'Brien, they say, for two years, to make sure of 'im. And when 'e 'ad word as O'Brien was on his deathbed, 'e hops rahnd with a carriage and collects the corpse afore it's cold, and just got out from under the noses of a gang of gentlemen from St. Bartholomew's Hospital, 'oo chased 'im all the way—a rowdy lot they are down there—and 'e locks 'isself into 'is workroom, and pops O'Brien into a boiler afore the cat could lick 'er ear."

"Good for Mr. Hunter! Pity he hadn't time to take more care, I see the boiling has turned O'Brien brown."

"Yes, sir, there's others 'ave said the same. But there 'e is, hafter all, and we're mighty proud of him."

"Don't blame you at all, he's magnificent."

McDonagh spent a contented-enough half hour with O'Brien and was summoned to the private room of Mr. Dane, one of the senior surgeons, who was elderly, businesslike, and impersonal.

"I may say I think you choose a wise course, Mr. McDonagh. I see you are but newly qualified, and some regular appointment is certainly preferable to—ah—potential private practice." His smile was wintry but sympathetic. "Moreover, you should, of course, acquire useful experience with the army or navy. Your credentials will be filed, and the correct procedure for you is to go to the medical division of the War Office—they are handling all the applications for both military and naval medical men. Good luck to you."

McDonagh took a hackney to the War Office, in defiance of his slim purse; he was tired of plodding about London. He emerged into Pall Mall two hours later with a fine black rage seething in him, which he had managed to conceal from the various people he had seen. Taking applications for surgeons? Reckon that were so, but exactly which office might be concerned, well, that were a puzzle. Here, Rob, d'you know where—? Might be you best go hup the stair to the general supply office, they'd know. . . . Forms for application? Well, yes, it was very likely, very likely indeed, that there would be new vacancies for surgeons—yes, army and navy both—but no recent general orders had come through here. Perhaps he had best go direct to the office of medical supply—oh, that was where he had been told to come?—yes, and see the senior officer. Mr. Whyte, would you kindly show the gentleman the way? . . . Most certainly, both arms of the service would be needing surgeons and were already taking numbers of applications. But Mr. McDonagh must be aware—ha-ha!—that government departments tended to caution and somewhat less than celerity in these matters. Yes, rearming and recruiting in all branches were going on, and the pace gave signs of stepping up a bit, with all this furor over the reputed massing of Bonaparte's troops and guns at Boulogne—what did Mr. McDonagh think of that, eh?

Damn impudent frogs, never knew when they were beat. Not that Boney should be underestimated indeed. Well, yes, Mr. McDonagh could fill out an application form if he wished, but as to when he might hear anything about an appointment to service—in any case, he would be examined first and interviewed, and as to when he might be summoned for that, there was simply no knowing. If Mr. McDonagh knew the War Office as the senior officer of medical supply knew it, he would realize that there never was any knowing. However, Mr. McDonagh was welcome to leave an application.

"I'm to report back then from time to time?"

"Oh, well," said the senior officer vaguely.

"Thanks very much," said McDonagh grimly. "I'll do so." By God, he would report back every day until they were so sick of the sight of him they'd give him a place to be rid of him!

And meantime— He had another meal and a few drinks at a tavern. He had discovered that it was impossible to get whiskey in London inns; if you wanted anything stronger than ale, you ordered gin, which added to his gloom. He drank the gin quickly to escape its flavor and mentally counted his money. He couldn't hang about forever waiting for a job, and if he would have starved in Dublin waiting for enough private patients, he would starve sooner in London.

Give it a fortnight, he decided philosophically; if the War Office hadn't placed him by then, he'd look for a quick job to tide him over, with an apothecary again or something like that. Sure to God even the War Office wouldn't delay overlong, when it was rearming all the other branches, to take in surgeons for the new ships and regiments.

And meantime, tonight, he would go to see Lauretta. He came out to darkness—the dusk was early at the tail of the year—and, stumbling on the threshold, cursed the crude, sharp gin; didn't go mellow in a man like whiskey, but he wasn't near drunk, nobody could say that. He found a hackney and told the man to drive to Queen Square.

That was where FitzEustace's house was, damn him. "Queen Square," Lauretta had said. "It sounds very elegant, does it not?" Doubtless it was. FitzEustace was a gentlemen, with landholdings outside Dublin but living mostly in London. Fitz-Eustace knew the best people; FitzEustace didn't have to work for a living. FitzEustace was a goddamned bastard.

When the hack set him down, he realized he didn't know which house in the square was FitzEustace's. He knocked at the nearest door and asked, and was directed to number four. He looked at number four doubtfully. "By God," he said aloud to himself, "the bastard must've wanted her dower." Thought FitzEustace was a rich man, but this didn't look like a rich man's house. It was of modest size and far from new; the square was obviously respectable, but none of the houses in it was grand. By God, a joke on pompous old Amison if he'd saved his daughter from marriage with one impecunious fellow to hand her over to another! . . . Shouldn't think jesting that way about Lauretta.

He knocked, and a parlormaid came and told him that Master and Mistress FitzEustace were gone out to the theater. McDon-agh swore, groped his way out of the square, and failed to find another hackney, lost in a maze of dark residential streets. He got back to White Cross Street at midnight, in a black temper.

His mother had had a piece of French bisque; it sat on the mantelpiece in the Belfast house. It was a shepherdess, in a wide hat and flounced skirt, with a long crook in one delicate hand. He wondered what had happened to it; no matter; but Lauretta always made him think of the fragile shepherdess.

He hadn't much talent for hiding his feelings, and probably Matt and Mr. DeLancey and a host of others knew how he felt about Lauretta Amison, from the first time he'd seen her away last year. Never said anything to him, which was just as well. All in white, she'd been, smiling and greeting guests in her pretty, soft voice. Amison was an acquaintance of Mr. DeLan-cey's; his son had been at school with Matt; the DeLancey household was not quite of social class to compare, but just now and then, when the Amisons needed a couple of extra young men for a dance, a stiff little invitation would be sent. Never for the dinner, only among the lesser guests asked for the evening dance afterward.

McDonagh had never been backward with females, but he'd

never met anyone like Lauretta either. You didn't think of her the way you thought of the kind of women that came to mind when you thought of, well, *women*. Well, he liked women, that kind, but it didn't mean one damned thing, very deep, of course. Different when it came to real feeling about it, to loving.

And damn it, damn it, it wasn't fair, when she loved him back, his darling, or said she did. A man with his way to make, maybe he hadn't comfort and servants and money to offer her, but if Amison had been reasonable, said, we'll give you five years to get somewhere—let him prove himself, he was willing to work and wait for Lauretta. Damn Amison and all social convention. Unthinkable not to have a daughter married at over twenty, as she'd be. And Lauretta being Lauretta, well, it was too much to expect her to defy her father and elope with him. She'd wept when she told him about FitzEustace, but she'd been even more terrified of running away—afraid of Amison, was the plain truth, damn him. A gentle-bred girl, and so little and soft she was, but damn it, to marry her to a man she scarce knew but as a casual caller ...

He'd been angry with her for being afraid, but he couldn't bear seeing her cry. Couldn't expect Lauretta to do such a thing as elope, she'd scarce had to make a decision in her life, and wasn't it for her sweet, soft nature he loved her? But—but—

At least he'd induced her to meet him to say good-bye, two months ago. Not the hell of a success it had been, he remembered gloomily. It was a cold day, and they met in the park, and she was afraid of being seen by some acquaintance. She'd cried again and said she was a coward for being afraid to run away with him, and she'd always love him dearly and remember him, and he was to forget her and be happy, and she couldn't stay because she was expected home for a gown fitting. Two days later she had sailed for England, to her fine London wedding, and McDonagh had gone out and gotten himself drunk.

He was cynic enough to tell himself now that he was a damned romantic fool and dreamer, to entertain vague fancies of making a great name and fortune for himself and FitzEustace conveniently dying off at the same time. Things didn't happen so, and anyway, surgeons never got hold of fortunes, however damned good they were—and he was a good surgeon, and he'd be better—they were lucky to earn a living wage.

But to hell with convention, he'd see her again at least. If she wasn't happy—how could she be happy?—damn it, she was young, she might settle down contented enough, soft and submissive as she was: if so, well, it wasn't McDonagh's part to make trouble. But he'd want to see and be sure.

Number 4 Queen Square. Not a very elegant house, as he'd imagined it. Wonder if FitzEustace was up to something. But by God, of course, it wasn't that FitzEustace had so damned much more to offer her; it was just that he was an English gentleman and a better match, money or no.

Damn the lot of them, bloody fine gentlemen, one day they'd know the name of Conal McDonagh.

McDonagh never paid much attention to clothes, but that morning he dressed for FitzEustace, damn him—just in the event the man was at home. He wanted and didn't want to be confronted with FitzEustace. He scowled at himself in the cracked glass, struggling with his neckcloth; nobody could call Con McDonagh handsome, but at least you couldn't miss him— he looked a bad-tempered tough in the glass, black hair needing trimming and perennial blue chin. The hell with FitzEustace, he'd look down his nose at provincial Con McDonagh no matter clothes or manners. But he donned his best gray breeches, narrow to the ankle and strapped over shoes, and his best blue coat, steel-buttoned and cut away to short tails in new fashion.

He presented himself at number 4 Queen Square at eleven o'clock, and this time was admitted; the parlor room where the maid left him was well enough furnished in somewhat heavy style. He stood in the middle of it, waiting.

When Lauretta came, she stopped just inside the door and said, "Oh, Conal," in a trembling voice. "I—I didn't know you were coming to London—you oughtn't come to see me."

"Well, damn it, as long as I'm here I can call on my acquaintances, can't I?" said McDonagh roughly. His heart twisted for her fragile slimness in a blue sprigged gown, her amber fine hair as always escaping to little tendrils curling about her face. She was a slight little thing, fair, and her blue eyes were swimming in tears, so that he caught hold of her hand and kissed it and swore again. "Love, love," he said, "don't cry, I never meant to make you cry! I just had to see you again, see if you're unhappy. Lauretta—"

"Oh, please"—and she drew her hand away with a little gasp—"you mustn't, Con. I—I—after all, I'm married now. You must just—we must just be friends, that's all. I'm quite well and happy, it's only that you startled me, coming in so unexpected. What are you doing in London?"

He told her absently. "Lauretta, is he unkind to you? Are you quite—quite contented?" he asked fiercely. "By God, if he's not—"

She colored easily and quickly, for little reason, and brushed her eyes with a wisp of handkerchief. "Oh, Con," she said unsteadily, "how can you ask that? I think I must be contented, my dear. James is always k-kind and thoughtful, you mustn't think he's not! I know I was a coward, for I d-did love you truly, but it's just as I told you, we must forget all that—it's not James's fault, and I mean to be a good wife to him—"

"Oh, I know, love," he said angrily, "I know! You couldn't be any other way and still Lauretta. Are you sorry I came? I don't mean to—to embarrass you, I just had to see you."

"It's all right, Con," and her voice was firmer. He saw, with angry pain and a queer mingling of other feelings, that she was already a trifle more mature, more poised now that she had recovered from startlement. "It's silly, isn't it"—and she smiled—"never to see each other again now that you're here—just because . . . I'm very glad you've come to see me, Con."

"Just because!" said McDonagh, scowling. "No, my God, I don't mean to make trouble for you, my darling, but if you can cut off loving so quick, I can't!"

"Now you're saying I'm heartless again." Her mouth quivered. "I'm not, Con, I did love you, I—I—but it's no use now, and—"

"And after all, it's not James's fault! All right, my love, don't cry for God's sake, I'm not expecting you to run off from your lawful wedded husband!"

And before she could do more than give him a tremulous smile, the house door opened and FitzEustace came in from some errand. He expressed himself as most pleased to meet an old acquaintance of Lauretta's—shying slightly under McDonagh's intensive black stare—and offered a glass of claret. And what brought Mr. McDonagh to London?

"Looking for a job," said McDonagh laconically. FitzEustace was a rather plump man of thirty or so, sandy and not unhandsome in florid fashion; he was formal and somewhat old-fashioned in knee breeches. "The government's rearming these days, and I think it likely they'll take on a good many new surgeons for the services."

"Ah, you are a medical man, I see. Why, I should think it not *un*likely," said FitzEustace cautiously. "I myself intend to enter the military if I may obtain a commission reasonably. I feel it to be the duty of every able and loyal man to offer his services to the crown in this parlous situation, when England is threatened with the unthinkable danger of invasion. The account in the *Times* this morning of Bonaparte's camp at Boulogne was most disturbing, most disturbing."

"Offer your services?" said McDonagh. "Well, it's nice to be able to forget money." Men like FitzEustace always raised a devil of contrariness in him.

"Ah, well, manner of speaking." And FitzEustace laughed awkwardly. "Er—I don't recall that I ever met you in Dublin, sir? Of course, I spend little time there."

"Oh, I'm the barest acquaintance of the Amisons," said McDonagh. "To tell you the truth, you're the only people I know in London, which is why you find me on your doorstep at an early hour."

"Really." FitzEustace gave him a doubtful look, slightly bewildered at a man who knew no one in London. McDonagh saw his mind working, provincial, upstart family, no money.

"Conal, it's too bad of you," said Lauretta. "You will make James think you are angling for introductions to prospective patients! Of course we are happy to welcome you at any time."

"I'm not thinking of setting up private practice yet, unless the War Office keeps me hanging about too long."

"Well, well, in any case," said FitzEustace with forced geniality, "you must take dinner with us one evening. Are you finding your way about the city easily? London can be confusing to newcomers, I know. Where are you staying?"

McDonagh told him, maliciously pleased with such a plebeian address, and FitzEustace gallantly concealed repugnance and repeated his invitation. "Very kind of you. I won't intrude longer on you now," and McDonagh rose.

"Do let us know what happens about your appointment to service, will you not?" Lauretta accompanied him to the door politely. "You're always welcome, as an old friend, Con, you know."

Oh, yes, he knew. Well, he wouldn't have Lauretta different. You couldn't pick and choose when it came to loving; it just happened. He wandered, brooding, down Holborn, and turned into a large jolly tavern called the Soldier. He ate cold beef and drank gin and decided that if he stayed long in London, he'd leave off the drink entirely, between such potables as gin and French wine; something wet was all you could say of either. Presently he set off for his projected daily visit to the War Office.

By the time McDonagh had an invitation to dine with Lauretta and her husband, he was wholly out of temper with the War Office, life in general, and Conal McDonagh. In his two weeks in London he had made a few acquaintances at a couple of taverns, notably the Black Bull in the shadow of St. Bartholomew's Hospital near Aldergate—some of the students and graduate surgeons. All that saved him from lunacy at enforced inactivity was the chance to talk shop with them. The newly qualified house surgeon, Arch Elliott, prophesied helpfully that it might be six months before he got anywhere with the War Office medical branch. "There'll be a lot of rigamarole to get through before you're even put on the list for call."

"Well, that's a hell of a lot of encouragement, I must say. I shall have to get a living somehow, practice or no."

"To quote one of my old professors," said Elliott solemnly, "no man, gentlemen, who enters the profession of surgery more

39

concerned with the remuneration he may earn than with the true passion of interest in his work can hope to become a competent, much less a great, surgeon."

McDonagh returned a suitable obscenity. "All very well for you to talk, you're getting wages."

"Sixty pounds a year and found, such as it is. And such private patients as may trust themselves to a new-qualified man."

"Well, it's something. You couldn't get the staff committee to take me on as another house surgeon, could you?"

" 'Fraid not at St. Bart's—no openings. They take on their own former students first. I'll tell you, though, you might try down at St. Luke's. It calls itself a hospital, but it's just a bit of a place, sixty or seventy beds. Old Street, opposite Bunhill Row out near Golden Lane. They put it up originally to house the overflow from Bedlam—"

"Thanks very much," said McDonagh. "It's difficult enough to deal with rational patients, I draw the line at lunatics."

"Oh, it's quite respectable these days! I know they keep a couple of staff physicians and one senior surgeon, and there might be a place for another man under him. No harm to go and ask. Play it up how you're the brave patriot eagerly waiting the call to serve your country—"

"And hoping to stay alive until I get it. Well, all they can say is no." McDonagh scowled again, absently, at the little stiff invitation card as he fetched out his wallet, where it reposed between the diminishing notes. "I'll try there, thanks, Elliott. What am I expected to wear to a formal dinner in London?"

"Gentleman's house?—butler, maids at table, and different wine with every course? How d'you come to know people like that? Knee breeches definitely, same as Almack's Club, they won't let you in in anything else."

"Well, damn it, they'll have to let me in, I don't own a pair."

When he left the Bull, he wandered up toward Golden Lane to have a look at St. Luke's Hospital. It wouldn't do any harm to present himself at least; and if, in addition, he could discreetly advertise himself as in practice among the other guests at Fitz-Eustace's and hope for a few private patients— Well, no harm in trying anyway.

3

It literally hadn't occurred to McDonagh that there might be the possibility of a job at a London hospital. Showed how provincial he was, he thought. There was just one hospital in Dublin, Queens', where he had had his practical training; it kept a permanent staff of six physicians and three surgeons, with a dozen assistants under each. He should have realized that in enormous London there would be several hospitals, places for many more staff graduates.

St. Luke's, when he found it, proved to be a very old building tucked away between two newer ones. Remembering the old original wing of Queens', McDonagh had dismal visions of hell-holes of operating rooms where all the available light came thinly from the wrong direction. He shouldered open a ponderous door and came into a small, square dark entry hall, absolutely empty and silent. Several doors led off it, the only open one giving onto a steep stair. He opened the next and revealed a cloakroom somewhat larger than the foyer, hung with top hats and cloaks. A little, wiry, leathery man with a crest of white hair was rifling the several pockets of a greatcoat hanging on a far peg. He glanced around testily.

"Yes, what'd'you want?"

"The senior surgeon."

"Oh, indeed? And what might be your business?"

"If it's any of yours," said McDonagh, "I'm looking for a place as assistant surgeon if there's one open."

"Oh, are you? Damn, I knew I had some left," and the little man triumphantly hauled out a bottle from the last pocket. "Where'd you train, young man?"

"Dublin. My God, that isn't by any chance a bottle of whiskey, is it?"

"It is, and it belongs to me," said the little man fiercely. He had the remnants of a thick Edinburgh accent; McDonagh put him down as one of the orderlies.

"Well, I was only asking. Have it sent down from Scotland, or is there a place in London you can buy it?"

"If you go to buying whiskey before you get a job, young man, you won't hold a job long. Who told you to come to St. Luke's, that there was a place going as assistant?"

"Is there, by God? Why, one of the house surgeons at St. Bart's just mentioned there might be no harm in asking here. What's the duty and pay?"

"Six and half days a week, one full Sunday off each month, and assist the orderlies in the autopsy room twice a week at the student lecture. That I make no doubt you'd be useful at, a grand big chap you are for slinging cadavers about. Take full charge of the buying, and the accounts must be strictly kept—there are four dissections a week, we've only a small panel of students, mostly acting as apprentice orderlies to earn tuition. We keep only the one assistant surgeon, who has two full wards. Thirty pounds the year and found, with a private room the other side of the dissection hall."

"They don't want much for thirty pounds, do they? How many orderlies would I have for the wards?"

"Nothing has been said," retorted the little man coldly, "about employing you, young man. Generally five or six, but Collins is frequently drunk." He drank out of the bottle, said, "Ah," and pounded the cork back.

"Well, you're a damned, cheerful, friendly soul, aren't you?"

said McDonagh, annoyed. "If the chief surgeon's anything similar, I don't know that I'd take the job were it offered."

"I," said his companion frigidly, "am the chief surgeon. Adam Gillespie, sir, is my name—if you're not ashamed of yours, may I hear it?"

"Oh, damn my tongue," said McDonagh involuntarily, "now I've talked my way out of the job before I begin. I beg your pardon, sir, but I'd no way of knowing— But damn, I call it an unfair trick to lead me on so!"

Gillespie sniffed and held out the bottle. "Have a drink— one," he invited. "If you'd set to kowtowing at me, I'd give you short shrift. Begin as you mean to go on. Let me see your certificate and hear something about you. I had an assistant trained at Queens' in Dublin once—hardly knew a saw from a scalpel."

"We get some Englishmen and renegade Scots there now and then," said McDonagh.

Gillespie sniffed again. "I won't be kowtowed at, but don't you go too far, young man! I happen to be in need of a competent assistant, as my former one cool as be damned walked off into military service t'other day—had the gall to excuse it by saying he had no notion they'd call him in so quick after he applied. But—"

"Why, that damned liar!—the senior officer at the War Office told me it might be six months before I was called! Another place where it depends on what influence you've got, I suppose! Or very likely they give preference to men with English names," said McDonagh bitterly.

"That I would doubt," said Gillespie. "If they did, they'd be perpetually short of medical men—half those in the service are Scots and Irish. Englishmen are generally too sentimental to make good surgeons, though they are sometimes competent physicians. So you want a job to tide you over before you follow my late assistant? Well, well, with all this to-do over the French, and half England getting into uniform, I daresay I must put up with it. Let me hear something about your qualifications." He leaned on the wall, hands in pockets, listening, and scowled at the proffered certificate.

"I came down for a drink," he said then abruptly, "before

doing an amputation. Don't like amputations—confession of defeat. Since I usually leave 'em to my assistant, suppose we kill two birds at once, eh, and I'll watch you do it, and if I think you're satisfactory we'll call you my new assistant."

"What, now?" said McDonagh. "I've not got my instruments."

"I can provide you," said Gillespie dryly. "One o' the temperamental sort, are you, that's got to have your own favorite steel?"

"Well, no. Of course, if you like." He followed Gillespie out, and they started up the stair. "What's the case?"

"Very nasty thing. Poor devil run over by a coach. Compound fracture, left leg, and both bones protruding. What'd you do with that when it was fetched in to you, eh?"

"Well," said McDonagh, irritated at this attempt to trap him with such an elementary question, "there's nothing to do but amputate. You can set a compound fracture if the flesh isn't open, if there's no wound. If there's an open wound with bone through it, you can set it, but it'll never heal, not once in a hundred times. You get blood poisoning, a lot of swelling with pus inside, and the patient dies if you don't amputate."

"And the good Lord only knows why," said Gillespie with a sigh. "One day we'll find out, you know. It starts to heal—that's the puzzle of it—and then in three, four days, poisoning. Yes, you're quite right, and it's the sort of simple little problem there should be more research on—why should the wound become poisoned with all the care we give it? Damn it, sir, by rights it should heal—why doesn't it? We can use this room," he added suddenly, and opened a door in the corridor they had entered at the top of the stair. "You might get the candles lit. I'll go and see the patient fetched."

It was quite a satisfactory operating room after all. McDonagh surveyed it approvingly when he had lit all the candles in brackets round the walls and two tall standards each holding eight tapers at head and foot of the table. The table was a convenient height and steady; the sawdust spread thick on the floor had been changed not too long ago, for there was little blood mixed with it; there was another smaller table to hand with a great variety of instruments spread out, and even a small hearth at one side of the room. McDonagh began to feel pleased with himself for the first time since he'd been in England, and at the same time the familiar, terrible, cold reluctance rose in him that was normal before he used the steel. He took off his coat, found a peg to hang it on, and looked at the hearth; a fire was laid, kindling and all. He took out his flint, knelt and lit the kindling. He went back to the table and selected a medium-sized cautery iron, wiped off a few rust specks with his handkerchief, and laid it on the hearthstone.

"Sweet heaven," said Gillespie behind him, "are they still cauterizing every amputation at Queens' Hospital?"

"I like it ready just in case it's needed," said McDonagh irritably. He wiped the cold sweat from his hands. "You can say what you like about the cautery, it's still the only satisfactory way to stop hemorrhage." He wiped his hands again; the sweat was drying on his brow; he felt it.

Gillespie looked at him interestedly. "I warrant you've a lightning hand, if not as quick as mine."

"Yes, I'm quick. Can you tell by the color of my eyes maybe?"

"By the sweat on your brow," said Gillespie. "You are, I think, the same sort of surgeon I am, Mr. McDonagh. There are some men don't mind it, but it's pain and grief to us to cause pain, and so we're quick to get it over."

"Well, it's one of the elementary lessons, isn't it, not just personal preference. We were never allowed over a minute and a half for a simple amputation at Queens', I can't say about other hospitals. Do you use anything else here for that except speed?"

"What d'you think of pressure on the carotid to deaden the senses?"

"Not much. You don't try anything with laudanum?"

"You know as well as I do, you give the patient enough laudanum to put him out of pain and you kill him. Or do they do that at Queens' too?"

"Might save a lot of wear and tear on the instruments at that," said McDonagh. He walked across to prod the fire. Two burly orderlies came in bearing the patient on a stretcher. McDonagh stood to one side with Gillespie while the orderlies shifted the man to the table. "You're a liar, sir," he said, "he's had something."

"He has indeed. He was chock-full of gin when the coach overran him, and he's now sleeping off the gin and a very small dose of opium he had when he came in."

The patient was not quite unconscious; he stirred and muttered. One orderly fetched a stack of clean bandages from a shelf by the hearth and arranged the pile alongside the instruments; the other stripped off the blanket. "Yes, damned nasty, couldn't do anything with that," said McDonagh. The breaks were below the knee, jagged bone protruding in three places, one bit broken off and possibly the missing piece embedded inside. "Has he bled much? I don't see any ligature."

"Nothing extraordinary."

The patient opened his eyes and looked up at them with vague alarm. He was a middle-aged man in respectable-looking garments, a black coat and once-white shirt; his left breeches leg had been cut away for the surgery. "For God's sake get his coat off," said McDonagh. "You ought to know enough for that, you men! Loosen his collar—he mustn't move about for a few days, and you can't pull and haul at him getting his clothes off after this. Get the rest of those breeches off. You can leave him his shirt, he'll need it in bed unless you keep your wards warmer than your operating rooms." He had forgotten Gillespie was there.

"Ow, Lord ha' mercy," mumbled the patient.

McDonagh rolled up his shirtsleeves, tried the heft of several scalpels on the table, picked up the smallest triangular saw, said, "My God, don't you ever reset the teeth on these things?" and decided on the third smallest; laid out the instruments he wanted in the front row, and chose the steadier-looking of the orderlies. "Here, you. Go over to the fire and stay by that iron—put it in and get it hot now. If I call for it, I want it ready in my hand in five seconds, understand?"

"Yessir."

McDonagh laid out in a row above the steels a dozen separated lengths of silk ligatures, the jar of adhesive cement, one pile of lint bandage cut in narrow strips, and another pile of linen bandage cut wider. "All right, tie him down." He took the thin length of whipcord, passed it round the leg six inches above the wound, knotted it loose, and began twisting it to a tourniquet with a wooden stick. The patient woke up wholly and protested.

"Ow, what the hell you doing?"

"You lie down 'n' be quiet," said one of the orderlies not unkindly. "All over in jest a minute, me lad." He tightened the straps about the patient's arms.

McDonagh wiped his palms a last time, selecting the right spot with a nice eye for getting far enough above the wound to be sure of clearing all the damage away and not so far above that he took off more than necessary. He took up a scalpel, and the patient said feebly. " 'Ere, what you off to do? Ow, my Lord—"

"Don't you worry, all you need to do is lie still, friend," said McDonagh. He nodded at the orderly across the table, and the man took a firm grip on the patient's thigh and knee above the wound. The scalpel laid open a precise line at a slight angle, one single jet of arterial blood shot out from below the tourniquet, and the patient yelled. McDonagh already had ligatures knotted on the exposed vessels; the blood stopped coming. He took up a neat flap of skin and tissue and anchored it above the cut with his left hand, and feeling for the little saw began to sever the bone. The patient was screaming and trying to struggle. The bone parted, the scalpel cut through the rest of the flesh and muscle, and the orderly lifted the severed leg and dropped it on the floor. McDonagh cut the knotted ligatures around the vessels and brought down the flap of skin across the raw stump; the orderly hauled the patient over on his side to expose the bottom of the wound, and McDonagh slapped adhesive cement on bandage strips and fastened down the flap. When it was well secured in place, he cut a slanted opening at the bottom of the several thicknesses of bandage, for drainage. The patient left off yelling and fainted, and Gillespie said, "Just under two minutes, Mr. McDonagh, not at all bad," in a dryly pleased voice.

"He's lucky to lose it below the knee," said McDonagh, looking at the tourniquet area. He loosened the knot and nothing happened, so he removed the twisting stick. After a moment the area turned from dead white to a more natural color, and then a red stain appeared through the adhesive bandage. "These damned things may be standard modern usage, but they're about as much damned use as praying over it. When they do the job, they're fine, but how often do they hold?" The five thicknesses of bandage strips were all soaked now. "Christ!" said McDonagh disgustedly, watching it. He took three larger strips and put them a dozen times round over the others, tied the last loosely, and watched again. A red stain came sluggishly through and grew to a patch irregularly circular, not covering the whole stump. He watched it for five long, slow minutes, in silence, and it did not grow anymore.

"Possibly all the gin is taking hold," said Gillespie. "Judging from his condition when he arrived, he should be all but pickled in it."

"Doubtless he'll think twice before going on a spree again," said McDonagh. "He's finished bleeding for a while anyhow. You'd better keep an eye on him close the next twenty-four hours," he added to the orderly. "If it breaks open, we'll cauterize, and be damned to modern methods." He turned away and remembered that this was not the old familiar operating corridor at Queens', and that he was here on probation. He wiped his hands on a bandage, feeling a little tired and pleased with himself. "Well?" he challenged Gillespie.

"Oh, very competent," said the senior surgeon. "You might have sawed somewhat higher up, you left a crack in the bone, but it will probably heal—a minor matter." The orderlies had the patient on the stretcher now and carried him out. "I should be pleased to try you as assistant, Mr. McDonagh. I think you will develop into a very capable surgeon. All good surgeons are fearfully bad-tempered at work."

The assistant surgeon's room opened off a corridor on the ground floor at the rear of the hospital; to the left of it was the door to the dissection hall, and to the right at the end of the corridor a door to a narrow alley leading up to Old Street. Gratifyingly there was a small hearth in the room, although if he wanted a fire between March and November (said Gillespie severely) he must buy his own fuel. He was entitled to three meals a day from the hospital kitchen and the free laundering of no more than two shirts and one pair of smallclothes per week; should he be one of those fastidious surgeons who covered himself with a linen surgical coat while operating, he might have it laundered once a month.

McDonagh was pleased; God knew the pay was nothing, but it was all clear, and he would be doing his own work while he waited for something better—he trusted—from the War Office. He brooded bitterly on the tale of Gillespie's late assistant while he fetched his belongings from White Cross Street to the hospital. Ten days, said Gillespie, fellow applies, is called up for an interview, and appointed to a regiment a week later. It was a damned ramp, unless the fellow had some influential relative.

He arranged his books on the small table which, with a straight chair, a chest, and a narrow bed, completed the furnishings of the room. It was only four o'clock; he might catch the senior officer still. Fired with indignation, he went out and found a hack. At the War Office he met the senior officer on the point of departure and told him bluntly what he thought of the medical department's lack of organization—if that was the reason for another man's preferment—or conversely its veniality.

"Well, now, really," said the senior officer, "I cannot listen to this. There is no favoritism implied, sir, in this extremely circumstantial case you quote. For all you know, this young man applied long before you. First come, first served. In any case, our examining board must be satisfied as to qualifications before an applicant's name is entered on the list for appointment. I may say you do yourself no good, sir, by making accusations of this sort."

"Oh, I don't expect any admittal from a government department!" said McDonagh. "You're always in the right! I can't enter a formal complaint, I daresay, but I'll ask you to record my new address, and you've not seen the last of me by any means. I'll be in from time to time to remind you of the date I first applied."

He walked back across the city to save the hack fare, which

laudable frugality was frustrated when he passed a bookshop along the Strand and, fatally, entered it. Almost at once he came on something new to him, a vilely printed thing entitled *A New Method of Operating for the Femoral Hernia*, by one Thomas Beddoes. It was overpriced at six shillings, considering its cheap binding, but he took it back to St. Luke's with him and began to read it over his first dinner there. He was pleasantly surprised by the dinner, which was more generous than most hospital meals in his experience.

He was in the middle of the meal and finishing the first chapter of the book when an orderly knocked on the door and told him there was a street accident brought in. "Overturned coach, sir. Three patients . . . Oh, Mr. Gillespie don't live on the premises, sir, any after-hours work is the assistant's business."

"Need I have asked?" said McDonagh sadly, and went out to the examining room. There he found a hysterical young woman with a dislocated ankle, an elderly man with what might be concussion, and the young woman's husband with a simple fracture of the arm. Both the conscious patients were volubly protesting their desire to be treated at home—persons of any consequence did not remain in public hospitals—my card, sir, if you will but send to my house for my second groom with the curricle, my own medical man will—

"That your coachman?" asked McDonagh, nodding at the other man. "Yes, well, he's a damned sight worse off than either you or your wife, sir. We'll keep him here. Send for your curricle if you like, one of the orderlies can go—in a hack, if you'll part with the shilling fare. I'll have you both fixed up by the time it's here, no need for your own surgeon." He shut up the woman by the simple expedient of jerking the ankle back into place, whereupon she fainted; while an orderly administered to her with hartshorn, he set the man's arm and bandaged it. "Ten shillings, sir, and it'll be four shillings a day inclusive for your coachman, unless it's necessary to do a trepanation, which would come to four guineas."

"This is quite outrageous!" protested the gentleman, nursing his splinted arm and beginning to regain some color. "The accident was Gregson's fault entirely, and he will forfeit his hospital expenses from his wages—and the farrier's bill, if either of the horses is injured! I had not expected such barbaric treatment even at a public hospital—"

"Please yourself, sir," said McDonagh. "We'll let you know how Mr. Gregson gets on." When the second groom with the curricle had carried them off still complaining, he examined the coachman and came to a gloomy conclusion about his chances. Hemorrhage from nose and ears, extravasation about the contusion above the temple, deep unconsciousness: in the old days, you'd do a trepanning job at once, but that wasn't considered so wise now. He decided to keep an eye on it for twenty-four hours, always supposing the man lived so long, and see if nature would come to their aid.

He read halfway through Beddoes and went to bed at midnight. Sometime later he was startled awake from deep sleep by a stealthy knocking at the alley door. Cursing, he got up, lit a candle, put on his greatcoat over his smallclothes, and went to answer. When he unlocked the door and pulled back the chain bolt, a tall shadow loomed up from blackness outside and asked suspiciously, " 'Oo might you be?"

"New assistant."

"Ow. Well, if you're in the market, we got two large in prime state."

"How prime?"

"Now, mester, Mr. Gillespie 'e's bin dealin' wi' us for years, an' know we don't go misrepresentin' merchandise. Four a week 'e take, barrin' the times 'e get allotted one from the hangman, an' never no complaints. We don't go diggin' up just any hole, mester—we picks 'n' chooses. Never anything over a week, as Mr. Gillespie knows, an' wuth the price."

"Well, let's see," and McDonagh stepped out into the alley. A couple of other shadowy figures clustered around a flat cart. The first man stripped back the canvas cover and McDonagh raised his candle.

"For Gord's sake, careful wi' that light! You want the watch down on us?"

"Oh, they generally turn a blind eye, don't they?" Both the naked cadavers on the cart were adult, and quite fresh, not more

51

than four or five days old. Both were middle-aged men. "Very nice. What are you asking?"

"Two guineas apiece."

"All right." Gillespie had said anything up to three guineas was usual, but it seemed a gross price compared to those current in Dublin, where a new corpse could be had for fifteen shillings. "Fetch them in." He went in ahead to unlock the dissecting room. There were already two cadavers there, ready for tomorrow's anatomy lectures.

Heavy breathing followed him; the men staggered in with the first body and heaved it up onto an empty table. "By rights," grumbled the negotiator, "you ought pay double for this 'un—in an iron box it was, the hell of a job to get into."

"Designed to foil ghouls like you," grinned McDonagh. "Think what an iron coffin costs the family!" He pried open the corpse's mouth. "Damn you bloodsuckers, you've stolen all the saleable teeth!" There was a great demand for sound incisors and front teeth, which were used for appearance's sake in making false dentures; wood or metal did for the out-of-sight molars. A good set of the six front teeth would bring ten shillings, and it was the practice at Queens' to salvage them and thus cut down the price of the cadavers.

The resurrection man looked astonished. "You are a new 'un, mester. That's our perks, like—quite the custom it is, we gets the ivories. On'y about one out o' a dozen still 'as 'em, any road."

"Oh?" said McDonagh. If so, London hospitals were prodigal with money. "Very well." The other cadaver was fetched in; he paid the men from the hospital funds, locked the door after them, and went back to bed.

If he had had any vague hopes of inaugurating potential private practice by introduction among a few gentlefolk at Fitz-Eustace's, they were dashed by his fellow guests at dinner. Again he acknowledged provincialism, ruefully; FitzEustace looked more important in Dublin than he was here. He scarcely moved in a dandy set, among the wealthiest class. Or maybe, thought McDonagh sardonically, he asked only his third-rate acquaintances at the same time as a lowly surgeon new out of

Ireland. The other guests, at any rate, were miscellaneous non-entities.

He devoted some effort to keeping his gaze from Lauretta, quiet and lovely in violet silk at the foot of the table, more poised and socially competent than the Lauretta he remembered, but still his darling. It was a little relief when the ladies left the table and he needn't take such care not to reveal emotion. Almost at once, however, he found himself as usual angrily and acutely embarrassed, not at but for his three companions, who commenced to bandy the risqué jests custom demanded be reserved for this half hour.

It was not, God knew, that he was a prude, but he felt vaguely that the sly jest and nudge in the ribs, over so straightforward a thing as sex, was unhealthy. Only Puritans at heart could so sniggeringly enjoy any reference to what they still thought of as sin. Embarrassed at his own embarrassment, which might look like prudery to them, and he the youngest man in the room, he scowled in silence at his oversweet port, forced to listen. They reminded him, with the shifting secret delight in their eyes, of newly adolescent youngsters who had just discovered there were two sexes.

Presently they exhausted the current fund of stories and passed to politics and the war. FitzEustace lamented the fact that military commissions were so costly and asked McDonagh if he had as yet had his application taken up by the War Office.

"I have not," said McDonagh, and added a few bitter remarks about government departments.

"Well, well," said FitzEustace, "in a general way that may contain some truth, but I must say I feel that in the present situation all loyal subjects should refrain from—er—undermining statements and criticism." He talked like that; in fact, all of them, like most upper-class men McDonagh had met, seemed to talk to impress each other most of the time. "Of course, as—ah—an Irishman, you may not feel quite the anxiety over Bonaparte as—"

"I'm sorry to disappoint you, but I've got no politics," said McDonagh. "It's six of one, half dozen of the other in any political issue or national either."

"Dear me, that is a somewhat radical statement," said the man across the table, a sheep-faced fellow in a striped waistcoat. He did not look offended, like FitzEustace, but analytically interested. "Don't you think, however, that men in your profession, sir, are almost bound to take the objective view of other matters too? Perhaps it's an occupational hazard."

"No, I don't see that—as many fools among medical men as others," smiled McDonagh.

"Well, it seems to me, you know, that the—so to speak—callous shell you are forced to develop in your own work—"

"Oh, do we?" said McDonagh.

"You mean," said the fair young man beside him, "g-getting used to d-dead bodies and so on, and b-blood? Mystery to m-me how you ever do, y'know. I saw a nasty c-c-coach accident once, and by Jove, I was sick j-just looking at the blood."

"I agree," said FitzEustace, "that the necessity of growing calloused to such things might very well make a man, ah, shall we say equally a trifle cavalier toward other established authority and tradition. No offense, no offense, Mr. McDonagh! perhaps a little cynicism is healthy, eh? Though I am bound to say, with all deference to your profession—and to digress from the original subject—that the numbers of these lawless resurrection men about these days is scandalous, quite scandalous."

"I s-say, gives me the grue to think ab-bout them," said the fair young man.

"Surely, when as I understand all the executed criminals are turned over to the anatomists, there is no need—"

"Well, you're wrong," said McDonagh. "Never enough cadavers to study, Mr. FitzEustace."

"Oh, come, I can scarcely credit that! And to those of us who keep any faith in religious doctrine, there must always be a certain repugnance at the wanton destruction of the Creator's handiwork—"

McDonagh looked at him blankly. He felt, ludicrously and angrily, like an adult strayed by mistake into a nursery, trying to meet the inhabitants on their own level. "Mr. FitzEustace," he said abruptly, "we had a windfall in a corpse today—an old coachman who died of a concussion. He'd no family to claim the body. We'll do the autopsy tomorrow. One day, sir, you may have the misfortune to suffer a concussion, and maybe your surgeon'll know better how to save your life because of this old fellow we could open up and take a look at. And if there is a God sitting up there somewhere watching all the bloody mess and nonsense He started down here, I just have a notion that He might think that was more sensible than letting a valuable piece of information rot underground on account of some damn fool superstition. Presumably, if any God did deliberately create us, He meant us to use the sense He gave us."

"Oh, really—" FitzEustace was outraged.

"I s-say," said the fair young man nervously, "all this talk makes me qu-queasy, y'know. And the port's finished anyway. Do let us j-join the ladies, shall we?"

McDonagh made an excuse to leave early. Before FitzEustace joined them at the door, he said to Lauretta, "I'm afraid I offended your husband tonight. And failed to apologize—not one of my talents! Probably because I was so damn out of sorts trying not to let him see I'm in love with his wife."

"Oh, please, Con," she whispered, trying to withdraw her hand.

"He'll not let you invite me here again, which may be just as well. You know I wish you all the happiness you deserve, Lauretta."

"If you're to keep on feeling so—so bitter about it, Con, maybe it is just as well," and her eyes were steady and sorrowful on him. And then her husband came up, coldly courteous, and McDonagh said good-night abruptly and set out on his long cold walk back to the hospital.

4

On Christmas Eve McDonagh took himself to the theater. Not as celebration, more in recompense. He had been just three months in England, and it looked as if he might stay a year before getting any advancement in work. It was not that he was so anxious to see bloody war again at first hand, but a military surgeon began at a wage of eighty pounds a year and might acquire a hundred with seniority; moreover, it would be valuable experience to have on his record, carrying some prestige. Aside from that, he might have been contented with his job at St. Luke's, for Gillespie was a brilliant man and could teach him something; but in three months McDonagh had grown a black hatred for London.

He had made a few friends here—Elliott and a couple of the last-year students at St. Luke's—but it was an unfriendly town, for anyone but wealthy gentlemen and their ladies. In Dublin men could sit over one drink in a tavern half the night, talking; here the landlord let you know you were expected to buy more or drink up and go. Any city was dirty; but London was the worst he'd seen, and the carelessness toward the desperate poverty in it, the cold blatancy of its crime, was somehow appalling.

On the right side of the ledger, true, was the fact that he'd been called up before the medical department's examining board, three weeks ago, and his name placed on the list for appointment to service. But he was warned that that might be slow in coming, there being many accepted applicants before him.

He went alone to the Covent Garden Theater to see an evening of farce and perversely bought himself a good seat in the stalls, but the overacted comedy on the stage competed for his attention with the curious, unusual, and exciting operation Gillespie was contemplating at the hospital. In one way McDonagh hoped a military appointment might be deferred for a few months; he wanted to see the outcome of that case.

About the middle of the evening he noticed the couple in the box just over him to his right. There was a very drunk young man and a very annoyed youngish woman. The man was noisy in drink and making loud sallies, which doubtless seemed excruciating to him, at the occupants of nearby boxes; after several attempts to make him behave, his companion sat very erect as far distant as the box allowed, fanned herself angrily, and paid him no notice. As the curtain dropped finally and the audience commenced to rise, McDonagh saw her disdain her escort's clumsy aid in donning her cloak and sweep out of the box ahead of him.

In the foyer of the theater a departing crowd milled to impede progress, waiting for carriages, for attendants to find hackneys. McDonagh edged around it by the wall and at the arched entrance giving on the corridor for the boxes, stumbled over a pair of outstretched legs. They belonged to the drunk young man, who was reclining against the doorpost, suddenly sound asleep and smiling sweetly. Men stepped over him and laughed, ladies drew in their skirts fastidiously, and the slim dark woman with him alternately prodded him with one foot and addressed maledictions to him in French. McDonagh looked at her interestedly and placed her without much difficulty. She was not so young as first glance suggested, somewhere in the mid-thirties, and her escort was hardly out of his teens. Her ensemble was proper, not gaudy or outré, and she had been discreet with cosmetics; but she was neither a lady nor quite respectable.

"You may as well leave off trying, madam," he told her. "He's dead out and'll just have to sleep it off."

She appraised him in one lightning glance. She had fine brilliant dark eyes and a mouth too wide for beauty. "I appeal to you," she said frankly, "is this not treatment of the grossest, to offer insult to me? When one escorts a lady to the theater, one does not—but definitely!—become incapably drunken. He is of gentle family, and I had not conceived such insult from him, this callow imbecile."

"Certainly if one expects any favor from the lady, it is not a thing one does to recommend oneself," agreed McDonagh amusedly. "I would advise you to wash your hands of him, madam, leave him where he lies, and allow me to find a hackney for you."

She gave him a swift smile. "But I have a heart, sir. He would undoubtedly take a fearful ague lying here on this cold floor, the attendants would not know where to convey him. Most certainly I do not give any favor to such a stupid young man, but I do not want his death on my conscience. If you would be so very kind to find a hackney, we will place him in it and tell the driver to take him home, and I will pay, for it is by no means right that you should take responsibility for this thing."

"If I could afford the gesture, you'd do nothing of the kind— as it is, it's just as well you make the offer," said McDonagh, laughing. "I'll find a hack, and then perhaps you would let me escort you home."

"You are poor? What a pity," she said regretfully. "Your kindness is all the greater then." When after some difficulty he found a free hackney, she watched with interested admiration as he lifted the young man into it and deposited him headfirst on the seat. "Tell the driver, it is number twelve Berwick Street. And"—as the hack started away—"I very much doubt that you will find another, in all this crowd."

"So do I. Let us walk along to the crossing and try there. And should we introduce ourselves?" He mentioned his name.

"I am Miss Fleur Galard, most pleased to do so, sir."

"Not Mademoiselle?"

"Indeed no, no longer! Since fifteen years my family is in

58

England, you understand, because of that *canaille* at home in France now."

"Ah, one of the aristocratic royalist families, no doubt."

She glanced at him in the dark; she had placed her hand on his arm lightly as they walked. "As you are poor and I need not masquerade with you, I think you mock me! There are many besides aristocrats who came to England. No, I am of the most respectable bourgeoisie as I think you know very well. And you? ... Ah, you are an Irishman? That is enchanting, I know them well. There are many Irish in France and now in our armies upon both sides, you know. I will make the confession to you, Mr. McDonagh, I myself, I have one grandfather who is named O'Donnell, is this not amusing? One does not talk of him, he was a common soldier and most unrefined, you know?"

"That must be a lie, the O'Donnells were princes in Ulster not so far back."

"Truly? So perhaps I am an aristocrat after all!"

He picked up a hackney at the next crossing, handed her into it, and asked the address. "It is King Street, number twenty."

"Number twenty King Street," said McDonagh to the driver, and stepped into the hack and slammed the door. The coach jolted off as he sank into the seat beside her.

"Now this is ungenteel, I did not invite you to accompany me."

"Why, it's plainly a gentleman's duty. London is dangerous at night. Suppose this hackman should assault you as you alight on a dark street?"

"You are droll," she laughed. "I have never seen a hack driver under seventy years old!" She leaned toward him and put a hand on his knee. "Mr. McDonagh, I think I like you. One must please oneself sometimes—with caution—and it is insupportable that because that young man is so stupid, I should spend Christmas Eve all alone. Also, I am hungry. If I ask you into my house, to have a little supper and a glass of wine with me, will you promise that you do not mistake my intention and make the tiresome scene?"

"Not this one time, I promise you."

"I think I must be very careful with you! It is only for an

hour. I go out at half past eleven, to meet some cousins and attend mass at the cathedral. You would perhaps join us?"

"I'm a heretic, Mademoiselle Fleur, as much as I'm anything—if I went there with you, my Protestant forebears would turn in their graves."

"Oh, horror! We will not risk it then," she laughed.

The house in King Street was small and set demurely back from the roadway; it was a neighborhood of good class, if not elegant. She brought him into a charming parlor, pleasantly and comfortably furnished, and issued rapid orders to a neat maid. In the blaze of candlelight she examined him more thoroughly and said, "You are younger than I thought."

"But never so callow as that one you began the evening with."

"No, I see you were never so young as that! Tell me, what do you do for money, since you are poor?"

"I'm a surgeon and working at a hospital until I'm called to military service."

"My God, I have saddled myself with a cutter up of corpses! Take that chair, it is comfortable."

"They all look comfortable," said McDonagh. "For a bourgeoise, you seem to do very well, Mademoiselle Fleur."

She laughed and shrugged, seating herself opposite him. "You do not mistake me—no, you were never in your life young and callow, my black Irishman! Perhaps I am sentimental tonight, to be frank with a stranger. Figure to yourself, we are a respectable family, but one must live, and a penniless foreigner in England—I am a practical woman. I am *demimonde*, yes, and I give value for money, I am honest, and I do very well, as you see. I say to myself eleven years ago when I am seventeen—you see how honest I am with you!—I must plan for the future, and I am very particular, I do not take any and all protectors who offer, no. I am under the care of Sir Adrian Neville first, a most wealthy and kind gentleman, and then of Mr. Henry Mortimer the banker, and until two months ago, of Lord Avery Conant. All very upright, correct gentlemen, and generous to me. By the time a woman like me is thirty years, her best time is behind her, and it is necessary to save the money before, that one may be secure and comfortable. This I have done. Lord Avery is so kind to give me this house, all my own, and I have saved and invested wisely. So I am now safe and may, if I wish, take no more lovers, but in any case—as always—I take only those I like." The maid came with a tray of sandwiches, cakes, and wine.

"And don't tell me," said McDonagh, "you choose one like that young fool you were with tonight?"

"Oh, that is a drollery! I will tell Avery I absolutely refuse! He is Avery's nephew, you understand, and Avery says to me he will be greatly obliged if I am accommodating to the young man, who is shy and backward in society—when he is sober!—uncertain of himself, you see?—that if he is given confidence by acquiring a mistress, undoubtedly he will grow to more maturity. I am quite willing to oblige, you comprehend that Lord Avery is still a good friend, though he is now married, I am glad to say to a charming wife. But when the fellow is so much more of an imbecile than I expected, I change my mind!"

"I don't blame you. You'd do better to please yourself and be generous to take a poor lover for a change?"

"Oh, oh, I said I must be careful with you! In one half hour I send you away, but now be comfortable and remember your promise. Do you smoke? Do not hesitate to bring out your pipe, I do not mind it."

"You surprise me—but I will."

"Why do I surprise you?" She raised her brows and smiled. "Oh, yes, ladies, they are very particular! *Do not smoke your horrid pipe in the parlor, it will ruin the curtains!—I have the headache, do not kiss me now!—You insult me, to be so crude!* That is why there are women like me, Mr. McDonagh, to be so easy and good to a man and make him comfortable in his own place. And now what are you thinking of, to look at me with such a black smile?"

"Why, I was thinking it's damned lucky I decided to attend the theater tonight."

McDonagh set out quite blatantly for admittance to Fleur's bed. He had lived a remarkably celibate life so far in England, which was possibly another reason for his discontent. Aside

61

from the money involved, one always had to take care with harlots, and certainly none of those who had accosted him in London was remotely attractive. Fleur was something else again, and maybe the answer to a prayer.

Apart from that she amused him; they understood each other. Some practical, blunt vein of cynicism both shared was instantly recognized between them. Oddly, aside from anything else, he liked her. Perhaps it was of boredom, living alone and quietly as she was, that she did not discourage his first visits, but he flattered himself that it might be different later on.

The third time he called on her was on his full free day, a Sunday. She let him in from a bitter-cold January wind and hurried to huddle again over the fire. "Brrh, what a day to make me answer my own door!" Her maid had this day out.

McDonagh divested himself of his greatcoat. "Are you flattered that I come out to visit you in such weather?"

"Not at all. I daresay you would go anywhere to escape your dreary hospital."

"I wouldn't call it dreary exactly, we're in the midst of a damned interesting experiment—"

"I beg you, spare me the details!"

"Oh, I didn't come to discuss surgery with you, Fleur." Their eyes met amusedly; she knew as well as he why he came.

"You will take a little brandy to warm you," and she moved to the wine cupboard gracefully. He admired her slender back, following her across the room. Not tall, she carried herself very erect, and affected stark white for contrast with her warm olive skin. Her shoulders were slim and taut under his hands as he caught her from behind.

"I don't need brandy for that," he said.

"You will make me break the glasses—Conal, no—do you not remember your promise?"

"I only made it for the one time." He twisted her around in his arms and kissed her. For a moment she resisted and then relaxed against him and broke the kiss to laugh.

"It is my own fault to let you come again. . . . Ah, no, this is no youngster! Do you grow so strong by manhandling corpses, Conal?—do not answer me that! Well, it would be a new experience for me, true. Barbarian, you need not stifle me!" She was prepared to conduct the amorous play and byplay, mannered, flirtatious, but he was in no mood for that. He kissed her again roughly, and she gave a little breathless shriek, and then something of his almost brutal urgency reached her and she stopped laughing and her arms slid warmly up around his shoulders. "Well, one must please oneself. I am magnanimous to you in your need."

"Oh, no, you were never so young as—say—that stupid boy at the theater, were you, Conal?"

"Let's say never so callow."

"Not in a million years, eh? But it is a big joke on me, you know."

"Mmm?"

"A very funny joke it is." She stretched luxuriously against him. "I have said I am an honest woman, when I am under the care of a protector I do not cheat him, that is not fair. But in between, I take what lovers I please, to amuse myself. And here is this brash young man, and I decide to be very generous and kind to him, to afford him some useful experience. Which is very, very good of me. And then I discover it is he who affords me the experience! How is it you become such a very expert lover so young, eh?"

"We just agreed, not so young as all that. Natural talent possibly," he said inattentively. He had just discovered a rather provocative birthmark on her right thigh.

"And there is the saying that practice makes perfect. You must have begun the practicing early then."

"Oh, fourteen or thereabouts, if it matters—and true enough, I've encountered a few more females since."

"You would say, when you can spare time from your work? I also think you must be a very good surgeon—a man skilled at one thing is apt to be skilled at another."

"I should hope so. At the moment I'm not thinking about the job."

"That one divines. And may I ask"—demurely—"how long you propose to keep up this tireless performance? Already I have enough evidence of your capabilities."

"As long as you like, lady. I seem to have been living a monk's life since I came to London. Hell and damnation, no, I've got to be back at the hospital for night duty."

"Which is just as well for me perhaps." She laughed and then drew a little away. "But your hands—your hands on me, I have the strangest feeling—"

"These bloody surgeon's hands—do you mind that?"

"I have the feeling you are naming over all the bones and muscles as you touch me."

He was amused. "I'll do it aloud if you like."

"Heaven forbid. The outsides of things are sufficient."

"It's a very nice outside, Fleur."

Suddenly she shivered against him. "Your hands, yes. I have the feeling they know too much, Conal—all there is to be known of a woman's body."

"About all bodies in general, lady—that's my job. Why the hell are we wasting time talking? There's another hour before I have to leave."

McDonagh said afterward that only Fleur and Asenath Nobbs kept him from lunacy that next four months.

Asenath Nobbs had been brought into St. Luke's two days before Christmas, accompanied by a tearful mother and a kind lady employer. Newly in the humble employment of general maidservant, Asenath had stumbled on the kitchen hearth settle and overset a pot of boiling water as she fell; the burns from that were superficial, but she had been knocked unconscious by the fall and lay several minutes with her face in the hot coals.

When they had got a powerful dose of laudanum down her and applied liberal amounts of tannin over the terrible raw surface that might have been a pretty eighteen-year-old face, they made a cursory examination for other minor injuries, and McDonagh grimaced as he spread salve on the water blisters. "This is one of those damned stupid, meaningless tragedies that makes you wonder why anybody ever thought there was a God, isn't it? She's a good, healthy girl, she may live another fifty years—with a face nobody can bear to look at."

Little Gillespie stood looking down at her vaguely. He grunted, "I wonder. I do wonder."

"You needn't. It'll heal, with luck, but you know what it'll look like."

Gillespie grunted again. They went out presently to soothe and inform the lamenting mother; the lady assured them she would gladly bear all expenses. "Up to what, madam?" asked Gillespie bluntly. "Would you let me keep the girl here for six months, say, at four shillings a day? I'd charge you no more, it's a chance to experiment.... What for? Why, to put her right again, to the best of my talent, and with God's help."

"I won't have no experimentin' on my girl—"

"It's for her own good, and likely that of many others, madam." The lady looked at him and seemed to be reassured; she calmed Mrs. Nobbs and repeated her offer. Gillespie was looking as excited as he ever did.

"And what's all that about?" asked McDonagh when the two women had gone.

"Something, by the living God, I have always longed to do," said Gillespie. "I daresay to a graduate of Trinity and Queens', the word grafting suggests only trees."

"You are some way ahead of me," admitted McDonagh.

"And yet the Italian Tagliacozzi knew of it in the sixteenth century. Amazing that no one followed it up, but of course, the church interfered—blasphemy to amend God's intentions! Tchah! There was an article in the *Gentleman's Magazine* nine or ten years back—Hindu method of repairing noses—not altogether satisfactory, I thought at the time, but interesting, interesting. Of course John Hunter did some experimenting along that line, as he did along most lines, but only on animals. If only the girl will cooperate! By heaven, I should like to try!"

"I remember that Hindu business, I saw the article in class. Eyewitness account by two British surgeons, wasn't it? There was a three-cornered flap of forehead skin brought down—left attached for the blood supply—but it can't have looked like much, you know. Nothing to take the place of the bone that was missing."

"No, but we needn't worry about that here. Skin has been grafted—not much and not many times—it's still in the experimental stage—but we know it can be done, with care and luck."

65

"My God, d'you think we could do something about that in there? Damned interesting to try, but I don't see how—does it really take hold and grow?"

"So large an area, that's the problem," said Gillespie. "The largest ever transplanted at once was round about an inch by two, I seem to recall. That's why I said six months—it'll take time—if it can be done—a little piece at a time, until it's all covered. We'll have to use both arms—"

Inevitably the news got about of a most extraordinary experiment going on at St. Luke's, and a constant stream of physicians as well as surgeons came to marvel and tell Gillespie that he was a madman to believe such a thing could be done. "She'll be a bloody celebrity before we've done," said McDonagh. "They'll put her on the stage and give us free advertisement."

Asenath was an intelligent girl, and cooperated. Dr. Tanner, the senior physician at St. Luke's, and indeed, all the physicians as well as the professional midwives, complained bitterly of the intrusion of surgeons into the medical section; the only women's ward was to all intents and purposes an obstetrical ward. "It's not decent," said the midwives indignantly, but in time they grew as interested as everyone else. "It's impossible"—Dr. Tanner snorted—"and you'll give St. Luke's a name for harboring lunatics on its staff, Gillespie." But he fell into the habit of calling on Asenath daily to see how the lunacy progressed. "Gillespie's an old devil to put you through all this discomfort, me dear!"

"I don't mind, sir, if it does what Mr. Gillespie says 'twill."

McDonagh was fascinated; this was something entirely new. Not that he would ever admit it to Gillespie, but he realized again that his Dublin training, while good, was not altogether as modern as it might be. Most professional men were scoffing at this operation as impossible, but at least they had heard of the few experiments in grafting, which he never had, aside from that one article.

A kind of breathless suspense built up at St. Luke's as January drew to a close. If Asenath suffered any of it, lying patiently with the underside of her upper arm bound fast to her cheek, she gave no sign; but her eyes followed the two surgeons hopefully

66

as they bent over her on daily visits—largely useless, for there was nothing to do at this stage but wait.

"That article about the Hindu," said McDonagh, "said butter—to soften the edges—"

"Tchah! I rely more on nature. We shall soon know—I hope to God I have not tried too large an area, that is all. If this first attempt succeeds in any manner, we'll know it can be done and go on."

On the twenty-sixth day since he had set the little flap of arm skin over the raw section of cheek and bound it in place, they went almost ceremoniously to the women's ward to complete the second half of the operation. "If only it has taken—if only it has taken!" All the surgeons in London had wanted to be present at this minute, and all the midwives and half the medical staff of the hospital were ready to crowd about and watch. Gillespie shooed them all away testily. As he reached to the first bandage knot, his hands were shaking; he stopped and took command of himself. The bandages came free, and there it was—an inch of firm set skin, still attached to the arm, growing on the upper cheek.

"Christ," whispered McDonagh almost in awe. "It does work."

"I told you." But Gillespie had to flex his hands nervously, controlling excitement, before reaching for the scalpel. "Just hold quite still, there's a good girl, this won't take a minute." Very gently he pared around the flap still attached, and McDonagh eased the inert arm down from the position it had held so long. The little square inch of skin was pressed lightly down, and covered with soothing salves, and fixed in place with adhesive bandage. "Ten days or so, and that will take hold. You see? It can be done!"

"There'll be lines of demarcation where they join, even without sutures—just little thin lines, you think? God, if we could do it in one piece, all at once! It's a damned miracle—"

"I told you," said Gillespie again in a voice wavering with triumphant relief. "Lines? Nothing to what those scars would be otherwise! It'll take time—time, such a large area on both cheeks, but you see it can be done!"

"Please, sir, my arm hurts," whispered Asenath. Hastily McDonagh attended to what both had forgotten, bandaging the little raw place on her arm.

Gillespie beamed at her, understandably proud of himself. "There now, you're going to be just as pretty a girl as ever you were before, Asenath. I'm afraid it means some time and discomfort, doing it bit by bit this way, but we know now it can be done. By heaven, you know, if we tried both arms at once—to save time and start grafts on both cheeks—I wonder . . ."

"Six months," hazarded McDonagh. "There's a good four or five square inches to be done on each side—more on the right than on the left—and then the nose bridge—"

Asenath began to weep silently. "Why, what's this, my girl?" said Gillespie. "You've been such a good, patient lass all this while, and doesn't it please you to know that you'll not be so badly scarred? Six months isn't so long out of a lifetime, you know."

"Oh, no, sir, but I'm afeared Mrs. Hamilton won't keep me place for me all that while, sir, and I'll be out o' work after."

"Most certainly," said Fleur, "you present me—me!—with new experiences in lovemaking. What a thing to talk about in bed!"

"But I thought you'd find it interesting," he said, laughing. "Should think any woman would. We've done all but one more graft on the right cheek—that's just been started—and a bit of the left one. The joining lines show still, but nothing to what the scars would've been—it's like a miracle! I never dreamed such a thing was possible."

"Ah, well," said Fleur resignedly, "some men, they like to talk about politics. I should be most interested, Conal, were they scars upon my face, and I am very happy you are pleased. But I do not like to hear about blood and raw incisions and the difficulty of keeping a bed-borne patient's digestion healthy while I am naked in bed with a lover. It is not at all proper or conducive to passion."

"You and Asenath," said McDonagh, kissing her, "are all that reconcile me to London!"

"I am flattered that you put me first!"

But before the final miraculous grafts were completed, McDonagh had notice to appear at the medical department for official appointment to service. That was in late April, and he swore as he read it and then laughed at himself. Never satisfied—five months ago he'd have welcomed this. Now, well, for one thing, he would never find so agreeable, attractive, safe, and complacent a mistress as Fleur with the armed services!

He broke the news to Gillespie, who said, "At least, Mr. McDonagh, I have managed to teach you enough to correct your deficient Dublin training that the men under your care may live to fight again."

"Go along, you old devil," said McDonagh amiably, "you're just jealous of the wages I'll be earning."

He reported to the War Office, and the senior officer, who had never quite forgiven him for his accusations of favoritism, welcomed him coldly. "Well, your appointment is here, Mr. McDonagh, and I trust you will be satisifed with it. I hope you have no objection to serving at sea rather than with the land forces? You are appointed to the naval frigate *Lively*, now lying at Portsmouth."

"Oh," said McDonagh, rather dashed, accepting the papers handed him automatically. "Well, that's quite satisfactory, certainly, sir. It's the same rate of pay after all, isn't it?"

"I trust you will earn it," said the senior officer. "A frigate is rather a small ship, Mr. McDonagh, and carries only one surgeon when it numbers any medical men in its crew at all." He sounded maliciously pleased about it. "I'll wish you good luck—and freedom from seasickness."

"Thanks very much," said McDonagh rather gloomily.

"You see you are to report to Captain Gates on the tenth of May, on board. I trust you can put your affairs in order and do so in the time."

"Oh, certainly." He never would have thought he'd be so reluctant to leave London. Gillespie swore at being left on such short notice, but it couldn't be helped. He began trotting around to St. Bartholomew's, Guy's, and St. George's, looking for a replacement.

McDonagh invested some of his savings in two new working coats, half a dozen shirts, and a pair of boots, indulged himself in a new amputating saw of more módern design, persuaded Gillespie to reveal the name of the tavern which imported whiskey for him, and bought some to take along. He went to see Fleur a last time, and she was flatteringly regretful.

"I shall never see you again. It is said sailors are never let ashore from vessels in the British navy," she said mournfully.

"What? Nonsense. Besides, I'm not a sailor. Technically speaking, I'm a civilian employee on board ship. And I only hope to God I'm not prone to seasickness. Only time I've ever been on water was crossing from Dublin."

"You will be a hero and experience many battles—"

"Well, not in a frigate."

"And if they do let you off the boat, you will come to see me again?"

"Well, that's a damned silly question," said McDonagh.

5

"You can be damned thankful," said the second officer of the *Lively*, a wiry young man named Warner, "that you missed spending the winter with us. My God, I've never seen anything like it, and I've been at sea since I was eleven. Cold? Enough to freeze the spit if you hawked over the rail! And never the smell of port for months. Daily drill, half the hands up top chipping ice off the canvas, keep us from turning turtle."

"Where were you making for, if it's not an indiscreet question?" asked McDonagh.

"Same place we're making for after tomorrow," said Warner with a sigh and a wink. "Round and about. Don't have any visions of excitement. It's a damned dull job, I tell you, patrolling up and down the Channel with one eye on Boulogne. I swear we'd all welcome a good fight. As it's been, we let off a few rounds whenever we come in firing distance—my good Christ, you ought to see the stuff Boney's got together there, troops, ordnance, supply wagons, horses—but so far they've not deigned to fire back at us, and I don't suppose we've done the hell of a lot of damage. Unless things begin to hot up some, you're in for a nice dull sea voyage for your health."

"Are you really sorry for not seeing action? Here, it's my turn to pay—same round again, waiter. Maybe they're expecting it to get a bit hotter, and that's why they've sent you a surgeon."

"Oh, we've had one," said Warner. "We don't generally carry a doctor at all in peacetime, you know—only the big hulks do—strictly a war measure. Prosy old fella by the name of M'Gilli-cuddy, and my good Christ, he was more of a parson than a doctor! Not an awful lot for him to do, you know, and as a consequence he went all hot and bothered over the couple o' cases of French pox we've got on board. Lecturing the poor devils about sin half the time. Transferred? Oh, no, we lost him overboard out in the North Sea."

"Good God, that's an encouraging thing to tell me!"

"Oh, you'll be all right and tight," said Warner. "Don't know what possessed them to send you to sea, though. That's the War Office, no attention to fitting the man to the job. There's not the hell of a lot of space aboard—surgeon gets any odd place below-decks, you know—and what they ought to do is sort out all the little 'uns to send the navy. The army now, space is no matter there, they can use you great hulking chaps."

"I can't say you're making me anticipate the trip," said McDonagh.

"Oh, I'm sorry about that—very glad to have you with us. As it is your first voyage, though, I might advise you to be on board well before sailing time tomorrow." Warner hesitated and then leaned closer over the scarred table in this dockside tavern, with the air of one imparting an unsavory secret. "Y'see, we let the common sailors go ashore. There'll be quite a shindy at the wharf, time they come back to the ship."

"Oh? But is that unusual? I should think, after that long at sea—"

"My good Christ," said Warner, "most o' the men on the big hulks haven't been ashore in years. Never see 'em again if you let 'em go, you know. That's the common hands, mind. Everything's brought to 'em when the ship's in port—no objection to fetching all the drink and women they want aboard—but they're not allowed off. Most line of battle ships abide by that.

We get a better class o' men, regular enlistments, not pressed men, y'know—a good many able seamen with time in merchants."

"I see. And yet they have to be repersuaded aboard?"

"Re—my good Christ, they'll be fighting to get up the plank first! Oh, I see what you mean—no, the mob I mentioned isn't crew. It's half the town after seamen every time a ship puts out, see." Warner grinned. "I don't reckon as most sailors—crew or officers—take much thought for day after tomorrow. You're in port such a hell of a short time, you see, don't seem to matter much what you do or spend on tick. I'm all right this time, I took a nice windfall off o' Dicky Turnbull at cards. Tell you what, you'd best just stop aboard tomorrow morning, not to get mixed up in it."

McDonagh took this advice, and appreciated it the next morning. The frigate was due to sail on a noon tide, and by ten o'clock the wharf was crowded with people all intent on apprehending the men off the *Lively* before they got aboard. The majority were creditors single-mindedly after their money, since the surety of a naval man in wartime was nothing to speak of, and they might not lie in Portsmouth again for several years. Once a man succeeded in getting aboard, he was safe, but to do so, he had to escape the clutches of every man he owed a shilling here and any girl who might have a grievance on him. Few would have managed it but for the interference unwittingly offered by almost the same number of peddlers eager to coax a last shilling or two from departing customers. These pushed and shoved about sailors and officers impartially, impeding progress but acting as buffers between debtors and creditors, urging the purchase of every imaginable object: wool stockings, jackknives, writing paper and quills and ink, religious medals, good-luck mascots, shirts and handkerchiefs, hair powder, clocks and watches, shoelaces, pocket mirrors, gimcrack jewelry, blankets, boots, and candles. The din was incredible, and grateful as the men might be for the unintentional protection, between the two sections of the mob they had to fight their way up the plank, cursing and breathless. When the company roll was called and the plank hauled up, the crowd on the wharf fell impotently silent, and the ship's cat, an enormous gray tom with long white whiskers, came to sit on the quarterdeck rail and gazed down at them with cold, triumphant arrogance—not unlike the expression on the captain's face.

McDonagh enjoyed that scene, and altogether thought he would enjoy this voyage. The *Lively* looked to him like a smart vessel, but her officers corrected this impression with dire prophecies of what might happen in any emergency. "She needs a complete going-over," admitted the first officer, Hyatt. "She's covered with scum on the bottom, there's hardly a lick o' paint left on her, and her canvas is rotten. She's not the only one. The Admiralty's been bent on saving money, up until war was declared last year, and a third of the navy ships afloat are as bad. We're told there's new stuff building, but who's seen any of it?"

"One good broadside would send us to the bottom," agreed Warner cheerfully.

"Now, now," said Captain Gates benignly, "no decrying of my command, sir! More beef, Mr. McDonagh? I daresay you've been told it's a pleasure to have you aboard. M'Gillicuddy may have been a competent surgeon, but I do like my sermons kept for Sundays! I trust we don't make you nervous with all this foolish talk?"

McDonagh grinned. "I have a notion you mean to, sir—ragging a landlubber. I'll take my chances with the rest of you, seeing there's not much else I can do about it."

"Oh, we won't be taking any broadsides, no fear—barring accident," Warner reassured him. "The French fleet is bottled up in the Mediterranean, most of it, with the admiral playing watchdog—and much joy he's taking of it, we can guess! That'll be a dull job too. As long as the admiral keeps Gibraltar, we're safe in the Channel—and in England. After all, thank God, there's no way to get into England save by water."

"If rumor's true," said Hyatt, "Villeneuve's fleet is a good deal larger. If it's forced to a fight in the Med—"

"It won't be," said Warner. "Or if 'tis, it'll be some way to the admiral's advantage. That's his style, as we all know."

The captain nodded, smiling. "No need to worry over Villeneuve when the admiral's got his weather eye open."

"You seem to have a good deal of faith in this admiral," remarked McDonagh politely.

They all looked at him in surprise. "Landlubber," said Warner. "But there, to a navy man there's only one man we mean when we say the admiral. Or don't you follow the news? It's Admiral Nelson we're talking of."

"Oh, yes," said McDonagh. The warm, fervent, almost boyish hero worship in all their voices stopped him dead from going on to say that he never followed the news because most of it was a censored pack of pronouncements from several equally venal parties, raising a furor over issues which, in the end, turned out to be quite unimportant. He had, of course, heard of Horatio Nelson.

He was gratifyingly free of seasickness, but as Warner had prophesied, the *Lively* might have been a pleasure ship cruising for her crew's health that summer. By the end of a fortnight the novelty had worn off, and McDonagh began to be fearfully bored.

He had what was called a cabin to himself; with vague memories of the big mail packet from Dublin, he was surprised to find this a flimsily devised room-by-courtesy, partitioned off belowdecks amidships by simple walls of canvas hung from the beams. The officers had similar pseudoprivate cubbyholes. The canvas walls could be removed in minutes, and those up on the flush deck would be, if sea battle were joined. Here, as on the line-of-battle ships—as Warner said—the midshipmen huddled in these drafty structures on the top deck, which would disappear as the ship was stripped for action. After surveying the small space where he would be expected to operate on the wounded—possibly in a rough sea and certainly in the hellish din of the guns—McDonagh could only hope they met no action.

The *Lively* left Portsmouth and made leisurely up the Channel in the clear, quiet summer weather, past Brighton and Eastbourne, and stood out a way there to come in sight and firing distance of Boulogne opposite. Boulogne had turned into an armed camp; clearly visible were the ranks of ordnance, the horse lines, the communal camps of bivouacked troops. Not much activity could be seen. "They're not wasting powder on us," said Hyatt. "Biding their time until Villeneuve slips past Gibraltar and can come at us with naval tactics." The *Lively* let off a few rounds of shot in the general direction of the shore and cruised on up past Dunkerque, made about in a sweeping circle that brought a view of Ramsgate on the horizon, and sailed back down-Channel past Boulogne again, as far as Le Touquet, and there made about and started back.

They heard frequent firing from the other British frigates on Channel patrol but saw no French navy at all. The crew had some occupation; the officers very little. They played cards interminably, exchanged reminiscences, and occasionally scanned the shore through glasses. McDonagh had never been so bored in his life.

On their fourth run up the Channel one of the guns got loose and skated dangerously over the deck, pinning a seaman against the rail. And that gave McDonagh no occupation since the man was instantly killed. Three days later he had a small windfall in the person of a sailor who had burned his hands on new rope, and a week after that they ran into a little unexpected rough weather north of Margate, and the third officer was thrown against a bulkhead and sprained his wrist. Apart from that, McDonagh might as well have left his equipment in London.

At least, as Warner said, the weather was mostly fine.

All summer they lazed up and down the Channel. McDonagh learned something about life at sea, won four pounds odd from Warner and Hyatt at écarté, and wondered why in God's name he had ever entered government service. All that reconciled him was the comforting thought of his eighty pounds a year, guaranteed whether he worked for it or not.

In the first week of September, off Margate, the *Lively* fouled herself on drifting wreckage in a sudden gust and began to leak a trifle faster than her crew could pump. "Well, this means dry dock, and past time," said the captain resignedly. They limped slowly into Margate and hung about for ten days, waiting for orders. Eventually a naval inspector arrived; the *Lively* was put up for extensive repairs; her crew was transferred elsewhere, her officers were sent off on leave to await recommissioning, and McDonagh with them.

He traveled up to London on the stage after a mildly wet fare-well dinner with Warner and hired a room at the Leicester Arms in Leicester Street. The stage got in at six o'clock; by eight he was knocking on the door of Fleur Galard's house.

"Now I know," observed Fleur, "why sailors enjoy such rep-utations."

"Enforced celibacy," he murmured. "Leads to all sorts of vices."

"Before you are emboldened to describe them to me, let us refresh ourselves with a glass of wine." She gathered her pei-gnoir about her, graceful as always, and rose from him to pad across the room to the table. McDonagh propped himself up against the headboard of the bed and watched her lazily. Re-turning to sit beside him and hand him a glass, she said, "You find me in a very nervous state, Conal. Indeed, you should be flattered that I pay any notice to you at all, I am so much—in the English phrase—at sixes and sevens. And I must break the news to you that it will no longer be *convenable* that you come and make love to me. It is all very awkward—"

"What? If you're trying to say you prefer a new lover," he said stiffly and angrily, "well, damn it, Fleur, you were ardent enough a bit ago. I—"

"Calmly, calmly! No, no, I meant to say, for this time being only. I like you very well, I am pleased to make love with you for the moment's amusement—we understand each other, do we not? No romantic nonsense is needed between us. It is nothing like that. It is quite true that I had almost decided to take a new protector, for I have a most flattering offer from a very pleasant gentleman, and one can always use more money. In that case, Conal, I should also—with regret—have dismissed you, for I am an honest woman, I do not cheat a formal protector."

"It is understood," he said in her own vernacular, smiling. "But?"

"But then I discover this very awkward and worrying thing—you would never in this world guess—"

"Not that you're pregnant? My God, I trust it's not that you have the pox?"

"What things you do think of, you are indecent! Well, I told you that I have family in England. My sister Elise, she was a great deal older than me, you comprehend—"

"All of four or five years?"

"*N'importe*," said Fleur, vague and haughty. "And she is married young in France. She loses her husband, whose name was Olivier, but she has a small daughter. Well, they come to England, twelve years ago, and Elise, she is also practical like me, but perhaps less to her personal taste—she marries, for the convenience, an Englishman, a respectable grocer who lives in Tunbridge Wells."

"Does this thrilling tale have any point?"

"It is what I am telling you. She is dead—no, no, not just now, four years ago—and this respectable grocer, he is as I suppose a good man, for he continues to shelter Madeleine. That is my little niece. So nobody thinks of it save to think Madeleine is provided for. And now suddenly she is not. She writes to me, she says the grocer is dead and has left her a hundred pounds only, and she must provide somehow for herself. She says she very much longs to know me, she is coming to London and hopes she may stay with me; she would have my advice for her future. In fact, I cannot—if I desired—tell her not to come, for she was to have started today, I had the letter but yesterday—"

"It sounds to me," he said, yawning, "as if your niece intends to batten off you shamelessly."

"Oh, but poor Elise's little daughter! She is only seventeen. I have some family feeling. No, it is not that I am so miserly as not to wish to help her! But Elise and her grocer, you see, they were of the most upright and did not at all approve of me. It is true Madeleine has no other close relative, there are cousins, but too distant to take responsibility. I do not—well, to be frank, I do not want to shock this young girl, I am quite embarrassed at the notion of having this respectable virgin as guest! And yet one does not turn away such a relative."

"So what will you do?"

Fleur laughed and shrugged. "I suppose you would not like to marry her, Conal? It is a pity she has no dower, for that would be the solution—a respectable marriage. Perhaps I shall find she has already a provincial sweetheart in Tunbridge Wells, in which case I shall persuade her to return and marry him! In any event, it appears that I am committed to entertaining her for at least a little while in London, and so now I will ask you how long you are to be here."

"I've no idea. I'm to report to the War Office tomorrow. They may send me to another ship at once or not for a month, but I don't suppose they waste money to keep us hanging about idle. Why?"

"Oh"—and she made a rueful, attractive *moue* at him—"you know a woman in my position does not go about much in society or acquire many social companions. The gentlemen I know, aside from yourself, I could scarcely approach in such a matter. It is that I will like to take Madeleine about London a little. It is her first visit to a city, and you appreciate that there are a few places where it is not *comme il faut* that we go unattended by a gentleman. The theater, and that most amusing street fair, and the entertainment gardens at Vauxhall, other places. If you are to be here, it would be very kind in you to escort us—"

"Oh," said McDonagh doubtfully, "well, I don't know—that is—"

"Of course," she added hastily, "you need not worry over the cost, Conal, I would pay for everything, I assure you."

He sat bolt upright and stared at her. "And what in hell ever gave you the idea that I was that sort of man?"

"What? I said only—"

"I heard what you said! My God, so that's what you think of me, is it? Offering me pocket money, thinking I'd accept pay for squiring you about, thinking to buy a—a goddamned *cicisbeo* for yourself! Well, you can think again, and be damned to your money!" He flung off the hand she put out, slid off the bed and fumbled for his clothes on the chair, blind with rage. "Damn you to hell, Fleur, is that how you've seen me all this time? Just waiting for the right minute to slip me my wages for obliging you? I'll be damned if I ever—"

"What have I said, what have I done? My God, I never meant to suggest—it is quite a logical thing to propose, do not be so foolish!"

"Logical!" shouted McDonagh, struggling into his shirt. "You damned well know what you can do with your logic! Thought you'd buy me, did you?—like any aging trollop that has to bribe a man—"

"You great rogue, I did not need to persuade you! I am insulted beyond measure that you say this to me—it is a filthy lie!" Suddenly she swung her feet to the floor, ran around the bed and slapped him fiercely. "Imbecile—villain! How dare you say such a thing!"

McDonagh dropped his waistcoat and shook her hard. "Just who the hell first insulted who? Offer me money, do you? Maybe you think an Irishman's easy bought on account of all of them selling themselves as mercenaries over half Europe—"

"Take your hands from me, you great ape! I would not give one sou for you were it asked—"

"Well, by Christ, you were never more mistaken, you little harpy! Go out and find another man to buy—wonder you haven't offered to keep me entirely, choose my breeches and shirts, educate my taste in wine—like any—"

"If you call me an *aged trollop* again I shall kill you, truly I will!" shrieked Fleur. At this point the door was flung open to reveal the maidservant, much *en déshabillé*.

"Oh, madam, does he murder you? Shall I summon the watchman?"

"No, no, all is quite all right, stupid! Go away—oh, my God, who can understand an Irishman? I never—Conal, listen to me, fool, you are quite mad to think this! Look at me—are you saying that I, *I*, Fleur Galard, who have pleased several of the highest and most fastidious gentlemen in England, cannot still with one snap of my fingers acquire what man I choose? I am kind to you because I like you, and now, when I try to be kind another way, because I have thought we are friends, you—"

"Kind? Goddamn it, Fleur, I don't know but that's a bloody worse insult than the first!"

"Oh, madam, I do think it will be best that I call the watch," quavered the maid. McDonagh slung his neckcloth on anyhow, brushed past her, and strode for the door furiously.

"Heaven deliver me from such imbeciles!" Fleur pursued him

into the parlor. "I apologize to you, Conal, I did not mean to insult you, though you are a great fool not to know it without my telling you—I beseech you, for the love of God, take this terrible scowl from your face and be sensible! And it is remarkably forbearing of me that I forgive you for calling me names, but I realize you did not mean them—you are a fool, but not that much a fool—"

"May I be damned if you'll ever see thirty-five again," said McDonagh maliciously. But he leaned on the door and looked at her. "Well, all right, I grant that—it'll be some time before you lack hopeful lovers! Maybe I overstretched the truth a bit there. But damn it, Fleur—"

"I have apologized, I have apologized! How in the name of the good God should I suspect that you would fly all to pieces about this? I will not speak the word money again—we treat it as an obscenity. Now, dare I say one more thing to you?"

"Oh, well," said McDonagh somewhat more amiably, "what is it?"

"Nothing about money, but if you would condescend to take two ladies to the theater one night, we would do you much credit with our finest gowns—and be most flattered to have the attendance of such a big, handsome young man."

"Now, my God, you needn't lay it on so thick," said McDonagh. He laughed and dropped his hat and coat. "Well, I apologize too, Fleur, but damn it, you shouldn't say such things to a man!"

"I frequently think," she said, raising her eyes to heaven, "that I should have done better to enter a convent. In any event, if I do take a new protector, it will be another Englishman—one can predict how they will behave."

At the War Office the next morning a junior clerk much friendlier than the senior officer surprisingly produced McDonagh's new orders at once. He was detailed to join the *Donegal*, a line-of-battle ship, at present part of the fleet in the Mediterranean; the frigate *Decade*, acting as dispatch courier and due in at Portsmouth on September twenty-fifth, would carry him out.

Irrationally he felt the Irish name to be a kind of good omen, and on what Warner called one of the big hulks there'd be better chance of seeing action; the little ships like frigates usually acted as naval scouts, taking only minor part in battles. He might earn his wages for a change on the *Donegal*.

He went around to the Royal College of Surgeons and inquired for a letter; in all the eleven and a half months since he had left Ireland, there had been no word from Matt DeLancey, and McDonagh had begun to think gloomily that there never would be. But the little cockney clerk beamed at his question and whisked open a drawer.

"Well, now, sir, it's not a service as we hencourage, you unnerstand, seeing as professional gentlemen, rightly speakin', did ort to 'ave their own proper addresses and not go roaming abaht like fly-by-nights. But oncet in a way, as it were in your case, sir, it do 'appen that a gentleman can't be exactly sure o' where 'e'll be a little while. Back in June this 'ere come, sir, and I kep' it careful against your haskin'."

"That's very good of you," and McDonagh produced a crown. He had meant to make it a half crown and was slightly surprised at himself for the impulsive and extravagant gesture, as well as at the unexpected warm relief flooding him at the sight of Matt's neat script on the letter. Put it away as catalogued past, he'd told himself: everything he'd known in that country colored with violence and tragedy. Respected old Mr. DeLancey, he had, and in spite of the slight difference in age, he and Matt had been friends, but life changed; his way and Matt's had veered apart. Now suddenly this letter in his hand brought an astonishing warmth of emotional memory to him.

He took the letter away and read it in the nearest tavern, hardly noticing the taste of the bitter English ale. The devil looked after his own, wrote Matt, and he'd had luck in Plymouth to fall in with some American sailors off a merchant out of Boston. Very nice fellows, and a Donovan and a McCarthy among them. He'd happened to be in the right place to help them out in a little fight—"Trust Matt not to stay out of a fight long," muttered McDonagh to himself—and they'd been grateful enough to take him in with them. "I'll not be so indiscreet as to give details, suffice it to say that the enterprise was not unconnected with the smuggling trade—surprisingly profitable, and as I reckoned my chances of starting fresh would improve corresponding to the capital I could bring along, I was damned glad of the opportunity." He had left the smugglers for good in March, having accumulated sufficient funds to live on while starting up a practice, and settled in New York.

"Don't let me make you envious, my boyo, but the signs are I've fallen on my feet here. Not a bad town at all. I've decent lodgings in with my consulting room, and there's quite an up-to-date hospital, where I'll be let to practice as well. Very decent old fellow named Van Houten, chief surgeon—been friendly in a stiff sort of way and asked me to dinner once. He's got a couple of good-looking daughters. Safety in numbers, I can't decide which one is prettier!"

"Well, damn," said McDonagh, smiling over that, "maybe Matt's better off than me at that!" He put the letter away in his pocket, to be answered at leisure, and strolled up to St. Luke's Hospital.

The orderly he met in the entry greeted him enthusiastically. "Come back to us, Mr. McDonagh, 'ave you?"

"No fear! I've a damned sight better job now. But I've some time to kill in London, and I wanted to know how Asenath Nobbs turned out."

"Ho, Mr. Gillespie's 'ad more attention over that case so 'e ain't fit to live with, sir. Wonder 'e can still get 'is old 'ats on. You'll find 'im up in the second operating room, sir."

McDonagh went up the stair and opened the door of the indicated room. "Would you like a consultation, Mr. Gillespie?"

Gillespie, bent over the table with his back to the door, did not look around. "Well, well, the bad penny. Shut the door, Mr. McDonagh, I don't want to take cold. Get the needle ready, Mr. Smith, if you please." The anxious-looking young man across the table, smiling timid greeting at McDonagh, was one of the second-year students. "What occasions your return from the wars?"

"I've not seen any yet. Had a little time to waste." He came up to the table and peered around Gillespie's shoulder at the patient, just in time to receive a neat, copious spurt of blood across his shirtfront. He swore and started back. "Damn it to hell and perdition, this was a clean shirt! Why didn't you warn me, in God's name?"

The patient grinned at him; a great hairy ape of a fellow, his grin was rather strained, but he affected unconcern for what Gillespie was busy at over his left arm outstretched and strapped down. "Yer didn't ort to put on a clean shirt when yer agoin' to visit a norspital, Doctor," he observed sensibly.

McDonagh smeared the blood dry with a handkerchief resignedly. "The mischief's done, and I only hope I don't get taken up for murder on my way back to the inn! That's very nice indeed—quite a big one, isn't it?"

"Nothin' dauncylike abaht me," said the patient complacently. "Whatever I does, I does big."

Gillespie was engaged in cleaning out a varicose aneurysm in the crook of the arm. He had the ligature on now, above the bulge; he stripped the vessels quickly and in another moment had cleared the block and had a tight pressure dressing bound on. The young student diligently collected the used instruments and began wiping them with discarded lint rags.

"I wanted to know how Asenath came out," said McDonagh.

"Oh, beautifully, beautifully," said Gillespie, loosening the tourniquet. "I never hoped for such a result. Of course youth was in her favor, but all the same it was something of a miracle. I really believe that in time the small lines will all but disappear. It opens up an entire new field, or I should say reopens it, for the technique is not new—fascinating possibilities, fascinating! Of course the old diehard conservatives will have none of it, tell me it was mostly luck—the damned obstinate fools! I met MacNamara in the street yesterday, and he had the confounded damned impertinence to say—"

" 'Ere, watch wot yer abaht wiv *me*," said the patient uneasily.

"Yes, I rather think you'll have to put on a second ligature," said McDonagh. There was a creeping red stain on the pressure bandage.

"I was very much annoyed. Tchah!" said Gillespie, applying the ligature. "Well, there you are, my man. When that's had time to set a bit, it'll be good as new. What causes it? My good man, your guess is as good as mine, have to confess we don't know! I'm afraid there's no rule of behavior I can recommend to prevent a recurrence. Might be anywhere else, too, if there is a recurrence."

"Well, you're a bloody cheerful cove," said the patient, getting off the table unsteadily with the orderly's aid.

"Be thankful we can do something about it," retorted Gillespie. He surveyed McDonagh, wiping his hands. "Well, well, you seem to have acquired a lot of brown. Been in the tropics?"

"Enjoying a pleasure cruise. But I've the promise of a chance at seeing some action, at least, from now on."

6

————•————

McDonagh wielded the brass knocker on Fleur's house door and waited for admittance, scowling absently down at the brick step. He did not feel at all in the mood to squire two ladies to the theater.

Buying tobacco in the Holborn Road this morning, he had met Lauretta. She was passing the shop as he came out; she was in the company of another young woman, and so they were forced to stand and exchange meaningless social talk a few minutes. You are looking well, Conal. I am so happy you at last have your appointment to service ... pray let me introduce my friend. . . Damned stupid mouthings!

She was four or five months pregnant. Somehow, irrationally, that had shocked him; vaguely he felt his shock to be shamefully adolescent and damned himself for a fool. It became her; she was lovely as ever, her amber curls shining in the sun, her blue eyes smiling at him, her soft voice gentle.

He struck the side of his hand hard on the doorpost, in a gesture of anger at unforgotten emotion and the pain it could still bring him. A damned fool, so he was; but it seemed at least that he learned lessons quicker than most men. One hard, sharp lesson in the vicious futility of patriotism, its essential fatuous absurdity—that he had had, in '98, and been cured; and one equally painful lesson in the futility of romantic love, and he was cured of ever falling in love again. But the fervent patriotism he had got rid of from his system; the other emotion still lingered in him.

The maid let him into the parlor, and Fleur was there, waiting for him. She was polished and a trifle flamboyant in white satin and lace, with her hair dressed high, and ablaze with an impressive collection of paste jewels. Surveying him approvingly, she said, "I move with the times always, whatever the fashion one must be of it, but I say again that I do very much like the new long breeches young men adopt these days. The line, it is so much more graceful! Do you not find something just a little ridiculous about tight knee breeches? And on fat men, devastating! What is this absurd name for the new style?—"

"Pantaloons." He took the glass of wine she handed him with a nod.

"Ah, yes, a quite silly name! Nevertheless, they become you, and especially with that blue coat. Some men must have the most excellent tailoring to make anything of themselves, but you need not be ashamed, you do credit to the least expensive garments."

"If we did not understand each other about money," said McDonagh, "I'd suspect you were out to wangle something from me, after such fulsome and unnecessary compliments."

"What, may I not be polite without being suspected?" Fleur laughed. "I am a little light-headed, Conal, with relief."

"Oh? How do you find you like this niece who's come to batten off you?" He was not much interested in Fleur or her niece at the moment; he was impatient to be off to Portsmouth and getting on to his new job.

"That is just it! She is yet dressing and will be here in a moment, so I will tell you quick—not that Madeleine is at all shy! It has been a little comedy, I so nervous of having her here. Indeed, I find her not the provincial little miss in any degree, but of very good understanding, though she is but seventeen." Fleur nodded, her eyes amused. "She will get on, this one. She has it all planned out for herself, how the wisest course is for her to adopt my own profession. Quite frankly she says she comes to me for advice and help, as the business proposition! She puts herself in my hands, for all she must learn. And it is true, which she realizes, that the coiffure, the style, the—how is it? —rough edges of a country upbringing must all be changed and smoothed before we enter the lists! But Maddi is very amenable, very sensible. It seems she is more like me than her mother! Poor Elise was so narrow of mind, so joyless. Possibly," said Fleur in a thoughtful tone, "that is why Maddi rebels against her upbringing."

"Oh, very likely." McDonagh laughed, somewhat intrigued. "So you turn into an amateur procuress?"

"That is insulting! We women must help each other. I am interested and amused. I think between us, with a small capital expenditure, we contrive to start Maddi off very well. Not too soon—as I have explained, she has a valuable commodity to sell, in a way, you understand, and we must make the best capture possible for her first protector, just the right man. Also, she is yet young and must acquire the polish—at least a trifle of sophistication, though not too much. Though for seventeen—and coming from Tunbridge Wells—she is quite creditable, you will find."

"Oh, did you want my valuable male opinion?"

"It would be entirely worthless," said Fleur amusedly. "She will not be aiming at the attraction of a straightforward young man like Conal McDonagh, but a rather special type. There is a type of middle-aged gentleman who feels he renews his youth by taking a young and innocent mistress to keeping, but most of that sort, they are tiresomely avuncular—it is not so much a mistress they want as a pretty young girl to play daughter. No, it must be a very special capture, Maddi's first. We will be in no hurry about it, for so much depends upon it."

"Like breaking in a horse?" suggested McDonagh, smiling.

"My God, men are indeed crude at times! The one we want, it is a man not too old, not too young, the sophisticate with perhaps the taste a little jaded, so that he will be amused to take a young innocent. But kind and of unperverted tastes. And of course, a man of wealth, who can afford to manage these affairs properly."

McDonagh said, "Crude, you say. I'd like to know what else that is."

"It is common sense," said Fleur. "And here is my little Madeleine." She turned with a smile as the inner door opened. "Come and be introduced to our escort, *chérie*."

"How do you do, Mr. McDonagh," said a cool husky voice. He responded automatically, somewhat taken aback—for no good reason—at first sight of Madeleine Olivier.

The hand she gave him was narrow and small-boned; she was tall for a woman, but very slender, and the narrow, sheathlike white gown she wore, high to the neck and fitted to the waist, accentuated her slimness. Her hair was dark, a smoky black worn in a loose, girlish style he suspected Fleur would soon change; but she had the very white skin of his own race, and her eyes were an unexpected gray, without any fleck of green or brown.

She looked back at him interestedly and divided a smile between him and Fleur, showing small, even white teeth. "What a pity this one has no money," she observed innocently. "But one can't have everything, and anyway I understand he belongs to you."

"That I do not," said McDonagh instantly, resentfully, and—to his fury—with some embarrassment. Well, no, he'd never counted himself a prude, and a moment ago he had been only mildly interested and amused at this situation. Now he was conscious of a sort of shock, and sudden surprising anger—at Fleur. The girl was very damned young; she was pretending to a veneer of sophistication, but it was obviously veneer. Brought up in a smallish country town, probably in a rigidly conventional household, she saw London and the exotic Fleur overlaid with false glamour, and the life of a demimondaine as wickedly exciting. Fleur had long forgotten seventeen; she said, *of very good understanding, not the provincial little miss*, but she gave the silly girl too much credit: Madeleine was seeing the surface of the thing, not the reality. Between her ignorance and Fleur's lack of imagination, they would ruin the girl's life, he thought angrily.

"But that is not funny—a trifle too gauche, my dear," corrected Fleur firmly. She was watching McDonagh with a little smile. "Come, let us be off or we will be late for the beginning."

McDonagh felt less than ever in the mood for taking these two to the theater. Unaccustomed and rather frightening emotion filled him, and that was pity. He had always said easily, myself's enough to worry about, and most often the obvious subjects for other people's pity had seemed to him merely weak. But this little idiot thought she knew what she was doing.

He sat between them at the theater, and the anger and pity grew in him for Madeleine's nearly successful attempt to behave as if attendance at the play were no novelty to her. What the hell did they think they were up to, these two, setting out deliberately to turn a respectable girl into a glorified harlot?

Astonishingly and infuriatingly he lay awake thinking about it, about Madeleine Olivier. Facing himself in the glass next morning as he shaved, he thought, well, to hell with it: it was none of his damned business, but he was in the habit of saying what he thought, and call it interference—which it was—somebody ought to interfere here. And he'd say it before Fleur if necessary, and to the devil with her if she resented it.

He walked up to King Street, to give the recurrence of temper time to cool down, and wielded the brass knocker briskly. The maid, greeting him nervously, told him that Madame was in her bath and not to be seen. "That's all right, it's Mademoiselle Olivier I want to see. Is she visible?" If he could get the girl to himself for half an hour . . .

The maid backed away, and he went past her into the little parlor. Madeleine was sitting before the fire over a fashion magazine. "Good morning, Mr. McDonagh. But not Mademoiselle, please. I couldn't help being born in France, but after all, I've lived most of my life in England, and while I'm sure a French accent does lend one cachet, I'm afraid I can't manage it, you know." She gave him her sudden smile, which lent her small features unexpected impish gaity. Her voice was rather deep for a girl's. He saw in her, briefly, the shadow of what she might become in ten years—a capacity for an elegantly sophisticated attraction she had—despite her lack of figure, despite her present occasional gaucherie.

"Miss Olivier, then," he said, and laid his coat and hat on the sofa and sat in the chair opposite hers. "Go away," he said to the maid, "and you needn't tell Madame I am here, to hurry her unduly." He trusted she would not; Fleur would be a nuisance now. When the maid had gone, he looked back to Madeleine. "I wanted to talk to you, Miss Olivier. I'm afraid I'm going to be rude, but there's no point in beating about the bush—not a habit of mine anyway—and I'm leaving London tomorrow and likely won't see you again for a long time, if at all."

She raised her thinly arched brows. "This sounds most intriguing! I am glad I came to London, there is something going on every moment. But I'm sure Fleur would like me to offer you a glass of wine—may I?"

"No, thanks, and neither do you want any. I—"

"How do you know? I find I quite like it. Mr. Bodge never would let me taste it, you know—"

"Mr. Bodge?"

"Good heavens, why the dreadful frown? Mr. Bodge was my stepfather."

"My God, of course," said McDonagh, momentarily diverted, "what else would a grocer in Tunbridge Wells be but Mr. Bodge? Nevertheless, you don't want a glass of wine now, for God's sake stop fidgeting around with the bottles and sit down and listen. I want to talk to you seriously before Fleur pokes her nose in at us."

Madeleine reseated herself, staring at him. "What about? Are you going to make me an offer?"

"I am not," he said irritably. "Now look here, Miss Olivier. Whether or not you know it, Fleur told me all about you—"

"She says you are a good friend," said Madeleine, raising her brows again.

"Stop interrupting." He plunged ahead bluntly, aware that there was no very tactful way to say this. "You'll have to forgive my plain speaking, but somebody has got to say it to you, and I don't suppose there's anyone else who will. I think you're making a bad mistake, which you'll regret, and Fleur's got no business encouraging you. You can't just blithely leap into a thing like this and reckon if you don't like it, you can get out again—because you can't. To be blunt about it, you damned well don't know what you're getting into, Miss Olivier." He smiled at her and essayed some cautious tact. "I won't tell you you're too young to know what you're doing, but I do think you haven't thought the matter through. You're seeing, oh, everything"—he gestured vaguely—"London, and Fleur, and her sort of life, through a sort of haze of glamour, and you just don't have any idea of the reality of it. I realize it may all look damned attractive to you at the moment, but it's not like that underneath, you know. It can be ugly and sordid and degrading, often. This is something you need to think twice and again about, that's all I'm saying to you, and I hope to God you will." McDonagh the reformer, he thought sardonically: a new role for him.

Her gray eyes had widened and then narrowed at him, but she showed no particular embarrassment. Now she broke in gently. "It's very flattering of you to be concerned about me, Mr. McDonagh, but is it any of your affair? I'm not exactly a child, you know."

He thought that was exactly what she was, but he said, "Of course not. But after all, you obviously can't know a great deal about—"

"And you do?" She laughed. She was sitting crosswise on her chair, swinging one foot slowly where it was crossed over the other; it should have been a hoydenish position, but she was an extraordinarily graceful creature and looked merely comfortable. "If we're talking bluntly, which you seem to think we are, I'd ask you just what suggestion you might have as to how I earn a *respectable* living? It's easy for you—or anyone—to say I ought to, but saying's not doing, you know. I've a sort of education, but I couldn't get a place as governess—I tried. And there's really nothing else for a female to work at, but domestic jobs—is there?—and I shouldn't be very good at that either. Mother was well enough bred that she thought it beneath me to know about polishing brass and cleaning floors, and if I apply, they look at me and say, Oh, but you're a lady, my dear, I couldn't have that in the house, not at all suitable, looking quite horrified, you know, as if I had three heads or were feebleminded. At least, that's what the one woman I applied to said. And I've only just a hundred pounds—or at least it's ninety-eight and eightpence, since we bought the stuff for a new gown—and I must earn some sort of living, you do see that. Mr. Bodge was very kind, and he would have provided for me if he could, but his business failed, you see. Everyone thinks—without really thinking about it, you know—that girls ought to get married, and that's that, they're off everyone's mind once they have husbands. But really, when we simply have to sit and wait for such a thing, which is what it comes to when one is situated as I was, with not many acquaintances—because Mother considered most of Mr. Bodge's much beneath her—and with no convenient relatives to invite me and chaperon me to places I might meet eligible young men—well, it just doesn't happen. I do think things were managed better in the days when fathers or uncles chose a suitable husband—at least one was never left on the shelf to fend for oneself. I should much prefer, of course, to be married to someone and have my own house, and children, and some settled sort of life. But husbands don't drop out of the sky into the laps of young females who have no dowers and are moreover of foreign nationality—you know how suspicious Englishmen are of foreigners, even if I have been brought up here and scarcely remember any French at all. And I have come to the point, Mr. McDonagh—which I daresay a man would never understand— when I am quite positively unable ever again to put on that brown merino gown, or the tabby silk that was turned for me when Mother had a new one six years ago, and which has been let down three times. I am also extremely tired of mending my one pair of stockings and putting cardboard into my shoes—it doesn't really keep the wet out, you know."

All this was said in a cool, rather expressionless tone, and in her candid gray eyes on him McDonagh was belatedly aware of more intelligence than he'd suspected. At the same time he recognized something similar to the hard, tough core he shared with Fleur the practical.

93

"I really think, after all, I will have a glass of wine," said Madeleine; she rose and poured it. "If you stop to think—as I have, you know—you must realize that it's very lucky I have a relative like Fleur. Of course, Mother would never hear her name mentioned before me, but she did talk about her to Mr. Bodge, so I knew quite a bit about her. I took a chance in writing and coming, but no one could be nicer or more understanding. I am not a child, and I know quite well I shouldn't be able to enter on such a career as I am, by myself. I really shouldn't know in the least how to start about it," and she laughed. "I should doubtless be tricked and exploited and altogether ruin myself, and perhaps end on the streets—which I do not mean to happen, I assure you. So you see it is very lucky I have Fleur to guide me. She says we shall invest a year in my acquiring what she calls polish and then set out to make the best possible capture at first. And it is all quite businesslike, I am to pay her back what she spends on me aside from my own little money, but not at interest, for she says that would not be agreeable to family feeling." Madeleine's smile was faintly mischievous. "I thought that was amusing—and so like Fleur."

"I—yes," said McDonagh. "Yes, isn't it?" He looked at her in rather helpless silence. "Miss Olivier, God knows I don't want to offend you or sound like a—a damned reformer, but—and I do realize the position you're in—but if you'll forgive me, it seems a drastic solution, damn it! That is, your reputation—"

"*Which,*" she pointed out, "is not a thing one can eat or wear."

"Look here," he said abruptly, "the case isn't so bad, it can't be. I know some people here who would be pleased to help you, I'm sure. If I gave you a letter to Mrs. FitzEustace, would you go there? They'd be kind, they'd take you in until you could find decent work—there'd be more opportunity for that in London, you know." An odd new thought crossed his mind on that, which was that he spoke the truth: Lauretta and her dry stick of a husband would be kind; they were conventional, righteous, Christian people. Something to be said for the orthodox—just once in a way, and taken in small doses, like opium, he thought with grim humor.

For a moment he thought she had not heard. "I did think," she went on dreamily, looking at her glass of wine, "of being a children's nurse. I do like babies. I used to look after Mrs. Ashling's; she lived next to us and was continually having them—rather nice babies, too, not quite like those I should like to have, all very fat and placid—the Ashlings both were like that anyway, very—very respectable middle-class English, you know? But the once I tried to get such a situation, the woman said, Oh, my dear, you're far too young, I couldn't possibly trust you. Which seemed rather odd to me, because after all, the nearer you are to the babies, so to speak, the better you'd understand them, wouldn't you think? But on the whole, while I like babies, I think I might find them very tiresome all the time when they were not my own. Oh, about your friends—I don't think so, Mr. McDonagh." She gave him an oddly benign smile. "I've quite made up my mind, you see. It is not, obviously, the sort of job I'd have chosen, with any preference possible. But it's only men, and not all of those, who can earn their livings, if they have to, at things they really enjoy doing and are—are concerned about, you know? I daresay you like being a doctor—"

"I'm not a physician, I'm a surgeon," he said in mechanical correction.

"A surgeon," she amended, "and that you always wanted to be, and so that's that, some people may think it is unfortunate to have to earn one's living, but at least a man like yourself earns it at work he is interested in, and no one—except a snob—thinks any the worse of you for working. So of course, it is impossible for you to imagine how it is for me, as a female, to be kept from it—except for such a career as Fleur's—and to know that self-righteous people will deplore it, which is maddening when it is really the only way I might earn a comfortable living. In any case, Fleur is quite right when she says—which I knew very well already—that men are all inclined to be fearfully idealistic and a little naïve."

Touched on the raw, McDonagh snapped back to that, "Well, that's the last word you could say about the man you're talking to this minute, my girl! You may think you've outgrown any illusions—I'll keep my face straight when you say that, if only

95

just—but I know something more about this than you do, and—"

"I don't doubt it," she agreed cordially, "from what Fleur says. But then that is only natural, you being a man."

"I am not talking about that aspect of the matter, damn it," said McDonagh.

"Well, if we're to talk on any other grounds than experience," observed Madeleine, "you are not all that much older than I am, sir. Possibly five or six years?"

"Call it about a hundred," said McDonagh wearily. "You've got the notion you're entirely grown-up and sensible, enough to decide a thing like this on its merits, pro and con. My God, you're hardly more sensible than a baby yourself—"

"Seventeen is not exactly infancy," she said.

And he said in sudden bitterness, "No, my God. God knows it isn't, always. Long before I was seventeen, I'd had my first girl and my first drunken brawl, and I'd seen too much bloody war—" He stopped abruptly, terrified. Not a war, a technical rebellion, and no amnesty ever granted. She'd roused his damned temper, and he had forgotten to guard his tongue. Enniscorthy: *a very pretty nasty hand with the knife*. And so now, fatal, mad to let her see he had said anything out of the way; say something else quickly, to make her forget it, take any emphasis from it.

He felt sudden sweat on his forehead. The silence had been too sharp and had gone on too long. He said roughly, quietly, "If you ever repeat that, you could get me hanged." And in his mind he walked back along Green Street in Dublin and saw a gallows with a man hanging. Another of the fervent patriots, the idealists, the damned fools.

He looked up and met her eyes. She said in a low voice, "Why, you're afraid—suddenly. Oh—"

He saw half understanding in her expression. He said, "I shouldn't have said that, I don't know why the devil I did. Forget it."

"I'll forget it, Mr. McDonagh," she promised gravely. He looked at her again and thought she would. There was quality in her, surprising and strong—or the promise of it. Again he was aware of a center of tensile strength in her, and this time, too, of honesty. He thought she meant what she said.

"I think I was a fool to come here," he said slowly, getting to his feet. "But somehow, damn it, it seemed a waste. You, I mean. If you're not quite so senseless as I thought—while we're being frank, I'll admit that much—" He heard behind him the rustle of Fleur's approach, and in the instant before her rather brittle voice accosted him in greeting, he met the polite smile in Madeleine's eyes—the expression she might turn on a prattling child or a boring dinner companion. Exasperated fury choked him, and Fleur said his name gaily.

"But you should know better than to call upon ladies in the morning, we are never at our best!"

He turned to face her. He said, "I only dropped past to say good-bye. I'm off for Portsmouth and parts beyond and wanted to wish you—both—good fortune until I see you again." If ever, his mind added, and, as he looked back at Madeleine, Good fortune—and better sense.

Undoubtedly he had been a fool—McDonagh the reformer, the rescuer of virgins! Could it possibly be, he wondered with an inward grin, that some of his righteous Presbyterian raising had taken root after all? What in God's name was it to him whether one girl lost her virtue?—and not even at his own hands, nothing to do with him.

He'd made himself look ridiculous, too, he reflected with a mental shrug, a solemn idiot lecturing her like a damned Methodist. Even now he wasn't sure what had prompted him: if it came to talking of morals, he didn't pay even lip service to many himself—only the important ones, the ones he valued: honesty, honor, integrity at his job. There were the hell of a lot of moral precepts in church creeds that didn't take human nature much into account. He'd always abided by the creed of live and let live, and he was damned if he knew why he'd broken his rule to lecture Madeleine Olivier on how she should live her life.

Or rather, on reflection, he did know, and why was he reluctant to look at it square? He wasn't used to thinking very long or deep about his own motives. Fleur—it was something to do with

Fleur. He liked her, casually, for what she was; as such women went, she was honest and amusing. You certainly couldn't couple an expensive courtesan with a street harlot; apart from anything else, they were different types. Oh, he'd enjoyed Fleur. So?

But there at the last, yesterday, he'd seen the brittle hardness to her, made the inevitable comparison with the girl. What the devil had Fleur reminded him of, absurdly? ... That old drunken cockney who came into St. Luke's with a broken ankle. "It's not that I'm orl that fond o' the gin, it's me 'eadaches, Doctor—orful 'eadaches I get, an' I only tike the gin to forget the pine like." Defensive: that was the word he wanted.

He laughed aloud suddenly, and his companions in the Portsmouth stage stared at him. There it was: you might not pay even lip service to the too rigid, superstitious old orthodoxies, but the awareness of them was still there. Every now and then rising to the surface on surprising occasions—in him, in Fleur, in everybody. A woman like Fleur was always conscious that technically she was a fallen woman.

So there were all the intricacies of the thing a bit clearer in his mind. He shared some of Fleur's inmost qualities, and he thought Madeleine, young as she was, shared them, too. It was no matter to him about Fleur—experienced, cynical, wise Fleur—he could take Fleur for what she was. But maybe, in Madeleine, absurd as it might sound, he saw something of himself seven, eight years back—the young innocent. Maybe his conscience was expanding, or was it a kind of instinct for the experienced and cynical to guard innocent youth? Call it unwarrantable interference and have done!

That satisfied him for the moment as to his own obscure motive, and he was able to leave off thinking about it. Whatever the ins and outs of the matter, nothing could be clearer than that it was none of Conal McDonagh's business.

And he liked women—in his leisure time—but he was some relieved to be getting on to a new job, back to his trade after a holiday.

7

"Obviously out of the question," said the chief surgeon of the *Donegal*. "I have never found that that technique was in any degree practicable, Mr. McDonagh." He said it pontifically, benignly, like a kind but firm governess correcting a pupil's paper.

McDonagh hung on to his temper. It wasn't that he resented an honest difference of opinion, but Clinton, damn him, never treated it like that; he always saw it as the foolish error of a slipshod young man without his own experience or wisdom. They had had this before, over the sailor with concussion ("I am surprised at you, Mr. McDonagh, obviously it is necessary to do an immediate trepanation") and he'd have brained the old fool if McKenna hadn't come up and eased him away. Just not done to question the chief surgeon's decisions; McDonagh would have earned a large black mark on his record, and it had been a near thing. To save himself, he had, as it now appeared to him, compromised his integrity: he'd simply walked away from the patient, who belonged to Clinton anyway, technically speaking. And Clinton had done a trepanation, and the patient had died eight days later. And McDonagh still felt that he was morally responsible for that man's death, because he had not been persuasive enough to hold Clinton off.

McKenna had said easily, "Ah, it depends a good deal where you trained and under who, you know—that sort of opinion. I grant you, it's the older school that says, Trepan immediately, but enough good youngish fellas agree with it after all. It's standard procedure in London Hospital. Not just a matter of personal opinion on individual cases."

"Well, by God, it should be—and it is with me! My God, a little elementary observation and a look at the death records would tell him different! You've got fifty percent less chance of bringing out a trepan case than any other operation. I've seen concussions before, you know—and followed results."

"All right, all right," said McKenna amiably. "So we both have. I wouldn't do a trepan here either, but neither you nor me's the senior surgeon, laddie."

And the man had died, yes, and maybe he'd have died anyway; maybe his time was up. But it stayed in McDonagh's mind that if he had kept his temper long enough to talk soft to Clinton and persuade him not to use the drill, the man would have lived. Contempt for himself had gnawed at him ever since, and now here they were at odds over the same sort of thing in a way, and it behooved him to remember the object lesson.

He didn't give a damn about Ensign Harry Lightfoot; it was the principle of the thing.

"With all deference to your opinion, sir," he said, feeling that it came out between his teeth, "I've seen several cases of this sort respond very well to the treatment I mentioned. I do think it's better to try for the lesser of evils, don't you? After all, it means the difference between retiring an active young man from service he's trained to and enabling him to carry on."

"If," said Clinton, "the treatment is successful, which is such a very slender chance that personally I scarcely think we need consider it." He smiled and shook his head at McDonagh. *These ambitious young men,* said the smile, *rushing in without experience to guide them!* He was a large bell-shaped man in the late sixties, with a narrow bald head, and he affected rather baggy knee breeches and snuff.

"I do beg your pardon, sir," said McDonagh very carefully, "but I don't think the chances are so bad as that." He felt as if he were balancing along the edge of a cliff. *For God's sake, don't lash out at him, take it easy, hold on!* "In fact, I think the chances are very good from what I've seen of such cases."

"Which can hardly be very much, eh?" countered Clinton good-humoredly. "It's a thing that happens chiefly with gunshot wounds, after all, and I understand you've not seen any action."

"There were two coach accidents," said McDonagh, "when I was at St. Luke's, and a few others I saw in training at Queens'. All of them responded very well." With that he managed to suggest that several surgeons he had worked with had decided on that treatment as a matter of course, while avoiding the direct statement that Mr. Such-and-Thus or Mr. This-or-That was a better surgeon than Clinton. He started to add that John Hunter's *Treatise on Gunshot Wounds* stated unequivocally— and stopped himself; that would leave the way open for Clinton to say something genial about new-qualified young men who were forever quoting textbooks, being without experience.

"Oh, yes," said Clinton inattentively. He leaned on the rail and stared across the harbor at the tiny island of Maddalena. "Four or five cases—not really much to go on, eh, Mr. McDonagh? I agree, it's a great pity for a young man to lose a leg, but these things happen."

"I'd be d—I'd be very sorry to see it happen here, sir, when there's no real need it should, as I see it."

"Oh, yes," said Clinton again. "You've said that several times before. Well, well, it's a matter of opinion, and I'm afraid I must plead greater experience and practical knowledge. I think we'll amputate, and be safe. The only question in my mind is, and perhaps I had best consult Captain Malcolm—will we keep Ensign Lightfoot aboard, or leave him in Maddalena to recuperate. There is no telling when we may get into action, you know—it may come at any moment, or, conversely, not at all—but in the event that we do, it would be rather a nuisance to have a helpless convalescent taking up space. Yes, yes, I believe I will go and consult Captain Malcolm, just to be on the safe side." He made off up the deck without another word; he had seen many years of service in the navy and was as surefooted on a deck as on land, for all his unwieldly paunch and spindle shanks.

McDonagh made a few profane remarks to himself, looking after him. Laurence McKenna strolled up from around the nearest bulkhead and observed approvingly, "You kept your temper with him anyway. I was ready to come up and forestall you from committin' mayhem." McKenna was the second junior surgeon of the *Donegal*'s three: a wiry sandy-haired man five or six years McDonagh's elder, with ugly good-humored features. He came from the county Antrim and had a fine amateur tenor voice.

"Mayhem!" said McDonagh. "I'd have thrown the old bastard over the side in another minute! I'll be damned if he takes off that leg! Doesn't he realize we've made any progress in the last forty years? No surgeon I ever met, damn his age, would amputate this case!"

"Oh, I quite agree," said McKenna. "But d'you think a two-to-one opinion'd mean anything to him? Gone to see the captain, has he?—tell you what, friend, suppose you and me go to see the patient." He grinned at McDonagh. "Seems to me the poor fella ought to have something to say about his own leg, y'know—and some of these regular navy men can be damned stubborn."

McDonagh looked at him and laughed. "I'm with you. Always a way to beat the devil round a gate!"

"So there is," said McKenna dryly as they started up toward the fore companion. "Trouble with you is, you never look for it until afterward—you just try to ram the gate down by bull force. All the celebrated Irish charm left conspicuously out o' you, wasn't it?"

"I wish to God I had some to use on Clinton," said McDonagh. He also wished he had a head for heights, looking at the gangplank ahead. It was one of several things—Clinton heading the list—he disliked about the *Donegal*; every time he had occasion to go from foredeck to aft, he suffered a minute of exquisite nervousness, crossing one of the narrow planks laid across the deep waist of the ship. Only pride kept him from detouring by the steep companionways when every other man aboard used the planks as a matter of course. The old *Lively*, being a frigate, had had a flush deck. He followed McKenna across now, carefully, resisting the impulse to look thirty feet down to the bottom of the waist, and breathed again on the other side. They went below by the fore companion and into the canvas-walled cabin next to the one they shared, where lay Ensign Harry Lightfoot.

Ensign Lightfoot, like many another man on present duty with the fleet in the Mediterranean, found life infinitely boring, and he had got up a party of young officers from the *Donegal* and the *Spencer*, both watering at Maddalena, to go ashore bird shooting this morning. Nobody knew or cared about seasons on a godforsaken Italian island, and it was something to do. Among them they had mustered three pistols and a musket illegally borrowed from marine armament aboard, and it was the musket—in the hands of an exuberant lieutenant off the *Spencer*—which had brought Ensign Lightfoot to grief. A wild shot had lodged in his thigh, smashing into the bone.

As they came in, he looked up a little wanly from where he lay on an improvised pallet bed. "Well, you bone sawers made up your minds to give me some notice at last, eh?" He had had some laudanum for the pain, and his voice was a bit slurred.

"Say your piece, Conal me boy," said McKenna.

McDonagh squatted down beside the bed. "Look here," he said, "Clinton's a blundering old fool, he's still doing things the way they were done forty years ago. He's made up what passes for his mind to take off your leg—"

That woke Ensign Lightfoot up. He went paler and tried to raise himself on one elbow. "What? My God, is it that bad? I didn't suspect—"

"No, it's not. I said he's a damned old blunderer. McKenna knows it as well as I do. We can put the leg right—as it'll ever be. I warn you, you'll go a bit lame, but it'll be perfectly sound in three months. The thing is, Clinton's the senior surgeon, and neither Larr nor I can dictate to him. It's up to you. If you raise a row and insist on one of us taking you on, we might manage it. Just say I told you I might be able to save your leg—I don't want to get into more trouble with Clinton than absolutely necessary—and insist I'm given the chance, see."

Lightfoot stared at him. "You can?" he asked anxiously.

"I said so, yes. All Clinton can say is that I'd no business speaking to you at all. But the mischief'll be done, and I'll apologize to him nice and meek." McDonagh grinned. "He's gone to consult the captain about leaving you to convalesce on Maddalena—"

"This dead-alive hole? My God!"

"—But he'll be down presently, all set to amputate. For God's sake stand him off."

"Christ, I'll stand him off all right," said Lightfoot faintly. "But if he's the say—he can just tell me I don't know what I'm talking about—if you can't—"

"You can be just as damn nasty as you like," said McDonagh. "Don't for God's sake quote me!—just go on letting him see you've got it into your head the leg can be saved, and you won't let him near you until it's been tried."

"All right," said Lightfoot. "All right, I'll try." His hand grasped McDonagh's sleeve urgently. "You—you can save it? It's not just maybe?"

McDonagh was no stranger to that look in a patient's eyes, the appeal for reassurance to ultimate authority. He had known medical men who, maybe for experiencing it so often, went to believing they were ultimate authorities, God's deputies and all-wise. Mr. William DeLancey had used to say it made him feel frighteningly humble, as if he posed on false pretenses. It had never affected McDonagh either way; it only made him furiously angry. "Looking at me as if I was God," he had said once to Matt. "How can I say anything for certain? How can any of us?" And Matt had quoted old Paré at him: *I dressed his wounds and God healed him.* Well, he hadn't any religion himself, but that was the core of the matter. You did your damnedest, the best way you knew, and then stood back and let nature take over the job. And sometimes, for no apparent reason, it didn't work. He resented being looked at as if he were omniscient, precisely because he couldn't be.

He said now, "Barring any complications, yes, I can put it right."

Lightfoot sank back, and his mouth straightened grimly. "I'll not let him near me. But for God's sake stay here, even if you daren't back me up too much!"

McKenna, who had been lounging at the entrance, hands in pockets, said softly, "And you'd both best prepare for battle. Here comes the old fella now."

McDonagh gripped Lightfoot's arm in encouragement and got to his feet. Clinton entered smiling, wiped the smile from his mouth, and made grave pronouncements to the patient. Lightfoot spoke up firmly as he'd been told, Clinton uttered astonished outraged bumblings at McDonagh, and McDonagh acknowledged as meekly as possible that he'd had no business discussing the case with the patient. Clinton told Lightfoot that McDonagh had not the experience or judgment to know whereof he spoke, and Lightfoot said his part over again and went on saying it. McKenna interrupted the third time around by drawing the chief surgeon aside deferentially.

"I do understand how you feel, Mr. Clinton, but it seems that the patient's got this notion firm in his mind, and I might say it's not all Mr. McDonagh's fault, sir, it was a very casual mention on his part, but you know how a patient'll seize on any little thing. You'd be bound to have a good deal o' trouble with him when his mind's set this way. It might be easiest to try the other first, just to satisfy him, and if it does go wrong, at least he'll likely be halfway reconciled that we did try, y'see, and be more tractable." He gave Clinton a sunny, expectant smile. "Don't you agree, sir?"

Clinton, eyeing McDonagh with dislike and suspicion, obviously did not agree, but under Lightfoot's half-hysterical threats to demand the captain's ruling, he gave way at last with bad grace. McDonagh swallowed his pride and followed him out to apologize again for unwittingly putting the idea in the patient's mind. "I assure you, sir, it was ony a casual word, I didn't think he could overhear—"

"Oh, indeed?" said Clinton huffily. "In view of our recent discussion, I don't know that I'll take that at face value! However, the damage is done, and I wash my hands of the case entirely, which I make sure was your intention! I only offer the prediction, Mr. McDonagh, based upon forty years of experience, that you will put the patient through a great deal of unnecessary suffering, all to amputate in the end, when blood poisoning sets in." He stalked away in offended dignity.

"And if that doesn't happen," said McKenna, "he'll never forgive you for cheating him of the chance to say I told you so."

"It's damned well not going to happen," said McDonagh. "Let's get to work on it and make sure." He turned into the next cabin to collect his instruments.

He had seen one bloody war, but it seemed this one wasn't being fought the same way, at least not yet. There was that great armed camp at Boulogne, just sitting there, and here in the Mediterranean, the French fleet lying in Toulon Harbor at anchor, while the English fleet, divided into blockading squadrons, patrolled gently onward from Brest to Gibraltar outside, watchdogs to keep the French penned up. This fleet in the Mediterranean, eleven line-of-battle ships, some frigates and supply sloops, was the last link in the chain. For eighteen months it had been patrolling here: lying at anchor, moving leisurely upward Toulon, back again, and wandering down the coast of Corsica to come to anchor again in the little harbor of La Maddalena off Sardinia.

The frigates were busiest, keeping the fleet's eye on Toulon in frequent runs up to scan that harbor, running fast with dispatches to Gibraltar, to England; the great capital ships had nothing to do but wait for possible action. Most of their little activity was contrived, and if the officers of the *Donegal* felt as the rest did, for that they credited their admiral, always concerned to keep his men fit and ready.

"Damned easy to go stale on a job like this, you know," the third officer Ashmund had told McDonagh. "Not one blessed thing to do but keep watch. You get slack, nothing ever happens, and then when something does, you're in no state to meet it—men fat and lazy, maybe a long list o' sick, and discipline gone to pieces. The admiral knows that—he's done his damnedest to keep the whole strength up to snuff. O' course, it's damned lucky the authorities are friendly on Sardinia—we can get ashore now and then, get fresh green stuff, water. The admiral's seen to it that every ship has a turn in harbor, every so often, and a little change at sea, moving around, to keep the men on their toes. But even so, it's a damnable dull job."

He went on, in almost the same words McDonagh had heard from other men, to praise the admiral: a great sea dog, Admiral Nelson, England's greatest, Nelson the hero of Cape St. Vincent. McDonagh listened to that idly, not much interested. He'd not yet, in the time since he joined the *Donegal*, seen the admiral; the flagship had never been in harbor at the same time.

If the officers and crew had little to do, the medical staff had less. He had discovered that naval surgeons were in a rather curious position, medically speaking. Since in time of action aboard it was surgeons who were needed, there were no physicians on naval staffs, but most of the time before and after action the surgeons were called on to attend complaints in the physicians' realm; bored, lazy, or genuinely ill patients came with vague stories of persistent headaches, constipation, loss of appetite, insomnia, various internal aches and pains.

"Damn it," he had said to McKenna, "don't they know the difference between surgeons and physicians? I never studied medicine, I don't know the names of half the stuff dispensing physicians use or what they use it for! I've made up prescriptions—worked for an apothecary in Dublin once—but I never troubled to remember much about it, and anyway, most of it struck me as damned queer medicine and not likely to do much either way."

"If you get any physician in an expansive mood," said McKenna, "he'll admit most of the good of a prescription is in the patient's faith."

"Theriac, I do remember that one. There was an old doctor, Trumble his name was, prescribed it for every patient he had, always trotting 'round for more of it, sometimes made up in a salve, sometimes to take internally—and what is it? I ask you— mostly ground-up vipers' flesh! And there was another one used to come in to buy mandrake root—"

"What," said McKenna with a grin, "an Irishman after an aphrodisiac?" He laughed. "It's shocking ethics, and we'd get in trouble on land, but we've all got used to it in the navy. Stock as many drugs as any apothecary. I've reached the point where I can mix up a purgative as neat as any doctor and never think twice about it."

"Well, you can go right on taking all such cases," said McDonagh. "My God, I might poison some poor devil!" But in self-defense he had had to familiarize himself somewhat with the stock of medicines.

Now, hauling out his case of instruments, his mind divided between grim satisfaction at victory over old Clinton and rumination on the surgical problem before him, he was in better spirits for anticipation of getting back to his own job. Clinton, saying it was obviously necessary to amputate! Implying that the four or five cases McDonagh had seen were unusual.

His mind went back over those cases analytically. And as he straightened with the case of instruments in his hand, the sudden sweat broke cold on his forehead; he had forgotten to quote one case to Clinton—the first he'd seen. His mind had shut down on it until this minute. Though, God, if he'd lost his temper with Clinton, it might have come out. And Clinton's expression would have been something to see. . . .

Enniscorthy. Oh, very damned lucky they'd been, up to Enniscorthy. Talk about war; that was war, savage, bloody, and no quarter. And not a scratch on either of them till then, two damn fool wild youngsters. And then—Enniscorthy, with the British Hessian regiments gone berserk with the bayonet.

They lay up in the bracken, hidden, he and Matt DeLancey, and saw the Hessians systematically murdering the wounded left on the field. He couldn't say to this day how he'd got Matt up the hill to hiding, to temporary safety. The ball had taken Matt just above the knee, and you could feel the bone was smashed. No surgeon to be trusted nearer than Dublin and William DeLancey, and that was a long terrible seventy miles away.

But he brought Matt home to Dublin, in a stolen farm cart, pulling it himself by night, lying hid up by day. Stealing what food he could pick up, and twice nearly caught. A tourniquet on the leg, torn from Matt's shirt, until it stopped bleeding. The damned rough track and the wooden-wheeled cart always starting it bleeding again. The downpour of rain that night as they lay in the open, partly sheltered under trees, outside Dunlavin village, and Matt delirious in fever, and that furtive-eyed fellow sliding up—got away off Vinegar Hill he had, where the Hessians had slaughtered too. Came at McDonagh from behind a rock, thinking to steal the food and Matt's pistol. Just luck, something making McDonagh dodge and turn.

I wonder if I killed him, McDonagh thought again. He did not much care; he only wondered. Gave him back some of his own medicine, anyway, and left him lying still in the rain.

But they came to Dublin in the end, to Mr. DeLancey, and the leg healed. Short, but quite sound.

War. England called this a war, with France. Sitting about on sea and land, damning Bonaparte for an upstart warmonger.

And when they came to Dublin, he and Matt, to safe shelter at last, there was news for him. News of the disastrous defeat at Antrim, and his father dead at the gates of the town, shoveled into a common grave with the other two thousand dead rebels, and Harry McCracken hanging on a gallows in Belfast ... *Oh, alas, says he, young Harry Joy for fifty pounds is sold.* ... Tired, tired to death—numb with it, and the news not really reaching him then—never been so dead tired before or since.

That goddamned cart, creaking and jolting and pulling his shoulder muscles loose—and Matt babbling light-headed nonsense behind.

"I thought you wanted to get on to it," said McKenna behind him. McDonagh started violently; he felt, as his grip relaxed on the instrument case, how tense it had been; his knuckles were white with strain. He raised a hand and wiped the sweat away and turned slowly to McKenna. McKenna out of the county Antrim, but he dared not say *Enniscorthy* to McKenna, for you never knew—you never knew friend from foe or fool from cynic.

"Yes," he said. "I'm just coming."

"I routed out a couple of assistants." Not orderlies, in the navy, and so far from being men with some rudimentary notion of how best to help the surgeon, the assistants were brawny part-time sailors whose main job was shifting patients about and holding them down by force for surgery.

"All right—good," said McDonagh. They walked down to the cockpit amidships, where the poor little devils of midshipmen crowded into canvas-walled cabins. During an action all these partitions would be taken down, and the space closed off in one square for the surgeons' operating room. The *Donegal* was a seventy-four-gun ship and carried nearly seven hundred men; space was at a premium. Operating tables would be constructed of planks laid over sawhorse supports; now this impedimenta was stacked along the port side, opposite the door flaps of the little cabins. The two assistants were wrestling down a couple of planks.

"Where d'you want it, sir? Turn out one o' the boys?"

"That won't do," said McDonagh. "He'll be some while on his back, and the more comfortable he is the better he'll heal."

"Also we want something at the bottom to tie it onto," said McKenna. "Keep it stretched."

McDonagh looked at him, snapping to interested attention. "I've heard of that, never done it or seen it. Do any good, does it? Doesn't it keep the bone apart from growing together?"

"Not if you're careful. About a pound's pull, just gentle and steady. Takes a big longer to knit, 's all."

"Really. But it stops it from shortening? Not altogether, surely, I can't believe—"

"Oh, Lord, no. But it helps. Depending on how much bone you cut out, sometimes you get only very minor shortening, half an inch or so."

"Well, I'm damned. We'll try it." He looked back to the assistants. "Bring all that right down to the patient, we'll leave him where he is in his own cabin. Fix up a bed well as we can out of the table, if you can call it that—he can't lie in a damn hammock for three months. Larr, you go and send a couple of men ashore, to beg or buy or steal some sort of mattress for it. Here's— what've I got?—seventeen shillings odd and God knows what in Italian money—I'll argue it back out of the stock fund later. Tell 'em to get the best they can, a regular thick pallet."

"Very good idea. And he'll have a nice view out over the water," said McKenna cheerfully, and departed on his errand.

McDonagh followed the men down to Lightfoot's cabin and

squatted beside him as the assistants set up the table. "Soon get it over with now," he said. "I'll tell you what we're going to do and what you can expect."

"Can I have some more laudanum?" asked Lightfoot restlessly.

"No. You've got quite enough in you now. Afterward, about an hour afterward, you can have some. We'll keep you as comfortable as possible, you know, but some of this you've just got to sweat through, there's not one damned thing we can do to help. Well, now, the ball's lodged in the bone, and it's got to be dug out. There's a certain amount of damage to the bone, it's smashed through, and some of it—I don't know how much—will have to be cut out. I'm going to do that, and then we'll put the whole leg above the knee in regular splints and wait for the bone to grow together. McKenna says if we keep a steady pull on it, it'll keep the leg from knitting as short as it would otherwise—we'll try that. I think it might be half an inch or so short, time it grows together. You'll go that much lame, but it'll heal quite sound, with luck."

"I see,' said Lightfoot with a thin smile. "Well, it's a damn sight better than losing it. You said, barring complications. What might happen?"

"What might always happen whenever a surgeon picks up a scalpel—blood poisoning. But even if it does, there are things we can do about that too, and nature often heals it on her own. We won't worry about that now."

When he got into it, half an hour later with the assistants hanging on to the patient and McKenna watching interestedly, he found the damage less extensive than he'd feared. He got out the ball; he dared not take too long to assess the injury, to keep the patient tense in agony, but he could feel that there was less ruined bone than he'd expected. He cleared it away, and closed the wound as quickly as possible, but took time to make interrupted sutures, for in a thing like this you could almost always expect some poisoning and suppuration. McKenna gave a little grunt of approval, passing him the lint pledgets to insert in the knots.

They applied the splints, and McDonagh watched then with

interest while McKenna with nice judgment arranged a complex system of ropes fastening the leg to an improvised footboard. The patient had fainted some while back, which made the rest a trifle easier.

"It's makeshift, but I think it'll do. And you know what we'll hear from Clinton if all on a sudden we get into action? Stealing an operating table and immobilizing it for months."

"Oh, to hell with Clinton," said McDonagh. He held a vial of hartshorn to Lightfoot's nostrils and added, "Just fetch that bottle we broached last night, I think the man deserves a decent drink. Well, there you are"—as Lightfoot's eyes opened—"all over, and we've got you tied up like a horse in stall, as you see. But it won't be too bad after the first fortnight, you'll just be damned bored. Meanwhile, here's a little reward for you, since you can't have any laudanum for an hour or so." He took the bottle of whiskey from McKenna and shot a generous portion into a wooden dispensing mug.

Lightfoot looked at it suspiciously but accepted help to raise himself and drink. "My good God and all the apostles!" he said faintly. "Never had any medicine like that before—take the top o' your head off—what the hell is it?"

"And that's the appreciation we get for sharing good Irish whiskey," said McKenna indignantly.

"Oh," said Lightfoot, sinking back with a moan, "so that's what it was—heard of it, of course—all I can say is, it explains a lot about that damned country. I'll stick to brandy and rum, thanks."

On the fourth day the symptoms of blood poisoning set in, and Clinton said triumphantly that he had told Mr. McDonagh, but all these self-confident young men had to acquire their own experience. McDonagh refused to let the assistants waiting on Lightfoot touch the wound; he went himself every three hours to wipe away the suppurating pus and cover the inflamed swelling with soothing oil and to loosen the sutures by removing pledgets as the swelling increased.

"I'll be damned eternally," he said to McKenna, "if I give Clinton the chance to crow over this! Of course, we've got blood poisoning—I never expected anything else—but we do manage to cure it these days, which Clinton evidently hasn't found out yet."

The swelling and suppuration went on increasing for a fortnight until all the sutures were let out as far as possible; then some of them broke through under the pressure, and a great deal of foul matter was discharged. McDonagh let it suppurate for half a day—"It won't hurt to leave it open that long, and it's a good chance to get rid of all this"—and when it seemed empty of matter, he closed it with adhesive dressings instead of sutures.

He was more interested in the news that Lightfoot had had a comfortable night than to hear that the flagship *Victory* had entered the harbor next morning.

Two days later the wound was still clean, the swelling was all but gone, and the pain much less. Ensign Lightfoot was on the way to recovery; now it was only a matter of time, to let the bone grow together.

Clinton came and looked, harrumphed in subdued tones, and went away without a word to McDonagh. "I told you, he'll never forgive you," said McKenna only half-humorously.

"I could put up with that," returned McDonagh, "if I believed he'd learned anything. But the next time he gets anything like this, he'll go right on and amputate as if he'd never seen this." He swore as the ship jarred and rolled and threw him against the side.

"I say, we're under way," said Lightfoot, raising up. "Must've been sudden orders. Lieutenant Ashmund was in a bit ago, he didn't say anything about—"

McKenna looked out the cabin entry in time to seize one of the little midshipmen hurrying past. "Where're we bound, d'you know? Anything up?"

"Yessir, can't stop, I'm sorry—they do say as the admiral's had word the French've got out of Toulon—we're all ordered to sea after 'em, crack on all sail!"

"Hell and damnation," said Lightfoot. "I get eighteen months of this damned boring patrol duty, and now when it seems we'll see some excitement for a change, I'm out o' action!"

8

Ensign Lightfoot had spoken too soon. They were on the move but, as it developed, a long way still from excitement. With word from the frigates that the French fleet under Admiral Villeneuve was off Corsica, the immediate English conclusion was that they were making for Naples or Sicily, possibly to naval rendezvous with their allies out of Spain. The whole English fleet put on all sail southwest, to intercept them. But no sign of the French fleet showed, and the second conclusion was that they had turned for the North African coast. Early February found the English ships, helped on with good winds, headed for Egypt.

They put in at Alexandria, and there some of the frigates they had scattered behind as scouts caught up with them. Villeneuve had put back for Toulon.

"Damn it, what're the frogs up to, leading a wild-goose chase?" was the consensus of opinion; but in obedient pursuit the English fleet turned and battled its way against adverse winds back across the Mediterranean. Villeneuve had anchored again at Toulon. The English capital ships came to rest and resupply at Maddalena and sent out their frigates to keep a close watch on the approaches to the eastern seas. The general feeling was that Villeneuve had made a trial run.

And there they patrolled and lay at anchor again, while the spring came on and Ensign Lightfoot's leg healed.

McDonagh was the first to admit that he was a single-minded man. In his concern for the surgical problem, the row with old Clinton had been a mere annoyance, and when he had got the case away from the senior surgeon, the business was over for him—that was that. He was constitutionally unable himself to hold a grudge past the time he regained his temper, and it always came as a surprise to him that other men could. It was borne in on him, during his patient's convalescence, that Clinton was nursing an outsize grievance on him.

Belatedly, and vaguely, he realized why. Clinton was an old man and perhaps not unaware of his shortcomings; his professional life was drawing to a close, and that frightened him as it would frighten any man. Maybe he had sufficient savings to live comfortably in retirement, or not; the fear and resentment went deeper than that. McDonagh was a symbol to him of all the brash young men who were coming up to oust him, the young men openly contemptuous of him, and of new ideas and experimental techniques he knew nothing about, which annoyed and puzzled him.

He was not a big enough man in himself to admit that he had been wrong, congratulate McDonagh on the patient, and let it go. From the morning when it became apparent that Lightfoot would retain the full use of his leg, Clinton brooded on his besting by one of these obnoxious young men, and nothing McDonagh did or said was right to him.

He found fault with everything he knew of Conal McDonagh, and since he could not find fault with McDonagh professionally, he found fault personally. With benevolent kindness he deplored the cache of whiskey McDonagh and McKenna shared, their occasional expeditions ashore. Not that there was much excitement to be found ashore; there was only one inn, the native wine was thin and nasty, and in such a small village there was no supply of professionally accommodating women, but it was a change. Every time McDonagh left the ship, Clinton catechized him on his return as to how he had spent his time. "I hope you won't take offense, my boy, but I do feel myself, as the senior on the staff, rather responsible for the good character of those under me." To McDonagh, who harbored a lifelong resentment of personal questions—"It's my own business, damn it!"—this was infinitely more irritating than Clinton's first sally, and he did not trouble much to conceal the fact.

"I tell you, he wants you to lose your temper and tell him to go to hell," said McKenna. "Then he'd have a complaint on you, insubordination to a superior. You just hang on to yourself, Con."

"I know that," said McDonagh with a reluctant laugh. "But he's damn irritating—talking at me as if I were ten years old and caught whispering in chapel!"

On the first day of April Ensign Lightfoot walked triumphantly across his cabin and back; McDonagh was pleased with him. It was evident that the shortening of the leg was slight, and Lightfoot even expressed satisfaction with his limp: "No need to explain how I came by it, you know! I'm bound to say that a visible wound does make people think higher of a man, for some reason!"

Most unfortunately Clinton happened to overhear Lightfoot expressing casual gratitude to McDonagh in talk with Lieutenant Wilberforce the next day. He met McDonagh on deck that afternoon and took occasion to speak to him about carelessness of dress. "I do realize that it may seem a matter of small importance to you, but the whole appearance of the professional gentleman is very definitely a part of inspiring confidence in his integrity. I'm sure you take the implication, Mr. McDonagh—a word to the wise."

McDonagh had been ashore with a couple of the younger officers for some rough walking exercise over the island and was at the moment clad in his oldest pair of breeches and boots and a shirt in need of both mending and laundering, minus neckcloth, coat, or waistcoat. He had, in fact, been on his way below to wash off the dust of the walk and change his clothes. He took some satisfaction in telling Clinton so, and damned him for an interfering busybody in less polite language to McKenna in their cabin later.

"Yes, well, all I say is, you go on holding your temper," said McKenna. "You've managed so far because you've got me to spill over at, but you won't have from now on, you know." He was due for leave, and a replacement was coming out with a dispatch frigate in a few days to take him back to England. "You watch it, Con. He's got his knife in you proper, and it'll be one thing after another. If the fleet gets into action, you two will likely find some real things to fight about. I don't say he could get you dismissed, but it wouldn't do you any good to have a senior's formal complaint filed against you, you know."

"I'd have a few home truths to tell the War Office—"

"The Admiralty," said McKenna. "Since they're stepping up recruitment and so on, the Admiralty's got its own medical branch."

"The Admiralty then. My God, any competent surgeon would realize the old bastard's years behind the times!"

"He's got a long and technically blameless record as a naval surgeon," said McKenna, "and rightly or wrongly, the favor's apt to be on the side of experienced elder men against cocksure young upstarts."

"All right, you've made your point," said McDonagh. "I'm not denying it, and I'll mind what you say." He certainly meant to; in a way, Clinton's malice was worse than childish and didn't warrant a loss of temper.

The frigate *Swiftsure* bore McKenna away for England and left in his place a taciturn middle-aged man by the name of Barstow. It had occurred to McDonagh that if the replacement surgeon were a man of Clinton's generation, to whom he could confide his grievance and hope for sympathy, he might rid himself of the festering grudge, but Barstow, while perfectly polite, seemed rather standoffish.

In any case, he was still largely an unknown quantity when, between one hour and the next, in a flurry of outrage, the whole fleet put to sea. The frigate *Decade*, back with dispatches from Gibraltar, brought the news that the French fleet had slipped through the strait six days ago. At once pursuit began, and the English beat their difficult way against east winds up toward Gibraltar all the rest of that month. Sir John Orde was lying outside the strait with five sail of the line and would doubtless have intercepted Villeneuve or at least posted scouts to keep sight of the enemy.

They anchored at Gibraltar on the sixth of May and, so far from making liaison with Orde, found that he had retired with his entire squadron to Brest, leaving not one scout behind to inform the fleet where the enemy was making. Rumor drifting down to the junior officers said that Admiral Nelson was in a fury at Orde. But while they hung about off Cape St. Vincent waiting for the admiral to decide on orders, information came to them; a Scotsman serving in the Portuguese navy rowed out alone in a rough sea to bring the news that Villeneuve's fleet had sailed three weeks ago for the West Indies.

The crew and officers heard that almost as soon as the admiral and his staff would be discussing it; secrets traveled fast aboard. That night at the junior officers' table, where the medical staff sat, Barstow offered the opinion that Sir John Orde would be bitterly criticized for his part in this action. "And it's a pity. Unavoidable."

There had been a good deal of bitter talk already about Orde, and that started more. Barstow peered at the naval men over his steel-rimmed spectacles and said mildly, "I'm not a naval man myself, gentlemen, but it seems to me it is only discretion for a commander with five sail of the line to retire before twenty-four line-of-battle ships. Eh?"

Next day orders were handed down: The Admiralty was sending out a reinforcement fleet—two capital ships and some seventy-fours and frigates—and despite the delay that Orde had already caused, the fleet was to wait for liaison with that force. On the eleventh the new ships arrived; the admiral (rumor said, in a fever of impatience) issued instant signals, and within two hours the fleet bore out to sea on the trail of the enemy across the Atlantic.

Barstow was a much-married man, and a good deal of his time was spent in the little cabin he shared with McDonagh, writing long letters to his wife. He also walked the deck solemnly, counting his revolutions, for sufficient exercise to maintain health, and before retiring punctually at ten o'clock, he read for half an hour in one of the several large tomes he had brought of early Christian theology. He was, in short, a damned bore, and McDonagh placed him professionally as one of those never-brilliant, never-incompetent surgeons whom nothing ever hurried or flurried and who could go on like a machine over a table for hours—invaluable in a busy hospital or his present position, but slightly inhuman. Not a man one would ever confide in or feel close to, and if he detected any of the truth behind Clinton's nagging of McDonagh, he said nothing, but kept himself apart from both.

Time did nothing, apparently, to soothe Clinton's resentment. All his faultfinding was so damned petty, McDonagh told himself, that it was absurd to resent it, he was being as childish as Clinton in showing irritation, but that was easier to tell himself afterward than to remember at the time.

They ran into high seas and dirty weather two weeks out, and one of the common hands slipped from a mast on his way up and fractured his wrist. McDonagh took him below to the little partitioned-off pharmacy room as a convenient place to apply a simple splint; Clinton was there compounding some dose. He stayed; he never said a word; but his expression and manner conveyed that McDonagh was an inexperienced, if well-meaning, first-year student who must be watched to see that he did not do something stupid.

McDonagh said nothing to him, and that was something of an effort.

Several days after that all three surgeons converged at the top of the aft companion on their way to five o'clock dinner in the officers' mess, and Clinton coughed solemnly at McDonagh. "Ah, Mr. McDonagh. I really do not like to sound prosing or overparticular, and I realize we are not exactly in society at the moment, but at the same time I cannot approve a professional man who is, um, perennially careless of his person. I notice that apparently you don't feel it necessary to shave yourself every day."

Involuntarily McDonagh raised a hand to his jaw. "I'm sorry

to contradict you, Mr. Clinton, but I do. If I'm to look clean-shaven twenty-four hours a day, it means shaving twice, and that I draw the line at." He stopped himself in time from adding, "If it is any of your damned business."

"Most unfortunate," said Clinton coldly. "It makes for a very slovenly appearance." He settled his own neat neckcloth and preceded the other two down the companion.

In his months aboard a line-of-battle ship, McDonagh had been horrified at the treatment of the common hands, a good many of them being pressed men who had been virtually held prisoners for years in naval service. Floggings were not uncommon, and the surgeons strictly forbidden to minister to the flogged men afterward; the boatswains and other noncommissioned men who were immediately over the common sailors managed to keep most of the men's pay by acting as go-betweens for purchases in port, and the men were accorded no more humanity in matters of hours of labor and decent accommodation than if they had been machines. No commissioned officer thought of addressing one of them in the ordinary way. McDonagh, in the course of administering occasionally to genuine medical complaints, had exchanged talk with a number of them. One of the hands before the mast on the *Donegal* was a man out of Galway, of low intelligence and humble nature; English was a second tongue to him, and finding someone he could talk the Gaelic to, he took to hanging about the medical office in all his leisure time, which was not much.

Clinton interrupted him talking to McDonagh one morning, and favored McDonagh with a grave lecture on the dangers of hobnobbing with low company, especially for a professional man. "I do realize, Mr. McDonagh, that in your native land these social standards are, ah, somewhat different than exist for Englishmen, but I am bound to warn you that that sort of thing creates a most unfavorable impression." He smiled almost expectantly.

McDonagh shut his teeth hard on an impulsive reply. Clinton thought to rouse him with that, good and hot; God knew he nearly had. After a moment McDonagh could think sardonically with one part of his mind that he had, in fact, very nearly fallen into the old trap of blind insularity, for the implied slur on his national breeding. The Galway man was scarcely a stimulating companion, but he was sorry for the poor bastard.

"I'll remember what you say, sir," he said to Clinton without a smile, and had the satisfaction of seeing the senior surgeon look briefly disappointed at the submissive answer.

All the way across the Atlantic he held his temper with Clinton, and sometimes it was a struggle; several times the old man came out with his subtle insults before others, though he took care to say nothing outrageous before witnesses, who might offer the later opinion that McDonagh was justified in retort.

Having no one to talk it out with, and in the enforced lack of other occupation to take his mind from it, McDonagh brooded over the situation, and by the time a landfall was made and the *Donegal* anchored among the rest of the fleet at Barbados, he had come to the conclusion that he was a fool to let Clinton bully him. If it came to a head, as he had told McKenna, he had a case against Clinton, at least one instance of incompetence: for no present-day surgeon of any ability would have considered amputation in Lightfoot's case.

There was substantiated rumor at Barbados that the French fleet had passed the week before, making for Trinidad; the English fleet set sail again south on its track and anchored there, having seen nothing of the enemy on the way.

On the morning of the day they lay at Trinidad, a seaman before the mast on the *Donegal* caught his hand in a winch. He was sent below for medical attention, and it happened that McDonagh was the surgeon summoned, being nearest at the moment.

He sent out a call for a couple of surgical assistants and examined the patient. The first two fingers were badly mangled and would obviously have to come off. The man was in great pain, and McDonagh mixed a stiff dose of laudanum for him while the assistants set up a table. Clinton came in as he was helping the man to drink.

"Ah, Mr. McDonagh," said the senior surgeon, peering at the wounded hand. "I take it that is laudanum you are giving the patient?"

"It is," said McDonagh shortly.

Clinton shook his head. "You have something to learn about naval regulations, young man. We carry only so much stock of drugs aboard, you know. It's not necessary or, I may say, salutary, to waste valuable anodynes on the common seamen, and it is never done. When we meet action, laudanum may be urgently needed in quantities for injured officers, and the supply must be conserved. I see this is a fairly simple, minor operation, and there is no need at all that the patient be given any anodyne. I must ask you to remember—"

McDonagh turned on him, goaded beyond control at last. The moment here, he was utterly unconscious of recklessness; he had had six months too long of holding his temper with Clinton. "I'll treat my patients as I damned well like, Mr. Clinton," he said hardly. "And I may say I'd like to have you on this table with a couple of crushed fingers—you'd be yelling for laudanum at the top of your voice! Since you think it beneath your august presence, Mr. Clinton, to talk with a common sailor, maybe you don't know that this man will be allowed one day off his duties to recuperate and then be expected to go back to work. I'd damn well like to see something like that happen to you and hear what you had to say about it! And as far as I'm concerned, Mr. Clinton, patients are patients, and if one of them needs a dose of laudanum, he gets it from me, if it should be the last dose on the damn ship and every single commissioned officer was waiting his turn for surgery, including the admiral! Now will you kindly get to hell out of my way while I get on with this?"

Clinton went purple and then white, but there was one sharp gleam of satisfaction behind the anger in his eyes. "This is rank and aggravated insubordination to your superior, insulting me before the assistants. I'll see a complaint is issued."

"Oh, for God's sake do what you like! Insubordination be damned, neither of us has any formal rank, we're supercargo until the ship's in action, you know as well as I do! I'll be more than glad to tell anybody from the captain up to the first sea lord of the Admiralty just what I think about you, Mr. Clinton. Meanwhile, I've got a job in hand, and I don't want any ham-handed blunderer of a so-called surgeon standing in my light making idiotic suggestions—is that clear?"

"I shall go to the captain," said Clinton, shaking with rage. "I refuse to stay on duty with you on my staff, I shall lay a formal complaint—"

"You can go to hell and discuss it with the devil, but for the love of Christ get out of my surgery!"

"You shall be summoned to answer—"

"All right, all right, you can try to get me locked up in the brig in ten minutes, but right now you can get to hell and let me finish this job!" shouted McDonagh.

Clinton bolted away clumsily, and one of the assistants said in an admiring voice, "Now that's what I call a nice hexchange o' compliments."

McDonagh grinned; he felt better for that little burst of temper than he had since McKenna had left. He said to the patient, "You just hang on now, all be over in two minutes," and nodded at the assistants, who took a firm grip. He took off the mashed fingers, applied adhesive dressings and a thick bandage over them, and waited to see if it would hemorrhage. "There you are. Take it as easy as you can, and if it starts to bleed you get back to me quick. I'll let you have some more laudanum in the morning."

He put on his coat, straightened his neckcloth, and went out of the little pharmacy to find, as he had expected, Clinton and Barstow waiting. "You will come with me to Captain Malcolm at once, sir—at once! I will not have you on my staff a day longer—"

"I'll be glad to go to the captain with you," said McDonagh coldly.

Barstow looked uneasily from one to the other. "Really I know nothing about this, nothing, I can scarcely be called as a witness for either of you—"

Clinton began to say something pompous about the whole medical staff, and McDonagh brushed past him and turned aft. In silence they went up the companion, across amidships to the partitioned cabins giving on the quarterdeck at the stern, where the senior officers were quartered. There a young ensign barred the way.

"I must see the captain at once—"

"I'm sorry, sir, it's impossible. Captain Malcolm—"

"Captain Malcoln and I are old friends, we have served the Royal Navy together for many years, and I have never found him deny me entrance to him at any time. This is a matter of the utmost importance, my man, he will forgive my interruption, I assure you." Clinton swept past the protesting ensign into Captain Malcolm's quarters like a strong breeze. "My dear fellow, I do ask pardon for interrupting, but I have a case to lay before you very urgently—"

The captain of the *Donegal*, a thin quiet man with shrewd eyes, glanced up from his table sharply. Another man sat there with him; there were maps spread out on the board. "I can't attend to you now, Mr. Clinton—later."

"This is of imperative urgency, sir—a matter of the grossest insubordination to me! I think you must agree that I have served as a competent surgeon on your ship for as long as you have held command and deserve some consideration. I must refuse formally to continue to act in that capacity while this—this impudent, incompetent, and rankly insubordinate young man remains on my staff! I wish to issue a formal complaint to that effect—" He stopped with a little gasp, which he turned to a cough.

The second man at the table had risen and turned to face them. "Really, Mr. Clinton," said Malcolm in an annoyed tone, "I cannot be bothered with any domestic squabbles amongst the medical staff at the moment! As you see, the admiral is with me, for private discussion. Pray oblige me by apologizing to him for intrusion, and bring this to me later."

"Oh, no, no," said the other man in a quick, high, brittle voice. "Take our minds off a minute, eh, Malcolm?" He laughed, and it sounded like a fox's bark. "These domestic squabbles can make trouble—don't want trouble, bad feeling—brooding—then in action, may interfere with the whole strategy! Don't laugh, sir, I've known it happen—some petty little circumstance starting everything wrong! What's the trouble, my man?" He showed bad teeth to Clinton.

McDonagh looked at him with surprised interest. So this was the great sea dog, England's naval hero, Horatio Nelson. Not what McDonagh might have expected, not by a long way. He thought, looking at Nelson, that the man must have an indomitable will to have made himself what he was. For he was a little man, and physically frail; he looked no more than skin and bone. His right arm was gone above the elbow, and his right eye was filmed blind. It was an almost fragile body, light-boned, a long, narrow skull with sparse flax hair turning gray, a nervous, tense little body, constantly in movement, violent in gesture.

And with a second glance McDonagh was somewhat incredulously amused, for here in foreign seas, in fleet action, the admiral was decked out with all his medals and honors, hung with apparent indiscriminacy on his fine blue coat. As he talked, he fingered them unconsciously, fiddled with his empty sleeve, smoothed his hair, and his one eye shifted from man to man like the eye of a marksman on moving targets.

"Well, well? Speak up and we'll get this settled! Insubordination, eh? This young fella? You must take it with a grain o' salt, young man—seems to me, looking back, very little ever happened to me at your age except bein' accused of insubordination! Leaders o' men never take kindly to regulations themselves, you know! Well? What's the complaint? How was you insubordinate, eh?" His one sharp blue-gray eye fastened on McDonagh.

McDonagh smiled at him coolly. "Why, Mr. Clinton came in as I was busy at a piece of work, my lord, and he was in my way—I told him to get out."

"He was," said Clinton, regaining the use of his tongue, "unwarrantably profane, my lord—he swore at me—"

The admiral clicked his teeth. "Bad, very bad. Seldom use profanity myself—unnecessary. Bad taste. But there are occasions, oh, yes. What else?"

"He was quite unnecessarily rude—and," said Clinton, "when I chided him for expending laudanum on a common seaman, he said—he said he would have done so even if the admiral were in need—meaning yourself, my lord."

"I beg your pardon," said McDonagh, "what I actually said—"

"What've you got to do with it?" demanded the admiral suddenly of Barstow.

Barstow shied back. "I know nothing of it, my lord. Mr. Clinton asked me—he said—"

"Said that, did you?" The eye was back on McDonagh. "Very

impertinent. Daresay you'd lost your temper and didn't heed what you were sayin', eh? He sounds like one o' these pompous bores that uses six words where one'll do. Is he?" He jerked his head at Clinton.

McDonagh saw a small smile quivering on Captain Malcolm's mouth. "He certainly is that, my lord—among other things."

Nelson gave his crack of laugh. "Very difficult to get on with 'em, I know! I've had to deal with some in my time. Know the only way to get the best of 'em, young man? Rank!—that's the answer. Get above 'em in station, and then you can be just as rude as you like but they can't answer back. Then they all say it's a mark o' your genius. Yes, yes, what's insubordination in youth is genius twenty years later—and a good thing too." He turned on Clinton. "You say you refuse to harbor the young man on your staff, eh? Well, Malcolm? Good surgeons, are they?"

Captain Malcolm said in a rather amused tone, "I've no complaint to make of either, my lord, of my own knowledge."

"Well, then, it's easy enough settled." Nelson raised an impatient shoulder. "Don't know what you expected Malcolm to do," he shot at Clinton. "Maroon the fella on an island?—we're half across the world from home! Not sensible, you know. What can't be cured must be endured. One competent surgeon's much like another. I'll exchange one with you, Malcolm, and that settles it. That satisfy you?"—to Clinton. "And you, young man!" He looked back to McDonagh. "Your senior was quite right about the laudanum, and you mind it! Any number o' common seamen to be had—officers are more important! Very well, we settle it so—you pack up your gear and come to the *Victory*, and I'll send one o' the junior surgeons to replace you. Now you all go away and let me get on with my business." Suddenly losing interest in the whole thing, he turned back to the maps.

The ensign guarding the entrance, who had lifted the canvas flap in the hope of hauling out the intruders, caught Malcolm's eye and herded the *Donegal*'s medical staff out with unexpected firmness. Clinton stuttered incoherently, "High-handed—I must say, in spite of his rank, deplorably inattentive to details—I cannot agree—"

126

"I shall be very sorry to see you leave us, Mr. McDonagh," said Barstow correctly, "but doubtless you'll find yourself happier away after this. And on the flagship, surely an opportunity for advancement—"

McDonagh looked at Clinton. "I can't say I give a damn where I transfer," he said, "as long as it's off this ship." He turned on his heel and went below to pack his belongings.

9

McDonagh had scarcely time to establish himself in new quarters before the fleet moved again, to Antigua. There information reached them that Villeneuve had started back to Europe, and within four days the English fleet was after him.

"And a nice season it is for a cross-Atlantic tour, I don't think," commented James Campbell, McDonagh's new cabin-mate. McDonagh was grateful for Campbell, a long, solemn, caustic Scot of thirty-five—grateful, as time went on, for more than one reason.

He had expected to be unwillingly welcomed as the inadvertent ouster of a known member of the staff, perhaps resented as a newcomer, and was surprised to be accepted with little comment. The reason for that, he deduced, was a curious one: he had come to the flagship under the auspices of the admiral—if Nelson had hardly heard his name—and as far as every man on the *Victory* felt, if Admiral Nelson thought it salutary to bring aboard a horned full-grown unicorn, they would have endorsed the idea enthusiastically. Moreover, there was greater formality observed on the larger ship. The senior surgeon, William Beatty, took his meals with the high officers, and McDonagh found himself casually taken into the group of younger men on the staff of six surgeons.

Between contempt and amusement, he also found that he was among a crowd of hero worshipers. The *Victory* was under command of Captain Hardy, an old friend of the admiral's, and had served as flagship for nearly two years now; the honor had perhaps made her officers a trifle light-headed, though from some of what he'd heard in London, McDonagh admitted that enough civilians in England shared the fervent and unquestioning adulation accorded Nelson.

Every time he had a glimpse of the strutting little figure, always bedecked with its medals, restless on the quarterdeck, he was surprised again, contrasting it with the many reminiscences and legends the junior officers' mess was never tired of retelling. And yet with all their childlike admiration, they were in awe of the little man, too; it was not a warm human love they had for him but an almost superstitious worship.

McDonagh found that even in the common hands, and remembering what Nelson had said about them, he was stirred to a contemptuous anger again for these stupid idealists. It was gratifying to find at least one man aboard—Campbell—who took a somewhat saner view of the hero and only smiled to hear McDonagh term him a pompous little bastard.

"He is that," he agreed in his slow unemphatic Edinburgh voice that reminded McDonagh of Gillespie. "But you've not seen much of him, have you, to listen to him, I mean? Well, nor have I, of course—humble junior bone sawer—but a bit more. I agree, an exaggerated sense of his own importance, but it's a very damned queer thing, you know—you listen to him awhile, and he has you believing it too. What's the word I want?—that French charlatan who got so much notice some years back—mesmerizes men, that's what the admiral does."

"Not me," said McDonagh succinctly.

Campbell smiled again and advised him not to say anything of the sort to Beatty, who was also an old friend of Nelson's—and a sentimentalist. That McDonagh already knew.

But he had an illustration of what Campbell meant a few days later. The day's routine, as far as the congregate of senior officers and the retinue about the admiral went, was invariable and strictly observed. By every dawn the little, erect figure of the admiral was to be seen on the quarterdeck; he rose and retired early and spent six or seven hours of the day pacing his deck, watching his fleet and what he doubtless considered his sea. Not long past dawn he shared breakfast with his officer staff, his two secretaries, and Beatty; in midafternoon they sat ceremonially to dinner in the admiral's partitioned-off dining cabin. An hour and a half later this august company emerged to the quarterdeck and paced solemnly while listening to a brief concert by the ship's band, composed of eight fiddlers, an accordionist, and three flutists.

Beatty had commissioned McDonagh that afternoon to mix up a concoction of his own devising as prescription for the admiral's distressing tendency to the ague in these cold waters. "He has never been strong, you know, a very frail physique—we must do all we can to guard him." McDonagh measured and boiled and mingled, reflecting gloomily that he might as well be a damned apothecary, so unspecialized was a naval surgeon's work; it would do quite as well to prepare the chinchona bark alone, all the other ingredients were likely useless and put in to make it look important. He came up from the medical stockroom with the bottle and heard the band-by-courtesy scraping and wheezing at *I'll Go No More A-Roving*, so it must be nearing five o'clock.

He was tired and bored with his hour in the stuffy little room below, and he went straight up to hand the bottle to Beatty, have it off his mind. The senior surgeon was walking back and forth with the admiral, Captain Hardy flanking the small figure's other side. McDonagh waited to be noticed.

"Will you not go in and sit down, sir?" Beatty was saying anxiously. "You must conserve your strength, you know."

"No, no, I do well enough, William! I have all the strength I need for the work I've to do, always have had—the creaking gate, eh? Don't fuss at me, there's a good fella. I'll not be taken until I've done what I was sent to do for England. Soon, it'll be soon, but not now, William. I'm safe awhile yet!"

"A premonition, Nelson?" asked Hardy with a smile only half-doubtful. He was a big hearty man in the fifties, looking to be good-humored and kindly.

"Premonition, premonition?" Nelson uttered his sharp, high laugh. "You dignify it! No, no—just, I've always known that—I was sent to do a job for England, England needed Nelson to save her. There's yet part of my job to finish, and when I've done it, no further need for Nelson!" He stopped suddenly and stood gazing out to sea. His one eye was sharp enough at close quarters, but shortsighted, and strained to the horizon, it was often inflamed; now he mopped at it with his handkerchief. "Not much work left in this, eh, William?—needn't dissemble to me, I've heard you muttering about it with Scott—I'll be blind in a year, unless my job's not done—if England needs Nelson, I'll be spared, I'll be spared—I know."

Hardy put a hand on his arm, turning him gently from the rail. He barely topped Hardy's shoulder, but as always he stood very erect, and he looked around with a rapt, vague expression on the two beside him. "Oh, I know," he said, "I know. Other things I've done in life, but that was no matter, no matter in the world. Nelson is here as—as England's second self, for just one purpose—none o' you need fear he'll be snatched away afore it's fulfilled!"

And for just one moment McDonagh even as an unnoticed bystander was caught by the fierce fanaticism of the little man into—almost—believing it.

He described the incident to Campbell that evening, amused and thoughtful, "I'm damned if he doesn't believe it, anyway."

"And the queer thing is he might be right," said Campbell. "Oh, he thinks a good deal of himself, I grant you, but he's an efficient fighting man, McDonagh—maybe he can be forgiven his sins for that."

"I understand," said McDonagh, wrestling with the cork of his last bottle of whiskey, "that he's collected a couple of sins, too. I noticed you rather shut me up at dinner tonight when I mentioned it. Is it one of those things not talked of in polite company?"

"In a way, in a way," said Campbell, laughing. "Implied criticism of the hero, you know. I understand it's a source of embarrassment to the news editors and official authorities. Heroes ought to be like Caesar's wife, it can be awkward when they're not." He took the bottle with a nod of thanks.

"What's the straight of it? He left his wife for another woman, I hear." McDonagh laughed. "My God, you wouldn't think a woman would look twice at him, would you?"

Campbell bent his long, dark, solemn face over his glass and drank, and then suddenly uttered one of his rare laughs. "And such a woman!" he said. He bowed his head in his hands and rocked with laughter. "You never saw anything like it in your life. Oh, yes, I've seen her—Lady Hamilton. Well, they say love is blind—it must be so. It was on my last leave in London—bit over two years ago. Saw them together in the Strand, just getting out of a hack." He went on laughing silently to himself.

"Well, what's the joke?" asked McDonagh impatiently.

Campbell sat up and wiped his eyes. "Did you ever see a Thames tugboat convoying one o' those great coal barges? That'll give you an idea. They say a dozen years ago she was a beauty—she was on the stage, you know, before she married—but she's spread a bit since. A great fat trollop of a woman, arms like hams—and one of those soft, silly, sentimental faces, too much paint and powder, lots of hair in too many ringlets, too many flounces and furbelows, you know the style. And the admiral fussing over handing her down the step, all anxious and attentive. If she'd missed her footing, she'd have squashed the little fella flat."

McDonagh roared at that picture. "I'll never let him impress me again! It's the damnedest thing how they always go mad after those great elephants of females, isn't it?"

"That's not the queerest thing about it by a long shot. I heard some of the inside story from a friend o' mine who was attached to the embassy at Naples—Hamilton was ambassador there, you know, for some while. How the admiral's wife may feel about it I don't know, but Hamilton was the complacent husband to end all. D'you know that the three of them lived peacefully together for years, until Hamilton died, sort of *ménage à trois?* It's a fact."

"I'll be damned," said McDonagh.

"I gather the orthodox lean to the view that a wicked wanton victimized the man of honor, and the more broad-minded regard it as the greatest romance since *Romeo and Juliet*," said Campbell, chuckling. "After that one glimpse—is there anybody outside listening? I don't want to be chucked overboard in mid-Atlantic—I can always cure a fit of the sullens by imagining them in bed together. Here, don't spill the whiskey, for God's sake!"

McDonagh set the bottle out of harm's way, shaking with laughter. "And yet you know," added Campbell, "there is something rather blatantly magnificent about the little man. For all his bombast and self-advertisement, well, there's more to him than just that. He's a very efficient fighting man indeed—for an Englishman."

The English fleet anchored outside Gibraltar on the twentieth of July; the captains shared the admiral's grave view that they had missed intercepting the enemy and that Villeneuve was making for Ireland as the first base for an invasion attack on England. There was rumor that Bonaparte was in Boulogne, ready to strike from there with his massed armies.

But in the second week of August cheering news arrived. The enemy had been sighted by a dispatch frigate and reported at home; the Admiralty had at once sent out a force under Sir Robert Calder, which had a brush with Villeneuve off El Ferrol and captured two of the Spanish ships with the French fleet. Calder had not followed on after his little triumph but lay off Brest discreetly; Villeneuve had put in at Vigo.

The rest of the English fleet started southwest for liaison with Cornwallis's ships, but the *Victory* turned for England, for the admiral had leave to discuss with the first sea lord. A fortnight's leave was granted all the officers.

"Going up to London?" asked Campbell.

"No—I don't know," said McDonagh. "Hardly worth it, is it, for such a short time?"

Campbell agreed. "Portsmouth's a town too. Glad of your company if you stay. I'm going to stop ashore at the Swan Hotel, they do you well. Always stay there on short leave. And I know all the brothels in town, be glad to introduce you—not that they're all so exclusive!"

"Yes, I'll stay," said McDonagh. "No point in going up to London for just a week." He realized suddenly that it was nearly a year since he had left London; it seemed scarcely possible. Brothels in Portsmouth, Fleur Galard in London. A harlot in Gibraltar, the friendly inn girl on Maddalena, and God, how he needed a woman now. He had enjoyed Fleur, but it seemed longer ago than last year. He was suddenly, in memory, sitting in her parlor again, hearing a girl's cool, rather deep voice saying, *She says we will invest a year in my acquiring what she calls polish and then set out to make the best possible capture.* ... He had a brief, very clear vision of Madeleine Olivier, that senseless and stubborn female, sitting sidewise like a hoyden on a chair by Fleur's hearth, smiling her sudden smile. He had lectured her like a damned parson; nothing to do with him; very likely in London now she was beginning to enjoy the first fruits of her career.

He removed his mind forcibly from that irritating episode, and just as unexpectedly it presented him with Lauretta, smiling at him in the Holborn Road, her soft voice saying his name. Lauretta, his darling, who belonged to another man, so forever Conal McDonagh would be running to the easy women, never one of his own to love true.

He stayed in Portsmouth with Campbell, and they made the rounds of the more exclusive brothels, got pleasantly drunk together in a tavern kept by a Tyneside Scot who stocked good whiskey, and came back aboard a fortnight later somewhat emptier of pocket and ready to sleep at night for a change.

The *Victory* put out from Spithead on the fifteenth of September, tacked around to Plymouth to collect two ships of the line, and made down-Channel to join the main fleet. Three days later they met a frigate on the way home from Gibraltar and learned that Villeneuve was lying in Cádiz Harbor, with the English fleet strung outside on patrol. The *Victory* put on all sail to join them, and a frigate ran ahead to warn the captains that they should fire no formal salutes when the admiral arrived, to warn the enemy.

Ten days later the flagship was with the fleet; with the four ships joining in the next week, the English strength was twenty-seven sail of the line. They lay patiently in a smooth sea, waiting for the enemy to move. And Lieutenant Barker of the gunners said pleasedly to McDonagh that night, "We'll see some action at last out o' this! The admiral means to force it to a fight this time, once for all."

Yes, they called it a war, McDonagh thought but did not say. Eighteen months, two years, of chase and search and wait, and not a shot fired. Action this time? He wondered.

They sat outside Cádiz for twenty days, waiting. The weather was clear and calm, the winds were slight, and the French cannily stayed inside the harbor. On the twenty-first day of waiting the signals came from the scouting frigates: the enemy was on the move. By late afternoon of the next day the intelligence was that Villeneuve's entire fleet stood out northwest, to gain sea room for turning into Gibraltar; the English fleet at once moved under all sail, southeast, to protect the strait.

"Oh, yes, friend," said Campbell, leaning on the port rail and looking at a choppy sea, "you're about to see a battle. At least we won't see the fight—hear about it secondhand from the chaps we're tending to below. Justify our wages for a change."

"And time," said McDonagh.

Every man on every English ship was alert for the arranged signals from the frigates keeping watch on the enemy, who were not within visibility: two blue flares on the hour, the French were running south; two warning shots, they were making west.

McDonagh was rudely awakened from sound sleep in a cold dawn the next morning by Campbell's urgent hand on his shoulder; there was a great noise of coming and going all about. "Better turn out if you want any privacy—we're being cleared for action."

"What, at this ungodly hour?" He got up, protesting; he had no time to shave or wash, barely to get his clothes on, before the canvas partitions were stripped away. The whole ship was alive and alert in frantic activity. He went up to the top deck with Campbell, to the port bow rail, and there, for the first time in all his months of naval service, he saw the enemy. Southwest, dim shapes through a rapidly clearing dawn mist close to the water, dipped and swayed the French fleet. He tried to count them but made out only that they must number roughly the same as the English.

"What happens now?" he asked through a yawn. "Should we get below?"

"Oh, it'll be some while before we see action," said Campbell. "Stay to see the first part of the show anyway."

Sailors, midshipmen, and noncommissioned men were running to and fro in seeming disorder, bawling orders, but there was some organization to it; the decks were being stripped end to end for action. The last canvas walls removed would be those making the senior officers' private cabins—Hardy's giving on the quarterdeck, the admiral's on the deck below. Now, by the time the sun was full up, the rest of the flagship was stripped; the same activity would be going on in the rest of the fleet. They could see men hurrying about the decks of the *Royal Sovereign* and the *Temeraire*, nearest to them.

The gunnery lieutenant came up and paused beside them. "Give you chaps something to do today," he said cheerfully.

"Will you?" returned McDonagh. "Looks to me as if the Frenchmen are getting away fast."

"Making back for Cádiz," said Barker, looking out to the dark smudges of the enemy. Every moment they were growing clearer as the mist lifted and the sun strengthened. "Going to be a fine day, but the wind's not so good. Dropping now. We'll get up to 'em before they make the harbor or anywhere near it."

"Where are we now?"

"Oh, a bit south-southwest of the cape—Cape de Trafalgar. Ought to be up with them by the time we're off there, unless we're all becalmed."

"Nice clear visibility for a fight," said Campbell.

"Oh, lovely. But we'll be in for some dirty weather tomorrow and next day; look at the swells—it's making up." The seas were enormous, if calm; the prow lifted smoothly under them an incredible way with each swell, dropped with a hurrying rush into each trough.

"How soon d'you reckon we'll be in action?" asked McDonagh.

Barker gestured. "Starting to form line now, but in this miserable wind it might be hours." He went on to see to his guns.

All morning McDonagh, fascinated, stayed at the bow rail, watching the slow-motion approach to battle. With ponderous deliberation, in the heavy sea and slight wind, the great capital ships began to maneuver into two lines for battle, in obedience to the fluttering signals from the flagship. Northward of the *Victory*, the *Royal Sovereign* headed the second line, and a kind of ragged order began to be made as one by one the ships took position—*Temeraire* and *Agamemnon* following the flagship; *Belleisle, Mars, Tonnant*, falling into line behind the *Sovereign*; the rest of them tacking and wheeling in a failing wind to come up. They milled and tossed in an increasing swell, the big hulks of the line, *Neptune, Leviathan, Conqueror, Britannia, Ajax, Orient, Minotaur, Spartiate, Africa—Bellerophon, Colossus, Achille, Dreadnought, Polyphemus, Revenge, Defiance, Thunderer*. The form of line showed even McDonagh, ignorant of naval strategies, the rudimentary battle plan: one line to cut in ahead of the enemy fleet; the other to attack the rear.

He walked down the port side to amidships; the entire ship was stripped now. Even the furniture from the grand cabin suites of captain and admiral had been carried away somewhere, and up on the quarterdeck—its whole expanse visible now from below—stood the small straight figure of Admiral Nelson, very fine in a bright blue coat brass-buttoned, with the sun striking gleams from all his medals. Captain Hardy was beside him, a signalman, and Beatty, and a couple of marine officers. The *Victory* staggered up, up to a swell with suspenseful slowness, and dropped only a little faster. There was almost no wind now.

The two fleets rode so in the deceptively smooth-looking sea for what seemed a long time; the French and Spanish enemy line was clearly visible now, a bare three miles ahead. Campbell came back with another of the junior surgeons, Aubrey. "I thought something was said about action," said McDonagh.

"It's this damned wind. We'll see something nasty when it starts," said Aubrey. "A slow breeze like this, it'll hold ships under fire from maneuvering, it'll be butchery when we get to it."

One of the marine lieutenants came up and made the inevitable remark about providing work for the surgeons at last. "This is going to be a bad one," he said. "I'd like to have your job today, tucked snug away below. This damned wind—it's another of the admiral's do-or-die actions. Nobody but the admiral would play it the way he's doing. Captain Blackwood's been begging him to go aboard the *Decade*, out of harm's way, but he won't hear of it. I wish to God he would."

"Why, is anything unusual up?"

"Unusual!" said the marine lieutenant. "Look at the signals—hardly enough breeze to fly 'em out straight. The other line hasn't a hope in hell of getting out to cut in ahead of the enemy—we're all going in straight for their rear, to push through the line. With the wind like it is, we'll be held direct in line of fire, and we won't be able to fire one shot until we're broadside to them. The admiral's hot to finish them this time—he—" The lieutenant stopped, looking curiously shaken. "He always seems to know when it's his day and his time. I think—he feels—this is the last time, and he's standing up there planning it all out cool as be damned—even Captain Hardy thinks it's madness to run up behind like this. 'I must scotch them once for all'—I heard the admiral say it—'it's my last day to do it.' And when the boat came to take Blackwood off, just now, he said to Blackwood, 'I'll never speak with you again, my friend.' "

"You mean he feels a premonition," said Aubrey with a troubled look.

The lieutenant said, "He feels these things—he's usually right—let's hope to God he's wrong today." He went on aft.

Slowly, slowly the great ships crept closer together in their lines, nearing the enemy almost at snail's pace. The admiral came down from the quarterdeck and briefly reviewed the forming lines of marines in their scarlet coats, on the poop. As he returned to his own deck, Beatty left him with a word and a handclasp and paused before his juniors at the rail.

"It is near the time we'll be needed below, gentlemen. Half an hour."

Campbell began to reply, but his voice was covered by a thin, ragged cheer from the deck of the *Royal Sovereign*, keeping pace with the flagship. Men on this deck too were looking up, smiling, to a new set of signals fluttering sporadically in the miserable breeze. The senior surgeon smiled slightly, but his eyes were grave. "I don't read signals, but I heard him give the order. He sends to the fleet to say that England expects that every man will fulfill his duty. He gave it to the signal officer, Nelson expects, and changed it only because the other signal is shorter. A strange and remarkable man—and a very great one. I do really believe he feels that Nelson is England." He looked out to the enemy line; he said, "There will be work below, gentlemen, do not delay," and vanished down the nearest companion.

Aubrey muttered something and went down after him. McDonagh stayed at the rail with Campbell, to see as much of the beginning action as possible; he felt half-mesmerized by this leisurely, almost ridiculously deliberate battle attack. In the very clear, bright sun of approaching midday, the French and Spanish ships were visible in sharp detail now. The *Royal Sovereign* and the *Belleisle*, in the second line, had a slight advantage of wind over the *Victory* and were crawling up on the enemy a trifle faster. In uncanny, suspenseful quiet, in this bright pleasant noontide, they rose and dropped with deceptive smoothness. McDonagh could even, now, make out the names of some of the enemy: the *Sovereign* was converging on a tall-sterned hulk called the *Fougueux*, and not far off was the *Santa Ana*, one of the Spanish allies.

Campbell said, "Why, that's Villeneuve's own flagship ahead of us, see the mast—the *Bucentaure*. Dead ahead, and our whole deck'll be held under fire from her for half an hour, as we come up, at this rate. Me for below and a nice stout deck between!"

"Yes, I'm just coming."

Suddenly a little puff of white smoke went up from the gunports on the *Fougueux*, and a moment later the crash of the shot carried across the water. Meant for the *Sovereign*, that was, McDonagh thought. The leading English ships were nearly on top of the French line now, and Campbell was very damned right—better get below. Almost reluctantly he turned from the rail. He had his hand on the rail of the fore companionway when he heard guns speak again, and the *Victory* staggered under him.

He looked up just in time to see the first line of scarlet-coated marines on the poop deck torn apart by a full charge of chain shot; he plunged down the companion before the bloody fragments began to fall, and as he ran, he thought, No work for surgeons there, but there will be—there'll be work for us this day, and plenty over.

"This damned wind—if we could get up broadside—" The lieutenant of marines almost sobbed in frustration, seeming hardly aware of McDonagh's probing finger after the ball in his shoulder. "Just slaughter—forty minutes under fire now, and we've not been able to fire a shot."

McDonagh found the ball, slapped on an adhesive dressing, and said, "There you are—better let one of us look at it again tomorrow."

"If I'm here," said the lieutenant, and started back to his post. McDonagh took a breath; for the first time in half an hour the team of surgical assistants, running back and forth, fetching casualties to the surgery theater below, seemed to have nothing for him. He looked around: Aubrey was just straightening from a table, shaking his head; Beatty was assisting another surgeon, couldn't see at what; Campbell at the next table reared up and roared for a cautery iron. An assistant moved leisurely to oblige, and McDonagh snatched it from his hand, cursing him for slowness. Campbell was sweating and bloody; he fell back, seeing McDonagh, and said, "Do the cautery, will you—need a minute to sit down if I can take it." The man on the table had an arm shot away below the elbow. McDonagh put the iron to it, and the man screamed and fought the assistants holding him, but he didn't know he was lucky there wasn't time for leisurely surgery and pressure dressings—some reason, cauterized wounds usually healed cleaner. The assistants carried him off. There seemed to be a sudden breathing spell, no more casualties being fetched in at the moment.

It was unbearably hot and close here in the cockpit, the surgeons' theater, with thirty men—surgeons and orderlies—working under pressure of speed, the fires blazing for the cautery irons, the air foul with sweat, blood, and vomit. They worked in the flare of hurricane lanterns making pools of light on each table. "It's all this time running up," said Campbell, "not able to fire back."

"Aren't we firing yet?" There was no moment's silence from the din of guns above.

"You'll know it when we fire." And at that moment the ship jarred and faltered; every man on his feet staggered and clutched for support. "God, what was that?"

Two assistants came in sidewise, supporting another casualty; one answered him. "We're up to 'em, grazed with the *Bucentaure* just now, be alongside in a minute—"

McDonagh leaped for the table; the man had taken a ball in the leg. He enlarged the wound and felt for the bullet, and just as he slid it out, he was deafened by a great roar and shock; the ship leaped under his feet. The patient said faintly, "Thank God, that's us—we can give 'em hell now, alongside—"

Again and again the *Victory*'s hundred and ten guns spoke. Casualties stopped coming in; all the surgeons took deep breaths and straightened to look about and take stock. It had seemed an endless nightmare of fearfully wounded men, but there were no more than fifty or so after all, from those agonizing long minutes when the *Victory* crawled up astern of the French flagship, unable to bear her guns for defense and taking direct charges down the length of her deck.

They stood waiting for more work, listening to the guns. A few more casualties were brought in, not enough to keep them all busy. Then the ship jarred again, sickeningly, sidewise, and they heard the ominous scraping of another hull against their own. A quarter of an hour crawled by while they listened to that and the guns, and then the panting assistants brought down two men with deep burns on their arms.

"Good God, are we afire?" McDonagh steadied himself on the table as the hulls scraped again, and began to spread oil on the outstretched arm.

"Not us, sir, we're hull to hull with the *Redoutable*, and we've fired her, but we're so damned close, and no wind—part of our rail caught too. Oh, Christ, you ought see what we did to the *Bucentaure*—raked her broadside, point-blank—so close, splinters off her and dust falling on our deck—never saw the like, I didn't, must've killed half her crew, she hasn't fired since, just drifting alongside—the *Redoutable* tried to board us, but we've shot away her whole fo'castle—"

"How do we look?" asked Campbell. "Took some damage that first half hour, didn't we?"

"Some, sir, not as bad as you might expect. Our mizzen topmast's gone."

"Where's all the musket fire coming from? Half the casualties we've had had musket balls in them."

"Oh, that's the French tops, sir—marksmen sitting up all the masts they got, afiring down on us, just like hail on the top decks, and the admiral and Captain Hardy apacing 'round the quarterdeck under it, God, it's a fearful thing to see. The whole deck's that slippery with blood, like ice it is, but we're on top of 'em now, we'll have 'em soon."

The rush of casualties started up again, and in the cockpit the air grew more foul and breathless. The lanterns were replenished to renew their fitful light and add to the stuffiness. Every five minutes the ship started and quivered as her guns gave tongue, and the surgeons swore at the need to repeat orders to deafened assistants. The casualties mounted and then again slackened off, and the surgeons had time to stand and listen to reports from patients and assistants about what was going on above. Between the separate thunders of the guns they could hear the little, faint, sporadic cracks of musket fire.

There was an interval then when no new casualties came in. McDonagh began to realize how tired he was; the effort of concentration and the pressure of speed, even for two hours, were exhausting. He leaned on his table, with a haggard, white-faced Campbell and a sweating Aubrey, and exchanged a little desultory talk. Aubrey said, "Seems it's nearly done with. Could have been worse. I make it roughly a hundred wounded—no telling how many dead, of course."

"Could've been worse," repeated Campbell dully. "I hope it's about over. God, I could do with a drink."

Aubrey was looking beyond him. He said on an indrawn

breath, "Oh, no, oh, my God, no—" and started forward. McDonagh turned.

Beatty was hurrying across to a little group just coming in—not assistants bearing this casualty: incredibly, one of the figures was Captain Hardy—and the casualty was a little frail body in a bright blue coat.

10

Beatty, grim-faced, gestured the others back and bent over the admiral where his supporters laid him. But all the surgeons came to crowd behind; Aubrey silently helped the senior surgeon cut away the bloody coat. McDonagh, looking over Beatty's hunched shoulders, heard Campbell beside him draw a sharp breath as the wound was exposed. Beatty's long steady hands, with their old man's chalky nails, gently shifted the slight body.

"Well—William?" The brittle high voice was as sharp as ever, only a little breathless. "Nothing to be done—for this—is there? Tell me, now—tell me!"

Beatty straightened. He said steadily, "My dear lord—I must tell you there is not—there is nothing to be done for you, nothing any surgeon can do. The ball has shattered your shoulder and spine and touched your lung in its passage."

"I knew—nothing to be done, nothing. My last piece o' work. I knew that—expected it."

"Oh, God," said Hardy in a low voice, "I must get back—look to him." He blundered out, wiping his eyes.

"I will give you some laudanum," said Beatty. "A moment—"

"No, no! Must stay—a bit—to learn how it goes finally. Don't—fuss me, William."

"As you like, my lord," whispered Beatty; tears were running down his cheeks.

Another man knelt beside the admiral where they had in their haste propped him against the side of the companionway, guessing it was useless to lay him on a table for attention—Dr. Scott, his private secretary and chaplain, an old man helplessly blinded by tears. He groped for his master's hand, whimpering, "Oh, my lord, my dear lord—"

"There, Doctor, there," came the brittle voice, "not such— fuss and tragedy, old friend. You need not—be so frightened for me, I have not—not been such a *great* sinner, Doctor—Where is Hardy? Someone—send to him, tell him—come. I must hear— how the battle goes."

Beatty nodded at one of the assistants, who went off snuffling unashamedly. "Oh, my God, sir, would that I might do something for you—my own life—"

"Never—mind, William, never mind."

To McDonagh, this whole scene suddenly took on the unreal quality of a scene watched from the stalls, of actors posturing on a stage. He found himself thinking that it was well produced, the lighting cleverly done and the chief actor putting on an excellent performance; just that last, indefinable aura of slightly implausible melodrama to betray that it was staged. Every man grouped about the dying admiral was weeping openly or surreptitiously; the chaplain was alternately praying and sobbing. With the appropriately smoky flare of the hurricane lamps striking occasional gleams from the bloody medals on the discarded coat and showing the glint of unaccustomed tears on manly browned faces, and the sweat of pain on the thin bone-white features of the doomed man, it might have been framed, frozen, for a canvas entitled *The Dying Hero*. And McDonagh thought, keeping himself out of this circle of strong emotion with conscious effort, that whatever playwright had manufactured the lines for the leading actor knew how to appeal to the popular mind.

"I must—stay—to hear how goes the battle," gasped Nelson. "Send for Hardy—"

145

The third officer came down the companion and knelt beside him: a youngish man, struggling to keep his voice steady against emotion. "It goes well, my lord—we have them—I think twelve or thirteen enemy taken. But this—is too great a price to pay, my lord."

"No—no! Never too high a price—for an English victory!" He was trying to raise himself straighter; his gasping voice rang suddenly strong.

"Get back," said Beatty, "give him a little air. Sir, a glass of rum and water, let me help you—"

"Send me Hardy—must tell him—" Suddenly he seemed to recognize the senior officer kneeling beside him; he clutched his arm. "Remember—my orders—anchor! Anchor after the battle—there's weather making, you'll be blown off your prizes and lose 'em—in the end. Tell Hardy—"

"Yes, sir, yes, my lord, don't fear or worry your mind now," and the officer's voice was thick with tears.

"William, William. Don't bury me—at sea."

"No, my lord, I promise you."

"Where's Hardy? I must know—"

The faint light streaming thin down the companion from the gun deck above was suddenly obscured. The captain of the *Victory* came tiredly down the steep treads and brushed through the close-packed crowd of men; he knelt beside Nelson and took his hand in both his own. "Nelson, my dear friend, we have taken eighteen of the enemy, and the day is ours—the enemy fleet is broken for once and all."

Nelson lay with closed eyes a moment, as if he had not heard; a thin smile tautened his mouth. "I bargained—for twenty—but that will do. Hardy—Hardy—"

"Yes, I am here."

"Codicil to my will—you witnessed—take care. Rely on you—as I said—I leave Lady Hamilton and my dear daughter—legacy to my nation, to be looked to—honorably. See to it, Hardy—see to them—meanwhile."

"I promise you, Nelson, I shall."

A little silence, and the gasping breath came more painfully. There were broken sobs from the old chaplain at his other side. Nelson turned his hand in the captain's to clasp it weakly.

"Good friend," he murmured, "oh, kiss me, Hardy!" The captain bent and touched his lips to Nelson's brow.

Oh, no, thought McDonagh, this is nearer farce than bad melodrama—the stage manager made a wrong move there. Still, the popular mind was always incredibly sentimental; it might go over well. He was watching fascinated, unable to escape the fantasy that the flickering lanterns were clever-arranged stage lighting, and these a company of actors supporting this week's leading character player. As the scene progressed, they all were grossly overplaying their parts—there was no need for Scott to utter such appalling loud sobs, or for the manly big captain to let his chin quiver so very noticeably, or for Beatty to wipe his eyes so ostentatiously.

Nelson was still smiling faintly; he half raised himself on Hardy's arm. "Thank God," he whispered, "thank God—I have done my duty—for England." One last effort to draw breath into the failing lungs, and he sank back into Beatty's arms.

There was one moment of stillness except for the chaplain's weeping, and then the chief surgeon rose to his feet. "Gentlemen, England has lost her greatest man," and his voice broke on the last word.

But this, said McDonagh's mind, is quite fantastic; the least sophisticated audience will laugh at it. In just a moment now the orchestra will begin the British anthem, and a large national flag will descend jerkily from the flies. He was vaguely surprised when all that happened was the complete breakdown of the chaplain and Beatty's gentle suggestion that he be taken away. A weeping lieutenant and the third officer led him out. Captain Hardy laid the inert arm he still held across the dead man's breast and rose unsteadily.

"I must—there are yet—orders to give," he said in a low voice. "Beatty, I would not distress any of us—further than we have been. But—he did not wish to be buried at sea. And the nation—will want to pay its respects. I must ask you—but you know what must be done."

"Yes, sir," whispered Beatty. "Yes, Captain, I will see to it." He applied his handkerchief again.

"Then, gentlemen"—Hardy looked about the silent, shaken

group—"I will ask you all who do not belong here to resume your posts and leave what is to be done to our surgeons. Let us remember him as he was, not as he is." He bowed his head a moment and in silence withdrew and went heavily up the companion. In silence, slowly, the officers followed him, until only the surgeons remained, with the assistants at a respectful distance. The noise of the guns had stopped, the silence was somehow shocking, and all the hurricane lanterns burned very low.

This was the moment, thought McDonagh, when the lights should drop dramatically as the curtain fell on the little tableau suspended about the body. Instead, after a long moment, Beatty moved unsteadily away to lean on the nearest table and looked slowly about the five juniors and dozen assistants. "Gentlemen," he said in a low, broken voice, "I—you must forgive me—I was his friend. I cannot—if some of you would bear with my weakness—"

They muttered shamefaced, reluctant sympathy, but no man said more or stepped forward. McDonagh hesitated, and looked at Campbell beside him, who nodded tiredly. "Mr. Beatty, Mr. Campbell and myself will oblige you." The others looked guiltily relieved.

"Thank you, Mr.—" Beatty gestured in weary apology for the unremembered name. "Perhaps it will not be—the task for you as for the rest of us—you are not with him so long. Thank you. You know what must be done—the assistants will show you—" He stopped, as if physically unable to go on, and made another eloquent gesture, and turned away.

Half an hour later, McDonagh was still mentally shaking off the effects of that scene, as he faced Campbell over the corpse. It was yet impossible to say exactly what he had felt, for the presence of the two assistants who had mournfully volunteered to stay.

The last shot had been fired, and by the pitching of the ship it was evident that some dirty weather was making up. The fleet would be busy now making secure its prizes; he reflected bitterly that it was a damned ramp, the regulations prohibiting a ship's medical staff from sharing in the prize money on the ground that they were technically civilians.

"Sir," said one of the assistants hesitantly, "if you was to say where—I mean, where it'll be best—to keep it, like—"

"Oh, well, I don't know," said McDonagh doubtfully. "I don't suppose we're likely to get into any more action, are we?"

Campbell shook his head. "They'll be partitioning off the cabins again here. Best thing to do is give it one to itself—against the side." He looked at the men, who wore uneasy, fearful expressions. "Here, you needn't stay, we'll not need you. If you'll just go and fetch the barrel and stand it there against the port side, that'll do, and you can go."

The men vanished with subdued thanks, and McDonagh said softly, "My good God in heaven, were you feeling the way I was for that farce?"

Campbell said, "Probably. The English are a sentimental race of men." His long face bore an expression of fastidious cynicism, looking at the body. "All the same, he made a good end, didn't he, the little man? You know, Con, he was as impressive as he was—sometimes—because he never knew he was being melodramatic. Perfectly natural and sincere way to act, for him. Say what you like about him, he was a patriot."

"A patriot!" said McDonagh. He said it savagely. "Oh, he'll go down in history as a great patriot—dying for his country—and nobody will remember or care about the names of the men who died today in the same battle. The men who were kidnapped into service and treated like animals and kept like slaves—the men who mustn't be given a little laudanum to ease them before an amputation because some gentry officer might need it for a headache—the men who did the fighting while he watched. Don't they count as patriots too?"

Campbell said, "They'll put up a fine brass plaque, friend, on the *Victory's* quarterdeck, and at the bottom, after all the fine words about the little fella, it'll say, *and those who fell during this action.*"

"Oh, very likely. Yes, that much they'll do," said McDonagh. "Say patriot, say damn fool."

The two assistants appeared, puffing, rolling a hogshead between them; they heaved and struggled at it, getting it upright in one corner of this smoky, echoing, darkening place, rather sinister now that it was all but empty, and the flickering light not reaching up to the beams that followed the contours of the deck above. "Well, I don't know that I go quite so far as that," said Campbell slowly. "All right, men, thanks, that's all."

Averting their eyes from the body on the table between the two surgeons, the assistants went out quickly. "Don't you?" said McDonagh. He began to strip the upper smallclothes from the corpse. "What've they done so glorious, let alone this battle today? Killed the hell of a lot of other men for the greater glory of national pride."

"And in the name of some abstract principles."

"Oh, principles! Now you're really talking about goddamned foolishness." McDonagh laughed, lifting the body while Campbell drew off the stinking wet breeches; expectably, bowels and bladder had evacuated involuntarily at the moment of death. "Those are what the fellows giving the orders sell to the ones do the work of fighting, aren't they? Convince 'em they're fighting for truth and righteousness. Here, I'll do that." He took the cloth from Campbell and began to clean up the corpse.

"There's lies told and wrongs done," said Campbell, "but you know something, Con?" He interrupted himself to ask, "Had we better weigh him down?" He went to peer into the barrel. "Three-quarters full—it'll just cover him, but he'll float a bit if we don't weigh him down. A couple of cautery irons'll do." They began to tie those onto the corpse's ankles. "You know something? At the end of all your talk about the lies and the senseless sacrifice and the dishonest politicians, all your wise cynicism, you come to, well, to this," and he laid a hand on Nelson's naked chest. "To a thing in a man that makes him say, and mean it, he's proud to die for his country. There's no answer to it—maybe there's no sense to it. But there it is."

McDonagh looked at him and laughed. He took the corpse's shoulders and Campbell took its feet, and they carried it across to the barrel of brandy and heaved it up and lowered it in. It settled down quietly; McDonagh watched to see that it did not rise above the surface, and slapped on the lid of the hogshead to wake echoes from the unseen roof. "Write him an elegy on that theme, Jamesy boy," he said. "I've seen patriots die before, the hell of a lot messier than he did. I've seen too many patriots die."

He was tired enough to sleep sound that night, though they pitched heavily in a gale. It was moreover a source of sardonic amusement to him, next morning, to be told mournfully by Barker that the gale had caused the loss or recapture of several enemy ships.

All but draped in mourning, the triumph of the battle turned to ashes, the *Victory* turned for home, leaving the rest of the fleet to bring the captured prizes in. Against adverse cold winds, she battled her way slowly up the Channel, taking nearly a month on the way; not until the fifth of December did she come to port at Sheerness. A committee of dignitaries from the Admiralty was awaiting her, to take formal possession of the dead hero's mortal remains and convey them to London to lie in state before, probably, a great funeral at the Abbey.

As a kind of by-product of the occasion, all the officers and the medical staff of the *Victory* were given two months' leave, to await recommissioning, for the admiral's flagship would be retired from service as a national relic.

McDonagh traveled up to London in an oddly irresolute mood. He was due pay and collected it at the Admiralty medical supply office; money was always pleasant to have, and as he'd reckoned when he'd first thought of entering government service, the rate of pay was good. But he couldn't so far agree with the senior surgeon at the Royal College who had said he would gain valuable experience in his profession. He'd been a naval surgeon for exactly eighteen months, and in that time he could almost have counted his patients on his fingers, aside from that last wild, bloody day at Trafalgar—and what was that, professionally speaking?—the simplest, most straightforward surgery, arduous only because you worked at top speed, one case after another.

Along with his pay he collected a letter from Matt DeLancey in New York, sent in care of the crown medical service and waiting for him at the Admiralty. He read it rather inattentively in an inn over a bad meal. . . . So Matt was to be married, was married by now—one of Van Houten's pretty daughters after all, good luck to it, and the practice doing well. Damn, he thought, maybe I should have thrown in with Matt and gone to America.

He went back to the Admiralty medical office, after rumination, and reiterated patient demands for some senior authority until he actually obtained appointment with one, who listened politely to him. "I quite see your point," said the senior authority in the end. "But there are, you know, many hundreds of surgeons, most of greater seniority to you, Mr. McDonagh, in naval service. I will say this"—he smiled encouragingly—"most of our younger men prefer service at sea, as being, ah, more adventurous—"

"Adventurous be damned," said McDonagh, "I've never been so bored in my life, most of the time."

The senior authority smiled again. "Yes, I do see your point—I saw some service abroad some while ago! Despite the briefness of your service on the *Victory*, Mr. McDonagh, that does give you some little prestige, if no more seniority, and that may help you in gaining preference. As I say, it's generally our elder surgeons who want shore duty, but I myself feel that it is salutary for the younger men, with more modern training, to see hospital service. They have much to learn from their elders— and the elders from them sometimes. I will tell you what I will do—I'll put your name down, in the lists for recommissioning, as with a request for shore hospital assignment. I can't promise you that you'll get it"—and he shrugged—"but at least there'll be the possibility."

McDonagh thanked him almost fervently. As he came out into the corridor, one of the clerks pursued him from the general office, waving a letter. "Beg parding, sir—overlooked this I did when I give you t'other one."

McDonagh thanked him; then, as he glanced at it, stopped dead still and swore in surprise. Thin, pretty feminine script he knew, which sped his heart in remembrance: Number Four, Queen Square . . . He ripped it open and a moment later uttered a little sardonic laugh to himself.

Half England had gone into mourning for its dead hero; the body lay in state in the Painted Chamber at Westminster, and preparations were under way for a pompous public funeral. All the newspapers had devoted half their space this week to highly colored accounts of the glorious victory at Trafalgar, and the poignant drama of the admiral's death in his hour of greatest triumph. It was, in fact, a slight breach of taste for the newssheets to give space to any more prosaic subject, and in order to fill up their columns, they had resorted to using somewhat irrelevant material so long as it was connected with Nelson. When the possibilities of eyewitness accounts of the battle and the tragic death were exhausted, there came analyses of the strategy, descriptions of the weather, an artist's scale drawing of the flagship, and the *Times* yesterday had published a full list of the men serving on the *Victory* during the action—not, of course, the common crew, but naval and marine officers and, as an afterthought, the names of the medical staff.

Eighteen months ago Lauretta's old acquaintance from Dublin had been merely a rather irritatingly brash young man it was necessary to show social courtesy; now he could confer some unusual prestige on FitzEustace.

McDonagh laughed again; he wasn't flattered. Of course, Lauretta, writing prim little sincere phrases, never thought of it so; that was obvious (if he had needed telling that she had not an ounce of deviousness in her) by her ingenuous *James says he is so looking forward to meeting with you again, so you see you did not make so bad an impression as you feared!* Oh, he could guess what FitzEustace was looking forward to! Invited to meet the small social lion would be every one of FitzEustace's grander acquaintances, and he'd be expected to entertain them with an eyewitness tale of the national hero's last melodramatic moments.

The devil of it was he couldn't get out of it, because of Lauretta. He could not say to her what he felt about it; he would have to accept FitzEustace's damned dinner invitation, and both for the chance of seeing his darling again and by reason of her presence, he would have to give the company what his host expected: a damned, solemn, silly, sentimental account of that death scene, which they'd all have eagerly pored over in the *Times* but would be thrilled to hear again from a man actually present.

He was annoyed, and at the same time he wanted to see Lauretta, however useless and painful it was. He went back to the Leicester Arms and said a few things to Campbell about sensation-mongers. Campbell was spending a fortnight in London before going up to his family in Scotland, and shared McDonagh's room. He laughed. "Who are they, bare acquaintances who hardly recognized you in the street last year?"

"Yes—no, a bit more than that, or different. I—Lauretta, Mrs. FitzEustace, I knew her in Dublin. I—her father wouldn't listen to me, damn him, he married her to this fellow."

"Oh, I see," said Campbell noncommittally.

"It's not Lauretta, wouldn't enter her head to capitalize on— friends. But he's a snob. And damn it, I shall have to go. I can't be rude to Lauretta, and—a damn lot more sensible never to see her again, but—" He shrugged moodily, turning away to fill and light his pipe.

"I see," said Campbell again. He let the silence go on until the subject could be considered changed, and said, "Like to attend the opera with me tonight?"

McDonagh cocked a brow at him. "Flying rather high, aren't you? I understand in the honest-to-God courtesan class you can't touch one for less than ten guineas." Only a few of the *haut monde* attended the opera for its own sake, and most of those only to show off fine clothes and jewels. Apart from these few gentry, the opera boxes were the professional showcases of the Fashionable Impures, the more exclusive of the available women, but those on show there aimed to capture the notice of fop, sophisticate, nobility, royalty—gentlemen of high society and wealth. Not a shopping center for two humble professional men, the opera.

"Oh, well, no harm in going to look," said Campbell reasonably. "It's always entertaining."

"Yes, all right," grunted McDonagh. That reminded him of Fleur; it was odd how emotions went. Well, he liked women; he'd enjoyed Fleur, but for some reason, coming back to London this time, he'd had no particular desire to go to see her, perhaps to renew their relationship. It was a combination of things, he thought, something as nebulous (and maybe as adolescent) as the discovery last year that she had a niece of seventeen, and his little shock and anger about that, Fleur taking it for granted that the girl was only sensible to embark on that career—and Madeleine herself, already under Fleur's influence, looking at him with bored eyes when he—

Well, no, not under Fleur's influence altogether; she had a stronger intelligence and self of her own than that. And damn it, they were probably right in taking such a sensible view, and what in the name of God was it to do with Conal McDonagh, who wasn't noted for his own rigid sexual morality and had no remote business criticizing anyone else's?

The fact remained, for whatever obscure reasons, he did not particularly want to see either of them ever again; the remembrance of both of them rather irritated him than otherwise.

And so, of course, there they were. Everyone arrived early at the opera house, and the intervals were long; it was more of a social occasion than anything else. McDonagh and Campbell had seats in the stalls, with a good view of most of the boxes. It was, as Campbell pointed out amusedly, rather difficult at first glance to tell the genuinely respectable gentlewomen from the courtesans, for these, the *haut monde* of the class themselves, were fully as fashionably and expensively arrayed. Only their professional assessment—discreetly as it was conducted—of the gentlemen who ogled, admired, dispatched notes by attendants, and came up to invade the boxes, betrayed their status.

"They give a ball every year," said Campbell in the tone of a scientist examining an interesting new specimen through the glass, "for the gentlemen of first fashion and wealth. The Cyprians' Ball, it's called. At the Argyle rooms. I understand it's quite an honor to be asked—a token that your fortune and credit has been found quite sound. That's a lovely piece up there, second from the right in the middle row."

McDonagh looked and said he didn't much care for blondes. He added that all these fops with their quizzing glasses and striped waistcoats spoiled the show of women. "Damned fools they all look."

"Some of our first families, with the bluest of blood," said Campbell solemnly, and at that moment McDonagh saw Fleur—and Madeleine.

He saw Fleur first, sitting near the front of the box, fanning herself indolently, in white as usual, showing a good deal of shoulder and bosom. It was a box almost directly over where he sat, and he had a clear, close view of her: the familiar small amused smile, the quick shift of dark eyes on everything to be seen. There was a gentleman in the box, leaning over the other occupant; he straightened to laugh and fiddle with his quizzing glass, and Madeleine Olivier came into McDonagh's view.

Between them they had accomplished a successful metamorphosis, he thought sardonically and angrily. She had no figure, a too tall, too slender girl, if with that fluid natural grace, but her gown, with its demurely high neckline and full sleeves, concealed the lack. Her smoky black hair was pulled back from her temples, dressed high to fall into a few careless ringlets behind, across one shoulder, with a curled fringe left on her forehead; it was devastatingly becoming to her thin high-cheekboned face, and yet artless—mannered casualness the effect. No, she was neither beautiful nor pretty, but a half-remembered line, unidentifiable, from where, school days or miscellaneous reading, slid into his mind: *There is no excellent beauty that hath not some strangeness in the proportion.*

An opera box: to show off both, or only Madeleine? Perhaps, then, she was still weighing possible protectors against one another.

McDonagh got up without conscious volition and made for the archway giving on the corridor behind the boxes. Campbell, who had followed his glance, caught him up to take his arm. "Here, where're you off to? Fellows like us can't barge in— all very exclusive these females are, at least as far as the cost goes—"

"Not so much as you might think," said McDonagh. He said it absently, but for the first time it occurred to him vaguely that he had been very lucky, or Fleur very bored, that time ago, that a courtesan of her caliber had favored him freely. He shouldered through the groups of men standing about in the corridor and, heedless of Campbell's warning protest, opened the door of the box and stepped in. "Decided to put yourself in the market again, Fleur?"

She rose up with a little consciously surprised shriek—no, one never took Fleur quite unaware—threw her arms around him and kissed him affectionately. "Conal, *mon cher*! How good to see you again! You are back from the wars safe, I am so happy. You remember my little Maddi?—and do introduce your companion!" A brief flash of smile at Campbell as he did so. "Allow me to make known to you Sir Almerick Dunstan. You look very well, Conal. How long are you back in London? Why have you not come to see us?"

"How do you do, sir," he said grimly to Dunstan, disentangling himself from Fleur. For no reason at all he felt fury rising in him for Madeleine, for this elegant gentleman, for Fleur's affectations.

Dunstan examined him for a long moment, with and without the quizzing glass. He was a middle-sized man of forty-odd, with a long, rather lined aquiline countenance, shrewd sophisticated light eyes, and graying hair in a Hessian crop. His suiting was a poem by the tailor: elegantly fitting knitted inexpressibles of cream color, molded to his lean waist and long legs, strapped over low shoes of mirrorlike gloss; discreet dark blue waistcoat; a rather high collar to his shirt, with a neckcloth exquisitely arranged *à là Trône d'Amour*, a perfectly cut blue coat, just a shade lighter than the waistcoat, sharply cut away at the waist to short tails, much padded in the shoulder. He wore a heavy gold signet ring on one hand, a cameo on the other, and his quizzing glass was mounted on a gold and ebony stick.

He looked McDonagh up and down, from his overlong-for-fashion crop that never stayed brushed smooth, his evening stubble of beard, his casually loose neckcloth, unpadded gray coat made by a Dublin tailor for six guineas and proclaiming the fact, to his black broadcloth pantaloons strapped over half boots in need of polishing. Dunstan smiled, dropped his glass on its gold cord slung about his neck, and said in a bored tone that he was delighted to make Mr. McDonagh's acquaintance.

"And you," said McDonagh to Madeleine, "are looking very well also, Miss Olivier."

"So kind of you, sir," she returned, smiling. Oh, they had done a piece of work on her, he thought: everything most discreet, only a touch of color high on her cheeks, looking like natural flush, the merest trace of lip rouge; the one beauty she possessed, besides her fine fair complexion, was her overlarge, candid gray eyes framed in long black lashes. He remembered Fleur saying, *I myself, I have one grandfather who is named O'Donnell....* Yes, the Irish said of eyes like those that they were put in with a smutty finger; the color of the winter sea off Derry head, pewter color, they were. At the moment they were faintly amused on him. He had forgotten the exact quality of her voice, too deep for a woman's and slightly husky. She was not beautiful; it was her eyes and her voice that made her distinctive. "Do tell us where you have been and what excitements you have seen with the fleet, Mr. McDonagh. I'm sure you've had adventures since we last met."

"A naval man?" asked Dunstan without interest.

"Thank you, no," said McDonagh, "few things so boring as life at sea. Both of us lowly surgeons in crown service, sir, and late off the *Victory.*" For the first and last time he took some pleasure in emphasizing the fact, giving him as it did some social ammunition against this highbred mannered fop. He was savagely amused at the brief malice in Dunstan's eyes, alert and aware for possible competition.

They exclaimed and questioned; they insisted that McDonagh and Campbell stay to share the box. Dunstan evidently was a guest, for he made no move to seek a seat below when the performance began. Yes, Dunstan was the quarry: for Madeleine? Of course. It was not for some while that McDonagh realized the instant motive behind Fleur's adroit maneuvering, as the summoned attendant fetched more chairs; he was as if casually placed at Madeleine's side, while Fleur devoted herself to Campbell at a little distance. The anger sharpened in him. Any tool to hand! Implied competition would always make the prize look sweeter.

In the enforced silence during the performance he began to wish passionately that he had not come, had not blindly followed impulse to invade here. He had finished with this thing last year. He had met Madeleine Olivier exactly twice and been astonished at himself and obscure motive leading him to attempt interference with her life; it was nothing to him personally, then or now. Why in God's name had he deliberately intruded himself here? He was conscious of Madeleine's scent, something different from the cloying perfumes most women seemed to like—what was it? Scent was the woman to him; his senses responded to scents more immediately than to look or touch. She moved slightly, close there, their shoulders six inches apart, and slowly brushed her fan, and a little breath of scent passed him, something spiced, different, and elusive. Bergamot, he thought, bergamot and perhaps rosemary, and very nice, too. At the same time, for no reason at all (seeing that it was nothing to do with him) he felt again, as he had felt for her before, exasperated fury—for her smile and the boredom in her eyes, for her passionless candor, for her assumption of sophistication.

He would get away; he would make some excuse and escape. . . . Campbell enjoying himself, shooting occasional questioning, humorous glances at him . . . Fleur, animated, whispering behind her fan . . . Be damned if he'd give this overdressed fop the satisfaction of leaving him in sole possession!

He stayed; he was caught. Fleur's eyes commanding on him: "Do us the favor to call tomorrow, Conal, will you not? Come and take a little luncheon with us, we will be so very pleased to receive you."

"I'm sorry, I don't think—"

"Oh, but you must, you will! I will not allow you to say no! Half past one, we will expect you without fail!"

11

————————————

McDonagh looked at the two of
them in exasperation, anger, and something like bewilderment.
"Look here," he said abruptly, "that's damned ridiculous."

"Not ridiculous at all," said Madeleine amusedly. "I think
Fleur's quite right, it will be just what is needed."

"Don't tell me you're having difficulty annexing Dunstan!"

"Oh, you mistake it entirely, you the crude and straightforward!" exclaimed Fleur. "It is a game, Conal, we are not harlots
to see the bargain made in two minutes! Indeed, Maddi could
have done well enough for herself before now"—and she
reached to pat the girl's hand—"but I am very particular of her,
as she is of herself also, I am glad to find. Sir Almerick will do
very well—"

"Oh, my God, yes, you're very damned careful of her!" said
McDonagh.

Madeleine laughed. She was all in blue this afternoon, another
high-cut, demure, yet sophisticated gown of some light, soft
stuff; again, sitting near in Fleur's rather overheated little parlor,
he was aware of her individual scent. "I confess I didn't realize it

either, but Fleur's right—it's quite like the game of courtship, you know. However crude an exchange it may be really, that is all elegantly covered up with flirtations and pretense. And just as a girl angling for a more regular suitor plays one off against the other, so do we. You can be of great help, Mr. McDonagh, by squiring me about a little—where Sir Almerick may notice it. He didn't like you at all, I saw that."

"Which is not surprising," said Fleur.

Suddenly the anger rose over other emotion in him, and he turned on her savagely. "If you want my opinion, you're a pair of harpies! I told Madeleine last year how I felt about it—yes, and damned myself for a fool afterward to interfere in what's none of my affair, you needn't tell me! But I'll say it again, and before you, Fleur—" He whirled on Madeleine—"you're a damned little fool, deliberately setting out to ruin your life by this. Oh, tell me again how impossible it is for you to earn a respectable living! You never tried in London, did you? Fleur's got something to answer for in encouraging you—"

"Now truly, did he do this? You said nothing to me." Fleur's eyes narrowed on him and Madeleine.

"Oh, quite righteous," said Madeleine, watching him. "Women already—shall we say debauched?—are one thing, but a respectable young virgin something else."

"That sounds very clever," said McDonagh, "and it may be damned funny too, but you're right. I don't like to see it, because I don't think you know exactly what you're getting into, even now."

"Well, it's nothing to do with you," she said indifferently, but her eyes held brief anger on him. "In fact, I find it rather amusing, for you sound as if you thought I was being coerced into it. In any event, I may do with my life what I choose, sir."

"Don't tell me," he said bluntly, "that you're looking forward to going to bed with that—that middled-aged fop—because I don't believe it." He had the unholy satisfaction of seeing her flush very faintly; despite her air of sophistication, a little crudity embarrassed her, and she was furious that it should be so, he saw.

She said coolly, "Not particularly, perhaps, but he is a

wealthy man and quite attractive, if one likes the type." The hand that held her wineglass trembled slightly with her irritation, but her voice was quite steady. "He's amused, he likes me, and I think he will make a very good offer, but it would be helpful to make him just a bit jealous. If he thinks I might give preference to another man, when he has felt confident that he could take me when he pleased, the offer may go up somewhat."

McDonagh came and stood over her; she tilted her head back to meet his eyes, bland and challenging. "You don't know a damn thing about it, do you?" he asked softly. "That's Fleur— her words in your mouth."

Her eyes were frosty with dislike. "There's really no need to discuss it any further. Since you're so far a Puritan to wash your hands of both of us—"

"On the contrary," said McDonagh instantly, "I have two months' leave and no plans whatever. Can either of you doubt that I would be pleased to be seen in public with so—decorative a female? But—"

"I greatly resent, Mr. McDonagh," said Madeleine in a gentle tone, "being looked at as if I were a painted trollop out of Houndsditch. However much you—as such a righteous gentleman—may deplore *sophistication*, you must agree that I have better taste than to advertise my calling by my face and dress."

"No, Conal, we will not trouble you," said Fleur firmly.

"Oh, you can't recant now," and McDonagh smiled at them, battening down his annoyance. "What I don't understand, I must say, is how you think Dunstan could possibly be aroused to jealousy over me. A titled leisure gentleman, with maybe a yearly income of ten thousand pounds—"

"Nearer fifteen," corrected Fleur absently.

"Trust you to know!" He laughed. "Dunstan, to think he was in any danger of being cut out for the favors of an available woman—who thinks of money first—by an eighty-pound-a-year professional man? And not a very high-regarded profession, socially, at that!"

Fleur rose and poured herself more wine. Her hand and her voice shook with irritation and temper. "Oh, this is camouflage! You think very highly of yourself, this sneering humility, it is only another way to proclaim it! What indeed makes you so righteous suddenly? So we think always first of money! You know as well as I, women like us are not harlots—we live by selling all that women have to sell, but we are not promiscuous street trollops! Did I think first of money when I was kind to you, eh? We may take money for our favors, but we do not stop being senseless female creatures, once in a way, like other women!" She drank half the wine at once, angrily. "That is, in fact, exactly why Sir Almerick Dunstan would be jealous, for he knows that women do not in the nature of things serve Mammon twenty-four hours a day." Her eyes measured him bleakly. "He did not like you, no. He pays his tailor in a month what you earn in a year. But he looks at you and he is jealous—never mind Maddi!—as man to man, for the twenty years you have on him—and the extra foot of height—and that you have shoulders to fill out a coat without padding. Your black brows and your long stubborn jaw that never looks shaven and the insolence in your eyes and the very way you have to move and stand, that is beyond all arrogant, and your voice that is deep and rough even when you are being polite—which is not often—it all says to him, and to everyone, this is a male creature of quality. To him it says, Of better quality than I—and he is angry, because he knows women, and that sometimes—even very often—the shrewdest woman in the world looks at *that* and forgets about money. And also he is angry, very plain and straight, because he is not that kind of man himself."

"I think Sir Almerick exceedingly attractive," said Madeleine, sitting very erect and studying her glass. "He has a great deal of elegance of manner—and manners."

Fleur drew a long, exasperated breath. "I agree with you—it is true—but some women have no sense whatever, as we all know. In any case, I—I beg your pardon to lose my temper a little over your stupidity, Conal. No, we will not trouble you with our affairs."

"Madeleine's affair, don't you mean? Maybe you're afraid she'd end by being as foolish as those women you mentioned? I can't say all that sounds exactly complimentary—I needn't be much of a man to be twice the man Dunstan is—but I take the point!"

"I assure you both," said Madeleine, "you need not anticipate that I should do that! I might say, Fleur, that some of us are neither so silly nor so susceptible as to prefer such—such—such blatant masculinity to more genteel behavior and appearance!" Fleur looked at her but said nothing.

"Damn it, you don't get out of it," said McDonagh. "You asked me! Don't make such a piece of work about it. I ought to do something to redeem myself, after being so naïve and righteous as to try to argue you into respectability!—hadn't I now? Not so arduous a task to squire you about here and there a few times where Dunstan can see us! I'll be glad to oblige, lady—where would you like to go tomorrow? Ranelagh? Perhaps to Kensington Gardens for tea? Would we be apt to run into Dun stan there?"

"You'll excuse me, I think I agree with Fleur," she said coldly and he took a step nearer her, smiling.

"Oh, no, you don't! Even if we don't run into Dunstan, I sup pose some kind acquaintance will see us and run to tell him. If what I've gathered of high society is so, these affairs are usually public knowledge among gentlemen and even provide occasion for private bets. I'll call for you at three o'clock. Don't keep me waiting, I've no money to waste on standing hacks. I think this may be a rather amusing way to spend my holiday after all."

Madeleine drew breath for speech, but Fleur interrupted her, with a shrug and a helpless gesture. "Very well. But twice or thrice will be all that is needful—"

"And quite as much as I should be able to agree to," said Madeleine hardly. "I shall not keep you waiting, sir."

He called for her the next afternoon still in that abrupt change of mood; a little cynically pleased (not for remembrance of Fleur's left-handed compliments!) at having, in a way, forced himself on her. Now he came to think, it was perhaps odd that he hadn't felt like discussing it with Campbell, and had been annoyed at the necessity for explaining where he was going. He had had to give Campbell some brief explanation of Fleur; and he liked the Scot, they got on well, but he'd be just as pleased when Campbell left for the north in a few days and left him alone in his rooms. . . . Contrarily he thought he'd enjoy his holiday this way—an amusing business.

Madeleine was ready for him and did not keep him waiting. She was fashionable in silver gray, a walking costume with its own small velvet hat; she had borrowed some of Fleur's paste jewels, he noticed. When he had told the hackman to drive to Kensington Gardens and seated himself beside her as the coach jolted off, she turned to him with a rather forced smile.

"So long as we must spend some time in one another's company, Mr. McDonagh, shall we call a truce?"

"Very happily," said McDonagh promptly, smiling back. "After all, the idea is that Sir Almerick should be convinced of our mutual attraction, isn't it? He'd not likely find it very plausible if we're seen in public looking daggers at each other!"

Madeleine laughed. "No, indeed! Truce, then—when we are in public."

"And you can get in some useful practice," he added, "exercising your wiles on me—while we're observed." Yes, it was contrary, but he was enjoying himself. Without much concern for why, he thought now he'd accepted her for what she was—or would be—and put that irrational issue out of his mind. Certainly she was a distinctive companion to be seen with.

She smiled noncommittally. "It's to be hoped I can—what was the word you used?—*annex* Sir Almerick fairly soon. Fleur's but waiting to have me off her hands, and out of her house, before taking a new protector."

"Oh, really? I can't say I'm surprised. She's a bit young to retire altogether."

"And one can always use more money." Her eyes were hard. "I now owe her nearly four hundred and fifty pounds, which I must make haste to earn and repay."

"Pity poor Mr. Bodge," said McDonagh, "he must be turning in his grave."

Madeleine's blasé assumption of casualness failed her, and she almost giggled. "Oh, heavens, don't put me in mind of it! And I'm dreadful to laugh. I was very fond of him, you know, he was such a kind creature. I—it's odd, when he was only a stepfather, but I really think I was—was fonder of him than of my mother." She looked thoughtful suddenly. "She thought so much about breeding, and what is done and not done, and what people will think and say. And I don't think her family was all that highbred—but I was always sorry for Mr. Bodge—she never allowed me to call him anything else, you see—because she was forever making rather horrid remarks about his business and his friends and his manners, as being *low*. And he never said a word back, poor dear."

"I see. And maybe you thought you'd show her just how low her daughter could go?"

"That's quite senseless, isn't it?—my mother's been dead for five years. And as to *low*, well, you should remember that one of my profession has risen high enough—both socially and financially!—to belong to the Duke of York."

"From what I've heard of the royal family," said McDonagh dryly, "I can't imagine she finds much pleasure in it."

"Heavens, I should think not! I saw the Prince when we were at Vauxhall Gardens recently. Anything less princely couldn't be conceived! A great fat thing, with a very rude loud laugh—he looks like a farmer in fine clothes."

"So you don't aim that high?"

"Heaven forbid! There are enough wealthy gentlemen who are more attractive."

As he handed her out of the coach at their destination, he said, "You see, we can get on quite amiably if we try."

She looked up at him, head on one side. "If *you* try, Mr. McDonagh. Now you're not snapping my head off every two minutes!"

"Oh, I've given that up as a bad job, Madeleine. You don't mind that I call you that? After all, if we're to make your fine gentleman jealous, we can't go on Missing and Mistering each other."

"Very true," she agreed sedately.

Kensington Gardens was one of the popular entertainment places which had sprung up in the nearer suburbs, and in good weather was crowded, emptier of company now in winter but still flourishing. There were sheltered tables where one might take a leisurely tea, and about the grounds pleasant walks, Punch and Judy shows, a performing bear, and other occasional amusements. Madeleine declined firmly to be taken to see the bear. "I've seen it once, and never again, the poor creature—so dreadfully thin and pathetic! And looking so human and yet *not*, if you see what I mean. I couldn't bear it! I think we had better just have our tea on the largest terrace—we'll be sure to be seen there." And not long after they were seated and awaiting service, she observed amusedly that the young man eyeing them from the second terrace—"No, don't look up now, he'll see"— was Mr. Algy Feversham, undoubtedly an acquaintance of Sir Almerick, and would bear the news that Sir Almerick's latest bit of muslin—or would-be bit—was receiving attention from a new escort.

"Then we'd better give him something interesting to see," said McDonagh, and leaned across the table to take her hand, smiling close into her eyes. "Just as a beginning."

"What a pity it's in the afternoon and I can't flirt with a fan," said Madeleine. "I believe he's scalded his tongue on his tea, he looks quite idiotic. Mr.—oh, I forget, we are to stop using formality!—Conal then—do you mind if I ask you something? Last year, when you were being so stupid to me, you said something and then told me to forget it. *Too much bloody war*, you said. And Fleur said you are newly come from Ireland. Was it a rebellion you joined, that you said that about hanging? Yes, I see it was. Dear me, you should watch your tongue—now I have you where I could get you in trouble, couldn't I?" Her gray eyes danced at him.

"Damn it, what d'you—"

"Oh, please, you're crushing my hand! Why, I don't mean anything—at the moment. I don't really suppose I could get you in trouble either, only on my word."

"Yes, I spoke a bit hasty there," said McDonagh grimly. "Devil sitting on my shoulder about it, so I'm like the man in Scripture—fleeing where no man pursueth! Damn silly. I'm done with all that nonsense anyway, for God's sake let's talk of something else. I like your scent, Madeleine."

"Oh, do you, I'm so glad. It is rather a chore to make it up, but one can buy only very common ones from the apothecaries. I'm become quite an apothecary myself—it's called cologne water of Portugal, oil of lemon and orange and rosemary—"

"And bergamot."

"Yes, more of that—and you put it with alcohol and let it stand forever—there, Mr. Feversham's going off, we've given him a new interest. Don't think me vain, but I've aroused a little attention in our circles, you know, I believe a good many gentlemen are curious to see whom I will favor first. What luck to see Mr. Feversham here, our first time out!" Her eyes danced again.

"Obviously Providence is on your side! But we needn't go back just yet," said McDonagh. He paid the waiter and stood up, not letting go of her hand. "We'll stroll about the grounds a little, just in case any more acquaintances of Sir Almerick are present." There was a curious excitement in him for having her to himself, for whatever surface reason; vaguely he put it down, his new feelings about her, to a number of little irrelevant things. She was not one thing or the other as yet—an available woman, but still an innocent. It lent a strange spice to being with her, for she need not be treated as a respectable girl. She had chosen for herself and must put up with that. The feel of her narrow soft hand, and its little reluctance in his, told him suddenly, incredibly, that despite her year with Fleur, it was as he had said to her yesterday—it was theoretical knowledge with her; the feel of a man's hand on her, however unintimate, was yet new. The strangest compound of pity, fury, and resentment flooded him like a violent tide. He pulled her to her feet almost roughly, and down from the terraces with their tables and scurrying waiters to one of the wooded walks.

She went with him meekly, and that pleased him and increased the little excitement. The path was shaded and winding, trees bare now and the place deserted in late-December chill. Out of sight of the terraces he stopped and pulled her around against him to stand in the circle of his arms. He was scientifically interested to find that her instant reaction was exactly that of any sheltered virgin of reputation.

"Leave me go!—what are you thinking of, to be so rude?"

"Do you really want to know?" he countered, and laughed. "Oh, no, you don't, Madeleine—stop fighting me, now—don't you think I deserve a little reward for obliging you so, to help you wangle a higher offer out of Dunstan? You're being silly, girl—a woman in your profession doesn't think much of giving away a few kisses, and you'd better get used to it!"

Her eyes hazed a little, meeting his amused eyes so close; she said, a trifle breathless, "I—suppose that's so, I—but you might—be a bit less hasty and rough about it, sir—"

"Oh, you'd better get used to that, too, Madeleine—we all come with different habits of lovemaking!" He felt her small breast under his hand, and he wanted suddenly to hurt her and suddenly to be very tender with her, the both at once, violently, and he tightened his arms and set his mouth on hers deliberately.

She relaxed against him, and at the far back of his mind he knew that she had never before been kissed with passion, and all the opposing feelings about her strengthened in him. He loosed her a little, and her eyes were blank on him; she steadied herself on his arm.

She said with a small gasp, "Well, now you have taken what you felt—just payment, may I be allowed to take a breath?" It was a gallant and nearly successful attempt at casualness.

" 'Please, Conal'?" he prompted softly.

"Please—Conal. You have qu-quite crushed my gown—"

"And that too you'd better get used to. Very well, I've had my pay—for today. I'll take you home." He laughed. "It's a pity to tease you, Madeleine."

"Tease me? Oh—"

"Never mind," he said, "never mind. This time next year you'll know well how to counter an attack like that—or give in to it more thoroughly!" And he said that with both amusement and anger. Oh, it was a damned comic, contrary thing in a man, and senseless, but something they all shared, maybe: whatever it was that wanted a woman willing and experienced and yet shied off being the first to spoil a virgin to make her that way.

He took her back to the city and made rather formal farewell. "Next Friday, shall we say? I'm engaged for Thursday evening. The Covent Garden Theater. I'll call for you at seven o'clock. Mind you wear your best gown."

"Very well," agreed Madeleine. She had been animated on the return journey, a little too much so; she did not look at him often. "That will be quite satisfactory—for our business arrangement, shall we say?"

He smiled. "Oh, I only ask very small payment, lady—nothing you can't afford! I'll see you then." He watched her into the house, still smiling to himself.

When he shook hands with Campbell at the stage station, the Scot said, "None of my business, but I think you were right when you said it'd be more sensible not to see Mrs. FitzEustace again. The way you've been cursing this dinner party—"

Well, no, he wasn't looking forward to that and hadn't been reticent about saying so. "Oh, damn it, I'll get through it somehow. Can't get out of it now."

"Send them a note you've been posted to the Outer Hebrides at a day's notice," suggested Campbell.

McDonagh laughed. "I'd like to! No, just one of those things. Every now and then—not very often, and not for very long—I think life'd be simpler to get through if Providence had made some other arrangement for regeneration, and there weren't any women in existence. Well, I wish you joy of Scotland at this time of year, it's cold enough here. Hope to run across you again one day, Jamesy boy—good luck with a new posting."

"And to you." But Campbell put his head out the stage window to add, "I withdraw my sympathy—you don't look about to drown yourself for unrequited love."

McDonagh smiled and lifted a hand as the stage pulled out. How could another man know what he felt or didn't feel? It wasn't that he was agonizing over Lauretta and his love for her all the while, but it was always there at the back of his mind, forgotten for a time while life went on in other lines, until something recalled it. She was the only woman he'd felt what was called romantic love for, and it wasn't a thing a man got over easy or quick.

It all flared up in him again, that evening, for facing her across a dinner table. She'd matured a little from the girl he had known and maybe grown even lovelier. She was wearing her hair a new way, drawn higher with more curls, but it escaped to curling tendrils as it always had, and her blue eyes were just as soft and smiling. . . . When the gentlemen joined the ladies after dinner, he managed to monopolize her for a moment to tell her so.

"Thank you, Con." She smiled at him. "I'm very well and

content. I—I have a dear little boy now, you know. I find I quite enjoy being a matron! It's odd how life turns out, isn't it?"

"Isn't it?" he echoed ruefully as she turned away to another guest. And just as he had foreseen, FitzEustace showed him off to the company as an eyewitness of the great hero's death, and he had to endure a good many silly questions and compliments, and conceal his real opinion of both the event and the man. That was the price he paid for seeing his darling again, and on the whole he thought it justified.

He went up to St. Luke's to see Gillespie; from the few months he had worked under the old man, he had some affection and respect for him, and he thought Gillespie had for him. At any rate, he welcomed McDonagh in his dry, undemonstrative way, and introduced him to a new assistant, Robert Meredith, a surprisingly handsome young man with a perpetual one-sided grin. McDonagh and he took to one another on sight, and Gillespie peered at them over the horn spectacles he wore for work and said, "You see, Mr. McDonagh, you accustomed me to having an impertinent, brash young man about the place, and I had to find another to replace you."

"He may be brash, but could he be as good a surgeon?"

"Why, damn you, and that from one o' these ham-fisted government bone sawers?" said Meredith indignantly. "You just ought to come upstairs with me and see the lovely hernia I did today."

"What," said McDonagh in surprise, "have they moved the dissection hall upstairs?"

Meredith aimed a mock blow at him, and Gillespie said, "No use, Robin, you'll never get the last word of him—he's an Irishman after all. If you'd like to watch us remove a few kidney stones, Mr. McDonagh, we'll be through for the day and I'll invite you both out to dinner."

"Damnation, I'm sorry, I can't, I'm taking a lady to the theater. Make it tomorrow." For a moment he would almost rather have been free to go out with them; then, thinking of Madeleine, the little amused excitement rose to the top of his mind. ... There were other days.

He escorted her to the theater, more interested in watching

her than the play—a silly piece of broad comedy. To his amusement and gratification—women infrequently had much instinc-
tive judgment about such things—she agreed with his unspoken
opinion. "I shouldn't mind its being vulgar if it were funny, but
it's not, is it?"

"Now what would you say if I said I thought it excruciating?
Fleur's neglected your education—never express an opinion
until the man you're with does so, and then agree! As a matter of
fact, I do agree with you. But the evening isn't wasted, hordes of
people must have seen us, and some who know both you and
Dunstan."

"That's so," said Madeleine, wafting her scent toward him
with her fan. "But however—businesslike—our arrangement
may be, Conal, you needn't sound quite so bored and indifferent
to any other aspect! I should like to feel that you don't find me so
entirely dull to escort."

"Whatever gave you that idea?" He laughed. "Quite the contrary! I've never been very good at turning pretty compliments."

"Oh, you needn't tell me that!" said Madeleine.

"Here, we'll be insulting each other again in a minute. Is anyone important watching us?" He leaned to her and laid his arm
lightly around the back of her chair; he had bought a box, and
now with the lights up during the interval they were in view of
most of the house.

"If they are not, they soon will be if you flirt much more
broadly. By the way, Fleur asks me to tell you that if you are
free for next Tuesday evening, perhaps you would care to make
up a party to attend a *bal masqué*—it's to be held in the public
rooms of the Chanson Restaurant and should be amusing. We
thought, you know"—she looked at him sidewise, with her
quick, elfish smile—"that perhaps Fleur's new candidate for
lover would like to join us, to make up the party—he's quite a
nice creature, a very polite gentleman, Mr. Saul Isaacs, a dia-
mond merchant in Maiden Lane—and then we thought that at
such a plebeian entertainment, there'd scarcely be any of Sir
Almerick's friends present, and he'd certainly not be there himself unless he were especially invited. So we have invited him, to
escort me, and you are ostensibly to escort Fleur—by now, you

know, he'll have heard that you and I have been seen about together."

McDonagh laughed; he was not much amused; he would not enjoy meeting that cold-eyed foppish gentleman again. He said, "Oh, certainly I'll come—quite a plot, I see. I'm to pay you violent attentions in his presence. And you are to—pretend to respond."

"Exactly. We needn't dress up for it, Fleur says—only masks, and we can provide you. I wouldn't have you out of pocket just to oblige me," said Madeleine demurely.

He was suddenly very irritated at her, but said nothing. In the hack as they came away from the theater, she chattered on about the *bal masqué* gaily; McDonagh interrupted her to say, "At least there are far more places to take women of your status than respectable girls—and no need for a tiresome chaperon! Public rooms in a restaurant—plebeian is a small word."

"Oh, yes, considered quite vulgar, but no less amusing!" she returned brightly. The hack creaked to a halt before the house in King Street, and he went up the step with her.

There was one of the few standard street oil lamps not far away, which was unfortunate, but he ignored it. As she reached to the knocker, he said, "Just a moment, Madeleine—you haven't rendered me tribute for obliging you this evening, you know!"

This time she did not flinch away as he pulled her into his arms, but she did give a little gasp of indignation as his hand came to her breast, and she held him off one moment. "You are the most outrageously irritating man I ever—"

"Knew?" He laughed. "But you've no experience to judge by, have you? Why, in ten years' time you may be looking back to me as a paragon of tenderness!" He bent his head and kissed her slowly, insultingly, enjoyably; and when he let her go, she stepped back and slapped him hard across the face.

"You little hoyden!" he said, and slapped her back lightly. "You see what you're learning?—not so easy a job it is as you thought—you'll earn your money!" He dropped the knocker on the panel for her and turned away. "Eight o'clock on Tuesday—tell Fleur I'll be happy to oblige!"

The hack driver had evidently taken that in with interest; as the house door opened and McDonagh came back to the road, he observed, "Wunnerful high-sperrited some females get, talking up to their betters. Thass right, mester, you want to give back as good as you get, make 'em respect you! Where to now?"

"The nearest tavern," said McDonagh moodily.

12

He dressed for the *bal masqué* that evening bitterly regretting that he'd agreed to go—to watch that bastard Dunstan licking his middle-aged chops over anticipation of Madeleine, grinning and posturing at her. Well, the devil with it, he thought, struggling with his neckcloth, since he'd got past that nonsense of trying to reform the girl, he didn't give a personal damn about it, but he'd taken instant violent dislike to Dunstan, and he was sorry for Madeleine. He needn't be; she knew what she was doing, or at any rate wouldn't be turned from her purpose now.

He swore aloud at the neckcloth, getting it tied somehow. Dunstan and his elegant smooth-fitting clothes! McDonagh grinned ruefully at himself in the glass. If he could afford Dunstan's tailor, he'd never carry the man's art with anything like such grace, he was aware. Dress himself as careful as he might, for some reason his neckcloths always worked loose and crooked, his shirts never stayed neatly pulled down into his breeches, his hair never stayed smooth, and his pockets filled themselves with mysterious miscellany to sag his coats. He cleared those of his best gray coat now, absently, of several advertising leaflets, an old receipted bill from a cobbler, a few halves of theater tickets, a folding magnifying glass he had not had occasion to use since laboratory classes at Trinity six, seven years ago, an old flint, and a bent sixpence. He checked his purse, dropping the sixpence into it, to be sure he had sufficient small change for vails to waiters, linkboys, and hackmen. Three pounds in notes, a sovereign, a sizable collection of smaller coins—that would do.

No, of course, the whole silly irritating business was nothing to him, in a few years he'd likely look back on it with a good deal of amusement, but just at the moment he could think of things he'd rather be doing than spending this evening watching that old lecher making up to an innocent less than half his age. Sorry for her!—so McDonagh was, when he thought of it, but also she annoyed him powerfully on occasion.

He got to the house in King Street early, but not before Dunstan, who eyed him with too gracious a smile, too cordial a greeting; evidently the identity of Fleur's escort had been revealed to him only at the last minute, and it had annoyed him, but he covered up well. He was suave in buff breeches and blue coat, his watch chain and heavy rings gleaming discreetly; he toyed with gold snuffbox and quizzing glass gracefully. McDonagh greeted him brusquely and began the evening's business by frankly ogling Madeleine in her daffodil yellow gown. Dunstan's eyes turned cold on him, and McDonagh announced cheerfully that he had told his hack to wait.

"I thought it best not to bring my own carriage," said Dunstan in a bored tone. "One can never be sure of the attendants at these places—on the rare occasions I visit such public amusement, I prefer not to risk my equipage or horses. And then it is rather a bore being driven—generally I tool my own sporting curricle, but couldn't ask ladies to crowd themselves into that, eh? Interested in horseflesh, Mr. McDonagh? I just picked up a prime pair at a bargain, good goers they are, only eight hundred guineas, cheap at the price. Drive at all, Mr. McDonagh?"

"Never," said McDonagh. "Too rough a sport for me, Sir Almerick—surgeon has to take care of his hands, you know. What a very lovely gown, Madeleine—you're charming in it."

"Oh, thank you, Conal," she returned prettily.

Handing the women out at their destination, McDonagh deliberately turned his back on Dunstan and made no polite demur as the other man perforce paid off the hack. After all, he thought, he might enjoy an evening of annoying Dunstan.

The Chanson Restaurant was one of the rather raffish French eating places which clustered about the streets off Piccadilly, along with, reputedly, a number of high-priced brothels flourishing in respectable-looking residences. Beyond the dining room, in the large attached public hall behind, the *bal masqué* was already in progress, with a thin crowd of revelers that would grow as the evening went on. McDonagh busied himself with helping Fleur and Madeleine remove their cloaks, letting Dunstan secure an attendant to lead them to one of the low little boxes set about three sides of the hall, where one sat out dances to watch the others and might be served with a variety of refreshments—all bad, he discovered—and flirted broadly across the little railing with strangers so inclined on the dance floor. He let Dunstan reward the attendant, settling the women in their chairs.

He felt rather a fool in the narrow velvet eye mask, but the little conceit became the women; it occurred to him after a while that this small effort at disguise of personality took the effect of somehow lessening their normal social restraint. Perhaps that was why *bals masqués* were popular. He watched the dancers, and these two women, thinking that. Fleur only shrieked with amusement when a couple passing the box executed a grossly vulgar step—ordinarily she was more fastidious—and Madeleine leaned forward, lips parted, watching the dance and seeming unaware of Dunstan's hand on hers.

McDonagh got to his feet abruptly and asked Fleur to dance. The orchestra, a small one, was unexpectedly good. He danced twice with Fleur, both country dances, before he turned to Madeleine. She demurred, "Oh, this one?" and expecting her to play up to him, he was surprised until he realized that it was a waltz. He laughed, and Dunstan turned an approving, amused smile on her; she flushed.

"Why, Madeleine!" McDonagh mocked her. "Can you have forgotten you're no longer a reputable little miss of Tunbridge

Wells?" He pulled her out to the floor with him. "It's only respectable women don't indulge in this shocking new dance! Have you ever waltzed? Quite easy, just pay attention and follow me." He put his arm around her and led her into the step.

Halfway around the hall she was silent, minding her steps, and then she said, "Of course I have—with the other girls, at school, and just for fun, to feel a little wicked. It's just that it seems strange—to dance so close to one's partner."

"Reason society frowns on it. Arm's length the rule in gentry circles, when there's waltzing at all. But isn't it easier to follow?"

"You're—a good partner," she said in a constrained tone.

Brazenly, aware that Dunstan was watching, McDonagh violated all the canons of good taste and pulled her up close, so that their bodies touched and swayed together. "There, you see, much easier to stay in step!" And for one strange moment he felt a little breathless himself, disturbingly conscious of her slim, taut body pressed to his. She was light and easy to guide, but he'd never before had the experience he had now, of feeling that he moved as one body with a dance partner, their very bones acting in unison, as one unseparated unit. It was upsetting and exciting; he was silent through the rest of the dance, and as he led her back to the box, he wondered if she had felt any of that too. She was rather flushed with the movement, and her hand shook slightly on his arm.

"Quick now," he said in a low voice, "sooner or later he'll go out to the cloakroom—that corridor there. You go out after him, as if you were bound to"—he grinned down at her—"straighten your hair or gown in the women's room, and I'll come after, we'll put on a little scene for him in the corridor."

Her eyes moved on his vaguely. "Very well."

Fleur shook her head at them as they entered the box. "Very naughty dancing, both of you! It is as well that we are not anywhere that matters."

Dunstan gave McDonagh a cold look and bent solicitously over Madeleine. "Wouldn't you like to sit quiet a bit, my dear, and have an ice and some punch?"

"That would be lovely," she smiled.

The ices were half-melted and insipid; the orgeat punch was thin. McDonagh disposed of his portion and carried Fleur off to the floor. "We're all three shortly about to desert you—whenever Dunstan goes to the cloakroom. Don't follow Madeleine, we want to put on a little play for him in private."

"Oh?" said Fleur. "You and Maddi decide to cooperate very well, eh? That waltz—quite indecent!"

"Don't call her by that silly name," he said without thinking. "Why must you shorten a lovely name like Madeleine?"

She danced a few steps in silence and said softly, "Maybe you are wishing it was the first form of that name, eh, Magdalen the reformed harlot?"

"Watch your steps," he said brusquely. "Don't be silly, Fleur, I don't give a damn either way. I don't like Dunstan, I'm glad to oblige in helping to relieve him of some money, that's all. Not that I don't think it's shameless of you to encourage the poor baby—talk about throwing a lamb to the wolves! My God, she'd hardly been kissed before."

"But she has been now? Perhaps we—or I—made a little mistake here in planning to sell her virginity. You would—what was the phrase you used, as in the training of horses—break her in very pleasurably, Conal, and give her a decided taste for her work!"

"Damn you, Fleur, damn you," he said furiously, impotently, "did I ever think you were anything more than a crude foulmouthed trollop? . . . I'm sorry, I don't mean quite that," as she stiffened against him—"never mind, I don't know what the hell I mean, let it go."

They came back and he sat between Madeleine and Fleur, listening to the fatuous compliments Dunstan whispered loudly to Madeleine, who flushed demurely and made play with her fan, obeying the rules of the game that said a really exclusive courtesan must act the discreet gentlewoman until an arrangement was arrived at. Dunstan led her off to dance again, brought her back, ordered more punch, and presently rose to excuse himself. In the blaze of lights in this public place McDonagh noticed with something like disgust Dunstan's sagging hound jowls, and the lines from nose to mouth corner, and a false tooth in his upper jaw, and the thinness of his absurd juvenile-cut hair. He had a sudden sharp vision of what Dunstan would look like on a dissecting table, stripped of his fine clothes, his wealth powerless to help him then, only a stringy middle-aged corpse discolored with corruption, waiting the scalpel that would show him to harbor the same viscera as any poor bastard out of a workhouse.

He watched Madeleine get up and drift out to the rear corridor where the cloakroom and supper room were. He went after her in thirty seconds. The supper room opened out directly across the corridor, with the gentlemen's cloakroom to the left, the ladies' to the right. It was yet too early for supper, and only a waiter or two scurried about that room. McDonagh caught Madeleine up as she entered the corridor and drew her up to the left a few steps, behind several long tables stacked on end against the wall, not yet set up for supper guests in the other room.

"How does it go?" he whispered. "Will you be annoyed at me for insolence, or pleased?"

She looked up at him blankly, as if she had not understood. He heard the door of the cloakroom open behind him, and crushed her against him and began to kiss her violently. She struggled and got an arm free to slide tight about his neck; when he took his mouth away she gasped, "Conal, oh, Conal," and sought it again blindly.

Like that, he thought; she was playing up well—learned easy and quick. And then a hand caught his shoulder from behind and he turned to face an infuriated Dunstan.

"Let her go at once, rogue! Offering such insult—" Dunstan swept Madeleine to his side.

McDonagh took a step toward him. "Are you telling me it's private property, Dunstan?"

"Oh, well, now, really, that's for the little lady to say, ain't it?" Dunstan gave a high humorless neigh of laughter, tightening his protective arm about Madeleine. "I'm saying you've no business offending her so crude, and—and she's but to complain to me if you do so again, I'll see something's done about it!"

McDonagh laughed at him. "Send your coachman and a couple of grooms to waylay me? Very careful not to threaten me here and now, aren't you? Why, you overdressed, finicking, goddamned little old fop, I could toss you out the nearest window with one hand, and I'd damn well enjoy doing it, too!"

"I'm sure," said Dunstan, showing his teeth, "that Madeleine needs no further demonstration of your rude force!" A couple of waiters came past, and a man on his way to the cloakroom, who eyed them curiously. "Come, my dear, this is a most unseemly scene, let me take you—"

"Thank you," and Madeleine moved away from him. "I am— I am quite all right now, Almerick. I must—straighten my hair, forgive me. I'll join you in the box." She walked away from both of them, very erect, down the corridor and entered the ladies' cloakroom.

Dunstan did not stay to prolong the quarrel, with McDonagh looming eight inches over him. He took snuff, snapped the box shut, and said with a cold smile, "I think you see that in a contest between penurious youth and well-provided maturity, my friend, your side must come off the loser! You are likely more accustomed to dealing with common street women, I daresay. A lovely little filly—entertaining—but no fool, you know. You haven't the stakes to play in this high a game." He strolled back into the dance room.

McDonagh went on into the cloakroom. Damn the lot of them; that was that; Madeleine would get a good offer, likely. The whole damned game was absurd, the way it was played among these high-society rakes and the women who catered to them. Pretense—veneer!—imitation of courtship, as Fleur said. It was a damned sight more honest on the lowest level, where the harlot sidled up and murmured, "Five shillings, mester, on'y five bob!" and you took her into the nearest alley. A damned lot more reasonable, too.

And now he'd go back and act sulky before Dunstan and dance with Fleur again and have to answer her questions, and next week, or the week after, he'd drop by to call maybe, and find that Dunstan had already taken Madeleine away somewhere. How did they arrange these things on this level? He had only a vague notion: a suite of discreet rooms somewhere, in a private hotel or a private house—an allowance paid into a bank.

A storm of red fury possessed him with appalling suddenness, he felt again her slender body pressed on his the first time he kissed her—just now when he ' danced with her—her arm around his neck, her warm mouth no longer quite so innocent. *Dunstan,* to have her first!—Dunstan, to know first the passion in her waiting to be waked—Madeleine, to belong to this old-in-lechery English bastard—

He leaned on the wall, shaking with that rage that came and went in a minute, leaving him weak and sweating with its force. What the hell, he whispered to himself furiously, what the *hell* was it to him, there were women to be had, never mind it, what damned contrary idiocy in him put any importance on this one? He took a breath and straightened. All right, he thought angrily, so he wanted her himself, he wanted her like hell, just that, her body to wake first, that was all, and this rage in him was just fierce resentment that his desire was balked. Thought he was a little more grown-up than that, to expend all this senseless emotion on one available woman, the kind not worth much emotion. Let it go, now he'd admitted the fact for what it was. Let it go and forget it.

He looked at himself in the glass, smoothed his hair and straightened his neckcloth, and went out to finish the rest of the evening according to schedule.

He did not see either of the women alone again that night; when they came back to King Street at two in the morning, Dunstan asked with chilly courtesy if he could drop Mr. McDonagh anywhere, and McDonagh said no, and walked off back toward Piccadilly alone. He had made no new engagement with Madeleine, and as it happened they did not know where he was staying; if they wanted to see him again, they could go on wanting, he thought. Been a fool to let himself be dragged into the business.

Deliberately he stayed away from King Street. He saw something of Rob Meredith; they went out sampling taverns together a few times, and often McDonagh spent the evening with him, when Rob was on duty, in the little bare room he had lived in himself, desultorily talking shop and other things. They celebrated New Year's together with a Gillespie quite unlike his workaday self, who revealed an unexpected fund of rather ribald songs in almost unintelligible Edinburghese.

And he called on Lauretta, properly after hospitality, at an hour when he hoped FitzEustace would be out. Lauretta he found playing with her infant in her sunny little parlor; she rose up flushed and pretty to welcome him and told the maid to fetch the nurse.

"Don't let me disturb you, it's an inconvenient time to come maybe," he said, feeling awkward.

"Oh, no, not at all, Con, it's always nice to see you. Besides, I'm happy to show off my darling Johnny," and she cooed over the little thing, holding him up for McDonagh's inspection.

McDonagh uttered all the indicated compliments, rather ill at ease because he was slightly surprised at himself (for once) for not having the appropriate sensations. All his frustrated love for her should have been sharpened in him for the sight of her, the sweet young mother, and maybe he should have been thinking that if he'd had his heart's desire, this would have been his son. Instead, he was a trifle irritated not to find her alone and unoccupied, and as for the baby, frankly he found it unattractive. He'd seen babies in hospitals, where only the lowest-class women went for delivery, that looked brighter and healthier; this fragile, white little thing, with its thin cry and pale blue eyes, looked exactly the sort of offspring FitzEustace would beget.

"He has such a sensitive constitution"—Lauretta sighed—"every least little thing upsets him, but Dr. Dyke says it's often so with very intelligent children. There, my pet—do be careful to keep him well covered up those drafty stairs, Mary, won't you?" The nurse bore the infant away. "Now, do tell me how you go on, Con. Have you received news of your new appointment as yet?"

"I'm to call at the Admiralty office next week to hear." He relaxed a little, alone with her; she listened sympathetically and gave him her soft smiles, and he began to feel that she was his darling, whom he knew, again. But presently, FitzEustace came in and was overcordial in his pompous way, pressing another dinner invitation; McDonagh made hasty excuses and escaped.

He was not enjoying his long holiday as he'd expected; he told Rob Meredith it was largely because he'd been on one long holiday for nearly two years. "That's all it amounts to, you know, at sea. I haven't done enough work to justify my meals, up to that last day at Trafalgar."

"You complaining?" said Meredith.

"Oh, well, damn it, we all grumble about working, but when you come down to it—" McDonagh shrugged. "I'd like a job to get my teeth in for a change."

He was lucky. When he called at the Admiralty medical office, he met the senior authority he had spoken to, in the corridor, and the senior authority smiled kindly. "Some new postings came in today, and in glancing them over, I see you've been fortunate, Mr. McDonagh. You are appointed to the naval hospital in Portsmouth.... Oh, I had nothing to do with it, only very happy to see such enthusiasm in a young man. Good luck to you."

McDonagh went on into the office and collected his official papers, his day considerably brightened for this news. He reread the brief directive as he emerged into the street: *To report upon the eighth day of February, 1806.* This was the twenty-sixth of January, and his leave was almost up. He tucked the papers away; he hadn't kept note of the days going by, and now, abrupt and immediate, it came to him that it was nearly a month since the evening he'd attended that damned silly *bal masqué* with Madeleine and Fleur.

Madeleine. It all rushed back over him, the various and contrary emotions he'd felt, and dismissed, and damned himself for. Well, likely it was all accomplished fact now; she'd sold herself to Dunstan. He'd sworn he was finished with both those harpies, but—well, call it a loose end, no harm in finding out. He made excuses to himself, half-angry. He did not go that day but indulged himself and spent too much money at that very exclusive brothel The Key in Chandos Street. He did not go the next day; but it stayed there, nagging at the back of his mind, and the day after that he walked up to King Street in the afternoon.

The maid let him in silently, and he walked into the parlor

ready to greet Fleur. Instead, he found Madeleine, sitting alone and apparently unoccupied before the fire. She looked around at him and said, "I heard your step—and quite thought I was dreaming. We had decided you'd been posted away suddenly." She was in the blue gown he'd seen before; she looked just as he remembered her, as if she'd never left this place, as if—

"Well," he said, "I didn't expect to find you here."

"Oh, did you come to—call upon—Fleur? I told you she's committed to a new protector."

"As a matter of fact," said McDonagh, "I came to find out how your little campaign ended, Madeleine." He sat down opposite her. "Should I apologize for not calling before? I thought our cooperative efforts had taken the intended effect and you were finished with me."

"Let me give you a glass of wine," and she rose to pour it, moving with that fluid, boneless grace. If he had known that she was here, he would not have come; now, for seeing her, all the hot desire and resentment flooded him again—a blind adolescent thing, he thought angrily, resentment only because Dunstan or anybody else should have what he wanted himself! He took the wine with abrupt thanks. Madeleine poured a glass for herself, sat down leisurely, and gave him her sudden smile. "Oh, you were very helpful, Conal. Almerick has made a very good offer, and I am to have a most charming apartment of rooms in Cavendish Square—an elegant address! In fact, I am to remove there next week, and I was just sitting here thinking about what stuff I should choose for the new curtains in the parlor."

"Oh," said McDonagh. "Oh, I see Or rather, I don't—for God's sake, why the delay? Didn't he begin to bargain with you after that absurd business at the restaurant?"

"Oh, yes. Quite satisfactorily. But the house was being refurbished inside, and Almerick was called away to his Norfolk estate on business. I'm to be installed, let's see, on the second of the month, for he's to come back on the fourth. I'm quite looking forward to it," said Madeleine.

"Are you, you little liar?" said McDonagh roughly. He rose and stood over her. "Are you? I don't think so. However much you may be looking forward to the money, I think you're dreading the man, an innocent like you! Never mind, Madeleine, you'll get broken in with Dunstan and think nothing of the next man—and the next—and the next. Practice makes perfect, you know."

"Do you sit up studying how to be rude, Conal?" she asked rigidly. "Or don't you need to?"

"Just natural talent," he said with a laugh.

She got up unhurriedly, and close there, he reached for her almost automatically, but she moved away. "Now you know what you came to ask, I think I'll ask you to go. You make me a bit nervous, because I never know where I am with you. Is it to be the upright angry gentleman this time, sternly telling me I'm ruining myself deliberately—or the rake who takes such pleasure in every casual female at his mercy? Did you enjoy yourself—teasing me, Conal—when I was a bit more innocent?"

"When!" he said, and laughed again. "You're nothing else now, girl—for a few days as yet anyway. And I wish you much joy in losing it, with your long-toothed lover who delays over estate business! My God, he's an importunate, romantic fellow, isn't he? Maybe that's an excuse for him to retire to take a course of aphrodisiac, d'you think? I wouldn't doubt it."

A little spasm of feeling passed over her expression, too fleeting to identify. She said very calmly, "Since you seem to be so concerned with examining my private feelings, and since we're being frank with each other, why, no, Conal, I'm not much looking forward to Almerick's lovemaking. But as you've just reminded me, practice makes perfect. If you should be in London again next year, or the year after, and we chance to run across each other, I might go so far as to forget about money for once and let you try how proficient I'll have become by then."

Without any conscious intention or plan, he hit her hard with his open hand across the face. He said, "You damned vixen, you're in the right trade safe enough!" And instantly was horrified at himself. What the hell was wrong with him, roused to such a pitch over a—Never struck a woman before in his life— he tried to think of some stiff apology, and the words clove to his tongue.

"Get out," she said in a whisper, a hand to her cheek. "Get out of this house!"

He turned and went without a word, as if he fled; and he fled gladly.

When he got back to the Leicester Arms, in as black a mood as had ever fallen on him, he met Rob Meredith just coming away. "Ah, well met, Con my boy! Gillespie and I are celebrating. We've got a healed trepan, if you'll believe it, never the suspicion of any blood poisoning."

"And when was the patient removed to Bedlam?" asked McDonagh.

"He's sitting up in bed rational as you or more, eating pigs' trotters," said Meredith, "and we're inviting you out to dinner. Had the news about your posting yet?"

"Oh, by God, yes, just what I wanted—"

"Tell us at dinner, I must get back. Seven o'clock, the Elephant in Aldergate."

McDonagh went into the bar of the tavern and drank gin moodily. He felt it was just as well he was leaving London soon. It was having nothing to do, a man stagnated and got himself into mischief; any little thing loomed important to him.

Whether it was some subtle influence of Meredith—who was one of those men who would go on looking an innocent twenty until he was dandling grandchildren—or possibly the consciousness of the compliment paid him by two young men apparently enjoying his company, Gillespie had shown an unexpectedly youthful side of himself to McDonagh these last few weeks. He and Meredith were awaiting McDonagh in the private dining room of the Elephant, and Gillespie recited incomprehensible verse by Burns over the preliminary drinks, in solemn high spirits. "It's the beginning of second childhood," said Meredith to McDonagh. "He's reverting to Edinburgh more and more. Only the other day he told me to *hauld* my *claish*, and this morning he informed me that my *trews* wanted mending."

"Second childhood my grandfather," said Gillespie. "You young fellows don't appreciate profound and beautiful literature. The greatest voice that Scotland has given the world—it'll take time before he's appreciated, poor fellow, he's not been dead long enough yet to be recognized. The language of the people—"

"It's no good writing great poetry if nobody can understand it, that's just what I say—oh, does anyone know how to read in Scotland? That's different, I daresay, if it is a written language."

"You're a cauf and a chiel without proper understanding," said Gillespie. Meredith produced a notebook and pretended to look up a translation, and the waiter peered at Gillespie doubtfully. "Oysters, my man, we'll start with aplenty of oysters."

"Very good, sir."

"For God's sake," said McDonagh hastily, "tell me about your wonderful trepanation."

By the middle of the evening both he and Rob were slightly bosky, nothing out of the way, just pleasantly stimulated; they had had some brandy after dinner, Gillespie scorning it and leading the way up to the Fallow Deer in Monkswell Street, a house kept by a Scot who stocked whiskey. "Must celebrate your appointment, Mr. McDonagh, you know." McDonagh never had seen and never would see Adam Gillespie any the worse for drink; the whiskey he took at the Deer affected his articulation and balance not a hair. He only quoted more Burns and presently joined the landlord in nostalgic—and perfectly tuneful—rendering of sentimental ballads.

"I freely admit," said Meredith somewhat thickly, "that the old fellow can put me under the table any time. I came to your damned whiskey late in life—delicate English constitution, raised like a gentleman on French brandy, I was."

"Nonsense, Mr. Meredith," said Gillespie severely, "why not be a man and admit it's your youth and poor judgment? I never overdrink because I know when to stop—I treat the *uisgebaugh* with respect, and it returns the compliment. At the moment I have reached my limit, I'll take no more," and he waved away the glass the landlord had refilled. McDonagh intercepted it.

"Oh, now, Mester Gillespie, you was juist in guid voice," said the landlord. "D'ye mind *Green Grow the Rashes*, now? Or *Corn Rigs?* That's a guid 'un—"

"Ah, that one calls for a verra expeerienced voice," opined Gillespie. Apparently in mutual accord they broke out happily together in melody.

> Green grow the rashes, O!
> Green grow the rashes, O!
> The sweetest hours that e'er I spent
> I spent amang the lasses, O!

McDonagh, in the landlord's absence of attention, refilled his own glass. "Here, man," said Meredith, "take it easy, we'll need to carry you home. You're three-quarters shot now."

"I am perfectly sober," said McDonagh very distinctly. "You're the one not used to the *uisgebaugh*."

> Gie me a cannie hour at e'en,
> My arms around my dearie, O!
> An' warldly cares an' warldly men
> May a' gae tapsalteerie, O!

"Though I blame Burns," said Gillespie, shaking his head, "for so far catering to a nice public opinion, when he set down our old folk songs, as to rewrite the less polite verses. No doubt he felt that if they could be sung in mixed company without offense, they would become better known. All the same—"

"Ah, you're reight, you're reight, sir," agreed the landlord. "All the flavor lost, so 'tis. That's a guid song, but I learned it a wee bit different, and no doubt ye did y'rself." They leaned together over the counter again.

> Green grow the rashes, O!
> Green grow the rashes, O!
> A feather bed is nae sae soft
> As the bellies o' the lasses, O!

13

———————

"Now look," said Meredith, taking great care of his speech, leaning on the door of the hack, "you'd best take thish hack, Con—tell man take you home—get there shafe, eh?"

"No, you damned fool," said McDonagh. "I'm perfectly sober. You're the one who's drunk."

"You're certainly nowhere near as full as he is," said Gillespie disapprovingly.

"That's right," said McDonagh. "You take him home and put him to bed. I'm fine—fresh air'll clear my head."

"Well, if you've made up yer minds," said the hackman. Between them McDonagh and Gillespie bundled Meredith into the hack, and it rattled off.

That had been only a few minutes ago, and he set out to walk back to the Leicester Arms. He wasn't any more than a trifle bosky, not on five doubles of whiskey. Well, maybe six; and the brandy before, but on top of a meal, the drinks before didn't count. He was quite steady on his feet, and he knew where he was and where he was going. Of course. A few minutes later he came into a wider street and recognized Piccadilly. Rob saying he was drunk—that was a joke—and he laughed, remembering how drunk Rob had been. Englishmen not used to the *uisgebaugh*. Funny little Gillespie. *A feather bed is nae sae soft. . . .*

That business this afternoon, he thought. Madeleine. What the hell had got into him? Hitting her—blundering away. Very bad, and he hadn't apologized. She was a damned irritating female and the sort you didn't use much social nicety with, even if she had been respectable—still was, for a while yet—but he ought to apologize to her. He'd feel better about it if he did that. Poor little innocent lamb, going to Dunstan.

He was at the end of Piccadilly; he turned and walked up toward King Street, past the occasional dim-burning oil lamps, to number twenty. The house looked all dark. Never mind, she'd be there. The vague thought crossed his mind that it was late, but likely they sat up late, in a back bedchamber or somewhere. Suddenly this was urgent in him; he wanted it off his mind. Madeleine, Dunstan. *A most charming apartment of rooms.* Damn Dunstan, damn him for the power to buy what Conal McDonagh wanted. Dunstan, to have her first. Warrant he was a clumsy, selfish blunderer with a woman—that sort—frighten her and hurt her, he would. None of Con McDonagh's business; she had chosen her bed.

He stood outside the house and looked at the dark front windows doubtfully. Only want to apologize, Madeleine—very sorry I was so rude. Just because I'm so damn jealous of Dunstan, taking you first. Don't care anymore what you do with your life—McDonagh the reformer!—but as you are an available woman, I'd like well, by God, the privilege his money can buy him—so I would, admit it. He was standing on the doorstep, and his hand was on the knocker.

Suddenly the door opened inward as the latch was drawn back, and he stumbled over the threshold because he'd been thoughtlessly leaning on the panel, into the feeble flare of a single candle.

"Oh!" she exclaimed in a little gasp. "I thought—Who is it? Oh, Conal—"

He collected himself and said formally, "I came to apologize, Madeleine. I was very rude—didn't mean to be—I'm sorry. I never meant to hurt you, I'm sorry."

"Oh," she said, and lifted the candle. "I thought it was Abby—the maid. She's very late. Fleur's gone into the country with Mr. Isaacs."

"I'm very sorry, Madeleine. Hope you'll forgive me."

"You've been drinking," she said, and she sounded amused.

Amused—always amused at him. Laughing. Righteous fellow trying to reform her; conscienceless rake, teasing her. He said with formal dignity, "Just a trifle castaway, that's all—sorry, Madeleine, just wanted to apologize." She laughed at him.

Never known a female who roused such fury in him or such immediate hot lust. All right, contrary, he thought: was it just because he knew he couldn't have her even if she was available?—that she came too high-priced for him? All the rage and passion and bitterness he had felt before swept over him as he stood there looking at her in the little light.

Late, it was late. She had got up from bed; she had a thin dressing gown caught around her, so close it showed the curve of one small breast. Her hair was tumbled a little, casual, and her face was pale without cosmetics.

It was the oddest way all the thoughts were in his mind at once, perfectly distinct and clear. He heard Fleur's soft insinuating voice: *You would—what was the phrase you used—as in the training of horses?—break her in very pleasurably, Conal, and give her a decided taste for her work!* He remembered her responding to him that night, her open warm mouth on his, and his impotent rage—another man to know first her passion—

She said, the maid out. And Fleur away.

She moved, and he was conscious of her scent, and she said, "It's late, Conal, you'd better go."

He shut the door and took off his greatcoat, dropping it on the floor. "Conal, it's late," she said coaxingly. "You can't stay now. I accept your apology, but you'd better go."

The blind hot desire was rising in him. He thought, so she was bent on turning herself into a high-priced harlot, and so she would, but not under the clumsy handling of an oaf like Dunstan—Con McDonagh the better lover any day—they'd find her eager and willing after McDonagh—

"Conal, please go home," she said.

Must mind what he was doing— She had backed a few steps away from him, and he put his foot on the candle she dropped and caught her close and began to kiss her rough and hard. "Girl, girl, don't fight me now, don't you know I've got to have you? Easy now—better for you than him I'll be—"

"Let me go—Conal, put me down!" But he picked her up, one hand over her mouth, and carried her across the parlor in the dark, avoiding furniture by miracle or accident, into the other bedchamber from Fleur's. He stumbled against the footboard of the bed, and she twisted away from him, but he caught her again. He had her dressing gown off now, and beneath it was only a thin night rail—no matter for stripping his own clothes, no time, no need—

"Let me go, please, Conal!"

"Oh, girl, don't fight me now, who would come, don't your neighbors know what sort of women live in this house? Madeleine, Madeleine, don't you know you've set me half mad wanting you—him, having you first—and bad for you, girl—let me come easy to you now, *gille mo croidhe, gille mo croidhe*—"

Those practiced hands of his, knowing just how to reach and rouse her—suddenly in his mind was the night they had danced, that was the way it should be, two bodies moving as one—but gentle and easy and loving with her at first, as it was needful. The love words spontaneous, unplanned against her warm breasts. And then her body arching involuntarily to meet his, her breathless moans on his name, her arms hard and tight around him.

And he took her in the greatest sensual joy ever with a woman—for whatever reason unable to prolong it as his usual habit with a woman, which worried him vaguely—the expert lover—but good, so very good—

He lay on her temporarily spent, and realized with utter surprise that the liquor had caught up to him.

Very damned odd. Couldn't remember how many doubles— didn't matter, he had a hard head— But half an hour ago he'd been quite clear-headed, in absolute control of himself, and now all on a sudden he felt to be as drunk as he'd ever been in his life. It was ridiculous, something wrong with that whiskey there'd been—

But a very, very fine feeling, having Madeleine the first time, her warm dear slim body as close as if they were one body—

She was holding him hard and warm, speaking in little gasps against him. "Conal, Conal, was it what you meant—always—that you loved and wanted—"

He laughed into her loosened hair, and drifting around in his mind now was the whole play in the round as it were, his own not too creditable motives and desires. He found he was muttering about that—"Paid him out, the bastard—and you too—have you first—nothing to do about it now—"

And she heaved him off violently, pushing him away with all her strength; he turned on his side and heard himself still rather witlessly laughing. "Oh, God damn you, Conal—get out, get up and get out of here, out of my sight—never want to lay eyes on you again, you goddamned rake and villain—damn you—" It was a little funny; what was she so angry about? She'd chosen her job for herself, and five minutes ago she'd been damn well enjoying it— Wanting to damn him up and down, some reason, but she didn't know the words, all she could say, *rake and villain*— It was funny.

A flint flashed, and the candle struck abrupt shadows from the ceiling and wall. She stood there at the far side of the bed; she had caught up her dressing gown, clutched it against her nakedness; her eyes were enormous on him, her hair all loose on her shoulders, and she was trembling violently so that the candle flame shook as if with fear. "Will you get out, get away from me—drunken beast, pretending—oh, my God, I could kill you."

"Now, girl," he said a little dizzily. "No way to act, all this temper about it—"

"I can't bear the sight of you—will you for God's sake get out of here—"

What with one thing and another, he wasn't in much of a state to go anywhere—very damn queer how the drink had hit him all of a sudden—but what the hell was she so angry about? Women—

He got up on his feet somehow and blundered out to the front of the house. He got entangled with something in the little dark entry hall; it was his greatcoat. He picked it up, tumult in his head for bending down.

He started rather unsteadily down the dark street outside, and now the drink was wandering around in him with a vengeance—very damned peculiar. At the corner of the street he stumbled against a man with a lantern: the watchman. "Sorry," he said, hearing his voice slurred. "Like to find—a hack."

"Yessir, that's what you need, if so be you've got coin to pay. I'll look for one, sir. Where was you wantin' to go, if you remember that far?"

"Leicester Arms," said McDonagh carefully. His head felt slightly clearer for the chill night air. But there had certainly been something queer about that whiskey.

"Yessir, I'll fetch you a hack from the stand up the next street."

McDonagh leaned back against the worn leather seat, shut his eyes, and tried to ignore the pounding in his head that was just not synchronized with the jolting of the stage. It was impossible to ignore the bright chatter of the two women passengers and the grunts, hawkings, and rattles of the old man reading the week's newssheets to pass the journey. The other man opposite leaned across and said sympathetically, "Not feeling quite the thing?"

"No—headache," said McDonagh shortly.

"Wet night maybe? You ought to have a drink or two when we stops at Chertsey, that'll fix you up. Not but what these stages're enough to give anybody a head, old rattle-shank things they be."

McDonagh grunted. As a matter of fact, he hadn't had a drink in three days. He'd had a head the morning after that bout, too, but this one was, he thought, a psychic head. That was damned funny; he was glad to be leaving London, to be getting on to a proper job of work.

Guilty conscience? he thought. Nothing to feel guilty about, exactly, no. Remorseful now, well, yes, he had been sorry. The hell of a head that morning, and he'd been rather horrified, remembering, in flashes and snatches. . . . Wonder if she'd told anyone yet, told Dunstan. Well, yes, sorry. He'd done some bad things in his life, a few times, he didn't think very bad, but he'd reckon that among them all right. Cruel, cold trick to play on the girl, never mind on Dunstan, serve him right, but Madeleine—liquor did queer things to a man sometimes. Couldn't undo it now, and one way, how could he be sorry for having known Madeleine? One thing the whiskey had told him true that night—better for her to know Con McDonagh first. It was done, good, bad, or indifferent, whichever side of his record it might go (if there was such a thing); he couldn't exactly wish it undone, but he'd been sorry.

He hadn't said so, or tried to. How could he? Only doubtfully possible way, a letter, and that was ridiculous. He'd never been very good, anyway, at writing down what he felt. *Not sorry it happened, Madeleine—just for the way it did.* No way to say it. So let it go, leave it.

"What you want," said one of the women brightly, "is a Dover powder. Good for almost anything they are, I swear. I do believe I've a packet in my reticule, you're welcome to one, I'm sure."

She was a large, muscular, red-faced farmwife, and McDonagh eyed her in sudden fright, doubting that he would have the strength to fight her off if she tried to administer it by force, as she looked capable of doing. The sort of woman who took competent care of an endless brood of offspring: he almost expected her to say, "No nonsense now, it's for your own good, open your mouth," and he most violently did not want one of Dr. Dover's powders, which he remembered to contain both opium and ipecac. However, happily she was mistaken in her claim, though the reticule was thoroughly turned out, and he was able to thank her peaceably for the intention and be left alone.

He broke the journey overnight at Guildford; the stage from there was due in at Portsmouth at five in the afternoon, but torrential rains had made the roads nearly impassable in places, and it was the middle of the evening when he was let down in the courtyard of the Swan. Perhaps the sensible thing to do was stop here overnight and report to the hospital tomorrow, but it also seemed sensible to save the night's lodging and meals; better to settle in where he'd be living. With some difficulty he located a hack for hire and was driven to the hospital.

It was a large square building in the west of the town, only a few streets from the harbor. He knocked and called for several minutes at a side entrance he judged would be used by the night-duty men before bolts were drawn reluctantly back and he was admitted out of the driving rain, and stood dripping in a shabby, dim-lit corridor.

"And who might you be?" asked his welcomer. He was obviously an old naval service man, boatswain or some other lower rank, given his porter's job on half pay maybe; he was sloppily dressed, and his breath carried a distinct flavor of rum.

McDonagh introduced himself wearily. "Where are the resident surgeons' quarters?"

"Ow. Top floor," said the porter. "You did ought report proper to Mr. Gunther, to be on the books like, afore turning up like this."

"I've been posted here. I'll be on the records already, surely."

"Ow, well," said the porter. "There'll be a room free, I dessay, where you can lie tonight—if they want change you about after, that's none o' my business. Reckon as I'd best go up 'n' show you."

"Thanks very much. I'd appreciate some help with my gear." He had all he owned with him, eighteen or twenty books, his clothes, his large flat instrument case.

"Ow, I've a rotten bad heart, can't to lift more than meself," said the porter. There were five flights of stairs, and the top floor, when they came to it, was dank and cold, as if no fire had been lit there this winter. The porter indicated a room which proved, when a half-burned candle was found and lit, to contain a lumpy-looking bed, a wooden chair uncushioned, a pine chest of drawers, a rickety table bearing a ewer and a chamber vessel with a crack in it, and a pine wardrobe in one corner looking like a coffin stood on end.

McDonagh looked at it gloomily and said, "Well, let's hope they do give me another room tomorrow."

"Ow, they're all the same this floor," said the porter.

"Bloody cheerful old boy," muttered McDonagh after him as he went off down the corridor with a vague promise to look out another chamber pot and more candles. Oh, well, shore duty carried a rise of ten pounds a year, and maybe they reckoned the wage slaves could afford to provide a few creature comforts for themselves.

In a hospital of this size, which used a dozen surgeons and as many physicians, the chief surgeon had an office to himself, on the ground floor. McDonagh went there to report himself the next morning.

He had found his way to the commissary by encountering the other residents in a body as he emerged from his room. Looking them over, as they were served a bad breakfast together, he didn't anticipate making any close friends among them. There was a diffident young man with spots and a nervous laugh, Bates; two quiet middle-aged men, Arnatt and Hoskins, who had the grayly despondent look of men mediocre in their work who had settled to terms with mediocrity and plodded through life unexpecting of anything new or strange; and an older man, Talbot, self-satisfied and by all evidence exceedingly vain of a Roman profile and an impressive head of silver white hair. He ran his hand over both frequently as if calling attention to attractions and even at breakfast—to young Bates's pink embarrassment and expressions of mild disapproval on the faces of the other two—revealed a stock of vulgarly lascivious witticisms. If there was a type of man McDonagh disliked more than a Bates, it was a Talbot. Bates's sort couldn't help being what it was.

It was Bates who plucked at his arm as they rose from the communal table, and advised him to be careful with Mr. Gunther. "What d'you mean, careful?" asked McDonagh. "I'm usually polite to senior surgeons."

"Oh, well, I meant, he's a bit of a stickler for formality and all that," said Bates. "You know. And well, it's mostly on account of your name. We—"

"My name? What in hell d'you mean?"

"Look, Mr. McDonagh," and Bates drew him down to the end of the corridor from the surly-eyed orderly clearing the table. The other three surgeons had gone out. Bates looked rather like a desperately earnest dog trying to communicate. "Look, I—I'd never dream of standing up to Mr. Gunther—I'm not much of a fighter myself, I guess, I just like to be left alone in peace to do my work, I don't go asking for trouble, as I reckon you can tell by looking at me." He uttered his nervous giggle. "But some things are fair and some aren't, and—I do reckon that all of us ought to try to work well together and get along. Maybe especially us who're residents—the other surgeons live out, you know, married men. When we read your name on the new posting, I said we ought to tell you, but the others shied off it, said it wasn't their business and let you find out for yourself. I don't reckon that's fair."

"What?" said McDonagh. "Tell me what?"

Bates took a breath and looked around apprehensively. "There's no trouble from Mr. Gunther—for us—long as we're up to snuff and remember to call him sir pretty often and go by his opinion. He's a very good surgeon, Mr. McDonagh—he keeps up with all the latest things, and all that—and he's fair. Generally he's fair to a man under him, gives him credit for what he does, see. I won't say he's not strict. You're supposed to attend church every Sunday, one thing, and wear a clean shirt every day, and he's a great one for keeping an eye on— on your morals, whether you go after women in the town and like that—but, well, that's just his regulations, it's—consistent, so to speak. What it is, Mr. McDonagh, he's not going to be as easy on you, I don't reckon, see. Because he—he just hates Irishmen."

"You don't tell me," said McDonagh, more amused than anything else. "Just on principle, every last one of us, good, bad, or indifferent?"

"Yes, like that," said Bates. "You see, he had a son, Mr. McDonagh. Just the one boy. I—I reckon he thought the world and all of him, see, and—you know a surgeon doesn't often make a fortune in his profession, and Mr. Gunther, so I heard, he scrimped and saved to give his son a fine education, and—and he even bought him a commission in the army—you know what that costs—because that's what the boy wanted. Well, I expect you know that about eight years back there was a big rebellion in Ireland, the rebels had a sizable army, and there was a lot of killing before it was put down."

McDonagh was silent, looking down at the floor. He said, "I know about that." Oh, yes, he knew.

"Well, Mr. Gunther's son was killed in it," said Bates. "He was only twenty-two, and I guess it near about killed Mr. Gunther, the boy being all he had. I do think, you know, if it'd been a regular war, he could have stood it—reckoning the boy died for his country, you know—but being as it was, he seemed to feel the boy was just murdered deliberate by a pack of outlaws. If you see what I mean. As I expect you'll see, he talks about it quite free, anybody who'll listen, but that doesn't seem to've—to've eased him about it at all, as you might think it would. He just hates every Irishman. He'll go out of his way anytime to insult or—or hurt an Irishman however he can, see. Why—" Bates lowered his voice even more—"one time we had a common seaman come in, an old fellow named O'Halloran, for stones in the bladder—simple sort of operation, and we were surprised Mr. Gunther said he'd do it. I assisted, Mr. McDonagh, and—" Bates turned paler—"I never want to see anything like that again! He kept him on the table forty minutes—you could see he enjoyed every second of it—I—I think he tried to hurt him as much as ever he could. And ordinarily—he's a good surgeon."

"I see," said McDonagh. "That's—well, I see what you mean. Thanks very much for telling me. What happened to O'Halloran?"

"Mr. Gunther cut too deep," said Bates. "I—I saw when he did, he knew what he was doing. Blood poisoning, and the man died."

"Yes, I see."

"He just hates any Irishman. A Catholic one worst, I—I hope you're not?"

McDonagh looked down at him vaguely and after a moment

smiled. Damn funny how the English were ignorant of English laws. "If I were," he said, "I wouldn't be here, Mr. Bates. It's against the law in Ireland for Catholics to enter trades or professions, didn't you know? Well, I shall have to go and report. . . . I appreciate what you've told me, I'll walk with care, I assure you." He turned away; and then, without turning back, he stopped and said, "Bates."

"Yes, Mr. McDonagh?"

"D'you happen to know—where Mr. Gunther's son was killed?"

"It was at a place called Wexford, I think," said Bates. "Why?"

"Nothing. Only wondered. Thanks for telling me," said McDonagh again. He went on down the corridor toward the chief surgeon's office.

Wexford. Oh, yes, Wexford town. The damnedest, bloodiest, most farcical business in that bloody war. So men like Mr. Gunther and Mr. Bates didn't reckon that a regular war. They should have been at Wexford town. That was all of war right there, the bloody nonsensical meaningless thing called war, in the name of glorious patriotism.

God in heaven, hadn't they been proud of themselves, taking Wexford, that army of desperate men! Not a regular war, no, that you might say indeed, about that aspect of it anyway. They came out with pitchforks and scythes and carpenters' mauls and clubs cut from the woods, the exceptional volunteer who had, maybe, a hundred-year-old pike or a matchlock gun. Half of them couldn't have said whether a colonel outranked a lieutenant, and several whole regiments were captained by priests, who knew no more of the art of war than the farmers they led. The Protestants of that United army as ignorant, and their officers.

But they had fought, by God, they had met the uniformed, equipped regular troops and beat them. They didn't know much about strategy; they were a crowd of farmers and beggars and peddlers and laborers, a scattering of wild young city men, a handful of landowners, and every last one of them a burning-hearted patriot with a blazing conviction he fought for a great ideal.

That was what happened to ideals—Wexford.

They were killing mad on both sides, it was hell broken loose—the priests, the Protestant leaders like Harvey hadn't a hope in hell of controlling them—any more than the British officers had of controlling their own troops. There was more blood spilled after the battles, in wanton murder, than on the field.

But Wexford—Wexford wasn't blood, it was whiskey. A god-damned farce, Wexford. Five thousand men in a confused, messy fight, and how many Irish and how many Englishmen dead outside the town and in it? (And among them one young man, with a new commission and a proud father, one dead man who was to reach a hand from the grave—queer, queer—to influence for good or ill one of the enemy who marched unhurt into Wexford. How had he died, how did he lie there? Bullet or pike or club—turning blind eyes to the sky, unmarred, or horridly mangled in some city alley? No matter.) They took Wexford, that army of hot-hearted patriots, and they were so damned pleased with themselves that they spent the night celebrating—and the next morning they lost Wexford to the fresh British troops who came against them cold sober.

Two thousand men had died at Wexford, to make a colossal joke for the history books. But that was the damned senseless sort of thing that happened to idealistic patriots who seldom (in the nature of things) had much sense any other way either.

A young man dead in a fine scarlet British coat, at Wexford. Con McDonagh had had the hell of a time at Wexford, that year he was sixteen and a half and as wild a patriot as any man he fought alongside. Not a mark on him through that fight—*a very pretty nasty hand with the knife*—and in the town after, he'd had a fistfight with a comrade-in-arms over a street harlot, and got the girl; she'd turned nasty when he couldn't pay—that had been funny, arguing with her—and he'd got roaring drunk with Matt and a fellow named Sullivan, the first time in his life. The hell of a time in Wexford, he'd had.

* * *

He put out his hand to open the door of the chief surgeon's office, and then he thought twice, and knocked on it politely before he turned the knob.

"Good morning, sir. Mr. Gunther? McDonagh's my name, sir, I'm posted new here—reporting for duty, sir."

"Come in, Mr. McDonagh," an expressionless, hard voice bade him.

14

"Interrupted sutures, I think, Mr. McDonagh," murmured the chief surgeon. McDonagh did not say that he had reached that conclusion too; he merely made the row of interrupted sutures, bandaged the wound, and stood back from the table in silence while the orderlies moved the patient to a stretcher.

"Quite competent," said Mr. John Gunther. "Really surprising—and gratifying." He looked at McDonagh with the merest vestige of a smile; his light, wide-set eyes were fixed and rather blank. "I might even say remarkable. Of course, it is a merely mechanical task. But perhaps we shall succeed in civilizing your race one day—with perseverance." He was a big spare man in the fifties, sallow-dark and bald, thin-mouthed, square-jawed. "That is all for you for the moment. I will ask Mr. Bates to assist with the spinal vertebrae case. You may return to your wards."

"Yes, sir," said McDonagh. He went out of the operating room, took off his surgery coat and hung it in its place in the anteroom, and wiped his hands on the communal towel hanging by the door. Bates slipped out behind the orderlies carrying the patient away; his anxious eyes, doglike, sought McDonagh.

"Mr. McDonagh," he whispered, "I—I thought maybe you'd care to go into town with me this afternoon, you being off, too. I mean, if it'd help to"—he grinned nervously—"blow off at me, you know—"

McDonagh smiled; he'd grown to like little Bates casually, with his eager good nature, a rather unexpected competence as a surgeon. "Thanks, but it's all right. I don't need to swear at him out of hearing, I don't mind him, you know."

"Don't you?" said Bates doubtfully. "Well, anyway, I thought we might go down to the Hard together if you'd like."

"All right," said McDonagh kindly. "I'll meet you at four o'clock at the gate." Poor anxious little Bates! Really wanted to go to sea, he did—wild about ships—his idea of how to spend his free time, go down to the front and look at ships in port. Rather like taking a very intelligent dog for a walk, to go anywhere with Bates, and that was an uncharitable thought, maybe unfair, but the way he felt. He'd spend an hour with Bates, to satisfy Bates's eager friendliness, and then drop over to the Seventy-four for a drink.

All the same, the little exchange with Bates had settled him a bit, from an hour's work under Gunther's eye. He had said he didn't mind Gunther, and in a sense it was so; in seven weeks he had come to where he scarcely paid note to Gunther's continual, bland, sneering insults, sometimes leveled at him personally, sometimes against his race in general. But to say Gunther didn't affect him at all, that was another thing. McDonagh would freely admit, if anyone asked him, that he was afraid of John Gunther, for good reason. Gunther was mad, and you did not lose your temper at a madman or hold him responsible for what he said and did; equally you did not enjoy being at close quarters with him.

No panel of examining physicians could certify Gunther mad and send him away to Bedlam; he was rational, maybe too rational. He was mad only on one subject. He was, moreover, careful, very careful. His gibes at McDonagh, the only Irishman on his staff, were not like physical assault, nor were they ever hysterically delivered. And a good many men had some violent prejudice they were voluble on without doing anything else about it. Oh, Gunther was damned careful about what else he did; he knew he mustn't arouse suspicion. Only Bates seemed to have noticed anything, and only the one case. Gunther had all the madman's awful cunning, and he had covered himself well.

Very likely, if it hadn't been for what Bates said to him, McDonagh would never have suspected any connecting link; as it was, the suspicion had grown, and he'd gone a bit out of his way to check on it—after the multiple fracture had died. A marine ensign named McCarthy, that had been; the amphibious service had no medical branch or hospitals of its own and was looked after by the naval service. That was an uncomplicated case, no surface wound, just a double break of the leg. He had set it himself; the man was in one of the wards he served. A little shock—it was a street accident, accounting for that—and later fever. Three days later McCarthy was dead. Why? Of what? It had been certified as virulent pneumonia, as good an excuse as any, when a patient slipped away like that, and the weakness and so on had looked enough like it. McDonagh didn't know, but he suspected something besides virulent pneumonia.

When he had seen the patient the second time, the morning after McCarthy had been brought in, the man had been alarmingly weak; the night before, there'd been that little fever, but now the patient had scarce strength to lift his head off the pillow, let alone talk much. All he had said, in fact, was in a low mumble: "Told him—takin' too much—too much—kind o' ham-fisted blunderin' old fella 're you, anyway?"

The man in the next bed was in pain, newly convalescent after exhausting illness; without any interest at all he said that one of the surgeons had come to see McCarthy, late at night, and pulled one of the death screens around the bed, stayed awhile— couldn't say how long. McCarthy's wife lived in Portsmouth and claimed the body, so it was never examined. Not to be opened anyway.

The body was never opened—to see how little blood was left in it.

Any surgeon in good faith might bleed a feverish patient,

though in McDonagh's opinion it usually increased the weakness undesirably, whether or not it broke the fever. But midnight was rather an odd time to choose.

The resident surgeons all had turns of duty at keeping the records, and after that—last week—McDonagh had gone back into the record books, through five years of surgical patients. He didn't think there were many to be laid at Gunther's door, but there was really no way to know for certain. No way to ask questions and check, without revealing this monstrous suspicion. There was *Joyce, Peter Flynn, 43, gangrenous leg amput* ... ("Oh, I knew a man by the same name once, I just wondered. Died, did he?" Bates: "Yes, he came out of the operation quite well, I remember. It was later he died—all of a sudden seemed to lose strength when he'd been doing fine. Funny how that happens sometimes.") There was *O'Halloran, Joseph Mary, 67, bladder obstr.*, he knew about him. There was *Donnelly, Sean Thomas, 24, knife wounds chest, groin, legs* ... ("Sounded like a dockside brawl, I just noticed it—get much of that?" Arnatt: "Oh, yes, I remember the case. Yes, it was—a drunken fight over a girl or something like that, I believe. These sailors, you know, ha-ha! Oh, well, they were extensive wounds, I seem to recall, but I was a little surprised when he died. Healthy-looking young fella. There was blood poisoning, of course, but that's to be expected. He just seemed to lose strength suddenly, you know, and—")

There was no surgery school at this hospital, no dissection room, no purchase of cadavers. Occasionally an autopsy was made, if there was no family to claim a body, but not often.

Such an easy way to do it, too. And Gunther was a good, modern surgeon, but enough of those still had great faith in judicious bleeding, to relieve pressure, lower fever, get rid of poisons; it lent itself to almost any sort of case.

McDonagh wondered almost academically how many men Gunther had murdered that way. The very cunning, the elaborate planning of it, told how careful he was. He probably held himself (with what iron control against temptation!) from taking more than one or two a year, three at the outside—any least vestige of suspicion he could not afford.

No, McDonagh was not ashamed of being afraid of John Gunther. If he knew Gunther's secret, sure in his own mind, it might so easily be only a fantastic suspicion, and it could never be proved. There was nothing he could do about it. And personally, he felt like walking very delicately under Gunther's light, wide-apart, cold eyes.

He met Bates and went down to the Hard with him and let Bates instruct him about the ships swaying at anchor, listening absently to a wealth of technical information. After a while he excused himself and walked up three streets to the Seventy-four. Even if he'd asked Bates to go along, Bates would have declined: he didn't drink.

McDonagh knew Portsmouth from that short leave he'd spent here with Campbell. It was Campbell who had introduced him to the Seventy-four, a house kept by a Scot named MacGregor. Beyond the faded sign, a once-handsome painting of a seventy-four-gunner with all sail up in a heavy sea, was a comfortable, warmly welcoming big public room with plenty of chairs, a corner by the hearth set apart for cardplayers, and whiskey to be bought.

"Have to stock whiskey in a naval port," MacGregor would say genially, "same as I do reckon landlords must in towns by army stations. Why, what'd England do for sailors and soldiers if 'twasn't for all the Scots and Irish serving her?" He greeted McDonagh now genially, a big sandy old man with a comfortable paunch, and had a glass poured for him by the time McDonagh was up to the bar. "Let off your halter lead awhile, Mr. McDonagh?"

"My month for night duty," said McDonagh. "Three hours short a day to make up."

"Goad, they do work you fellas."

"Keep us out of mischief," said McDonagh with a rather forced grin.

"Aye, something in that. Will I be meeting you at the kirk tomorrow?"

"Now, man," said McDonagh, "I was made to sit through a hellfire sermon every Sunday until I was past fifteen, and I draw the line at voluntarily letting myself in for any more. If it's not taken by now, it never will! I also draw the line at letting authority dictate to me about my private life. Regulations promoted by the chief surgeon that we're supposed to attend some service, and I went once to learn the minister's name and where the place is if I'm asked, but that's self-protection. My God, I've only eight hours off a week and one full Sunday a month."

"Well, noo, I wouldna say I don't agree," said MacGregor thoughtfully. "And I'm a kirkgoing man maself, too, but I do juist admit that if, say, the town council was to make it law I had to attend every Sabbath, by Goad, I'd stay away to show ma independence. No call nobody's got to tell no man what to do and not do in his private time."

McDonagh shoved back his glass for refilling, and with another friendly word MacGregor went off to a new customer. McDonagh drank half his second whiskey and brooded awhile over the rest of it. Between one minute and the next there descended on him a black gloom of despondency.

He didn't much mind Portsmouth—one town was like another, though there was no theater here, nothing in the way of amusement to speak of—and the hospital job was one to get his teeth into all right, enough patients to keep a surgeon busy. But he was going to loathe every minute of his life here, he foresaw already. Just one of those things, everything about the job was wrong except the actual work, and that had the satisfaction taken out of it by Gunther, by the need to work under Gunther. But it wasn't all Gunther. God knew, that would be enough, but on top of Gunther, there were the other surgeons; none of those he worked with were likable, give-and-take, companionable fellows to spend off-time with; Bates tried too hard to be friendly, in too humble a way, and the others were a bit stiff, much older men. The damn rules and regulations were stiff, too; mostly Gunther, that was. That hellhole of a cell they gave him to live in: ice on his shaving water every morning now, and he knew well in summer it would be an oven, at the top of the building. It was just the whole damned situation—he felt it was about as bad a place as he'd ever be in, and for tuppence he'd get out and go back to London to starve trying to start a private practice, only you had to sign up for four years in naval or military service. He was caught here, Christ damn his luck, that was all; he'd have to sweat it out best he could. Couldn't apply for a new posting now for two years; he was trapped here for two years. The thought of it made him reflect dismally that it was just too damn bad he'd ever walked alive out of Enniscorthy.

He finished the whiskey, feeling horridly sorry for himself, and then shook off that mood with a rueful grin. His own fault, but God, he'd rather have stayed at sea! Still, here he was, nothing to be done about it.

He beckoned MacGregor. "You'll lose a customer if you can't provide me with a private bottle. I'll die of pneumonia in that icehouse the hospital calls a resident surgeon's bedchamber, or be found stiff and stark some morning frozen to death."

"Och, noo, Mr. McDonagh, that'd be a great pity indeed. Sure you can buy it off me—glad to oblige—four and six the quart, and it's not cut stuff, you know better, though I don't say it all crossed the border strictly legal."

"I don't give a damn how it gets here so long as it is here, thanks, MacGregor."

He slipped the bottle into his pocket and walked moodily back to the hospital. As he came in the main entrance, back into the familiar aura of infection and sickness, wet sawdust, and dirt-engrained old wood-floored corridors and wards that permeated even the ground floor of the building, the porter on duty called his name. "Letter for you, sir."

McDonagh took it without much interest. Strange script, cheap notepaper, his name spelled wrong. He ripped it open; it was a brief, formal invitation to dinner from Mr. and Mrs. Osborne. Osborne? he thought. Oh, yes, Osborne was one of the nonresident surgeons; he was seldom in either of the wards McDonagh served. An effort of memory brought a vague impression of a tall, stooped man, forty-five or so, with a bald patch and steel-rimmed spectacles. Social gesture, welcome to new member of staff. He would have to accept and probably find himself the only guest under forty: a stiff, boring evening.

He mentioned it casually at dinner, or what passed for dinner in the hospital commissary. "I expect it's the standard social gesture to a new staff member?"

To his surprise, Bates beside him turned an embarrassed pink, and Talbot across the table sniggered. "Oh, yes, I was wondering when you'd receive that. Dear me, she must have catechized poor Osborne—just to be sure she didn't waste time—first. Eh, Mr. Bates?"

Bates turned brighter pink and filled his mouth, mumbling. "What's all this about?" asked McDonagh.

"Oh, I wouldn't dream of ruining your ideals, Mr. McDonagh," said Talbot, smoothing his hair, "or spoiling your anticipation." He sniggered again and plunged into the retelling of a joke that was for once funny as well as vulgar. Eyeing Bates, McDonagh dropped the subject, rather intrigued.

He was on night tour with Bates this month; there was seldom much actual work to be done, but they were supposed to be on call, and to pass the time McDonagh had taught Bates to play écarté. His conscience would have kept him awake at night if they played for money. Bates, the son of a Methodist preacher, had been strictly reared, and his nervous habit of glancing behind might betray his inner conviction of a stern parental eye still on him; he had scarcely seen a pack of cards before and still occasionally confused the clubs and spades.

As they sat in the chill corridor end that night, one of the tall wooden death screens shutting off some of the draft and a couple of candles flickering feebly on the cards on the too small table, McDonagh asked casually, "By the way, what was all that about my dinner invitation?"

"Oh, dear," said Bates uncomfortably, and turned pink again. "Well, really, you know, I—I don't like to be uncharitable. Gossip isn't a thing one ought to—that is, well, Mr. Osborne's a very fine man, most senior next to Mr. Gunther, you know, reputation of the highest. I"—and Bates unexpectedly grinned and confessed honestly—"I like him because he's like me, you know, or I'm like him. I mean, we both—if he feels like me—we know our jobs, we aren't really as—as dithering as we seem, it's just that we—I—can't put up a good *show*, if you see what I mean, Mr. McDonagh. Maybe it's something to do with looks. It's all very well to say it's what's inside you that matters, but what you look like does matter, you know. I don't reckon a man like you's ever given it a thought—never had to. I mean, you're big, and well, you look like what—what women expect a man to be—if you'll forgive me—and as for other men, well, they'd think twice about acting nasty to you, you don't look the sort that'd take much off anybody. People, they're peculiar about these things. That is, they say—women and men both—as it's things like being kind and generous and charitable and—and Christian that really matter. But that's not how they act. They'll turn around and admire a man more that's maybe not like that at all, if he's big and quick to speak up for himself and brash with the girls, and—like that."

"So they will," said McDonagh with a smile. "It's called human nature, Bates."

"Oh, I know. You can't expect people to be *reasonable*," said Bates humbly. "But you know, men like me—and Mr. Osborne—we've got feelings, too." Bates looked down at his cards, and his voice dropped. "I—I mean, we notice pretty girls, too, and we'd like to—to have them admire us and make up to us . . . and people in general to seem to think something of us, our opinions and so on. But they look at us, and we don't make any impression on them, you know, they just think we're poor things and don't pay us much notice. But we're just the same as other men—inside like."

McDonagh felt depressed. It was, of course, all too obviously true. And he couldn't say something hearty and comforting to Bates about anybody liking him once they knew him, because it was a lie: there was no harm in the man, probably the hell of a lot more moral worth than in Conal McDonagh, but, well, he was the kind of man you wished to God would swear once in a while, or take one drink too many, or ogle a woman, just so you'd know he was there, as it were. McDonagh wondered sadly if Bates had ever so much as kissed a girl; between the Methodist preacher and Bates himself, it didn't seem likely. Poor little bastard, he thought. He said, "Oh, well, I know what you mean, but you just want to assert yourself a bit, man, let people know you're not to be trampled on."

"Mr. McDonagh," said Bates mournfully, "men like me, we just aren't made that way."

"Well, anyway, what's all this got to do with my invitation?"

Bates was still looking down at his cards. "Well," he said slowly, "you see, Mrs. Osborne, she's—she's not a very nice woman, I guess."

"Oh?"

"I don't know, you understand. There's a little gossip about her, on the quiet. Mr. Talbot mostly. Hinting, you know. And when I was first here, last year, I was invited to dinner—the Osbornes and the Winters and Mr. Howie and his widow daughter, they always have the new members to dinner, I understand, sort of a welcome, like you said. But Mrs. Osborne, she—she didn't exactly act like you'd expect, she's sort of gay and too young, if you know what I mean. She is a bit younger than him, I guess, but not really young, she must be as old as thirty-six or seven, I reckon."

McDonagh laughed, thinking of Fleur. "I might comment, but not knowing the lady I won't malign her virtue. Make up to you, did she?"

"Well, no," said Bates, looking at him uncomprehendingly. "She—as a matter of fact, she seemed to be sort of disappointed—"

It was unkind, but McDonagh couldn't help laughing again. "People often do," said Bates rather miserably. "I just thought she acted a bit young for her age, and being a professional man's wife, and all. But Mr. Talbot will have it—he's always making jokes about it—that she's on the lookout for lovers. Because—her husband's—well, no good to her—that way. Rather bad taste, I think, when he doesn't know—"

"As far as you know! Maybe Mr. Talbot has information, shall we say, inaccessible to you." McDonagh grinned.

Bates said, "Well, I did think she didn't act very kind to her husband. A bit like Mr. Osborne was a tiresome little boy she couldn't be bothered with, and ordering him around."

"I see. Well, I must say I'll look forward to meeting the lady, to compare opinions," said McDonagh amusedly. Bates looked at him in silence, with embarrassed speculation. "My God, man, don't ask the question! If she was Circe herself, I trust I've better sense than to get involved with a woman married to a man I'm technically working with. Asking for trouble! But at least I can tell you whether Talbot's hints are based on fact."

And Bates said, "I guess you can, Mr. McDonagh. I guess you'd know—about a woman."

Oh, damn, thought McDonagh, the poor little bastard, but you really can't base a friendship on pity and nothing else. He said abruptly, "Well, let's get back to the game. It's your play."

After that he accepted the invitation feeling slightly more enthusiastic about it—if it was mainly curiosity—and on the evening appointed sallied forth to the Osbornes' house in the town with some anticipation.

He hadn't been in the house five minutes before he knew where he was with Eunice Osborne.

She was a small plump woman, with high color, black hair and black eyes, and a little pursed-up mouth. A nervous robin of a woman, a little too bright and gay, a little too skittishly dressed, using too many gestures and extravagant phrases. McDonagh reckoned she would get up out of her coffin to flirt with the undertaker, and she might find enough men here and now to be interested, for she had provocative curves and a forthcoming way of displaying them. In fact, if she hadn't happened to have a husband—a man was a fool to get involved with a married woman—and if that husband hadn't happened to work in the place he did, McDonagh might have been mildly interested. As it was, his interest was academic.

Oh, he'd known women like Eunice Osborne; there were enough like her, and with some of them it was just surface play, they were technically faithful wives. But he was surprised and shocked (half because he'd have said he was cynical enough not to feel either reaction) when she cornered him alone, about the middle of the evening, across the room from other guests. "What a relief," she said, "to meet a man I needn't use one-syllable words to." With a careless wave of her fan: "I think you're on night tour now, aren't you, so you're free in the afternoon. Shall we say four o'clock tomorrow?"

He stared at her for a moment. Her black eyes were bright as a bird's on him, her little crumpled mouth wet and open, and she giggled softly, foolishly. "I think we'd have a very nice time together, Mr. McDonagh."

He felt afterward that he must have looked at her, ridiculously, much as little Bates might have. Something besides surprise came over him, and that was revulsion. He said, "Thanks very much, Mrs. Osborne, but I'm an independent man, I'm afraid. I prefer to buy it and not put myself under obligation." He turned and walked over to his host and a group of guests, and took care not to be caught alone with her again. Oddly he was somewhat shaken for a second time to find absolutely no change of expression in her eyes on him the rest of the evening.

He'd never run across quite so casual a promiscuity before. And he appreciated a willing woman as much as the next man, but there was something rather grotesque about a woman as willing as all that.

He came back to his dank cell of a bedchamber, that midnight, and had a couple of drinks to warm him, and went to bed. It was his night off from ward duty.

And he had a dream—a terrible dream.

He dreamed that he stood on the edge of blackness, looking into a circle of light falling on a great dance floor. Only one couple dipped and swayed there, waltzing to an unseen orchestra. At first he thought the woman was Eunice Osborne, for she wore the same gown as she had worn, a plum-colored gown cut very low at breast and sleeve and tight to her figure. Then, as they swirled past, he saw that it was Madeleine, in Eunice Osborne's gown. And her partner was Sir Almerick Dunstan, but not the Dunstan McDonagh had seen on a dance floor before. It was the Dunstan he had seen, angrily and vindictively, prepared for the dissecting table. A stringy, naked middle-aged corpse, discolored with beginning decay.

More than that—for, as the dancers broke apart to execute an impromptu *pas*, he saw with horror that Dunstan had got up off the table after the dissection had been started. The first great incision had been made, chest to genitals, and the twisted ropes of the intestines were spilling out, hanging in coils like serpents, writing with life of their own; the lips of the incision gaped wetly. Then the capering corpse with its fixed grin had clasped Madeleine to him again, all that corruption and slime and filth was pressed against her, and they went swaying and circling in the dance. McDonagh tried to scream out to her, but he could not utter a sound; he was held dumb and powerless here to watch.

First she was laughing up into the corpse's face, gay and enjoying the dance, and then, when they came past again, she was weeping slow and silent, and she turned to McDonagh as she danced by and cried softly to him, "Oh, Conal, Conal, was that why?—you never said it to me, please say it to me—" And he tried to go to her, to wrest her away from the bony arms of that awful thing, yet something held him from moving, though he felt the sweat start from his struggle to escape and go to her. It was such a very ugly gown; she shouldn't be wearing that gown.

He was possessed by the greatest horror he had ever known, and at the same time a black sorrowful guilt of remorse settled over him, and he felt the rain of hot tears flowing down his face. But worse was to come, for the next time the dancers passed it had changed again—not Dunstan, still guiding her with his cadaver's fixed grin and his revealed guts all pressed tight against her—but she turned again and looked at McDonagh. She smiled at him, a narrow lascivious smile, and her mouth was open and wet, and her eyes too bright. She said, "Tomorrow at four, Conal, you needn't pay me this time, Conal, such a good time together, Conal," and she made a lewd beckoning gesture.

He shook cold and violent with horror, loathing, fear and guilt crawling over him like live things, like the slimy serpents of Dunstan's pink intestines. He tried to scream, to run; he was blind with terror and the river of tears flowing.

He woke abruptly, covered with icy sweat, and lay for an unknown time trying to shake off the clinging terror of the dream. After a long while his heartbeat slowed and the sweat dried on him; he could move convulsively and sit up. After another while he reached out and fumbled for the candle, and got it lit.

He had left the bottle of whiskey on the bed table; he had a drink straight out of it, and when it hit his stomach, he could draw a long breath, and the taut shaking of his body quieted a little.

God, he thought, God.

It didn't hit him all at once like the whiskey. It was as if the dream had unlocked a door, and now the door was opening slowly, quietly on a place he'd never seen before.

Liquor did queer things to a man. . . . Remembered, he had, in flashes and snatches, more or less what had happened. Said to himself honestly he didn't feel exactly guilty—because she'd chosen her own way: what did it matter, in what order men came to her? Maybe not much—now.

Not street harlots, said Fleur angrily. No. Oh, God, Dunstan had been nearer the truth when he said; *Accustomed to dealing with common street women.* Madeleine, for all her pretended coolness and casualness—hadn't he thought it often enough?— theoretical knowledge, still in a very real sense the respectable girl from Tunbridge Wells, that night. *Women like us, this level of exchange, an imitation of courtship.* So it was. Imitation of romance, lend the exchange a little grace and piquancy.

He had remembered what he'd thought and felt, in a jumbled sort of way. Remembered her struggling and trying to soothe her, murmuring soft, endearing words to her, handling her gentle and slow the way it was needful, and her sudden involuntary response, little breathless gasps on his name—not just for any man clever enough to rouse her. And not ten minutes later, was it, his drunken tongue unguarded, what had he said?—just now remembered—*Paid him out, the bastard, to have you first.* She had thought it was all pretense, a cold, calculated trick, that he hadn't wanted her, only to play a trick on Dunstan and her together—nothing more.

Had a right to be in a fury at him, hadn't she! It just came clear to him this minute. And it wasn't so—Dunstan hadn't really mattered a damn to him, only that another man should— It was Madeleine, he'd been mad with wanting her for herself, that wasn't any pretense. He wanted urgently, agonizingly, to tell her so now—too late—that had been real, he hadn't pretended anything he didn't feel. Too late now, too late.

Too late to be sorry, he wasn't sorry—she'd chosen her way. That was no matter, that aspect of it, no guilt there; if not Con McDonagh, some other man. But he'd treated her like a harlot, as if she didn't matter a damn to him in himself, or she thought he had, and maybe that was the worst thing he'd ever done in his life. Because it was a lie—he had wanted her for herself, he would still want her—only she came too high-priced for Con McDonagh—mistress to a man like Dunstan.

It was all a confusion of half thoughts and feelings in him, maybe not making much sense on the cold facts—only he seemed to be seeing it right way around, somehow, for the first time, and he was appalled at himself, for his stupidity for it up to now. Maybe it was a damned senseless way to feel; she was Dunstan's kept woman now, and she'd go on to some other man and another after that—she wasn't a woman any man owed much nicety of manners—but you couldn't go by the ortho-doxies altogether, ever. Depended on the way you felt. She was on the other side of the line now, apart from the women a man might feel genuine romantic love for, the women of any lasting importance to a man. But she wasn't a mindless, crude, insensi-tive alley trollop. He wanted, with a kind of terrible pain of ur-gency, to apologize to Madeleine, to make her believe how wrong she was about him. It wasn't a lie, he had to say to her; I meant it all, please believe it wasn't a lie, I wanted you more than I've ever wanted any woman before all my life, I never took such passionate pleasure with any other woman, it wasn't just that you were a woman, it was that you were Madeleine, please believe me.

Never say it to her now; no way to say it and make her believe it. Never would be, would there?

"My God," he whispered to himself, "how much of a fool can a man be?" But there it was; it was done, and there was no help for it now. She was not now, even eight weeks, ten weeks later, the same girl; maybe it did not matter so much to her now. A man made bad mistakes; he did bad things he didn't mean, or understand the badness of at the time; he just had to go on from there, hoping he'd learned something, trying to forget what he'd done, for it did nobody any good to brood on it.

"Oh, God, Madeleine, I'm sorry," he heard himself say aloud. Presently he snuffed the candle and lay down again in the dark, but it was some time before he slept.

Something odd and disturbing commenced to happen to him then. All right, he'd said to himself, I did a hellish cruel thing to her, I'm sorry and shamed for it, but it's done; no use to brood on it. It wasn't that he expected to be able to put it right out of his mind, but he wasn't going to let it dominate him either.

In the days and weeks after that, he came to a place where what he had done lessened in seeming enormity to him; he no longer felt such an agony of remorse for it. But something worse and utterly unreasonable came into its place. He kept seeing Madeleine and Dunstan in his mind. It was not a waking fantasy, not that his imagination kept evolving them much as they would be now, in London, attending the theater together, having meals together, even going to bed together. At intervals during the day, sudden sharp visual scenes presented themselves to him, that was all, and every one of them was rather like that dream, and quite horrible to him—and entirely without sense.

He saw Dunstan doing disgusting things to her, and sometimes she was laughing and sometimes weeping. Sometimes Dunstan was dead, and sometimes quite a normal live man. He saw Dunstan strangling her once. He saw Madeleine standing over a sleeping Dunstan with a knife in her hand, and in the flashing instant—all these irrationalities lasted—he saw without any surprise at all that it was the knife he had lost on Enniscorthy field, the familiar black bone handle with a crack halfway down, and an eight-inch double-edged blade.

As he walked through the wards and talked with the patients, and stood over the operating table under Gunther's cold eyes, and played cards with little Bates or Talbot—as he went through all the motions of his present life, these meaningless hallucinations came to him. A flash, and it was gone; he might not hesitate between two words, but a wave of horror had passed over him.

Once, as he took up a scalpel and bent over a patient on the table, it was suddenly Dunstan's corpse there.

There had been a man brought into Queens' once with a concussion; it wasn't an extraordinary case, you saw it rather often, of course; he'd been thrown from his horse, and gone about his business quite rationally, apparently unhurt, for twenty-four hours before suddenly dropping unconscious. McDonagh felt vaguely as if the same sort of thing had happened to him, delayed shock of some sort, for some reason, and if the curious symptoms hadn't been so upsetting, he would be angrily amused; as it was, he sometimes wondered in a sweat of fear if he wasn't going as mad as Gunther.

Two or three times a week these fantasies kept him from dropping off to sleep easily; he was distrustful of taking laudanum, knowing how easily one could become addicted to it. But he found that a stiff drink of whiskey served much the same purpose of settling his mind for sleep, so that was all right.

The disturbing symptoms went on, waxing and waning, for nearly three months, up until the middle of June; the year turned, and the short, clear, nostalgic-scented summer nights came, and he slept, but he often dreamed and woke sweating from unremembered nightmare, so that he took a drink and a smoke to settle himself again for sleep. Then, suddenly, the little irritating strange visions left him in peace, but with another irrational obsession at the back of his mind, and that was that somehow, one day, he must try to explain to Madeleine, to make her understand. It might not matter so much to her now, but he'd never be quite free of the whole episode until he did that, tried to make what amends he could.

Meanwhile, he dragged through gray, dull days in this hellish, companionless job which infrequently offered anything interesting. He was absently kind to little Bates, he kept his hands and voice steady under the madman Gunther's rapt eyes, he suffered intense boredom and restlessness for the dearth of any sympathetic, sensible, like-minded man to talk with and spend leisure time with, and he came up to his room at night exhausted not with work but with black dissatisfaction of life, and had a few drinks alone to induce sleep.

Every month or so he picked up a fresh bottle from MacGregor. But June hadn't grown old before he found with mild surprise that the current bottle was getting low. Better get two next time, he thought, have enough on hand. Maybe one of the orderlies had discovered it, came up to steal a few drinks? Find a hiding place for it, be on the safe side.

He finished dressing, thinking that, and took up the bottle, looking for a good place to secrete it. A minute later he found he'd absently poured a drink; he swallowed half of it, put the rest back, and took himself to task. Conal, my boy, you'd better take care, drinking before breakfast—and alone—very bad indeed. The *uisgebaugh* is a fine thing to a man as long as he stays the master, but once let it get the upper hand, and you're done.

He hid the bottle in the pocket of his greatcoat in the wardrobe and went down to breakfast.

15

━━━━━━━●

The navy lieutenant's name was Michael John Ryan; he was thirty-six, with twenty-three years of naval service behind him, a big, cheerful man beginning to thicken a bit about the middle, and he had a blond wife named Emily who lived in Plymouth and three sons and two daughters. McDonagh knew all that and a good deal more about him before Ryan had been twenty-four hours in hospital. He had come in consequent on a badly set broken leg of four years back; it had given him pain and lameness since, and the surgeon technically in charge of him, Hoskins, had decided to try a course of hot fomentations and massage before attempting the drastic procedure of rebreaking and setting the bone.

Ryan came in the week a heavy chest cold spread among the men in that ward; all but two of them were hawking and snuffling miserably, and most running a slight fever. Ryan came down with it three days later, and was slightly less cheerful when McDonagh saw him next morning.

"I'll tell you, a good stiff glass o' whiskey 'd fix me up," he said. "Hot, you know, mulled like. Fix me up proper."

McDonagh grinned at him. "Reconcile you to the cold anyway. Look, don't breathe a word to anybody, but I'll fetch you down a drink late tonight. Least I can do for a Belfast man. But if you whisper about it, I'll be mobbed."

"God bless and preserve you," said Ryan. He was the twenty-ninth Irishman at present a hospital inmate. McDonagh knew; he'd kept a check. And that was about all he could do.

In the nine months he had been at the Portsmouth naval hospital, two hundred and sixty-seven men with Irish names had been admitted as patients; MacGregor had something in his contention; the services all numbered a good many Irish and Scots. Of that number, thirty-nine had died. It was impossible to check back on all of them; in the wards McDonagh entered, only five Irishmen had died, and he was certain that three of them were natural deaths. The other two might—just might— be laid to Gunther.

He'd done some thinking and brooding about them, about Gunther. No way to get at the man, no way to challenge him, stop him. Gunther behaved in a perfectly rational way always; he was just damned cunning. If McDonagh brought his suspicion into the open, it would do Gunther no harm—gain him sympathy against an overimaginative young man. Gunther had everything on his side: authority, seniority, tenure, experience. Nobody at all would believe such a fantastic thing of him. Oh, Bates had been right in saying that Gunther was not reticent about his personal tragedy. Gunther made no secret of his still-sharp sorrow for his beloved paragon of a son wantonly murdered by an uncivilized race of renegades; he offered his bitter memories and his vindictive opinions to anyone in hearing. And maybe that was, contrarily, more evidence of his cunning, for nobody would believe he would find action necessary as well.

McDonagh was afraid of Gunther the madman, and he was also angrily, cravenly afraid of himself—of what he would do or not do, if action was forced on him. Impossible to turn a blind eye; impossible not to be aware, automatically, of which men in which wards might be targets for Gunther. And if he ever knew for certain—before or after? He was afraid he would be a coward and do nothing; he was afraid he'd be a fool and get into some nameless danger he couldn't get out of. He had once given some thought to going to Osborne, who was next senior to Gunther, but, Osborne!—an older Bates, ineffectual.

Oddly enough, Gunther wasn't on his mind that night. He'd sat here in his room, which was beginning to be a dank cell again after three months of being an oven—God, how had he withstood nine months of this purgatory?—and had some drinks, and found he was brooding over Madeleine again. . . . Back in June he'd tried, hopelessly, to write a letter, but that was no good. Nothing was any good to make amends, but if he could see her again, to try—He shook off the mood with an effort; once he started thinking about Madeleine, now, his mind just went around and around it in a futile circle, it was senseless; why couldn't he put it behind him, for God's sake?

He remembered his promise to Ryan; he put on his coat in lieu of a dressing gown, for the cold corridors, slid the bottle into his pocket, and went down three flights of stairs to the second ward. It was dark, except for a glimmer of candlelight behind a screen at one end of the room. He thought nothing of that until he came up to it, for it was Ryan's bed, and Ryan wasn't really ill, he might easily be sitting there reading late, waiting for McDonagh and his promised drink.

So it was sprung on McDonagh like a trap, what he'd been most afraid of, and he walked into the scene without having any lines ready.

Ryan was half-propped on the pillow, and John Gunther was sitting on a stool beside the bed. "Oh, evening, Mr. McDonagh," said Ryan easily. "God ha' mercy, have I got you bone sawers that worried over me, two o' you calling out o' hours?" He gave McDonagh a dropped eyelid that said, Stay till this old bastard goes off, I'll not give you away!

McDonagh said, "Evening, Mr. Gunther—Ryan. Just dropped by to see how you were feeling." He had gone absolutely cold, and the whiskey he'd had moved sickly in him.

Gunther said in an expressionless tone, very quiet, "I must occasionally check upon your patients, Mr. McDonagh, to be certain they are receiving proper care. One may educate a savage up to a point, but still he will need supervision." How clever he was, not to change his attitude.

McDonagh saw the shape of the little wedge-bladed bleeding knife in Gunther's breast pocket, and pushed half under the stool, one of the metal buckets used in the operating rooms for receiving amputated or excised material. It came to him with absolute irrelevant certainty that there was a wad of folded bandage in its bottom, to deaden any sound of liquid dropping. He had walked in on a murderer as he was about to kill, and there sat the victim, a little feverish and uncomfortable, but on the whole cheerful enough and innocently anticipating his drink of whiskey. Possibly Ryan was to be recorded as another case of virulent pneumonia. Gunther couldn't know McDonagh suspected him, or could he? He was foiled tonight, but what of tomorrow night and the night after? Not only Michael John Ryan; what about Tom Kavanagh four beds down, or James Grady in the bed by the door, or Patrick Burke under the window?

Quite frankly McDonagh was terrified, and unashamed of it. It was said a madman had superhuman strength when roused, and wouldn't any direct move against Gunther rouse him?—any revelation that there was suspicion? Ryan was the only fit man in the ward besides himself this moment: could the two of them handle Gunther if he went berserk?

While he noticed and thought all that, he was moving and talking casually; without conscious plan, his body seemed to know what to do. He stepped around Gunther, up to the bedside. He said, "Oh, you're looking fine, Lieutenant, well on to recovery. Fever down, too. I don't think we'll have to bleed you—for that or anything else."

"Well, I should hope not," said Ryan.

Gunther got to his feet and just stood there, silent. All McDonagh's muscles tensed, ready. One part of his mind told him that Ryan, at least, was safe now; Gunther couldn't try it on Ryan after this. And that little exchange had not revealed any suspicion to him; it was a perfectly ordinary remark to have made. He would have to accept defeat here, and make another sneering little remark perhaps, and go away. And, please God, go away. After all, that was the principal effect you wanted to achieve, to all intents and purposes alone with a madman at dead of night: to get him peaceably to go away. Wasn't it?

McDonagh's mind said to him in agony, Don't say it, don't say anything more.

He straightened from Ryan's bedside and looked at Gunther. For the first time he saw a little of the madness in Gunther's eyes; Gunther didn't look mad, to be foaming at the mouth or anything as definite as that; just, his eyes moved, uneasy and shifting. McDonagh said, "In fact, we seem to be getting past this little plague quite well. I don't think there's a patient in the ward that needs bleeding. Is there, Mr. Gunther?"

Oh, God, now he'll know; what have you done? Ryan was looking between them, a little puzzled. Gunther stood there a minute, and then he reached up and took the cupping knife from his pocket. He looked at it, and looked at McDonagh; then he turned and walked away. He went out into the darkness of the ward, and out of the ward, and shut the door behind him very softly.

McDonagh sat down carefully on the stool. Don't alarm the patient: first rule for beginning students. Couldn't give Ryan his drink right away, hands shaking so he'd spill half the liquor. "What was all that about?" asked Ryan, and yawned. "You seem to have offended the old boy. Who is he? He's not the other ward surgeon, the one that saw me first."

"No. Chief surgeon."

"All that about savages—he don't like you, hey? Had a little trouble with him—brash young junior?" Ryan grinned shrewdly.

"Something like that," said McDonagh.

"Bit old-fashioned maybe. See a lot of that in any job, I reckon—old men can't get used to new ideas, won't hear of any change. Did you bring my drink?"

McDonagh handed him the bottle. By the time Ryan handed it back, he was ready for one himself. He'd had, well, he hadn't counted the drinks, before he came in; he'd been feeling just pleasantly relaxed, but all of it had died in him, and he was cold sober now. They handed the bottle back and forth several times.

"Man," said Ryan, "I hope you've not an operation to do in the morning."

"Damn, I'm sober as a judge," said McDonagh. "But I'll let you have the last drink, go on. Ought to have scotched your cold by now."

"Pity to kill the bottle on you," said Ryan politely.

"Oh, that's all right, I can get more. Pleasure to have someone to drink with for a change. Now you ought to sleep anyway. See how you feel in the morning, we'll get busy on those fomentations."

"Damn 'right," said Ryan a bit thickly. "Don't want to waste time here—more 'n I need to."

McDonagh said, "We'll fix you up." He put the empty bottle in his pocket and went quietly out of the ward. Behind him the room darkened as Ryan snuffed his candle and settled down in bed. The corridor outside was all dark, too, except in one place at the end where the stair came down beside a tall window. The glass was old and dirty, but late moonlight filtered through in a short path. McDonagh walked up toward the patch of light, toward the stair, and just as he reached it, something moved in the shadow beyond.

He stopped. He thought, Whiskey—just a little drunk he was. If Gunther attacked him now, he wasn't in the best state to defend himself. His hand closed on the neck of the bottle in his pocket.

Gunther stepped out of the stairwell. He looked very tall in the deceptive light; his face was in shadow; he stood there motionless. When he spoke, his voice was curiously ordinary, even conversational.

"You're what they call Nemesis," he said. "Aren't you?"

McDonagh could not have spoken to save his life, and maybe it was to save his life.

"Aren't you?" insisted Gunther. He sounded, suddenly, like a persistent child asking questions. "It's only lately I've begun to suspect the truth, you know—that the Other Side is strongest. It seems a terrible thing—to me—but it's true, isn't it? They always get the better of us—the good men, the righteous and godly men. We think we've found a way to get around them, to circumvent them, to take just vengeance, but they always prove the stronger. They always know. Just as you know. You are one of Them, aren't you, sent here to stop my taking my just ven-

227

geance? That's very strange, I never suspected you at all. But you are, aren't you?—one of Them, from the Other Side—one of Satan's emissaries?"

"Yes," said McDonagh. It came out in a whisper. "I am—one of Them—sent to stop you."

"It's a very terrible thing," said Gunther, "to know that They are always strongest, that They will always emerge the masters. We're told lies about it, and that's not right. But perhaps only a few men ever suspect the truth. It really is very odd. I was so pleased with my just vengeance. I thought I had found a way at last to fight back against Them in the holy war, God's war against the Other Side. I was even planning somehow to include you, you know. If only you'd fallen ill some way. I never thought—until just now—and then I saw They knew and had sent you to foil me."

"Yes," said McDonagh.

Gunther nodded once, sharp and abrupt. He said, "A terrible thing. Never to be able to get back at Them at all, to know any victory. No prayer, no faith strong enough against Them. But having learned the truth, I must admit defeat, that is all." He came forward, and McDonagh sidestepped him and stood tensely ready. But Gunther walked straight past him and on down the dark corridor, to the downward flight of stairs at the far end, and vanished.

McDonagh hauled himself upstairs by the banister, broke open his reserve bottle, and went to bed drunk.

He was awakened by a hand on his shoulder and Bates's breathless voice. "Oh, Mr. McDonagh, do wake up! Please, Mr. McDonagh—"

McDonagh opened his eyes, shut them, swore, and clutched his head. Bates was standing over him, still in his nightgown with an aged woolen dressing robe over it, his hair all on end. "For God's sake, don't shout at me," mumbled McDonagh. He sat up very carefully.

"I'm sorry to disturb you, but oh, Mr. McDonagh, a dreadful thing—we'll all be wanted, I daresay, give evidence—Mr. Talbot found him just now, being up early—he—er—was on his way to the privy—"

"Don't dither at me, Bates," said McDonagh. "Especially at the crack of dawn. Did you wake me up to give me the glad information that Mr. Talbot's bowels are in a healthy state?"

"Oh, Mr. McDonagh, it's Mr. Gunther—he's gone and hanged himself! In his own office, with the door open, and all the candles burned down, he must have been there half the night—"

McDonagh dropped his hands from his head. "I'll be damned," he said. "I will be damned." Ignoring the pounding hammer in his head, he threw off the blankets and got out of bed with an involuntary groan, reached unsteadily for his smallclothes on the chair, changed his mind, and picked up the bottle from the table. "Here, we can both do with a drink. I will be damned." But a great weight seemed to have been lifted from him; it was a solution, maybe the only one for Gunther.

"Oh, no, thank you, if it's spirits I never—"

"Here, drink," said McDonagh, and all but held the bottle to Bates's mouth. Bates drank, coughed, gasped, and thanked him feebly. "I suppose someone's sent for Mr. Osborne?"

"Yes, Mr. Talbot sent an orderly—I expect we'll all be wanted—"

"Yes," said McDonagh. He took a second drink and began to feel somewhat less like death. His eyes focused on Bates, who was staring at him as if mesmerized. Abruptly he realized that he had gone to bed naked, and stood here shivering in morning chill in the same state, and there was something shameful, oddly embarrassing, in Bates's eyes on him; he felt vulgarly too large and hairy in front of Bates' tousled pink-and-white skinniness. "All right," he said, "I'll dress and come. Someone had better call a magistrate, too. You go and tell Talbot I'm coming." Bates went almost thankfully.

McDonagh never told anyone about Gunther. There was no question or trouble about the suicide; Gunther was known to be a bitter, unhappy man. McDonagh said nothing to the magistrate about his midnight meeting with Gunther, and nobody thought to ask Ryan anything. There was a flurry over covering up social scandal; the local rector was broad-minded. McDonagh attended the funeral with the rest of the staff on a dismal day of driving rain; he did not say a prayer for Gunther's soul, because he was entirely unsure that there was such a thing in a man or anything at all to pray to. But in his mind he pronounced a little epitaph on Gunther.

All for Wexford town! All for the colossal joke, the pointless fury of Wexford.

Osborne succeeded Gunther as being next in seniority. No radical changes or innovations could be expected from Osborne; the only difference it made to McDonagh was that he was freed of a weight of worry and fear and had more time to brood on his own private concerns. And it made a little difference later on, too, for it was bad enough to get involved with the wife of a senior colleague, but the chief surgeon of the hospital—well, that was a graver mistake.

He never intended to have anything to do with Eunice Osborne. Very likely he never would have, but for a combination of circumstances. He was paid quarterly, but he'd got through quite a sum of savings in London, and since coming to Portsmouth, he'd had to buy a few new clothes, sundry odds and ends. Figures never meant much to him; he didn't keep personal accounts. Now and then that winter it occurred to him that one way and another MacGregor at the Seventy-four was getting quite a bit of Con McDonagh's money, but what was four and six a bottle? In any case, the money went somehow. God knew he didn't have much free time to spend with harlots, even if they'd been expensive in a naval port. But you wanted to take care with those—especially the inexpensive ones—and, well, maybe Fleur, or familiarity, had lessened his appetite for that sort of woman. Rather like cut whiskey, he thought vaguely: not the same lift.

At that he probably wouldn't have got himself involved with the damned woman if she hadn't inadvertently caught him at the wrong moment, when he was just full enough of drink to be pleasantly stimulated, on top of himself, feeling vaguely amorous. It was his free Sunday, and he met her in the street. Her black eyes glistened moistly on him, and her plump little curves, seen through the whiskey, looked more enticing than they later proved.

He ended by going home with her. She had both Osborne

and her servants well trained, evidently. Maybe Osborne had just shut his eyes and walked away from it long ago. He spent most of his time at the hospital anyway. The couple of servants were stiff nonentities; Eunice simply took McDonagh through the house to her bedchamber and shut the door.

"No one ever thinks of disturbing me here"—she smiled—"while I am *at my devotions*, as our ancestors used to say, did they not? My household knows better," and she tittered at him.

When he got back to his hospital cell that time, McDonagh looked at himself in the glass ruefully and said, Never again. Just a bit too low even for Con McDonagh.

But she wouldn't leave him alone once she'd got her claws into him; she was insatiable. She knew when he'd be out; he came to believe she lay in wait for him, and she was there to be had, free and willing, when he wanted a woman. The odd thing was, he couldn't say he took much pleasure with her. He went through the motions, that was all, and he thought every time he did that he lay with her for the habit of an appetite—and because it was what you did with a woman like Eunice, rather automatically, when you found yourself alone with her. He didn't know whether Osborne knew the identities of her lovers, or if he cared anymore; the man acted quite normal to him, the same as to the other surgeons. He couldn't say he was much interested in what Osborne thought or felt.

Nothing, not the absence of the madman Gunther, certainly not Eunice Osborne, made his present life any less dissatisfying, any less boring and gray. Whenever he took his mind from his actual work, it went straight to that maddening, reasonless obsession about Madeleine, and hastily he put that at bay with whiskey, the only weapon against it. The days went by in a meaningless series of mechanical duties; when he thought, it seemed incredible that he had been in Portsmouth eleven months, a year, fourteen months. (Had she left Dunstan yet, for another wealthy lover? Try to conjure up nameless face and figure, the man who might have right to her now.)

It was one morning in April, suddenly, that he was brought up short to see with brief, awful clarity where Con McDonagh had got to in his life.

There had been some survivors picked up from a lifeboat, off a storm-sunk frigate in the North Sea, and brought ashore at Portsmouth. Most of them were suffering only from exposure and starvation; but one man had gangrene started in the foot from frostbite, and it was necessary to amputate a few toes. He was taken into the operating room an hour after he arrived, and McDonagh came in with Bates to do the amputation. There was no need for an assistant—it was a simple operation—but Bates had a rather annoying way of trailing McDonagh about.

McDonagh looked at the patient, laid out what he wanted in the way of instruments and dressings, and nodded at the orderlies to strap the man down. He wouldn't trouble with adhesive bandages or ligatures but cauterize and have done with it, such a small area. He stationed an orderly at the fire with an iron, and took up the scalpel for the initial incision.

With the steel over the patient, he stopped, and suddenly found himself weak. His hand was shaking visibly; he couldn't properly focus on the wound area; he couldn't judge exactly where to begin the cut. He was, in fact, too full of whiskey to judge anything, to embark on any delicate manual job.

He leaned on the table. God, he thought, I didn't know I'd come to a pass like this. Never realized, until just this minute. He tried to think, futilely, about the whiskey. He'd gone past the point, long ago, of feeling guilty about that first necessary drink or two first thing in the morning. Usually a slack time in the wards about ten, he'd got into the habit of slipping upstairs for another drink then. And at the noon hour, before the meal in the commissary, and after. Nuisance going upstairs, and in the last month or so he'd been carrying a bottle on him, for a private drink in the privy or an empty corridor corner. But it hadn't seemed all that much, or all that serious, just something to help him get through the day, that was all; he was never drunk on duty; he wouldn't go that far, he couldn't—

But he didn't dare touch this patient now. God knew how much damage he'd do, hand shaking like that, sudden sensation of queasiness in his stomach. He had enough sense left for that anyway.

"What's the trouble, Mr. McDonagh?" asked Bates.

McDonagh laid down the scalpel. "You take it, Bates," he said. He was sweating, and his tongue felt thick and clumsy. "Little touch of—of indigestion, maybe, I'll be all right, but I'd better not start this—right now. You take it." He looked up as he moved from the table, and caught the wise grin the orderlies exchanged. Dim anger moved in him; even the damned orderlies knowing . . .

Bates seemed to think nothing of it. He said, "All right, I don't mind," and came forward. "I hope you're not coming down with something? Feel sick, or a headache? There's been a cold in the first ward—"

"I'll be all right," said McDonagh. "Don't fuss, I'll be all right." By God, he'd better be; he meant to be. Pull himself up sharp on this; no future in letting the *uisgebaugh* get control over him. Never realized how much he was using; an insidious thing the way it crept up on a man. He'd take care, watch it, after this.

He tried. That experience frightened him, and he tried. But he found he couldn't get through the day without it; if he didn't steady himself with a few drinks spaced out, every man who saw him would mark his hands trembling, the state of his nerves. Had to have enough to keep steady, put up a rational appearance, but he would taper himself off gradually, cease to depend on it, he thought. He would do that for a week, keep check on every drink, deny himself half those he wanted; then on his free afternoon, or his full Sunday, conscious that he had no responsibility for a while, he'd make up for it and usually get to bed drunk.

And there was always Eunice, if he went out—meeting him in the street, sending him little private notes. The goddamned woman was a millstone around his neck, he didn't want her, he wasn't interested—but there she was; he couldn't get free of her. Must cut out all the whiskey, couldn't go on like this. Only one drink tomorrow morning, get him through to noon, and only one more before five o'clock. Ration himself sensibly, soon get over depending on it. . . . He had to come up at ten o'clock for the second drink, or he'd never have gone through ward examination without betraying himself, and he had to have another in the middle of the afternoon, and after dinner, on top of a meal, it was safe surely to have a couple more—had to sleep.

Osborne called him into his office one morning. "I don't like to chide you, Mr. McDonagh," he said, blinking nervously behind his steel-rimmed spectacles, "but I believe you were responsible for keeping last month's records? Yes, well, it is rather—er—carelessly done, you have missed copying several accounts."

"Sorry, sir."

"It is, after all, a simple task," said Osborne apologetically, "though perhaps I'm rather fussy over exactness—but—er—none of the other juniors seems to have difficulty with it."

"I'm sorry, sir," repeated McDonagh.

Osborne looked at him and suddenly got up to step closer. "Mr. McDonagh, you've been drinking, haven't you? Now, really, that is a thing I cannot approve—on duty, too. I must, I really must ask you never to do such a thing again."

Oh, go to hell, you little rabbit, thought McDonagh wearily. He very nearly said it. Damned prim little old-maid spinster of a man, no wonder his wife looked elsewhere, scared to death to say anything but *I really must ask you!*

"I am surprised at you, Mr. McDonagh, really, I must say. I—I am sorry to see a capable young man drifting into such bad habits. I must ask for your promise not to drink in working hours. I would like to say, at any time, but I—er—should dislike to seem to interfere unwarrantably with the personal lives of my staff. Well, Mr. McDonagh?"

"Oh, all right, all right—sir," said McDonagh irritably. He looked at Osborne with dislike. He wanted suddenly to say to him, You'd be better occupied, you little cow-hearted bastard, keeping your damned hot harpy of a wife off other men's necks!

"I trust you will be more careful in the future," said Osborne, weakly overlooking the impertinence. "I would advise you not to attempt any surgical work until you are quite sober. I have no objection to a friendly glass in leisure time, but drinking on duty I will—er—not condone. That is all. I will give you the—er—benefit of the doubt this time."

"Oh, thanks very much, sir," said McDonagh, and went out.

Take care Osborne didn't catch him out another time—or anyone. He must try to taper it off quicker; no good going on this way. Ought to break off with that damned woman, too, finish the whole thing. The trouble was, it looked so easy, nothing to it but a little willpower, when he had a few drinks in him, and then, when he hadn't, and his whole being was in dire, awful need of it, he'd think, One, just one, just carry me over a bit—and that led to more. Got to stop it, do better than this.

The following Monday he had a savagely pounding head from the night before, and turned over two operations to Bates. When they came out of the operating room, Bates said nervously, "Mr. McDonagh, I guess it's none of my business, and you know I don't mind doing your work—but you—you are drinking a bit, aren't you? I mean, that's why you—that is, at least you realize you shouldn't work on a patient, when—It's not good, Mr. McDonagh, you're not looking yourself at all, or well—"

"I'll be all right," said McDonagh doggedly. "I'm stopping it, I'm trying to stop it. Bates. You're a good chap, cover up for me. Appreciate it, but don't worry, I'll be all right. In another month or so—manage to taper it off, see?"

"Well, I'm sure I do hope so. You're not looking well at all. If—if there's anything I can do to help—"

Bates was a good little bastard, meant so well, if only to God he wouldn't look at you like a dog whose master was out of sorts, wanting to help by licking his hand or offering a head to pat. "Thanks, Bates—good chap—but I'll be all right."

In the middle of the week after that Osborne came into the operating room one late afternoon; an emergency had been brought in, a nasty open compound fracture, and McDonagh was watching Bates take off the arm. When the chief surgeon came in, McDonagh straightened up and made a little play about handing ligatures and dressings to Bates, make it look as if he were assisting, however unnecessarily. Osborne stood to one side, watching until the patient was carried away, and then he said quietly, "Mr. Bates."

"Yes sir?"

"I think you—and Mr. McDonagh—were operating this

morning. Would you mind telling me how many of the four cases you—er—operated yourself?"

"I—well, really, I can't say I recall offhand, sir, I—I think we split them between us."

"Are you—ah—certain? The orderlies say that you did them all and have, in fact, been doing a great part of Mr. McDonagh's work for him."

Bates looked at him dumbly and wet his lips. McDonagh said, "So the orderlies are carrying tales, are they? Not enough to do, they've got to go spying on the staff!"

"Mr. McDonagh," said Osborne, "it is my responsibility to—ah—oversee the surgeons under me and make certain that they are doing their work competently. I do not like to pry into a man's personal life, and—er—the orderly in question who approached me did not do so in any—er—spirit of slyness or gossip. He happens to be a responsible man, and he realizes that the hospital is—ah—responsible too, for the welfare of its patients. I cannot say that I think any patient is very safe in the hands of a drunken surgeon—"

"And just why in hell d'you think I've kept my hands off my instruments if not for that reason?" exploded McDonagh at him. "Take me for a fool? All right, I've been overdrinking a bit, but I know it, and I'm stopping it—I'm taking care with it now—give me a month, I'll be all right again! I could name the damned Methodist that carried tales to you, too—and I'll be glad to tell him what I think, damn it—"

"Mr. McDonagh, two months ago I detected you drinking on duty, and by what I learn from the orderlies, you have since—er—exhibited no symptoms of behaving any better. In fact, I am told that you appear more or less continually under the—ah—influence of spirits. That is a thing I really cannot tolerate, young man, we have our patients to consider—"

"Please, sir," said Bates in a low voice, "he's—Mr. McDonagh realizes, sir, he's stopping it, it's just that—I guess—you can't stop all at once, but he's trying—if you'd—another chance—"

"He has given no evidence of it, Mr. Bates," said Osborne, "although I appreciate your loyalty to a colleague. Quite the contrary, in fact. Mr. McDonagh, you really must realize that this constitutes a very black mark on your record. I am willing to give—er—any man a second chance, but it appears to me—from what I have learned—that you have had innumerable chances to—er—pull yourself together and have failed conspicuously to do so. Moreover, in other aspects your entire moral character—"

"Moral character!" shouted McDonagh suddenly. "You're the hell of a man to talk about moral character, Osborne! Clean your own house first! Maybe if you were man enough to've kept your damned tart of a wife off my neck, I wouldn't've got to where I am now! The goddamned harpy—don't you know half Portsmouth's been in your bed, or don't you care? Standing there preaching at me—By God, so I am halfway drunk, I'm six times the man you are all the way drunk, and if you point out the bastard carried tales, I'll lay him out and another like him, with more drink than this in me too! Expect me to go down on my knees and beg you for another chance, don't you? I'll be goddamned if I ask a favor of any man like you—can't even manage his own wife proper—"

Osborne went sheet white. But except that his voice shook when he spoke, he spoke calmly. "Mr. McDonagh, that is enough. I cannot retain you on the staff of this hospital, you are not fit either physically, mentally, or morally to be kept in crown service, and I shall so state in my—ah—official report upon this disgraceful business. You are dismissed from duty as of this minute. If you care to, you may plead your case at the—ah—Admiralty, but in view of what I shall have to say about you, I doubt that you will meet much leniency."

Bates was twittering agitatedly in the background; neither heard him or paid attention. "D'you want to know what you can do with your Christ-damned hospital and the Admiralty, too?—tell you for tuppence!—don't know how to God I stayed here so long, I swear—crowd of old fogies twenty years dead without knowing it—I don't give a damn for your damned job—"

"You will be off the premises within an hour," said Osborne rigidly, "and I shall send a full report of this—er—scene to the Admiralty at once." He turned and went out; he looked as if he might be sick at any moment, his balding brow wet with sweat, his eyes glazed.

"Oh, dear, Mr. McDonagh," said Bates in a whisper, "you

shouldn't—you really shouldn't have said all that. Mr. Talbot says—Mr. Osborne hasn't—hadn't—any notion at all of how his wife carries on, you know. And—"

"Oh, damn the lot of you!" said McDonagh furiously, and pushed out past him.

"Now look, Mr. McDonagh," said MacGregor, distressed, "I keep a decent house, I always have. I don't say the men don't get a bit over themselves now and then, but real out-and-outer drunkenness I won't have. I can't let you have another drink, sir, you're blind now, and I don't like to do it, Mr. McDonagh, but I'll ask you to go off back to your hospital and not come back here until you're sober, sir."

"Oh, hell, go to hell, MacGregor," whispered McDonagh. Hospital. Never go back to the damned hospital again. He lurched up to his feet.

MacGregor grabbed at him. "Here, sir, you can't go like that. By Goad, I'd never forgive maself—maybe your job lost on you—look you, sir, you come into the back room and rest a bit, sober yourself up afore you're seen—"

"Leave me go, I'll get out o' your damned house!"

"Now, Mr. McDonagh, you let me help you—"

He snarled and shook the man off, nearly fell with the effort, and clutched at a table.

"Here, what's this, having trouble with a customer, MacGregor?" He knew that voice—couldn't think whose—

"Well, I am, sir, if you'd just lend a hand, get him to the back room—never forgive maself if he got in trouble through me turning him out like this. Hold up, he's going out on us, well, that'll make him easier to handle, manner o' speaking—"

An unspecified time later McDonagh found he was still alive, if only just. He lay for a while gathering strength to open his eyes, did so, moaned, and shut them. Room he didn't know—stiff parlor, religious pictures—felt like a sofa under him. Someone put an arm around him and told him to drink; he did so, thirstily. Queer medicinal taste, nasty.

"That'll pick you up in a minute. Just lie quiet. My God and all His archangels, you really did yourself proud this time, didn't you?"

Knew that voice. He opened his eyes again, however painful it was. After a minute he smiled, with effort. "'S Larr. Larr McKenna, off the old *Donegal*. Good—see you 'gain, Larr."

"I can't say the same for you, Conal me boy. I hear you're stationed at the hospital here. 'S matter, don't they give you enough work to do?"

It all rushed back into his mind again, endless circle, disgrace, couldn't trust himself to touch an instrument; report to the Admiralty, dismissed—dismissed—dismissed for incompetence, neglect of duty, drunkenness, irresponsibility. Never thought come to such a pass as this—Con McDonagh who meant to build a fine career for himself—black mark on your record, Mr. McDonagh—

"Oh, God, Larr," he said. "I'm in the hell of a place, Larr—will you lend me a hand for God's sake—"

16

McKenna went up to the hospital to collect McDonagh's belongings for him; he was new ashore and not on leave, for his ship was in port only for resupply, but he had twenty-four hours free. "Any money on you? You can pay MacGregor for a room for the night?" Yes, McDonagh could do that, and he had twenty-three pounds odd in the Portsmouth bank.

When Larr had gone, McDonagh went up shakily to the room MacGregor hired him; the potboy fetched him up water, and he sluiced his face, and sat on the bed with his head in his hands. After awhile he got up, went across to the wavy glass, and had a look at himself.

He remembered that night in Dublin when he'd arranged for Matt to get away, saying, nothing here for any man; money to be made in England. Meant to make something of Con McDonagh, he did—not for just the one reason, but to show old Amison. Lauretta, Lauretta, his darling. Old Amison maybe knew what he was doing. Wasn't it a damned good thing he hadn't given Lauretta into the care of this irresponsible drunken oaf? Landed in England he had, almost exactly four years ago, with twenty-two pounds odd on him, and the hell of a lot of plans and hopes. Come to be making ninety pounds a year at a good secure job, and thrown it away, and here he was with a pound more in his pocket than he'd had four years ago, and a large black mark on his record.

He looked at this Conal McDonagh in the glass and didn't much like what he saw. This McDonagh had turned twenty-five last February, and he looked ten years older. Of course he hadn't had much appetite lately, he'd dropped weight, there were lines in his face and his clothes hung loose on his big frame. He hadn't shaved in two days, and his eyes were red-rimmed and blood-shot. The hand he raised to his loosened neckcloth was shaking visibly. He was two hours awake from a drunken bout, and already he needed a drink, he needed a drink like hell.

He said aloud to himself, "All right, you senseless bastard, that's enough. This is where you begin over again."

McKenna brought his packed bags up presently. "I hope I got all your personal instruments. There was a funny little fella, Bates, helped me—almost crying, so sorry he was."

"Bates," said McDonagh, "poor little Bates. He tried. Must write and thank him. Thanks, Larr. Will you do just one more thing? Here, I've got enough on me—go and get me a ticket on the London stage. The one leaving at noon, I must get to the bank and close the account before I leave."

"Look, man," said McKenna, "have you a place to go in London? Don't want to barge in, but you've not much money, have you? Let me—"

"Let you nothing. I'll be all right. I'm going to pull up, Larr, I bet you ten to five I'll be worth double your wages in ten years, by God. See? I'm not done yet."

"That's the boy, Con. But if ten pounds'd be any help—"

"Ten pounds is always a help, but I'll not take it, thanks. If I haven't any money, I can't buy whiskey."

"I'll buy you a drink now."

"And I'd sell my soul for it, but I won't take that either, thanks, Larr. I said this is where I pull up."

McKenna looked at him for a moment and laid a hand on his

shoulder briefly. "Stay by it, Con. Where'll you be in London? I may have enough leave coming to get up to town in a few months."

McDonagh was silent and then said, "Ask for me at St. Luke's Hospital. If I'm not there, they'll know about me."

He went up to London on the stage, and he thought he'd never finish the journey alive. He felt like death, twelve hours —twenty-four—thirty-six without a drink. It was all he could do to lift his bags across the inn yard at the Guildford change. In London he didn't try; it needed all his strength of mind to stay upright while one of the ostler boys found a hack for him.

"Here, sir, you do look bad," said the hackman, concerned. "Let me help you in—where to, sir?"

"St. Luke's—Hospital, please."

"St. Bart's is nearer, sir, if it's a doctor you're wanting—"

"No. St. Luke's, please." He leaned back and shut his eyes, hardly aware of the smells and sounds of London passing. He thought muzzily of Gillespie and Meredith; he thought, friends, might offer a drink—mustn't take it, must explain. Gillespie singing over the bar in the Fallow Deer that night—stone cold sober, and Rob drunk as a lord—Oh, God, don't think about that night—that night . . . Madeleine. . . .

"Let me help you in, sir, you're weak as a cat."

"Thanks—very much." Impersonally diagnosing his own case, he wanted to reassure the man, It's only hunger, not the plague; couldn't eat all yesterday. First thing to do, get to a place where I can eat. The weakness put foolish hot tears in his eyes at the familiar dark, shabby entry hall. "Just put the bags down, thanks." Laboriously he found sixpence on top of the fare. The man asked if he shouldn't call someone, looked relieved when an orderly came in. McDonagh dredged up the man's name with effort. "Pinner," he said, leaning on the wall. "Pinner. Want— Mr. Gillespie—or Mr. Meredith."

"Why, Mr. McDonagh, my God, sir—here, let me fetch you a chair—"

He sat slumped in the chair, concentrating on staying in it, until a hand fell on his shoulder. He looked up slowly into the boyish, innocent, handsome face of Rob Meredith with its unexpectedly shrewd, steady eyes. "What's up, Con?" Rob didn't flinch at the look of him, and McDonagh knew what he must look like. Gillespie came up beside him; he said nothing at all, but looked down at McDonagh gravely.

McDonagh essayed a smile between them. "Look, the two of you. Don't really need telling—what's wrong, do you? I've come begging, Mr. Gillespie—want a place to stay—get on my feet again. I've been dismissed—derelict on duty—damn fool I've been, you needn't tell me that. But I don't mean to stay down, burden on you from now on. Give me three months, that's all."

Gillespie grunted at him and reached a hand to his wrist. "Your pulse is verra slow, Mr. McDonagh—you're in need of a stimulant. What'd you say to a good stiff drink o' whiskey?"

McDonagh said, "Look, you old bastard"—trying to grin at him—"don't try to be funny, no Scotsman ever had a sense of humor."

"What you need at the moment," said Meredith, "is a meal. No, I know you're not hungry, but you'll get it down if I have to spoon-feed you." He looked at Gillespie.

The little Scot swayed back and forth on his heels; he hadn't taken his eyes off McDonagh. He said, "Not me nor Robin nor any man on God's green earth can be of much help to you now except Conal McDonagh."

"Now did you think I was asking for that kind of help? Know that—as well as you do. Want a bed and a place to sweat through it, 's all. And no kind moral opinions on what a Christ-damned fool I am."

"Oh, well, we knew that anyway," said Meredith.

"That infectious fever patient died this morning," said Gillespie, "up in the second medical ward. I'll ask Dr. Tanner can we borrow the bed to move into your room, Robin."

"Do that indeed," said Meredith. "And if he's farther gone than he seems to think—but he always had the hell of a high opinion of himself—the mortuary's right next door, we'd not have far to carry his vulgar bulk. Come up, Con my boy, up on your feet now, you know the way, but let's take it easy—I don't want to rupture myself carrying you—that's the boy, one foot in front of t'other—"

* * *

Mostly in the little room at the rear of St. Luke's, where he'd lived first in London, he sweated through it. It was bad, but even then he knew it wasn't as bad as it would have been later on. He had been on the liquor, really to have it master him, less than a year, and he wasn't as pulled down in permanent health as he might have been. The first month was the worst, while the liquor worked out of his system.

He lay there or paced the room, wrestling with it, exhausting himself with the exercise of iron control, and in his bodily weakness the fantasies visited him again: Madeleine, Madeleine and Dunstan, what he had done to her, God, why must it haunt him like this? Senseless, absurd. A woman like that. Other fantasies, too, unconnected. He went back in nightmare, sleeping and waking, to the bloody fields before Enniscorthy, he pulled that damned farm cart through dark dream country, Matt babbling nonsense behind, he woke trying to scream, trying to run from the gigantic British Hessian, scarlet-coated, coming at him with a bayonet. And lay sweating in aftermath of terror, if he was alone, a long while, not so long if Rob spoke from the other bed to tell him where he was.

Once he had a strange dream, another sort of dream. He was just a youngster, and at a picnic in the country outside Belfast. He didn't remember his mother, but he knew in the dream that the lady with him was his mother. She was smiling and soft, in a white gown, and her black hair was brushed the way Madeleine wore hers, pulled back with a curled fringe. His father was there, too, a big, ruddy man with laughing, bright blue eyes, and the green summer country all about was warm with sun. He knew they were dead; his father was dead at the gates of Antrim from a British musket ball and shoveled into a common grave, and so were a thousand other men, and McCracken was hanging on a gallows in Belfast, while all the desperate bloody fighting in the south had gone for nothing, nothing, the priests and the Protestant leaders all hanged, too, or broken on the rack, and he would spend the rest of his life dumbly, stubbornly hauling at that goddamned cart, to get Matt home safe to Dublin. He knew all that, but for an instant of time he was immeasurably comforted at being there with them, at the innocent, small pleasure of a child on a picnic, and their loving smiles on him. He woke with his face wet with tears and was sorry to wake.

He read doggedly to pass the time, keep his mind occupied. "Don't feel you have to stay with me, Rob—not a child, you know." He got through the first month, and he was still alive and feeling increasingly stronger. Then he went walking around the city, anywhere at random, miles, to tire himself physically and create hunger. He picked up the weight he had lost and began to feel like a Conal McDonagh he had known.

He came back to the hospital late one November afternoon and met Gillespie and Rob just coming down the step. Rob stopped, looked oddly guilty for a flash, and said something genial. McDonagh surveyed them and laughed. "You're on the way to the Deer for a drink, aren't you? For God's sake, I'm not so sensitive—trot along and enjoy it! Pity I'll never join you again in my life—I won't dare."

"Now that's just where you're wrong," said Gillespie sharply. "You won't come with us now—we'll give it another month— but you'll come to the Deer with us, or alone, again, Mr. McDonagh, and sit peaceably over a couple of drinks and walk out without a back look. It's not as if you'd been an old fellow with forty years of tippling behind. I daresay with that kind the only thing is for them to leave it alone altogether. But you, you've mastered yourself, Mr. McDonagh, but if you stay afraid the rest of your life to take one drink, you're still not master of the liquor. Which is not sensible. On Christmas Eve you'll come out with Robin and me, and we'll have a few quiet drinks in a reasonable way, and you'll go to bed sober, but you'll know you're master, and it'll never be on top of you again."

"Well," said McDonagh thoughtfully, "maybe so, Mr. Gillespie—maybe that's the way to do it."

One afternoon he found he was only a few streets from Queen Square, and after a short debate with himself he called on Lauretta. He was looking more himself now; he'd not shock her. And sitting with her in her little parlor, seeing her soft, slow smiles and the amber, curling tendrils escaped sweetly from her ringlets, he could almost feel that these four years were a dream, that she was not wife to another man but still his own dear.

"You look—older, Con," she said. McDonagh smiled a little bitterly.

"And I was just thinking how much the same you looked—as the girl I knew in Dublin. Do I? Well, maybe reason for it." He had no reticences with Lauretta, and he told her, in short, angry phrases, how it had been with him.

"But you're—all right now, Con?" and her eyes were anxiously sympathetic, a little puzzled.

McDonagh said, "I'm all right—that way, yes." Suddenly he leaned forward and took her hands in his: small, short-fingered hands, with little pink nails, and soft. His own looked twice the size, holding them, and they resisted and then lay acquiescently in his palms. "Oh, Lauretta," he said lowly, "I thought—when I was down like that, maybe your father knew what he was about—not to give you to my care, my darling. But now it's in my mind—that if I'd had you, everything would have been different for me, and I'd never have got to that state at all. If I'd ever had—my heart's desire."

"Oh, Con, please," she said in a shaken voice. "We can't go back in life, you know. You mustn't—mustn't keep thinking about me that way. I do wish you'd find some nice girl to marry, my dear—it's true a wife would keep you steadier—"

"So easy to say, my darling." He kissed the little hands and let them go. "But I won't worry you, Lauretta, try not to worry you." He didn't know whether it was better to see her or just have her there at the back of his heart all the while without seeing her.

"But you are better, and you'll soon be back at your work?"

"Oh, yes, soon," he said. Back at work. It was a frightening thing to have to think about. Where and how? Needed capital to keep yourself, start a practice. Better to have a regular hospital appointment. He was not needed at St. Luke's, no room for him there; he wasn't known in London elsewhere. He had not held an instrument for nearly four months. It was not that he felt any nervousness about first taking on a patient again after this sorry interim, but there was bound to be—even though he was himself again—a certain self-distrust until he knew surely.

As it happened, in the event he hadn't time to feel nervous. He was sitting in the little rear room, smoking over a book, that next afternoon after he'd seen Lauretta, when an orderly knocked and looked in, the man Pinner.

"Oh, beg parding, sir, but I hoped—Mr. Meredith he must be up in the first operating room with Mr. Gillespie—"

"Yes, they're doing a rather complicated job on some kidney stones, why?"

"Oh, damn," said Pinner unexpectedly. He was breathless and flustered-looking. "It's an accident, sir, just fetched in—bleeding something orful, great spouts like—I and Jack, we got tourniquets on, but—"

McDonagh put down his book and pipe. Without stopping to think, automatically he said, "I'll come." He ran up the stair ahead of the orderly, and once he was in the second operating room, there was no space for examining his emotions. The patient had several deep gashes in left arm and leg, two of which had severed arteries—thank God the orderlies had had sense enough to get tourniquets on—and for five minutes he was too busy to think consciously of what he was doing. He had the cuts stitched together and pressure dressings on before he realized fully that he was standing over an operating table at work again. And then he did not feel either especially pleased or nervous; it seemed quite normal.

He was all right in himself again. He could stroll up to the Deer with Rob tonight or tomorrow and sit companionably over a couple of drinks and come away. And how much of that was due to the fact that he had friends to talk with here? He couldn't say in addition, a settled feeling in life, because that he didn't have now any more than he'd had in Portsmouth, but he had a better feeling about life here. So he was whole again, and living on friends, and what the hell was he going to do about that? He'd had official, cold notice of his dismissal from Admiralty service; in seeking a new job, he couldn't very well give his naval service in reference—not if he hoped to get the job. Yet for some reason he didn't brood about it; he felt superstitiously that something would turn up. Even a long letter from Matt, with all his latest news, boasting about a new son, increased practice, plans to buy a house—it didn't make McDonagh jealous or sorry for himself. For the moment, for just a little while, he was drifting, and content to drift.

For nearly a year he had urgently, anxiously wanted to see Madeleine again, but since he'd been back in London, he had made no move to do that, for a reason he didn't examine deeply. It was that violently, bitterly he would be shamed to present himself to Madeleine as the man he had been two months ago: have her see him like that, how low he'd gone, maybe to rejoice over it. When he found Madeleine, to make what apology he might, it would be as the Conal McDonagh she remembered.

And that was an ambiguous thought . . . the McDonagh she remembered! Not a very attractive specimen at that, the one that would have stayed in her mind.

Drifting, so he was, this fortnight, these three weeks since he had known for certain that he was back to himself and whole, as if waiting for something to show him the way. On the last day of the year, as he finished dressing, as he looked back at his reflection, knotting his neckcloth, he knew quite suddenly that this was the day he would see Madeleine. He would go to see Madeleine and say what he must say to her, and after that his conscience, which had been obsessed with her so reasonlessly, so ridiculously, would be satisfied. The whole episode would be over, and he could go on to the next part of his life free and clear.

She had said to him, an apartment of rooms in Cavendish Square—he remembered the very tone of her voice on the words. Not a very full address, and that was some time ago—for a woman in her profession.

He walked up to King Street after breakfast and knocked at the door of number twenty. As he stood waiting for admittance, he remembered the last time he had been here, that night, and his self-disgust at his stupidity was as fresh as the first moment he had, belatedly, realized what he had done. And he thought that if Fleur knew of it, she might be in no hurry to tell him where Madeleine was.

The maid hesitated to admit him. Yes, Madame was in, but— McDonagh said, "Not alone? Never mind. I'm on an innocent errand, I'll explain myself," and brushed past her into the parlor. This low little cottage house, its one floor of intimate rooms, awoke memories in him mostly self-derogatory. Before the fire Fleur and a middle-aged dark man were lingering over breakfast; the man's eyes were alert and curious on McDonagh, and Fleur's briefly angry.

McDonagh nodded at the man. "I'm sorry to intrude, sir, and it's business only, I assure you! Miss Galard can tell me something I want to know, that's all, and then I'll leave you. You're looking well as usual, Fleur."

"Well, I see we must make the best of your intrusion, Conal," she returned amiably enough. Had Madeleine not told her then? "This is Mr. Isaacs, I make known to you—Saul, a most brusque and frequently irritating young surgeon, Mr. McDonagh, who is given to these rude social gestures."

Mr. Isaacs smiled and said, "Women make so much of these things. Do not mind her, sir, but sit and have a cup of chocolate with us."

"Thanks very much, no," said McDonagh, smiling back. "I'll ask my question and depart in peace. I want to know where Madeleine is, Fleur."

Her eyes narrowed on him. Elegant as always, and as attractive and desirable, she was yet beginning to show her age a little, in betraying lines about mouth and eyes. "And what do you want with Maddi?"

"That," said McDonagh, "is none of your affair. Nothing wrong, Fleur. There's something I want to tell her, that's all. Where is she? Is she still with Dunstan?"

Fleur looked away, down at her half-full cup of chocolate. "I made a mistake there somehow—I do not know how or why, it is queer. Bringing you into that business—still, halfway it was you putting yourself into it, was it not? I know nothing about such matters, but I once knew a man—an alchemist—who told me there are certain things, certain powders and liquids, you comprehend, which will mingle quite agreeably, and then there are others, you put them together and *pouf!*—the explosion. It was something like that, yes."

"Stop nattering and tell me the address," said McDonagh irritably.

She shrugged. "After all, it is nothing to do with me anymore, is it? She may not be pleased, but I will tell you. It is number seven Cavendish Square."

"Thanks very much. I won't intrude any longer then." He had finished with Fleur a long while ago; leave her to her own life.

The tall, old house in the quiet square had been cut up into separate apartments, according to the numbers on the front door. Number seven was up one flight of stairs, its door at the front on the left; he wielded the brass knocker once and waited, with no conscious thoughts in his mind, again only shameful memories.

She opened the door herself. He said brusquely, "I daresay I'm the last man you want to see, Madeleine, but I've something to say to you, so I had to come." She stood there rigid, looking at him without expression, indefinably looking a little older, a little harder, but still just as he remembered her, tall and graceful. She did not speak. "May I come in?"

She looked at him a moment longer and then suddenly turned and retreated into the room, leaving the door open. He went in and shut it behind him. He couldn't have said afterward what the room was like, whether well or shabbily furnished, whether large or small. He did remember that there was a hearth, because she walked across and stood by it, with her back to him. She was wearing a yellow muslin morning gown, and her erect, slender back looked stiff.

She said in a hard, expressionless voice, "Have you come, perhaps, to ask that I redeem my promise—and let you try how proficient I am become from the little provincial miss you knew?"

"I didn't come here to have a fight with you," said McDonagh. Always she could raise irritation in him. "I've something I want to say, that's all, Madeleine, please just listen to me. It's— I'm damned if I know how to say it right, but I'll try. You've good reason for thinking what you do of me—or you think you have. I don't need to tell you I was in liquor—that night—and I don't say it as an excuse. But—well, I'm not usually so thick-witted, or I like to think I'm not. Maybe you won't believe me, Madeleine, but it was quite a time after, all of a sudden, I realized what I'd made you think. That—that it was a planned trick—on you. That's not so, and I just wanted you to know it. The other thing I said to you, that was so. I wanted you—I wanted you like hell, Madeleine, it wasn't pretense about that—I meant that. If you thought I—tried to make a fool of you, making you—want me—if only for a little while—just to get back at Dunstan—well, that's a lie. I never planned such a thing at all. I just—I was there, and you alone like that—and my God, I wanted you, I couldn't stand thinking of any other man having you—first. That's all it was, Madeleine, and I was sorry afterward. Not for having you, but—the way it happened, to make you think that. That's all I wanted to say to you, and I hope you'll believe me."

She turned slowly to face him. She was always pale, but she looked paler now. "Is—is that—the way it was, really, Conal? You did—want me? I'd like to—I do believe it, I—" Suddenly she smiled, a brief half-sad smile. "I should have known that you're not the sort of man who thinks very far ahead, wouldn't plan such a thing, but I—" She stopped as if she'd finished the sentence.

"Madeleine—"

"Yes?"

McDonagh felt sweat on his forehead. He hadn't known he'd feel like this, seeing her again. Once he'd admitted to himself that most of his irritation at her, that time before, had been on account of his physical desire for her, he'd understood himself better in relation to her. Perhaps Fleur had gone to the heart of the matter an hour ago, with her alchemical properties; something about Madeleine, physical or otherwise, made him want her harder and hotter than any other female he'd ever laid eyes on. But apart from that, just now, a strange, desperate feeling possessed him for just a flash, gone so quickly there was no identifying it—familiar and not familiar. Wanting something else, something different, about her or from her. It was the sudden childlike feeling that came over a man, flooding his whole being, sometimes, only for one heartbeat—a vague wanting, nostalgic, hungry, immediate, for something, for everything—not knowing what was hungered for.

"Yes?" she said again. She looked the same, not much older,

not much harder—yet. But he thought she was thinner, or perhaps her hair was drawn back closer, to show the hollows beneath her high cheekbones.

"Are—are you still—with Dunstan?"

"Can't I offer you a glass of wine?" she said. He didn't want it, but he was too occupied coping with all his feelings to say so. Wanting her so, right now, so terribly. She moved over to the table to fill two glasses, and he saw that her hands were shaking slightly; she was not so calm as she sounded. The strangest mixture of feelings came on him for that, satisfaction, renewal of desire, and something he couldn't identify at first because it wasn't a thing he felt very often, and that was humility. "Why, as a matter of fact," she said, "I have just left Almerick, and am looking about to decide on a new protector."

And McDonagh said, because he was obscurely frightened of ununderstandable emotion in himself, "If that's a hint, I'll have to disappoint you, lady. I'm afraid you'd come too high-priced for me."

Her eyes went blank and then hard on him. She handed him his glass and drifted back across the room. "Yes," she returned in an expressionless voice, "I daresay—and it was not a hint. Do you know, I—I am surprised that you thought enough—of the matter between us—to come here and explain. What did it matter, Conal? This man or that—to be first, second, or third?"

"It was the way the whole thing happened," he said angrily, "you know that. I—my God, I never meant you to think that! And oh, God, Madeleine, I couldn't be sorry for it, but—"

"Couldn't you?" she said softly, not looking at him. "I—I couldn't either, Conal. I—it—made it all different. I—" She looked at him once, briefly, with a little gasp, and away. "I—went to Almerick—because I'd promised—and I owed Fleur all that money—I didn't want to, Conal, I hated it—"

"Did you?" he said stupidly, still busy with keeping down crude lust. "Yes, from the little I saw of him, I wouldn't say he was a very accomplished lover. You'll need to be a bit more cautious this time, choose a man with more finesse."

She put her glass down clumsily, suddenly, spilling a little wine, and turned her back on him. Her voice shook. "Yes—yes,

I must. If it's—any satisfaction to you, Conal, you were quite right—that first time, telling me I was a little fool to choose this career. And when you said—I would earn my money hardly. But as I said to you, one must live, and only very fortunate people really enjoy what they must do—to live."

And there were all his feelings changed again, different and quite unidentifiable, oh, damn this female who had the power to put such emotion on him, for no reason at all—"Madeleine, if you mean—my dear—"

"Oh, no," she whispered, "don't call me that." She swung around to him again, and now her eyes were bright and hard. "I'm not your dear, Conal. I'm for the having of any man with sufficient money, and as you point out, you have not. Yes, I will be careful in making a new arrangement. Several gentlemen I have met—this while I have been kept by Almerick—have made me offers, but I'll take my time deciding among them. Though I expect it will be Harry Burdoun, he is by far the wealthiest. Oh, everything you said to me was true, Conal—does that please you?—but it is far too late to put myself back to—to that Madeleine Olivier who came up to town from Tunbridge Wells. I have paid back Fleur what I owed her, and—this is really very funny, when one stops to think of it, you know—I have some modest savings that would constitute a respectable dower. Only in the acquiring of it, I have made something of myself—that no man in his right mind would ever want to marry. Isn't—that—so?"

"Oh, my God, Madeleine," he said helplessly, angrily, "I'm sorry—tried to—but try to tell any stubborn child the truth and be believed! Now it's too late, now that's so, it's just as I told you, you're caught."

"Oh, but you needn't feel sorry for me," said Madeleine. She was still trembling a little, he saw; she took up her glass and drank off the wine quickly. "As I say, one has to live, and this is quite a good living—and a profession I can now claim some modest experience at, if I am still a beginner, so to speak. I expect it's strange, but I don't feel wicked from—from a religious view, you know—I'm afraid my morals were sadly neglected that way." She smiled. "I expect I'd have been brought up in the

Catholic church, but Mother discovered it was thought very low-class in England, you see, and she thought more of the neighbors' opinions than anything else. No, it's merely that perhaps I'm not made the right way—for this career. However, one does get accustomed to anything, and it is quite a good living."

McDonagh wanted appallingly, furiously, to hit her, to swear at her, to reach for her any way and get her close. A faint breath of her remembered scent came to him. He said sharply, "I wouldn't be too certain you don't enjoy the job, when you talk that way."

"I'll tell you something," she said in a very low voice. "Something *I've* wanted to tell *you*, Conal. Perhaps it will please you. It wasn't Almerick's fault—that I loathed every minute of his lovemaking. It was your fault, Conal. You spoiled me for Almerick."

"Well, my God, that's not very surprising," said McDonagh. "I said he wouldn't be much accomplished in that line."

"Perhaps," said Madeleine, "you've spoiled me for any man, I don't know, Conal." She looked at him blindly, hazily.

He read that as invitation, and all the hard-repressed hot desire exploded in him, and he reached for her, stumbling forward. Madeleine backed away across the room. "No!" she exclaimed. "I won't—I won't let you again—I won't let myself—shameful, when it's only— No, Conal! I mean it this time!" And she actually snatched up the poker.

He stopped where he was. "Oh, aren't you in the right trade!" he said viciously. "Know just how to get a man stirred up, and then keep him at arm's length—to push up the price!"

"Oh, God," said Madeleine, "I can't bear any more of this— go away, Conal! No, I don't know if you made it wrong for me with anyone else at all—there's only been Almerick—but I will try, I will know, with the—next—one. But it doesn't really matter, because it's too late now, isn't it? It only matters to me now—none of your affair."

"You're damned right," said McDonagh, "it's not. And you're having hysterics over nothing, like all women—never heard such damned sentimental nonsense in my life!" He had forgotten every emotion now but intolerable anger at her for frustrating his awful need—this damned female, what was there about her?—only another available woman now, if an exclusive one, but—"You judge that by two men? Look around careful, Madeleine, and take a lively young man for your new protector, and you'll find out how much you can enjoy your work! I don't say you'll find one as good as me on any street corner, but—"

"Get out," she said. "Please go away. I—I can't talk to you anymore. Very likely you're right. And thank you"—there was faint irony on that—"for calling to explain that to me. Good-bye, Conal."

McDonagh was so angry, still in the grip of physical desire for her, so confused and irritated at his own unaccustomed sensations, that he was temporarily speechless. He picked up his hat and strode out and banged the door behind him.

17

McDonagh never remembered consciously how he came to be in Lombard Street, at dusk. He had walked blindly for miles after leaving Madeleine, until he found he was in a lather of sweat inside his greatcoat, and took himself in hand, slowing his pace. He turned into a tavern he was passing and had a meal. What sort of fool was he to let himself get into such a state, all over that maddening girl who didn't mean a damn to him—a girl like that? All right, he'd behaved wrongly to her, he'd been sorry about it, and now he'd seen her and said so, and the whole thing was done with, so let it go and forget it, for God's sake! It was done; it was finished.

He began to feel calmer, he could look at it objectively, and maybe for a connected reason (all his loose ends of life tied up, as it were) he began feeling more actively concerned over what he was going to do professionally. When he left the tavern, he walked up to St. Bart's to see if Arch Elliott was still resident there and if there might be a place open. He didn't have much solid hope there would be. He did find Elliott, casually pleased to see him again, and over a drink at the Bull he frankly told Elliott the situation he was in.

"My God, McDonagh, I'd like to help you, but I'm not on the committee, you know. There's no job open at the moment, anyway. You can put your name down for consideration when there is, but—" Elliott shrugged.

"Yes, well, I hadn't really expected anything else. But I'd better do that, just on the long chance." He went back to the hospital with Elliott and spent half an hour making out an application form that would very likely be of no use whatever. ("Employed St. Luke's October 1803 to April 1804—what have you been doing in the succeeding three and a half years, Mr. McDonagh?") But the gesture had to be made. . . . He began to feel rather dispirited and in no mood to face Rob or Gillespie; he went out walking again, down by the Embankment, and stared into the Thames, brooding, for a while.

When the early dusk began to come down, and with it a thin fog, he found himself walking slowly up Lombard Street. As he came past a house halfway down toward Gracechurch Street, a man passed through the doorway, and there was a brief showing of light as the door opened and shut; the sounds inside filtered out louder to the street for a moment. McDonagh stopped and turned to the sheltering house wall to strike a light for his pipe. It was a tavern—some jollification going on, customers gone to singing.

His pipe caught, and he straightened, putting the flint away, and wondered what had suddenly, piercingly, brought vague nostalgia of memory in his mind. Then he smiled and went up to the inn door, stood listening. There was at least one Irishman in there, and he was doing the singing. In a good loud voice, too, and with great feeling.

> Oh, list to the lay of a poor Irish harper,
> And scorn not the strains of his old withered
>   hand!
> But remember these fingers they could
>   once move sharper
> To raise the bright strands of our dear native
>   land.
> It was long 'fore the shamrock, our dear
>   isle's loved emblem,

Was crushed in its beauty 'neath the Saxon
   lion's paw,
I was called by the cailins of village and valley
Bold Phelim Brady, the Bard of Armagh!

There was a private soldier leaning against the doorpost. He looked at McDonagh with mild interest. "Nice voice, an't he?"

"Well, loud and on key," said McDonagh. The nostalgia still moved in him dimly; he remembered his father singing that ballad.

"Ah," said the private, "what more can you hask? Passes the time it do, on a long march like—when we're not amixed up with some other troops, that is—'im bein' the colonel, there can't no un say nothin' about its bein' undignified, you see. 'E acts more proper—got to—when we're along of another regiment."

At a patteran or fair I could twist my
   shilellagh
Or trip through a jig with my brogues
   bound with straw,
And all the pretty maids around me
   assembled
Loved bold Phelim Brady, the Bard of
   Armagh!

"Parding, sir, but you 'appen to 'ave the time on you?"

McDonagh fetched out his watch and held it to the light from the door. "It's just on six."

"Thanks, sir," said the private rather mournfully, turning up his collar against the chilling wind. " 'Alf a nour more then. Stations me 'ere and says, Fetch me hout at 'alf parst six, 'e says. It an't that 'e gets drunk, for 'e never *do*, but 'e loses track o' time. And never think to hask 'ave I got a watch, to know. But that's Colonel Devesey for you."

"I see," said McDonagh, amused. "Well, I think I'll have a drink myself. I'll tell you when it's time if I'm still here." The private thanked him gloomily, and McDonagh went into the house.

The singer was sitting at a table near a welcoming hearth, and he had evidently created an atmosphere of goodwill about him. Four uniformed private soldiers stood about listening and smiling, the landlord was beating genial time, and the two or three other customers were not obviously annoyed. McDonagh strolled up to the bar and ordered a half of ale; he didn't care for ale particularly, but gin he couldn't drink, and the ale at least was less potent.

Although I have traveled this wide world over,
Yet Erin's my home and a parent to me,
Then oh, let the ground that my old bones
     shall cover
Be cut from the soil that is trod by the free!

And when Sergeant Death in his cold arms
     shall embrace me,
O lull me to sleep with sweet Erin go bragh,
By the side of my Kathleen, my young wife,
     oh, place me,
Then forget Phelim Brady, the Bard of Armagh.!

"Oh, that's a lovely song, that is," pronounced one of the soldiers. "I remember me old da singin' that un, as I make sure Johnny here do, too. Beg t' interjooce ourselves, sir—Mick Callaghan from Wicklow, and this here's Johnny me brother, and that's Patsy Milligan from Cork, and that's Brian Carmody out o' Kerry. Pleasure to hear a lovely Irish song sung right well, and don't tell me by an Englishman either."

The singer beamed at him and said, "By damn, no! Desmond Devesey, my good fellow, out o' Roscommon, and let me buy you all a drink. Landlord!" He was about fifty, a solid, square, beefy man with a bush of wild hair and very bright blue eyes in a brown face. He was not in uniform, but dark civil dress.

McDonagh came up to the table. "I echo Callaghan, sir—remember my father singing that, a good song. Mind if I sit with you?"

"Sit down, sit down, another Irishman always welcome! Let me buy you a—ah, I see you already have one. Name, sir ... Oh, ah, didn't I know you were an Irishman the minute you walked in the door? Now here's another good song you'll all know, join in the chorus, don't any of y' be shy, now—" Devesey threw back his head and with magnificent attack embarked on the verse in a roar.

> Let the farmer praise his grounds,
> Let the huntsman praise his hounds,
> And the shepherd his sweet-scented lawn!
> But I, more blest than they,
> Spend a happy hour each day
> With me charmin' little crùiscin làn,
>   làn, làn!
> With me charmin' little crùiscin làn!

Five voices joined willingly on the chorus—

> Gradh mo croidhe mo crùiscin,
> Slainthe gael mo bhùirnìn!
> Gradh mo croidhe à cùilin, bàn, bàn, bàn!
> O, gradh mo croidhe mo crùiscin làn!

By the time all four verses had been sung, they felt friends all around, and Devesey was charmed with them. He wasn't drunk indeed, only mellowed, and he liked to sing, and he liked praise for it. He insisted on buying another round, and then he sang *Brennan on the Moor* and *Cockles and Mussels.* One of the Callaghans said *The Rakes of Mallow* was a lovely song, and they all sang that, Devesey the loudest, and then he sang *Garryowen* and all nine lugubrious verses of *Barry of Macroom.* McDonagh with difficulty got out of accepting a third drink and was just reflecting somewhat guiltily that he really had no business sitting here thoughtlessly enjoying himself—there was a childlike enthusiasm about Devesey that was insidiously infectious—when Devesey, draining his latest glass, set it down with a thump and exclaimed, "Oh, grand, grand! Excellent accompaniment, all of you—*now*, all together, let's have a *real* song—" And throwing his head back, he embarked exuberantly on *Boyne Water.*

> *July the first, of a morning clear, one thousand*
> *   six hundred and ninety,*
> *King William did his men prepare, of thousands*
> *   he had thirty—*

The battle of the Boyne having resulted in a Protestant victory, it was a mortal insult to give vent to that ballad anywhere in earshot of a Catholic, and McDonagh lunged frantically across the table and clapped a hand over Devesey's mouth, too late. The four soldiers sprang up in a body, breathing fire.

"Sing the *Boyne Water* afore honest Irishmen, y' damn Protestant!" "Oh, let me at the blackguard, Mick, out o' my way!" "The *Boyne Water* he sings at us, does he, I'll teach him sing—" The biggest soldier swung clean on Devesey and knocked him out of his chair, and Devesey scrambled up, shook his head, and, yelling curses, went for his attacker with both fists.

"He's drunk, he didn't know what he was doing!" shouted McDonagh, grabbing at one of the Callaghans, who had collected an empty bottle from the nearby bar. "You fool, stop it now, he didn't—" He ducked the bottle, connected with Callaghan's jaw, and Callaghan staggered back, bounced off the table, and let out a roar.

"Ho, t'other un's another bloody Orangeman!" He lunged at McDonagh, brandishing the bottle.

The door crashed in, and the private from outside came at a run. He was willing, but he wasn't big, and it was a confused fight. The landlord was jumping up and down yelling that he'd call the watch. McDonagh took a cuff on the head that made his ears ring, slipped on the wet floor and sprawled his length, and was promptly kicked in the ribs. He got up and bawled at the private, "Get him out, run for it!" They were three to four, and discretion was the better part of valor. He pulled Devesey off one of the Callaghans, and they retreated slowly to the door, Devesey making strenuous efforts to get back wholly into the fight. The fog had thickened, by the grace of God. "Run!" shouted McDonagh to Devesey. "Run, you damned fool!" He and the private pulled Devesey along between them, down a few turnings, and presently stopped and panted. No sounds of pursuit could be heard.

Devesey turned to the soldier and asked quite calmly, "Is it half past six, my man?"

"Well, there," said the private, "if the time's not gone clean out o' me 'ead, Colonel, sir, I do beg parding."

"In any event," said Devesey, settling his neckcloth, "I have wasted enough time enjoying myself, I must get back to that damned paperwork. Let me see, you said your name was, ah, yes, Mr. McDonagh—I do appreciate your cooperation, sir, against those vulgar and crude sons of the south! How fortunate that you chanced to be there. What part of Ulster do you hail from, may I ask?"

McDonagh said resignedly, "Belfast. And they told you they were southrons, why in the name of God you did such a damned fool thing as to start the *Boyne Water*—you aren't even drunk as an excuse!"

"Well, well," said Devesey guiltily, "I was a bit carried away perhaps. It's a good tune, isn't it, a damned good tune! Now I'll tell you what we'll do—where are we?—oh, well, keep on walking, bound to come somewhere in time—you must join me for dinner. No, no, I'll take no refusal! I'm entitled to a little innocent enjoyment on my leave, surely—even if there is that tiresome appointment at the Horse Guards in the morning, must have the report ready to hand over, bunch of fat-arsed old nannies down there at the War Office! Never mind that, come along. My man, I won't need you now. Get back to my rooms and occupy yourself usefully polishing my boots or something, eh? Yes, yes, come along, Mr. McDonagh, we'll find a decent restaurant. I'm quite ready for dinner, and I daresay you are, too."

"Well, it's about time you were in," said Rob, looking up from his book. "I was beginning to wonder—"

"If I'd forgot all my moral resolutions?" McDonagh grinned. "No, I've been—I think—arranging my immediate future. In a sort of roundabout way." He sat down on his bed and suddenly laughed, thinking about that ridiculous scene. He began to describe it to Rob. "Met this private outside the door, see, he told me—and I only went in because, well, it sounded amusing— And then Devesey all on a sudden commenced to sing the *Boyne Water*, and of course all hell broke loose—"

Rob looked at him blankly and asked why. "Oh, Lord, of course, you're a benighted Englishman. Well, it's about a battle the Orangemen happened to win, you see, and singing it before a southerner's about equivalent to calling him the son of a Queenstown harlot, so there was a little dustup, and we had to run for it—"

Rob looked at him indulgently and said, "You hotheaded Irishmen. What's that got to do with your future?"

"Well," said McDonagh, "he's a nice old boy, curious as a monkey, and he turned me inside out over dinner, wanted to know all about me, so I told him. And he says I should meet him at the War Office—which he calls the Horse Guards—tomorrow morning, and apply for army work, and he'll back me up. Says they won't take any note of the Admiralty business, now the medical services are separate, account of there being rivalry between the two branches, and if there is, I'm just to say it was rank jealousy got me dismissed and he'll back up the story, but anyway, they're in need of surgeons and likely won't ask too many questions."

"That sounds reasonable, I must say," said Rob thoughtfully.

"And if it's not," said McDonagh, starting to laugh again, "I wouldn't put it beyond Colonel Devesey to raise such a row that I'll be taken in just to settle him down!"

He was not far wrong. Colonel Devesey of the Seventy-third (Light) Foot was a man of sudden, violent impulse; as McDonagh suspected, knowing the type, he might lose interest in you day after tomorrow and go on to some other enthusiasm, but once he conceived a notion for maneuvering matters or men about, no power on earth could deflect him. He shepherded McDonagh up to the medical supply office in a rush; to McDonagh's relief the senior officer he had dealt with here before had apparently been supplanted, and it was a strange authority who was peremptorily informed that Mr. McDonagh was to be taken on at once on the army medical rolls and instantly posted to the Seventy-third.

"But, Colonel, our regulations—the young man must be interviewed, his credentials—"

"By damn, anyone can see he's an excellent surgeon, excellent! No delay, sir, don't you know the country's at war? Must have enough surgeons with every regiment!"

"But, Colonel—young man, you're welcome to file an application, it's quite true we're in need of more surgeons—"

"Fuss and bother!" exclaimed Devesey. "Now you listen to me, you, whatever-your-name-is—Mr. McDonagh has had most unfair treatment from the Admiralty, mark that! Of course, we know they're all damn fools up there, letting a good surgeon go! You will know how to ignore whatever such blunderers may say, I trust! Forms, interviews—must have regulations, I daresay, but nine of ten times it's a damned waste of labor!"

McDonagh got a word in peaceably to the effect that his credentials were on file, and he would much appreciate an interview. "Yes, well, if you will make out an application—"

"Now mind," said Devesey, "I return to the regiment end o' next week, and it would be convenient if Mr. McDonagh could go along, all officially on the rolls."

"Well, really," said the senior officer feebly, "I scarcely think—"

It did not, of course, come about quite so quickly as that, but somewhat to McDonagh's astonishment, it went almost as smoothly. He expected to be catechized rather sharply at his interview, and meant to tell the story honestly, whatever effect it might have—only sensible thing to do. To his surprise, the examining officer only said dryly, "I see by your records that you ran into a little trouble during naval service, Mr. McDonagh. Well, well, these things will happen to young men, and it's a pity to take a man's good name away for one error. Every dog allowed one bite, eh?"—and asked him no questions about that at all. He was told that a posting would very likely be given him within a month, as recruiting and supply were being stepped up in pace. "Can't say more now, all rather indefinite, but there may be an expedition fitted out for action rather soon, at least all the signs point that way."

McDonagh went back to St. Luke's, still surprised at the ease of his acceptance, and waited only twenty days to receive official orders for duty. He was attached to the Twenty-second Foot, at present lying at Saffron Walden.

"Well, well," said Rob, "your fiery colonel will be furious that they didn't send you to his regiment!"

McDonagh laughed. "He's probably forgotten all about me by now. And I don't know but I'm just as pleased. Life might be just a trifle too exciting, lived alongside Colonel Devesey! All the same, I'm damned grateful to the old boy. I'd never have tried for it, never thought about it, if he hadn't happened along when he did."

Rob cocked a brow at him. "Think you'll like army life?"

"I'd damn well better," said McDonagh only half-humorously. He added awkwardly, "Don't want to embarrass you, but you know I'm grateful—to you and Gillespie—what you've done. I didn't look a very promising gamble, I don't suppose."

Rob grinned. "It's surprising how often long odds pay off. I wouldn't lay a wager second time around, Con."

"No, well, there won't be a second run," said McDonagh.

He left London on the tenth of February, two weeks before his birthday, still feeling slightly dazed at the magic with which destiny had manipulated matters for him. Wryly he thought, thinking of Matt, that maybe the old adage was right—the devil looked after his own.

McDonagh's first sensation about army life was irrational and in a sense amusing. He must, he thought, remember to tell Matt about it when next he wrote—as the only possible confidant. He found he was almost passionately grateful that the Twenty-second Foot did not wear scarlet coats, but blue and buff.

A number of regiments were lying in camp at Saffron Walden when he came there, among them a few Hessians and troopers, and passing close to a file of the former, on his way to find his quarters, he felt the sweat on his forehead and the tenseness in his muscles. Absurdly he wondered if any of those men had been at Enniscorthy or Vinegar Hill. Near ten years ago, but the past had such a disconcerting way of creeping up on a man unawares.

But on the whole he settled down happily enough with the regiment; maybe because he had made up his mind to do so. The other surgeon attached to the Twenty-second was a middle-aged Welshman, Evan Morgan, easy to get on with, if of a melancholy disposition; there was very little for them to do, but Morgan thought wholesale military action was coming.

"Bound to, you know, Mr. McDonagh, and it'll be Spain. Boney's got a stranglehold on the country, and the hell of a big army pouring in there, by all accounts. There's rumors of an expeditionary force being sent to engage him. Though of course, we might not be included in it. But if so, we'll have plenty to keep us occupied indeed."

McDonagh said vaguely, "Oh, well, in the lap of the gods, I daresay." He should have been bored, but he wasn't, particularly. The officers and the medical staff, which included a physician, Dr. Twelvetrees, were quartered in the town comfortably enough. It wasn't much of a town, but he got acquainted with several of the younger officers, and they found sufficient amusement among them, with cards and an occasional dance arranged with the aid of regimental wives and daughters. McDonagh had never been much of a horseman, hadn't needed to be, being a townsman, and a couple of lieutenants, Buckley and Prince, took him in hand over that.

"Got to ride in the army, old boy, you know. You'll thank us later on!" Most fine afternoons found McDonagh borrowing a nag to jog about the countryside, if he hadn't work to do; he grew rather to enjoy it. And from time to time there was work to be done at the efficient small temporary hospital tent at camp: accidental injuries on maneuvers and the like. He was feeling entirely himself, physically, by then; rather surprisingly he enjoyed that four months at Saffron Walden.

Possibly more than anything else he enjoyed the occasion when with the aid of a medical orderly he hauled Prince and Buckley roaring drunk out of a tavern, applied drastic sobering remedies, and delivered a severe lecture to them. "Well, my

God, I never knew you were a damned Methodist!" said Prince resentfully, clutching his head. "Ought to be ashamed of ourselves, indeed! Who asked you to pronounce solemn judgment?"

McDonagh laughed, offering him more black coffee. "You've no idea how pleased I am with myself. I see I'll have to tell you why or you'll never speak to me again!"

"Damn, I reckon you've a right to be," acknowledged Buckley when they had heard why. "Maybe I'll take your lecture a bit to heart after all, McDonagh."

In May rumors began filtering down that action orders were on the way to them, and a number of wild speculations ran like gossip through all the regiments. Britain was going to invade France—no, Denmark, that expedition last year to capture the Danish navy was the first move—no, they were going to Germany, attack Boney from there. Early in June definite news stilled all rumor and set the quartermaster's office working overtime. Just as Morgan prophesied, it was Spain. A large expeditionary force, of which the Twenty-second was a unit, was to embark next month for Portugal, the objective being to deal with Bonaparte's armies across the Spanish border. The force was to be under the command of the new lieutenant general Sir Arthur Wellesley.

Morgan said thoughtfully, "Quite a little name Wellesley made for himself in India, and he commanded that force that took the Danish navy last year, didn't he? I understand he's regarded as one of the more brilliant of the younger tacticians. An Irishman, I believe—"

"Don't say that to any other Irishman," said McDonagh. "I won't take it as an insult because I got over any childish black-white patriotism long ago. His name's not Wellesley, it's Wesley, at least that's the form most of the family use—yes, they're a powerful family in Ireland—he's chief secretary there now, political influence. Maybe he was born there, Mr. Morgan, but don't call him an Irishman."

Morgan smiled and said, "Got over all your patriotism, Mr. McDonagh?"

"Yes, damn it, don't know why I said that. What the hell does it matter?" It did not matter; ridiculous to sound so touchy.

Only, the powerful Wesleys or Wellesleys were a symbol, in a way, of all that lay behind the bloody field of Enniscorthy—another of the wealthy, influential English robber baron families that owed their first gentryhood to land stolen and sharp business made and native Irish exploited and oppressed, in a nation not their own. All right, he had got past any childish patriotism, the unthinking sort, but he could disapprove objectively of that, couldn't he?

In spite of the shortness of time for preparation, the officers and the medical men were allowed brief farewell leaves. McDonagh had ten days in the middle of June and went down to London.

And there, damn it, he found himself mildly in the grip of his obsession again. As if there were yet a loose end to be tied up somehow. He put it firmly out of his mind as irrational; he entertained Gillespie and Rob, and he called on Lauretta. She was sweet and soft to him as always; but there were anxious shadows under her eyes, and she sighed over the war.

"James is entering the army too, you know. Oh, yes, he has succeeded in obtaining a commission quite reasonably, in the Thirty-fourth Dragoons. Of course, his regiment is not yet under orders, but oh, Con, it will be, won't it? I'm so worried. For—for both of you, everyone we know as well, but—it is so dreadful that there have to be wars, so many young men killed—" And she said as he left her, her eyes swimming in tears, "I'll pray for your safety, Con."

He came away and walked restlessly about the city, almost sorry he had still six days to waste here before rejoining the regiment at Portsmouth. He had done all he wanted to do in London, all but the one thing.

"Oh, hell," he said to himself disgustedly on that thought. It was finished. What else did he have to say to Madeleine, for God's sake? But reluctantly he let his feet carry him up to Cavendish Square.

A stout, bald man answered his knock, and looking at him, McDonagh wanted to murder him. *That*, and Madeleine! The next minute he made a silent apology to the fellow. "Oh, nobody that name here. Must've been the tenant afore my wife and me, sir." He looked at McDonagh doubtfully, as if regretting the sir. "I did hear that the owner o' the building had kept this suite for some fancy woman he had in keeping—no offense, if that's not her you meant. But that were four, six months gone, and if 'twas that female, well, you know, they move about quite a bit."

McDonagh thanked him. So that was that, and let it go. What did it matter? He had finished with Madeleine; let her go her own way and live her life as she must.

Because he did, after that, put it behind him, of course, coincidence took a hand.

Larr McKenna was on leave, and McDonagh had arranged to meet him for dinner, his last day but one in London. Larr had an interview at the Admiralty that afternoon and had said carelessly, "I'll meet you in the park across the way—it's fine weather, you can amuse yourself ogling all the nursemaids and governesses airing their charges if I'm late." And half past four found McDonagh strolling aimlessly through St. James's Park doing just that.

He did not have to look twice to identify Madeleine, sitting alone on one of the wooden benches. He knew it was Madeleine with one side glance, by the curve of cheek, the line of shoulder, turned away from him where he stood. He stopped and swore to himself, and then he went over and sat down on the other end of the bench.

She looked around, and sat very still for a moment, and then started to get up. "Please, Madeleine," he said. "This is the most senseless damned thing ever happened to me, but I want to say something else to you, please listen. I—you've left Cavendish Square, I went there. Are you—that is, you've taken another protector, I expect. Where—"

"I don't think that's any of your business, Conal McDonagh," she said softly, remotely. Oh, she looked just the same, and he found he wanted her the same way.

"No, it's not, I'm sorry," he agreed. "Just—will you listen to me a minute, Madeleine? I'm a damned fool, which you don't need telling," and he grinned at her forcedly. "Never thought I was such a sensitive plant! But there it is, I want to say—"

"If it is anything like what you said to me the last time," she said, "you may as well go away now, I don't want to hear it."

"Damn it, listen, will you? I'm sorry—I will not lose my temper with you—don't know why to God—"

And she interrupted suddenly, looking squarely at him, "No, I shouldn't have said that, Conal. What you—what you came to say was honest, and—I was—glad you told me that. I'm sorry, I'll listen." Once again, as when he had met her first, he was aware of a quality in her like a quality in himself, something essentially blunt and honest, resilient and tough.

"It's the damnedest thing," he said, "how for some reason I always do lose my temper, Madeleine, when I'm talking to you. Don't mean to. And I swear to God I won't this time, because—because that's what I wanted to say to you. When I saw you that last time, it happened the same way, I came to apologize and for some senseless reason I lost my temper and lashed out at you, said things I didn't mean. I was sorry afterward. I am sorry, Madeleine. Look, I'm attached to the army now, and I'm about to leave England, for God knows how long. I may not see you again. I just felt—that I'd left you with a bad feeling about me, and I wouldn't want that. I know I'm quick-tempered, I try to hold it in, times, but it gets away from me. I say things I don't really mean. I hope you won't hold it against me, Madeleine, that's all. That you'll—have a better feeling about me."

"Than you deserve?" she said. But she smiled, and it was very briefly her old impish smile; for just a flash her gray eyes danced the way he remembered, and he caught his breath against the urgent desire to reach for her. "I know you do that. Thank you—for apologizing. It's all right, Conal. You can't help being—what you are—any more than I can, or Fleur, or—or anybody else. It's all right."

"Are you—are you well situated?" he asked after a little silence, trying for a light tone.

"You know, I don't think I'll tell you how I am situated," she said coolly. "It's none of your affair. Perhaps I'm just secretive."

"Maybe you don't want to be bothered with me again. I can't say I blame you! I don't want to pry," he said. No, he didn't; he just wanted her, herself. No, he didn't particularly want to know what man had the right to enjoy Madeleine now, whether he was old or young, whether she had found out that there would be, after all, men who could rouse her to passion as well as Con McDonagh. Suddenly, violently he didn't want to know that.

"Oh, hell and damnation," he said aloud to himself. Damn the fact that he wasn't due pay for three months; he'd go up to that exclusive house The Key tonight, with or without Larr, and satiate himself on a woman. That was all that was wrong, it wasn't just Madeleine; it was his need for any female.

"What is it, Conal?" she asked, looking at him.

"Oh, for God's sake," he said roughly, "you don't need telling, do you? I'm just envying your new lover—and wishing I had a fortune to be eligible for your high-priced favors!"

"Do you still want me, Conal? How—how do you want me?" she asked. She leaned forward to him, and there was an expression in her eyes new to him, and her voice shook a little.

He stared at her uncomprehendingly, said, "Well, you ought to know by this time. Never mind, women are women, aren't they?'" He laughed and got up. "I'd better leave you or we'll be insulting each other again. But I'm glad I met you to say this, Madeleine. I—I didn't want to leave such a bad feeling about me with you. I was damned sorry—afterward."

She sat back with a little faint sigh; she looked up at him, and then suddenly she got to her feet and stood close to him. "Conal," she said, "I—I wish you s-safety and good luck. You're going with the army into action, you said."

"Why"—he was somewhat embarrassed, taken aback at the little dramatic gesture—"thank you, Madeleine. Surgeons generally stay behind the lines, you know!" Resisting the impulse to step back from her close, lovely scent and warmth—or a lot nearer—he laughed. "Who knows, maybe I'll win a fortune in plunder and come back wealthy enough to make you an offer as a new lover!"

Madeleine stepped away from him. "Oh, no," she said. "Any man but you, Conal. If you offered me a million pounds. No."

"Oh, that's unkind!" he jested. "I thought you'd decided I was the best you'd tried! Why—"

"I don't want," she said, "to lose my temper either, with you. I think I might—in just a minute. Never mind, Conal, put it down to female foibles! And I must go now. I do wish you good luck always." Swiftly, impulsively, she reached up and dropped a light kiss on his cheek, and took up her reticule, and smiled at him again, and started away down the path. And then she looked back and added, "In case we don't meet again. Thank you, and good-bye, Conal."

He watched her down the treelined path until she passed around a turn from his sight, but she did not look back again.

18

There was a Portuguese outside, not far from the window, singing to a guitar, one of their leisurely subtle-rhythmed melodies. The low liquid notes of the guitar and the soft tenor quavering sentimentally, about true love never fading, made a background of sound and color in McDonagh's mind. Familiar—expectable—it seemed to him that ever since he'd been in this damned place, he'd been trying to cope with dirt, sweat, blood, flesh rotten with gangrene, food rotten with weevils, every variety of insect in existence, all savage, indifference, poor equipment, lack of nearly everything— and all the while, somewhere in the background, thin, melodious guitar music and a wavering tenor.

God, he thought at the back of his mind, God, I hope that leave comes through soon. Two years next month, with no more than two weeklong leaves. Entitled to a month or two—or three—enough to get back to a civilized country for a change.

"For God's sake, give me more light!" he demanded. The orderly beside him silently stepped back to fetch the standing candle sconce nearer. "Look at it, just look at it! Two weeks ago

I could have saved it. This is the kind of thing we put up with."

One of the two visiting naval surgeons across the table said, "Er—yes, much advanced, bad state—why didn't you try cutting lower down a fortnight back, instead of waiting?"

"Before God, because the patient wasn't here, damn it! Trundling in a stretcher somewhere up by Portalegre! For God's sake, hold him down, will you?"—to the orderlies. The patient, a youngish captain of troop, was in a fever, muttering and twisting restlessly. "So don't tell me I'm a bungler, do the amputation with the man in this state. Sooner it's done, the better, and we'll just hope he doesn't die of shock. Maybe you see now what we're up against here."

"Not so good," said James Campbell. "We get some damned hectic times on board during a fight, but at least we get patients fresh, so to speak—as you know," and he smiled. The other surgeon off the *Mars*, newly in at Lisbon with fresh troops, looked blank, and McDonagh laughed grimly.

"That's about it. All right, get that iron ready, let's get it over." He whipped on a tourniquet, stripped back a flap and ligatured the vessels, and took off the leg that needn't have come off two weeks ago, before the gangrene was so far advanced. It was a long while since he'd been so careful to use sutures with or without pressure dressings; he cauterized the whole area, and put on a thick bandage, and let it go. "Don't ask me," he said to Campbell, "why we don't often get blood poisoning when the wound's cauterized. The fellows mulling over experiments in nice quiet city laboratories, they'll find out one day, I expect. Every time I use an adhesive dressing—when I can get them—instead, I lose the patient or have him occupying a bed four times as long. Well, there he is—take him away—is that the last one? Thank God!" He wiped his hands and straightened, feeling at the tired muscles in his back. "Come down with rheumatism next thing if I don't get some leave soon! Well, come up to my quarters, I'll find a drink for you."

The older naval surgeon declined apologetically. "If you could tell me where I might find Mr. Shotworth—we're taking Major Dunning back on the *Mars*, you know, and I believe Mr. Shotworth's been looking after him. I want to find out what treatment he's been having."

"Oh, yes, that chronic knee." McDonagh yawned. They had come out of the operating room into the great square forecourt of the hospital; this had been a civic palace of some sort and instead of doors was opulent with tall archways, floored with tile and stone, and all the stairways were narrow, dark, secretive-twisting spirals going up inside the walls. "The second arch down," said McDonagh, pointing, "you'll find a ward that Shotworth serves. Somebody ought to know where he is, but don't try to ask any of the Portuguese orderlies, because you'll get tangled up in what they think is English. If he isn't in the hospital, he'll be at the *cantina* across Roly-Poly Square—"

"Er—?" said the surgeon.

"Well, that's the nearest the British army gets to O Rocio! Right up the street, you'll see the tile pattern to mark it, wavy black-and-white lines all across, that's Roly-Poly Square. The biggest *cantina*, on the north side, where all the officers go. You'll find him all right." The surgeon went off, looking dubious, and McDonagh took Campbell's arm. "Good to see you again, Jamesy, damned good. They keeping you busy at sea?"

"Oh, tolerable. I must say," said Campbell, "rather be there than here, what I've seen of Lisbon! Do you seriously mean to tell me the army's got no surgeons in the field at all? Where's the fighting now? There looked to be the devil of a lot of work going on, fortifications and breastworks, up the north side—are they expecting siege, or what?"

"Oh, my God, if you want to know all the ins and outs, you'll keep me talking until dawn! Here, this way." Some of the surgeons had quarters on the top floor of the vast building; McDonagh led the way up one of the narrow stairs, half turned to go on talking. "No, I don't mean they've got no surgeons at all. The chief medical officer's been agitating for field hospitals ever since we landed, but the commander—damn his fussy, cold, arrogant British soul—won't hear to it. Too much impedimenta, he says, totally unnecessary! Certainly we've got a fine, convenient place here, as you can see—excellent base hospital—and a death rate, and an amputation rate, fifty percent over what they ought to be because we just don't get the patients soon enough. Take that man I just did. He's been fifty miles up north, one of the British officers with the Portuguese guerrillas, and he

275

took that ball in the leg three weeks ago. If there'd been a field hospital, he'd have had proper treatment at once. As it was, he wasn't fetched in until this morning. He was unlucky, there aren't any surgeons with the Portuguese. With our troops, well, there's a surgeon for about every thousand men, in the field, and some miscellaneous stretcher-bearers competent to tie a bandage. The men with minor wounds, who needn't be sent to the depot hospital, get decent treatment, but God pity the fellows hurt bad enough to be sent back! Emergency treatment, and then a trip of a fortnight or so back here—it's a damned disgrace, in a supposedly civilized army."

"It doesn't sound a very sensible way to look after the wounded," agreed Campbell. "How d'you ever find your way around this rabbit warren?"

"Oh, you get used to it—here we are." As one progressed from the ground to the third floor, the rooms were smaller and smaller, apparently constructed for the more junior clerks; here on the top floor two long stone corridors crossing each other gave onto a number of small square rooms. "I," said McDonagh, "have two to myself, having been one of the earlier residents. Oh, my God," he added as he opened the door. The first room, overfurnished for Portugal with a chair, a chest, and a tall rickety dresser-cupboard, was a good ten degrees hotter than the corridor, principally because Rosara was squatting over a blazing brazier, cooking stew, and had left the window shut. McDonagh shouted reprimands at her, which elicited only a placid smile and a good deal of Portuguese in return, swore resignedly, took Campbell into the bedchamber, shut the door between, and flung up the window. "Not that it helps much, but it gives the illusion of fresh air. God, this climate. If you'll excuse me, I'll take off my shirt. Oh, it's not so bad really except in summer—hot like this twenty-four hours a day."

"I see," said Campbell with a grin, "that you have picked up Portuguese in a double sense."

"Know about four words of it. Oh, Rosara? You don't need to talk with a woman for that," said McDonagh amusedly. "Practically every British officer in Portugal's picked up one of those. Several, in fact, as the army moves around. The poor devils of

276

peasants, they've been chivied hither and yon by the war, you know, and a lot of the women are glad to get a decent living and a little fun out of attaching themselves to a Britisher—or, I suppose, a Frenchman on the other side. They'll cook your meals and keep a fairly respectable place for you and not ask much. Had Rosara nearly a year now, she's a pleasant girl enough, if only she liked open windows a bit better—I expect the natives are used to the heat. Not a bad cook either—d'you know, they've got a dish called *olha-podrida* that's exactly like Yorkshire pudding—" McDonagh broke off and sat down at the head of the bed, leaving the foot to Campbell. "I'm babbling, sorry, sheer tiredness, I expect. I'm due for leave soon. I hope to God it comes through."

"You look as if you could do with it. All the glorious victories in Portugal have been splashed over the news at home, but I must say"—Campbell gestured out the window—"Lisbon doesn't look as if it were worrying about the war. Everybody on holiday and having a marvelous time!"

McDonagh said wryly, "Everywhere but at the base hospital." He got up and rummaged in the wardrobe for a bottle of the thin, sharp Portuguese wine and the single pair of glasses he owned. "I won't apologize for this, we've got used to it."

Campbell tasted it and said it wouldn't be bad if it were iced. "For God's sake, don't talk about ice! Yes, everybody comes to Lisbon for a holiday. The British have taken over the city—did you notice the resemblance to Margate in August? Regimental wives sketching pretty little watercolors in the streets, parties of sporting huntsmen riding out after quail, and even, by God, nursemaids with babies in prams promenading on the seafront. It's the damnedest war *I* ever saw, Jamesy."

Campbell laughed. "This is all a revelation to me, I must say. We've been having a nice quiet cruise in the North Sea, and reading all the news accounts of the major war action here. Somehow I had the impression that the general was running it quite efficiently, and adding to his laurels. Frankly—well, you appall me with your tales of one hospital for the whole army, and that—" He waved helplessly at the window.

McDonagh grunted and strolled over to look out. It was just

after seven, the time on a summer evening when Lisbon ventured out for sociability after the rigors of heat during the day. The street was crowded with people, all wandering leisurely up toward Roly-Poly Square, the central gathering place, and the great majority of the crowd was British. All the officers financially able had fetched their wives out, often families too; a few had married Spanish or Portuguese girls. The wives had acquired servants, carriages, horses, and trunkloads of souvenirs; everyone, men and women, had obeyed the craze for acquiring pets and trailed about accompanied by leashfuls of Italian greyhounds, Maltese terriers, or braces of sporting hounds, and such outré acquisitions besides as billy goats, monkeys, and parrots. The women were fashionably clad in British style; less could be said of the men. No official attention was given to uniform; most uniforms had worn through and replacements were unobtainable, and officers and men alike wore whatever they could buy or their fancies dictated. You could identify the officers by their obstinately clung-to swagger sticks and chevrons of rank sewed on civil dress. "Appalling," said McDonagh. "I could think of less cautious words." He drained his glass, turned, and began to tell Campbell what he thought of Lieutenant General Sir Arthur Wellesley, Baron Durou of Wellesley and Viscount Wellington of Talavera. Root, line, and branch he cursed him, and when he had exhausted his vocabulary, he drew a long breath and added, "Damn, I feel better for that. Now run off and tell the intelligence officer there's a traitor in our midst."

Campbell grinned at him. "You never did take kindly to authority, Con."

"I don't take to that kind of authority," said McDonagh.

"You should see—you must know—what the newspapers are saying about him. Great, brave patriot, true-blue Englishman, just the man to win glorious victories against the upstart Boney."

"Patriot!" said McDonagh. He was silent, and then looked up from refilling his glass. "Damned odd thing, James, your turning up—manner of speaking. I've thought now and then lately about little Nelson—laying him alongside Wellesley, you know. I didn't think such a hell of a lot of Nelson as a man—he thought too high of himself, cocksure, brash, overconfident fellow—"

"Mmm, yes," said Campbell sedately, "we always detest our own qualities in other men."

"No interruptions, please," said McDonagh only half humorlessly. "But anytime I'll take a Nelson—he was at least sincere, if simple—in preference to a Wellesley. He's a coldhearted bastard, James. One time, I remember, I was told that surgeons all grow callous shells to suffering. Don't know about you or any other, but myself, it's not so much that I get used to it—it just makes me so damned furious when there's nothing I can *do* about it. What the fellow meant, I suppose, is that we get used to thinking about patients as—maybe—not quite human anymore, just cases. But damn it, Jamesy, if that is so, at least I'll say that I look at a patient *as* a patient, not first as a major or a captain or the son of a duke—or the son of a costermonger in Whitechapel. ... He came in here last week—" Absently McDonagh turned out the pockets of his coat over the foot of the bed and found a packet of the little Spanish *cigarillos* he'd come to like. "Try one of these, they're quite good—mild. He came in here last week, just casual inspection, you know, happening to be in the neighborhood, as it were. With the chief medical officer. Most of us expected to trail him around—he didn't do more than glance into the wards—and answer damn fool questions. Something was said about the death rate—chief hinting for field hospitals again, I expect—and Wellesley says, 'Oh, well, in the nature o' things, mostly common soldiers, what? No loss as men—scum o' the earth they are—but they serve as cannon food, o' course. Must try to save as much o' my cannon food as possible, but concentrate on the officers—that's the thing—one good officer worth a thousand of those thieving bastards, y'know.' "

"Yes," said Campbell after a pause, "that's the typical British officer, isn't it?"

"No, I wouldn't say so. A lot of the junior officers are damned good men, conscientious, look after their troops. God knows there are enough rough fellows pressed into service—or old regulars—with somewhat elastic morals about mine and thine—and other things. But they've done the fighting, while he looked on—the way generals do. He's a womanizer, I hear—wouldn't doubt it—and a damned tough man in himself, I'd say—I'm not saying he's a coward because he's not—and maybe a brilliant general, I couldn't say about that. But he's cold all the way through, and he's the hell of a lot more interested in the fortunes of Arthur Wellesley than in serving England as a patriot. At the moment the two happen to coincide, that's all."

"He sounds extremely typical to me," said Campbell in his slow Edinburgh drawl. "But I understand the army's been moving around quite lively the last two years here. You mean to say you've been stuck in Lisbon the whole time?"

"Oh, no, I was in the field awhile. We've having a respite now, fortifying the outskirts of the city from Tôrres Vedras down—about the only fighting going on now is by native guerrilla troops. It has been livelier, yes. I was mostly in the field until a year ago—up to just after Coimbra and the Douro fight. Sweat and dust and mud and rotten food and marches of thirty miles a day—dead boredom and dead tiredness—and then a fight and me the only surgeon for forty cases all fetched in at once. Oh, it was war—just say that and have done, as senseless and nasty as war always is. And I'm talking too much about myself. Tell me what's been happening to you, Jamesy."

Oh, it had been war, and he hadn't enjoyed it, but talk about a job to get your teeth in! No, he didn't know a great deal about military tactics, but that first six–eight months, it had looked to him like one confused, hasty fiasco after another. Apparently the War Office agreed, sending for Wellesley and a couple of other commanders to answer for their failures and staggering losses and the ill-conceived Armistice Convention of Cintra.

Of all those battles, McDonagh would remember that at Roliça as the prototype; watching it from baggage camp, he thought to himself that that untrained horde of United Irishmen at Wexford had had better sense of cooperation and organization. Units here and there starting premature attacks alone; men panicking suddenly in the front and retreating through their own lines. And the casualties up as high as fifty percent—a nightmare for the surgeons. The nightmare needn't have been so long or so bad if they'd had all the equipment they needed, but what did you do, just what could you do, when you were issued a couple of yards of uncut cotton ligature instead of the hundred yards of silk you needed, and there was no transport for the wounded except stretcher-bearers on foot, and half the time, God, not even enough fuel obtainable to keep fires going for the cautery irons? They said Wellesley was furious that he'd been given no wagon train; in the end the quartermaster's branch bought farm wagons and donkeys from local natives to transport supplies—all very well, but they didn't buy enough to transport the wounded, oh, no, food and ammunition and the guns were more important! Well, maybe Wellesley was a brilliant general, but if he wanted to get on with his damned patriotic victories, he'd have done better to arrange more care for his wounded. The war was his business, but the medical staff had to cope with the results.

The general's attitude filtered down to the surgeons through the chief medical officer's assistants. Now, two years after the British army had landed in Portugal, the newspapers in England might be lauding Viscount Wellington as a national hero, but there wasn't a surgeon or physician with the army who did not feel to be having a bitter personal feud with him. He was always reluctant to increase in any way what he called the impedimenta accompanying troops, and God knew there was enough of it. Officers took along their wives, in carriages or on horseback, and leashes of hounds for fox hunting when they bivouacked, and native servants. The common soldiers soon collected a ragtag of Portuguese women camp followers, and there were a number of regular soldiers' wives too. But my God, for Wellesley to point bitterly at all that and say testily they couldn't burden themselves with field hospital equipment in addition—! First things came first. After a battle, then at least one group of men saw what the surgeons were talking about: the wounded.

But that never changed, from Roliça to Vimeiro to Tôrres Vedras, to La Coruña, to the river Douro. And in between the battles the surgeons had to turn to the aid of the handful of physicians with the troops in the field, to cope with the Guadiana fever and dysentery and a hundred lesser ills that beset men in a difficult and unfamiliar climate.

After Coimbra, when they crossed the Douro—more by luck than good management—and defeated Soult, McDonagh was violently, angrily relieved to be sent back to the medical depot in Lisbon. There, and how ironic that was, was this fine, large, airy, admirably equipped hospital, a full staff of physicians and surgeons. All that was humanly possible they could do for the casualties fetched in—and most of those were still brought on foot by bearers, maybe on the way a week or two, so that wounds comparatively slight, or repairable to a high degree at the moment of occurrence, were festering and poisoned when the hospital surgeons first got to them. And the officers' wives following the troops in their private coaches!

Oh, let England applaud Wellesley, who could by one decisive order have changed that.

But at least at the depot hospital McDonagh felt he was accomplishing something constructive. Or as constructive as possible in the middle of such meaningless violence as this war.

Lieutenant Sutherland . . . McDonagh passionately resented losing a patient, but he resented Lieutenant Sutherland doubly. He had a grievance on fate he'd be long forgiving, for Sutherland. . . .

The lieutenant was with Stewart's Light Infantry, one of the few regiments that pursued the French retreat at Douro. There had been some last-minute skirmishes, hand-to-hand fighting in that, and Sutherland had evidently run across one Frenchman with some fight still in him and a liking for the knife. When Sutherland was fetched in, he had lost some blood; they weren't mortal wounds, but nasty—both cheeks viciously crisscrossed with deep gashes. Long ago the few surgeons in the field had forgotten about the tidy official intentions of regimental medical staffs; in the shambles of cleaning up after a battle, the surgeons from rearguard regiments which had suffered light casualties went to the aid of those with heavily decimated troops. McDonagh happened to get Lieutenant Sutherland, and did a rough-and-ready job of stitching up his face cuts.

"Will it leave scars?" Sutherland kept asking anxiously. "Please try to fix it so I won't be scarred—will it be bad?"

"Now, you're not a vain young lady, lieutenant—scars of honor to show, you know! It won't be so bad, no." It wouldn't have been but for the damned thick cotton sutures. Now that was a place adhesive dressings were really useful; if he'd had those, even such deep gashes would have healed clear and smooth, only faint lines left. As it was, the heavy sutures left great puckered marks; the wounds healed well, but not prettily. Sutherland convalesced in camp, and McDonagh had ample opportunity to observe his progress, but afterward the proper regimental surgeon took over, and McDonagh didn't give much thought to Sutherland; there'd been so many more difficult and dangerous injuries.

He had just received his transfer, from official attachment to the Twenty-second to the great depot hospital, when the Eighty-eighth surgeon wandered into his section and asked apologetically if he'd mind stepping over to talk to Sutherland. "I believe you were the one sewed him up? ... Yes. Well, he's fearfully cut up about being left with scars, seems to think if you hadn't been in a hurry—"

"Damn it," said McDonagh, "nobody could have brought it out different, with this damned thick cotton stuff."

"Oh, I know, but if you'd just explain to him—he won't listen to me." McDonagh went to see Sutherland and talked to him about processes of healing and the lack of proper equipment.

"Look, Lieutenant, I can understand how you feel about it, and it's a damned shame, but just one of those things. You mustn't be too sensitive, the scars aren't that bad."

"Oh, my God," said Sutherland wretchedly, "it isn't me, Mr. McDonagh. I wouldn't care much about it. It's—it's on account of Sophia—my wife. Home in England. She—she's awfully sensitive, she just can't bear—any blemish like this. I've seen her shrink away from—from people—scarred not half so bad. It was her one fear when I came out, that I'd be—I can't go home to Sophia like this—"

McDonagh said soothing things to him. Privately he thought the young lady would be the better to have her foolish foibles squelched, and that the lieutenant was making mountains out of molehills. But how much use his reassurance was, he found out two months later, when Sutherland was brought into the hospital, an attempted suicide. They never, thought McDonagh, hunting for the slippery little ball between the man's exposed

283

ribs, knew certainly where the heart was. Damned funny when you thought about it, a soldier—couldn't even kill himself, how could he aim right at an enemy?

And Sutherland burst into tears at finding himself alive, with McDonagh bending over him and telling him he was a damned fool, but not enough of one to make a job of it, that he'd be all right. "*Not* all right—don't want to be! I can't go home—to Sophia—like this—"

"Well, damn," said McDonagh thoughtfully to himself. He went away and talked to Shotworth and Tebbs, who served that ward with him. He wrote to Sutherland's colonel and got grudging permission to keep him in hospital. And with some excitement and trepidation he started some skin grafts on the scars. It was a more difficult job than little Asenath Nobbs had presented; the scars were healed and had to be scraped raw again, deep enough to erase the suture marks. But Sutherland was eagerly cooperative and stoic, and he was young, of strong constitution, and healed quickly. The experiment succeeded beyond McDonagh's wildest expectations, and he came in for some flattering praise from the other surgeons, who couldn't quite believe it. Neither could McDonagh; he'd tried quite large areas at once, and every one took beautifully: it was something like a miracle. There were faint lines, but not too noticeable, and all the ugly puckering was gone. Oh, he was pleased with Sutherland, almost as pleased as the lieutenant was with himself! He showed off his prime patient all over Lisbon and wrote excited boasting letters to Gillespie and Matt.

Sutherland rejoined his regiment, which was bivouacked near Badajoz, on the severe representations of his colonel; there was sporadic effort to discourage unnecessary visits to Lisbon on the excuse of needed medical attention, and although he was due for long leave shortly, he was ordered back to camp for the interim. McDonagh saw him off, feeling the obscure pride of the creative artist who has breathed life into clay. Sutherland, in some odd way, reconciled him—almost—to the gangrenous limbs he couldn't save, the ill-fed, feverish men whose weakened constitutions made them victims to relatively minor wounds.

In Christmas week, a month later, a sergeant of the Eighty-eighth came in with a broken kneecap from a mule kick, and McDonagh asked him casually about Sutherland—if the truth were told, ready to do a little more boasting. "Oh, Lieutenant Sutherland, yes, I knowed him, sir. The pore young fella, we lorst him matter o' a fortnight back—he were detailed to go out with some o' these here native gorillas, as they call 'em, and ran into the French up the river. Took a ball in the spine, sir. A pity it was, we was all sorry—a very good young orfcer he was."

It would be a long time before McDonagh forgave destiny for Sutherland. But nothing about a war made much sense anyway.

He was fairly comfortable here in his hospital quarters, more so than the staff members sent here later, when quarters were no longer available in the building. They had made what arrangements they could in town, in private houses; a few of them had come by the inevitable Portuguese women that way.

It was hard to say, McDonagh reflected humorously, whether those women were taken on primarily as servants or mistresses. They were useful as both, and in his own case, he reckoned, he appreciated Rosara more as the former than the latter. Probably the other way around with the officers, who had not as many tiresome domestic details to think of. There was no commissary for feeding the staff communally at the hospital, and they had to find themselves, whether they lived in or out. Rosara, able to bargain at the local markets, trotted out cheerfully with the handful of coins McDonagh gave her every few days and produced relatively appetizing meals on her brazier. She also made up the bed, dusted the few sticks of furniture, and swept the floor occasionally when she thought of it. If he wanted to make love to her, she came to him with the same impersonal placidity with which she mixed up a stew or wielded a broom, and that was very much the same way he felt about it himself.

He hadn't, even if it had been a habit with him, either the time or the inclination to think much about himself here these days. For two years he'd been working too hard to have thought to spare for yesterday or tomorrow; the immediate job to get through today was enough, and most days he went to bed exhausted and slept soundly

But in the last few months the spate of casualties had slackened off, with most of the army concentrated in or about Lisbon. The officers said wisely that old Douro—the natives' name for Wellesley—was playing for time, getting all these heavy fortifications up during the lull in action; for any concerted major attack it was vitally important to continue to hold Lisbon, for supply to reach them by sea. The only fighting going on now, as McDonagh told Campbell, was by native volunteer troops in guerrilla units, here and in Spain. Some of those had British officers with them, and most of the casualties coming in now were those men. Even if anyone had been interested in trying much, it was difficult to get the Portuguese into hospital; they distrusted the foreigners' strange methods of treatment, and died or recovered by their own medical customs.

With more occasional time to think and feel personally, McDonagh began to realize how very tired he was of this hand-to-mouth existence in which the only real occupation was grim work. His only two leaves from duty had not been long enough to get away from Lisbon, and so far from enjoying them, he had found himself eager to get back to routine where he had something to do at least. God, if he could have enough leave to get back to England for a month or six weeks, to a civilized place where there were clean, fresh food, paved streets, theaters, shops, pretty women, people talking about something besides gangrene and festering pus and amputations! He would be due for long leave in June, but whether he'd get it was another question.

It had been a welcome break in the monotony to look up from that patient as the bearers brought him in and see Campbell there, just as surprised to see him. The *Mars* was to be in harbor only two days, but while she was in, he and Campbell saw a good deal of one another; he showed Campbell around Lisbon a bit, and they caught each other up on their personal news. Any small thing served to lighten the drab routine of this place; he felt a trifle more his old self for seeing Campbell again, not an automaton set to mechanical work as he seemed to have been for so many months.

He went down to the front to see Campbell off the morning

the *Mars* sailed. "Good luck with your leave, Con. I've some time coming up too, not enough to get home, but London anyway, July or August. Maybe we'll meet."

"Nothing I'd like better, but don't count on it! I'm not really due for leave until June, and it may be another couple of months before it comes through. You know how government departments are—like God, they move in mysterious ways."

"How true, how true," said Campbell. "Well, anyway, look after yourself, Con. One thing"—and he grinned—"you're apparently cured of the drink permanently. If anything looks guaranteed to drive a man to drunkenness, it's what you're coping with here! Rather you than me."

McDonagh agreed gloomily, shaking hands with him, and since for the moment nothing was demanding his attention at the hospital, stayed to watch the *Mars* out, wishing he were on her.

When he got back to the hospital, he went through his wards, changed a few dressings, and dropped off an armful of soiled dressings at the doorway of the vast kitchen, for the laundresses. For perhaps the hundredth time he demanded the head laundress and, through the medium of the one Portuguese orderly who had grasped more English than *yes, no,* and *latrine,* explained that the cloth must be washed thoroughly, no stains left, washed with soap, not just pulled through river water. She nodded and smiled cheerfully. But yes, it should be done as he directed! And day after tomorrow, thought McDonagh, he'd get them back, all neatly folded, with dried pus and dark bloodstains still on them here and there. Probably not important; any medical authority knew that laudable pus aided healing, but the damn things stank abominably.

He went up to the great entry hall to see if there were any new arrivals. There was one, just brought in evidently, still lying on a stretcher. A private soldier was talking to one of the recording clerks on duty, who glanced round at McDonagh with relief.

"Just about to call one o' you, sir. I don't rightly know if this ought to go in with surgical or medical records, sir."

"What is it?"

"It's stones in the bladder," said the soldier insistently. "That's what it is, for sure. Me brother had just the same kind o' pain, an' that's what the doctor said it were. He's had it now couple o' days, come on suddenlike, *which*, while I'm bound ter say *wasn't* like me brother's, well, the same *sort* o' pain it seems ter be—kind o' sharp and sudden, right in the guts, lowdown, you know—an' I says ter him, Sir, I says, it's stones in the bladder, just like me brother, see. Nor he wouldn't come to the hospital right off—be all right, he says, just indigesting like, he says, but 's morning he were orful bad, as you can see, and I took it on meself to bring him, me bein' his batman, see—acause it *is* stones in the bladder, and one o' the bone sawers can reach up and fetch 'em out, way they did with me brother—and he got over it just fine and never a sick day since."

"Well," said McDonagh, "if it is, he belongs in surgical, Matcham. But let's have a look at him first—not that I'm disregarding your diagnosis"—with a grin at the soldier—"but a second opinion's always a good idea, you know!" He moved over to the stretcher and squatted down for a better look at the man twisting in restless pain there.

It was James FitzEustace, and he looked up at McDonagh with glazed, unrecognizing eyes.

19

McDonagh straightened. He said to the clerk absently, "Get some bearers and send him up to the fourth ward." Without another word he turned and went up there himself. It was one of the smaller wards, on the second floor; when he came in, he looked about to see who might be available. Tebbs was exchanging some cheerful talk with a convalescent patient; McDonagh jerked his head at him, and Tebbs sauntered over.

"What is it? Either a feast or a famine here, eh? Too much work or not enough. Something new in?" He was an ugly, good-humored young man with wiry red hair: a very good surgeon.

"Well, there is," said McDonagh, "and since you're yearning for work, I'll hand it on to you. Following me up—here it is now," as the bearers came in with the stretcher.

"You sickening for something? You're the glutton for work around here."

McDonagh said nothing, but went down to the bearers. "Any empty bed—that'll do, that's all." He stood with Tebbs looking down at FitzEustace. . . . Hadn't known the man was in Portugal. No reason he should have, but—and FitzEustace couldn't have been in Lisbon long, he'd have seen him somewhere. Never mind that, no matter.

"Oh, God, oh, Christ," whimpered FitzEustace, twisting on the bed, clutching himself; he was white and sweating with pain. They looked at him, and at each other.

"Well, better give him something to settle him down anyway," said Tebbs, and went off to the pharmacy room. McDonagh watched FitzEustace tossing and tensing in evident agony. Tebbs came back with a glass and said, "Stiffish dose, but I'd say he can do with it." Between them they supported FitzEustace to get the laudanum down. It was indeed a heavy dose; within five minutes his body began to relax; he drew several long breaths and lay still, breathing regularly.

McDonagh drew Tebbs to the foot of the bed. "I don't want him as a patient, I can't take him. Never mind why—personal reasons. I'll stand alongside and watch, I'll consult with you, but he's all your responsibility."

Tebbs looked at him with mild curiosity, speculation. "All right. I won't pry, except to ask maybe if you're afraid you'll cure him—or kill him. Personal reasons—ha! Love or hate, eh?"

McDonagh laughed shortly. "My God, I don't know if I could tell you." Hate? He didn't hate FitzEustace; the man was too much of a nonentity to warrant that strong an emotion. Nor was it, certainly, anything so forthright and simple as that he feared the temptation to mistreat the man as a patient, even to murder him. Just because he was Lauretta's husband. That was simply silly, a thing out of bad melodrama. Medical men had too long and rigorous training at—and you might say an instinct for, or they wouldn't be medical men—fighting on the side of life, to turn to death easily. The name of John Gunther slid into his mind, and he smiled slightly, ruefully. He said, "I don't want to be responsible." That came closest to his feeling. For if FitzEustace died, if—

He took himself up sharply. If knowledge, training, experience could do anything at all, FitzEustace wasn't going to die.

Tebbs stepped back to the bedside, and McDonagh followed him. The patient was lying easier, though the sweat of pain was still on his face. "Better," he gasped, "thanks." The laudanum was taking hold of his mind as well as his body; but his hazed eyes focused on McDonagh with difficulty, and he smiled weakly in recognition.

Tebbs laid his hand gently on the abdomen. "Tell me where now. . . . Here—a bit lower down?—ah. Yes." FitzEustace had gasped and tensed again as weight came on the pain. "You lie quiet awhile. Here, we'll get you more comfortable, get your breeches and shirt off." FitzEustace was too weak, between the pain and the laudanum, to help them much, even to lift himself. They stripped him to his smallclothes, leaving him uncovered in this heat, and moved a few beds away.

"What d'you think?" asked McDonagh. "Looks like ileus."

"I'm afraid that's an academic question," said Tebbs. "Would you laugh if I said, Something wrong inside, and left it at that? Ileus, yes. But we just don't know much about that, do we? Guess—try. There's a place there, you saw—right side, down lowish—feels hard, queer. If it was in a little different position, I'd say hernia or intestinal obstruction. Pity it isn't. That I could do something with. Go up through the anus and cut a piece out o' the gut. But it's not that, of course. Being where it is, we say ileus, which means—well, what?"

"Yes, I know. Seen much of it? What d'you think's best?"

"Well, you must've seen some cases, too."

McDonagh grunted. " 'In the month of November 1711,' " he quoted drearily, " 'as I was dissecting the body of a malefactor in the public theater at Altdorf—' Oh, yes. First time anybody suggested any reason for the symptoms, when Heister looked at that cadaver. Not sure that's what it is. What's called an impasse. You can't ask a cadaver, Do you recall ever feeling a severe pain about *here*? And you can't cut open the patient with the symptoms to have a look."

" 'The vermiform process of the cecum,' " Tebbs went on dreamily with the classic quotation, " 'preternaturally black, adhering closer to the peritoneum than usual.' Interesting to see. Yes. Well, the operative point is that at least the malefactor didn't die of that—obviously it had happened years before the German was dissecting him. If that's anything at all to do with what we call ileus and let it go at that. I've seen a few cases back in London Hospital. A woman, just the same as that"—he jerked his head at the patient—"rigid spot in lower right abdomen, severe pain, nausea, so on. And a young man, not long after. Both of 'em recovered after a bit and seemed perfectly normal."

"Mmm. Saw one myself, at Queens'. Woman, too. Died. What'd you do for it?"

"What did you? Put 'em to bed and observe progress, with judicious doses of opium to keep the pain down, purgations and clysters."

"Yes. The chief at Queens' tried hot fomentations."

"Ah," said Tebbs thoughtfully. "I don't know—it sounds and feels, somehow, like an inflammation of some sort—in which case, might be better to use iced pads. You think? Held continually on the area?"

"That," said McDonagh sarcastically, "is the most academic idea you've had yet. Ice. In Lisbon, at the end of May."

"Hell and perdition!" said Tebbs. "I'd like to *know*, that's all. I sometimes think that's the real reason a man wants to be a surgeon—insatiable curiosity. I hate these things we don't know much about."

They stood there in silence a little, both brooding. "Do you suppose one day we'll be able to cut open the abdomen on a living patient? If we ever find something to send a patient unconscious—deep enough not to feel the pain—God," said McDonagh violently, "if we ever can! Not only this kind of case, but all sorts of things we just have to stand and look at now."

"Yes. Some things we can do and some not. Impossible shock to the patient, cutting there—just one of the things out of our range. If we ever can, you and I'll never see it. Well," said Tebbs, looking back at the patient, "ice, no, not any more than in hell. But cold springwater—maybe, cloths wrung out and held on? Couldn't do any harm, anyway. We'll hold off on a purgative awhile."

"It's your decision—we can try."

When the ward orderlies commenced to fetch in the dinners for the dozen convalescents, and McDonagh realized what the hour was and that he was hungry, not much change was visible in the patient. Shotworth had come in in the middle of the afternoon, looked with mild curiosity, observed the cold cloth pads, and said, "Whose idea is that, in heaven's name? Oh, I don't interfere with another man's case, but you young fellows with your new ideas!—half of 'em useful, I daresay, but t'other half mad! Much better stick to the classic treatment. I've had some occasional success with a strong tobacco clyster—just mention it."

As soon as the first dose of laudanum had worn off, the patient commenced to have pain again; when it was safe, they gave him a small dose of opium undiluted; that was standard treatment, and he responded somewhat better than to the laudanum. However, he appeared to be raising a slight fever.

"I'm going to be up all night with this," said Tebbs, "and maybe tomorrow night too—can't trust him to the orderlies. I hope you'd like to spell me, or stay for company at least."

"I'll stay," said McDonagh. "No better, no worse, except for the fever, but that's expectable, of course."

"Yes. I think we may as well leave him while we can and have a meal." Tebbs looked down at the patient thoughtfully. Fitz-Eustace was uneasily succumbing to the opium, only partially conscious now, turning weakly and restlessly from side to side. "He'll be coming out of that by eight o'clock or so, and then we'll try a purgative."

They separated for their respective quarters; McDonagh climbed tiredly up to the top floor of the building. All his mind had been concentrated on the physical aspects of the case; his emotional temperature at dealing with Lauretta's husband he had relegated to the background, and he was unprepared for the wave of feeling that struck him as he opened the door on the first of his two rooms.

Rosara was kneeling before the brazier; she looked up and said something placid in her own tongue, went to fetch a plate and spoon from the dresser, wiped both perfunctorily on the hem of her gown. The room was stifling. He saw it suddenly as Lauretta might see it, or anyone of civilized sensitivity—as, by God, he should have seen it himself a year ago—and disgust and a kind of impersonal astonishment at himself took possession of him. The squalid, dirty, bare room; the nameless mess she had been cooking—the malodorous stale air in this stuffy little place—and this woman—how in God's name had he withstood it, living like an animal? Always considered himself medium fastidious, he had, too. The woman, how could he—she was dirty, she was stupid, it had been a long time since she was young. He must have been mad, putting up with this, saying it wasn't bad—casual crude jests with Campbell about the practicality of combining housekeeper and mistress! God—he leaned on the door, and in his mind he saw Lauretta's sunny little London parlor, and Lauretta smiling at him, so neat and fresh and smelling faintly of rose sachet.

He shook his head blindly at this stoutening, dirty slattern and turned away. She shrugged indifferently and commenced to eat the dish herself. McDonagh escaped down the stairs, still wondering angrily at himself, and went up to the biggest *cantina* across Roly-Poly Square. Thin liquid notes of a guitar from one corner, friendly loud talk among a crowd of young officers. There were a few men he knew sitting about, but he only nodded at them and chose a table alone, ordered a meal at random, a bottle of the thin wine.

As he sat eating, not wanting the food now, hunger dead in him for the sudden self-disgust, a small party of men came in and sat down not far off; the talk died momentarily, and glances went that way—curious, respectful, admiring, interested, smiling. The commanding general and a few of his staff. McDonagh looked at Lieutenant General Sir Arthur Wellesley, and a curious, confused connotation of thoughts drifted through his mind, below the surface that was concentrated on himself, and Fitz-Eustace, and Lauretta.

Not a weakling, no. Easier to see through if he were. He was a tall, spare man, looked about forty but might be older, great beak of nose, a careless dresser—a rather high, sharp voice with the note of arrogant authority in it. His eyes followed the Portuguese girl who served them, and McDonagh thought coldly that if he were a woman, he'd as soon be ogled by a snake; the eyes had the same lidless, fixed look. . . . Wellesley, chief secretary for Ireland by political influence. The Wellesleys—Wesleys—arrogant gentry living lavish off tenant farms and people exploited and property stolen, in a land not their own. *The Saxon lion's paw.* Wellesley, his high, neighing laugh echoing in the hospital corridor: *Scum o' the earth they are.* Damn Amison, damn him, wouldn't marry Lauretta to any but a gentleman with a fine high-sounding English name ... *Life's anguish is more than I can dree, since ...*

He drained his glass and left half his meal, went out of that place quickly and back up the street to the hospital. He passed two Hessian troopers in worn, stained, faded scarlet coats, and he'd been two and a half years with the British army, but he still felt all his muscles tense as he passed there close to them.

FitzEustace went into a high fever that night. They withheld any opium after eight o'clock and gave him a purgative of calomel. Two hours later he was in agony, screaming with pain, and they gave him more opium. At two in the morning the fever rose so high that Tebbs bled him. In the humid, fetid atmosphere of the summer night, in the ward of ill men, they worked over him, trying everything on him old and new. The fever continued to go up; they wrapped him in blankets to induce a high enough sweat to break it. They gave him another purgative and administered a tobacco enema. Toward dawn he seemed to fall into a coma, and they left him in the care of the steadiest orderly to snatch a little sleep and visit other patients, only to be called back in midmorning to find him moaning with pain again.

"Oh, *how* I hate these things we don't know about!" said Tebbs. They went on going through the motions of effort, as McDonagh said wryly, trying everything all over again, the standard treatments out of the textbooks, all that day. In the middle of the evening the patient, still in high fever, full of opium, wasted from purging and exhausted with pain, fell into a deep coma, and at three in the morning he died.

"Well, so that's that," said Tebbs, straightening with a long breath. He looked at McDonagh. "Didn't do much good for you to turn him over to a really competent surgeon, I must say.

Damn, I hate to be beaten like this. . . . Whatever your personal reasons, McDonagh, you don't look much cut up about it."

"I didn't give a damn about him personally," said McDonagh wearily.

"Um. Well, now that the stable door is firmly shut and locked, I'd like to have a look inside—what d'you think?"

McDonagh said, "I suppose we can. He'll have to be buried here, his family's in England. There wouldn't be any fuss raised." And then he sat down on the bedside stool and laughed. "Oh, God, that's funny, that's very damned funny! He disapproved so of it, 'Interfering with the Creator's handiwork, Mr. McDonagh, disgraceful, wanton!' What's that standard line from all the best romantic novels—*Little did I wot*—"

"Here," said Tebbs, "you going hysterical on me?"

"No, I'm all right. Only suddenly seemed so damned funny." FitzEustace, looking outraged at him over the dinner table. "All right," he said abruptly, "he was your patient, you report to his commanding officer, it's the Thirty-fourth Dragoons, far as I know. May have just come into Lisbon, I had no idea he was here, I know that. I don't suppose you'll have trouble getting permission for an autopsy, we'd better do it this morning." In summer in Portugal the sooner a corpse was underground, the better.

There was a little difficulty about locating the commanding officer—the regiment had landed at Lisbon only a fortnight before—and it was afternoon before they could do the autopsy. "Well, there you are," said Tebbs sadly, looking at a mass of inflamed, ruptured tissue. "Why should it be so, and what else ought to be done about it?"

"You tell me," said McDonagh. He prodded at it thoughtfully. "If it ever *is* possible to do an abdominal incision—well, I've cut out the hell of a lot bigger pieces of gut and had the patient recover well. I suppose you could just cut this out. It doesn't seem to have any particular function."

"That's reaching into the future a long way. Well, I suppose we'd better fasten him up nice and tidy, the regimental commander has to see him before the funeral—regulations. When is it?"

"Four o'clock, the coffin should be here soon." McDonagh handed him the sutures. "I'm attending. Not that I enjoy funerals, but—You have any idea how soon official notification is sent out? I mean, does it have to go through the War Office or direct from the regimental commander?"

"War Office, I should think, why?"

McDonagh looked down at FitzEustace, naked and shrunken and looking as if he'd never been alive, roughly sewed up the middle with coarse stitches, already discoloring with beginning corruption. "I'll have—to write," he said dully. "His wife—I must write Lauretta. Hate like hell to—get in with the news first, and yet, well, maybe it'd come better from me at that."

"Oh, I see," said Tebbs interestedly. He looked from the corpse to McDonagh. "Not exactly a formidable rival, or was he?"

McDonagh was silent, and then he said, "He had tenant land, and a house in Queen Square, and a respected English name. Maybe that's the only epitaph he needs—from me anyway. You hand him over to the coffin merchant, will you? I need a drink."

That was a difficult letter to write; he'd never been very good at setting down what he felt in writing. The first draft he wrote, he found he was detailing the progress of the disease and the various treatments tried, as if he were describing it for a medical journal. He tore that up—impossible, mad, to inflict all that on her, and besides, it sounded rather as if he meant to imply defense of himself. Equally it was impossible to get any sincerity into expressions of sorrow and sympathy. "Oh, hell!" he said, tearing up the second draft. Maybe because of his profession or just because he was Conal McDonagh, all the conventional attitudes to death and funerals (like the conventions as they concerned a good many other things) always irritated, bewildered, and amused him. Both damned sentimental and damned silly. He didn't know and he didn't care whether FitzEustace (or anyone else) had a thing called a soul, to be wafted away to some vague place for reward or punishment—it seemed a farfetched idea—but you didn't enter on philosophical discussion about souls to bereaved widows either. And of all things he was bad at doing, at the top of the list came the social duty of parroting conventional clichés about anything.

In the end, he produced a rather wooden letter, he thought, telling her the bare facts, that the man had had a peaceful death (quite truthfully, since he'd been unconscious for several hours before), and describing the regimental funeral and the small cemetery west in the city. He added, with some trouble over the right words, all the usual correct phrases of sympathy and, as an afterthought, that he might be on leave in England sometime this year and would, of course, call on her.

After he'd sent the letter, it seemed to be an accomplished fact for the first time, and he sat down and thought about it, with a strange, almost reluctant excitement gradually filling his mind. FitzEustace was dead; Lauretta was a widow. Could it ever be possible, *was* it possible, that Con McDonagh was to have his heart's desire? It was a supersitious fear in him, dangerous even to think about it, to bring it out in the open and look at it. Pretend the possibility wasn't there, as if it were a shy forest beast he tried to lure to him, careful not to frighten it away. And that was ridiculous, for him, who tended to drag things ruthlessly into the light of day for examination, but the way he felt.

She would have had his letter sometime at the end of June, and in June he applied formally for his long-due leave. He heard nothing about that at all. The lull in military action continued; Lisbon sweltered through the summer and suffered such a plague of dysentery that the surgeons were pressed into service alongside the physicians in the medical wards.

In July, late, McDonagh had a letter from Lauretta. It was a short letter, and he read it over and over, reading so much into it that was not there. In conventional, rather prim little phrases she thanked him for his letter, which had reached her before the official notice—*I cannot tell you how greatly I appreciate that it was so, Conal, for that cold official communication seemed so very soulless.* She was greatly indebted to him for telling her of the services and describing the place where her dear husband was laid, and when next he should be in England, she would, of course, look forward to seeing him and hearing of that melancholy occasion in more detail. She was well, yes, though this sad news had depleted her for some while, as he could understand. She was pleased to be able to tell him that her dear son improved much in health, although it was sorrowful to reflect how happy his dear father would have been to know that, how proud of him, and that the dear child would lack a father's affection. *And thank you again, Conal, your letter has been a little comfort to me, that all possible remedies were tried and that at least he had a peaceful passing.*

Oh, a conventional letter, but—but—He waited and fretted in an agony of impatience to hear about his leave. Seeing her, he could know better. Of course, to approach her so soon was—but damn it, there'd be so little time! Perhaps only a month in England, less, with the time wasted going and returning. (Don't think or plan about it: dangerous.) Offend her? She *was* conventional, his little darling, couldn't help it with her sort of upbringing. But if he could know for certain—even though of course, she'd want to wait—Oh, God, was it possible to think that Con McDonagh might one day have his heart's desire?

That time of waiting, in the intolerable, continual, humid heat, tried him hard both physically and mentally. Sickness was rife, from rotten food and bad water, and the wards overflowing. There was enough for all the medical staff to do, and he should have been able to sleep sound when he got to his quarters, but he lay awake in the heat thinking of Lauretta, of London again, of going to see Lauretta. Of perhaps—perhaps . . .

He lay alone, for that one brief shocking revelation of the squalor to which he had descended had been enough; he had sent the Portuguese woman packing, and she had gone as indifferently as she had come. He waited out this time here as he might spend an interim in the impersonal hired room of some tavern, impatient to have the time done, to get on to the next important part of his life.

That summer was a foretaste of hell as far as the heat went; he thought of his months in that little cell at the Portsmouth naval hospital—he had thought summer in England hot! Like everyone else, he sluiced off dust and sweat three times a day, a useless procedure, and drank the sweet half-chilled wine punch the

Portuguese were fond of, which was only an aggravation to thirst, and grew more irritable every day.

In the first week of September he had a genuine case of bladder stones, and the patient, weakened by dysentery, had a difficult convalescence. For several nights McDonagh, not so much worried for the patient as unable to sleep and restlessly making occupation for himself, went up to the ward at midnight to supervise the changing of dressings on the suppurating wound. Tebbs was on night duty that week, and they would make a little pretense at enlivening the monotonous routine by going out to the balcony at the ward end, drinking a glass of the unsatisfactory punch together.

"Heard anything about your leave yet?"

"Is there such a thing?" returned McDonagh gloomily.

"God, a good rain would break this for a bit anyway. But another month should see the end of it for this year."

"That's a cheerful thought. Sounds like eternity right now."

"I know. About this time it's really got to you, you can't sleep, appetite's off, everything at odds. God's practice effort at hell, this must've been."

McDonagh agreed dispiritedly. When he left the ward, he was just as tired as he'd been all these last weeks, but he knew he wouldn't sleep; the night was breathless, as if this part of the world were held in suspension, in a vacuum. He went out of the building and walked around it to the main grounds or what passed for them in Portuguese construction: a strip of earth walled in, overlooked by the iron-balustraded balconies above, giving onto the medical wards. There was an illusion of air a little fresher, even moving, out of doors. A few lights showed still from the ground-floor windows, but most of the hospital was dark. A gibbous moon was just rising in a blandly clear sky. McDonagh leaned against the wall and lit a cigarillo; his mind was blank with exhaustion and yet past the point of rest.

Damned country, he thought tiredly. Dirt, heat, sweat, insects, illness—and always slow guitar music in the background ... But that music wasn't a guitar. A man singing, somewhere— up there, one of the top windows this side of the building—

It was like an auditory illusion, nothing that could be real, a thing only he was hearing. Thought just now, he had, that it felt as if time were suspended, breathless, here, so all time could blend, perhaps, and he was hearing out of the past something that had once been uttered and since had drifted lonely in time. He thought he could place it as coming from one of these windows, but that was illusion, too—must be. A single voice, lifting clear in the distance somewhere, on unheard words, and a silence, and then something very improbable, which was most definitely an illusion—for this was Lisbon, a stifling, sweltering Portuguese night, and it was the current year of 1810, a modern time.

Not a guitar. The even thinner, but sweeter and sharper, notes of a hand harp, and a man's voice rising above that. A very clear, firm, resonant tenor—and the melody was one of unresolved minors, instead of the saccharine sentimentalities of this foreign music—and the man was singing in Gaelic.

> *If I might have my heart's desire, it would be*
> *that I were now in Ireland,*
> *Looking up at the Mourne Mountains as they bend*
> *like mothers down to the sea by Rosstrevor,*
> *Or if I might stand looking out over the Lough*
> *of Belfast,*
> *With a million glancing lights on its little waves,*
> *happiness would be in me,*
> *That I might lie again with my darling, the*
> *pulse of my heart.*
> *If my heart's desire were granted me, I would be*
> *going about the village of Mooncoin on*
> *the Suir,*
> *Or drinking in a good tavern by Rosslare in the*
> *county of Wexford—*
> *In the north or the south of Ireland, little*
> *difference to the lone keening in my heart*
> *These many long nights and days, for the hunger*
> *of my heart's desire,*
> *That I might lie again with my darling, the*
> *pulse of my heart.*

The last slow notes faded out almost in a whisper, repeated: *gille mo croidhe, gille mo croidhe.* As if they indeed had come a long way in time to reach this moment, as if time had called them back to their proper place. For they did not belong to this year of 1810, this modern time. That might have been one of the old chieftains' bards, three, four, five centuries back, the kind of music those men had been famous for.

He did not quite believe that it was real, that he had heard it. Then his cigarillo burned his fingers, and he dropped it. Illusion, yes—was it? Very tired, so tired, his mind playing tricks, maybe.

Quite suddenly all the accumulated exhaustion of months claimed his body, and he felt he could lie down here on the hard-baked earth and sleep for a week. His mind was utterly blank of anything but the insistent need for rest. He found the door and somehow got himself up the stairs to his stuffy, bare rooms and half fell across the bed and slept. He slept sound, dreamless, and well until the next midday and woke feeling that he had come to life from a dream of death. It was raining steadily, and the open window let in fresh, cool air.

He dressed and went downstairs, and was beckoned by the recording clerk on duty, waving a long official envelope at him. His long leave had been approved; he was to have October and November to do with as he liked.

20

"After all, we're having rather a slack time just now, sir, and—well, damn it, a week's a week! Just asking you to stretch a small point, you know, sir."

The chief medical officer relaxed to a faint smile, and McDonagh thought with relief, By God, the old boy's going to play along! "It is against regulations, as I hope you realize, Mr. McDonagh. However, I'm quite sure that in your place I should be doing some special pleading also! I will—er—stretch the point, and write you an authorization to the captain of the *Tourney*."

"That's very good of you, sir, thanks very much."

"Er—yes," said the chief medical officer. "You might oblige me, Mr. McDonagh, in return—I know it is another small point—and try to say *sir* with less obvious reluctance. Yes, I shall have the note for you this afternoon."

McDonagh departed the office, jubilant. He was entitled to transport to England, in any available naval ship, but nothing now in harbor or expected was bound for England, to coincide with his leave. The *Belleisle* would come in, in a fortnight or so,

303

and could take him back; but his leave began in six days, and to waste a week waiting for transport! As it was, he could now get off tomorrow on the *Tourney*, a fast frigate, and hope for a quick voyage, with a week in hand.

For the distance it was not too bad; they had good winds up the coast of Portugal and were delayed and sent out of their way only a day or so by storms off southern France. The *Tourney* left Lisbon Harbor on the twenty-fourth of September and made past Spithead into Portsmouth three weeks and three days later.

McDonagh was the first man off her. He went straight up through town to the Swan, to ask about stages, and that was possibly both rude and cowardly of him. Being in Portsmouth, he should take an hour to call at the hospital, to see Bates if he was still there, buy him a—no, he didn't drink, of course—but just be polite enough to thank the little fellow. Damn it, he had; he'd written him a short letter from London; he hadn't any desire at all to see Bates again, or any of the others. Life, he thought tritely (with a grin for the triteness), was a bit like a journey on a stage, itself: you passed different places and saw different people out of the window, and some of them traveled with you for a while; but you couldn't go back and make part of the journey over, and essentially you were making it alone.

He was in luck; there was a stage for London in two hours, and he was on it, after a meal and a drink at the Seventy-four— for old times' sake, he said to himself sardonically. All that unaccustomed philosophizing started a train of thought in his mind, and he stared out at the Hampshire countryside and thought vaguely about life. Remembered Lauretta saying something about a good wife making him *steadier*. Well, it was true enough he'd not lived a very settled life these last years since coming to England, but that was in the nature of his job after all. It wasn't that he was unsettled in himself, was it? Of course, there was something in what she said.... Quite suddenly he thought of Barstow on the old *Donegal*, that much-married man, writing long letters to his wife in the little stuffy cabin. Didn't mean because a man roamed around on that kind of service, he was *unsettled*—whatever that meant. A good many of those men had families in England. Was it bad luck, dangerous, to think about that? But he couldn't stop himself.

A man ought to look ahead sometimes, try to see where he was going. . . . He hadn't done much of that these seven years. Hadn't really been able to, things happening to take him a step or two on, this direction or that. He ought to think of it now, because of Lauretta. If—yes, well, *if* it were possible at all— even to think *perhaps* . . . Eighty pounds a year with the army, might come up to a hundred or a bit more. It was a steady, secure job, but he didn't know that he'd want to go on like that. Rather be placed permanently in one spot, hospital staff work, private practice on the side, and of course, more money to be made that way—if you were lucky, and good. He thought Conal McDonagh was both. This was October 1810, and he was committed to military service through February of 1812; then, if he liked, he was free. He thought if he could manage to put aside some savings against that time, in case he couldn't find a place open on the staff of a London hospital at once—but eventually, with his record and experience, he would almost certainly find a place, and the big hospitals paid eighty or a hundred a year, and he could match that or more with decent private practice.

Oh, he couldn't help thinking about it anyway. . . . *Steadier*, she said. A man ought to try to plan, not just drift. And Con McDonagh was a good surgeon, but he'd be the first to admit that he had faults other ways: got himself into trouble now and then, did himself no good professionally, from his quick temper and contempt for the social niceties and flouting of convention. But the other side of the ledger, he didn't think he'd be such a bad bargain. Was it unlucky to think about it?

She had said once she loved him. He had kissed her in the dark of the stairwell, one evening the Amisons gave a dancing party, and told her he loved her, and she had trembled against him and kissed him back shyly. Damn, damn Amison . . . Met her in the park to say good-bye, and she had cried and said she loved him dearly but meant to be a good wife to Mr. FitzEustace, and he was to forget about her and be happy. The little French bisque shepherdess on the mantel, so delicate, so fragile. ("Your mother was very fond of that, Conal, I always take care of it because she loved it." Wonder whatever became of it, when all the property was confiscated?)

It seemed to him, in a muddled sort of way, looking back, that everything that had happened to him since had happened as it had because of that. All been different, better, happier, *steadier* (yes) if he could have had his darling safe to himself. And maybe now it was all going to come straight and right for Conal McDonagh at last.

It was the damnedest thing, he was amused at himself; he found he was delaying, nervous as an adolescent, that first afternoon, taking unnecessary pains with his dressing, deciding his nails needed clipping. Putting off the minute he would know. He took himself in hand and out of the Leicester Arms; and in Lisbon he'd thought longingly of a civilized town again, but now, walking through London, he scarcely took note of its crowds and busyness and smells and sounds, for thinking of Lauretta.

And then, damn it, when he was ushered into her parlor, he found he wasn't the only visitor. Another man—quite a negligible man, one he'd met before, where?—the fair-haired, stammering young man who had been at the dinner party that night when FitzEustace was so outraged. He couldn't remember his name, but Lauretta supplied it. "You remember Mr. Ringwood, I'm sure, Con." She was in mourning, of course; it accentuated her fair fragility, put gold lights in her amber hair.

"Dear Con, so good to see you again," she said, smiling at him. "Do sit down. Mr. McDonagh was—was one of the surgeons who attended poor James, Adrian. He was so very kind to write me and—and tell me how it all was."

"Oh, I s-say," said Mr. Ringwood vaguely. "You j-just home from Portugal then? M-must seem good to be back, what? Yes, a t-terrible thing ab-about old James—not even in b-battle, what? I mean to say, not that it's any less *s-sad*, y'know, but well, after all, in a war, that is, I mean to say—"

The damned idiot sat there nattering, hadn't the common courtesy to go away, when he must see that Lauretta wanted to talk privately to McDonagh—did she? He uttered brusque replies, and Ringwood wriggled uneasily under his black looks and stammered all the more.

"You must tell me more fully of it, Con," she said gently. "Adrian was James's cousin, you know, and will be concerned to hear, too."

My God, he didn't want to talk about FitzEustace, go over all that again, but he had to, doing his best to summon the correct grave phrases, Ringwood nodding solemnly and heaving sympathetic sighs, and Lauretta looking down at her clasped hands. Talk, talk, talk about FitzEustace! The man was underground, it was over, and all this just reminded her. He supposed a woman couldn't be married to a man for a few years and not have some concern for him, whether she loved him romantic or not—she'd hardly be in the mood after this to listen to— But damn it, it didn't appear that he'd have the chance to talk to her alone today anyway. This goddamned foppish cretin sitting there as if he meant to stay until Christmas!

She gave them tea presently, and after tea she had the nurse bring the little boy to her, and McDonagh's angry impatience increased until it was intolerable, for the white-faced child saying "Uncle Adrian" in a timid voice, and Lauretta discussing his health with Ringwood. "You remember how ill he was in the spring, it's quite providential he recovers so well, indeed, he's been playing in the park all morning, haven't you, darling? I let him go out with Mary only on fine days, of course, and some of the big boys are so rough, I do worry rather. But Dr. Dyke assures me that he will continue to grow in strength, when he has made such a good recovery. Darling, you mustn't be shy of Mr. McDonagh, say how do you do and let us see what lovely manners you have."

The child muttered miserably and leaned against her with his face turned away. Oh, *just* the wretched little rat of a youngster FitzEustace would beget! thought McDonagh.

And presently she was saying apologetically, "I am going to send you both away if you'll forgive my breach of manners— Dr. Dyke tells me I should rest for two hours before dinner, though I'm quite well really, but I do get tired rather easily, it's silly of me, I know. Thank you both so much for coming—it is lovely to see you again, Con, I'm so glad you have come home safe." And more conventional, meaningless little phrases—of course, she couldn't say anything real with this fool here—and there was nothing to do but go.

On the pavement outside Ringwood said nervously, "Oh, er, be v-very happy if you'd c-come to the club, have a g-glass with me, Mr. —er. What?"

"Thanks very much, no," said McDonagh without much effort at politeness, and waited until Ringwood, looking relieved, had stammered farewells and started off toward Piccadilly, so he could choose the opposite direction.

After that he couldn't very well call the next day, and he went up to St. Luke's to see Rob and Gillespie, took them out to dinner. Gillespie, he thought, looked older and shrunken somehow, his crest of white hair thinner. The next day he spent rather dispiritedly walking around the city, bought some new shirts, neckcloths, and handkerchiefs, and handed over his watch to be repaired. "Dear me, sir, whatever have you been adoing to it? . . . Oh, ah, I do see a few the same, to be sure, now you tell me—gentlemen as has been in a climate like that there. It's all the dust, like, in tropic parts. Not but what it's a good watch, sir, and I can clean it up proper, but if you was thinking of a new one—some very fine timepieces we got in just now . . . Oh, I quite understand, sir, I'll have this 'un running proper for you in three-four days."

Damn, he wasn't going to enjoy this holiday at all if it went on like this. Until, unless—only the one thought in his mind as he came back to England, and to hell with the proper conventions, he had to know for certain one way or the other. The next afternoon he walked up to Queen Square again.

The maid kept him waiting some time in the entrance hall, but eventually came back and ushered him into the parlor. Lauretta rose and gave him her hand with a colorless greeting; when the servant had gone, she said repressively, "Con, you shouldn't have come alone, again. I—I don't mean I'm not pleased to see you, but I am in new mourning, and I should not receive gentlemen alone, any more than I should go to the theater or a ridotto or give a dinner."

"Oh, damn it, Lauretta, can't you see how meaningless all that is? Whatever you do or don't do afterward doesn't change how you felt for— I'm sorry, I know women think more of all that, maybe, but— It's just that I had to see you."

She told him to sit down, so she was going to let him stay, at least. "—For a few minutes only. Perhaps it seems meaningless to you, but then you—you never were the sort of gentleman who paid much lip service to social customs, were you? It is important, you know, for how people think of you. Of course, it's not—not anything to do with the person, I agree with that— perhaps I'm not quite so conventional as you think, after all! A good many people who very correctly go into mourning for the proper period didn't really feel at all affectionate toward the one they're mourning for. But, well—don't you see, Con, what people think of you is important, and it's an accepted custom, everyone would think very badly of me if I—"

And that seemed to imply to him— He said quickly, "You do feel like that, Lauretta? I hoped—that is, of course it was an arranged marriage in a way, not your own choice. I—"

She sat up a little straighter, looking at him earnestly, his sweet Lauretta, so lovely even in the ugly mourning clothes. "But you mustn't think, I never meant to say—I had a deep regard for James, truly I did."

He dropped that subject hastily and smiled at her, trying to find the right words, to summon persuasion and tact. "Lauretta, I'm going to offend you more, and I'm sorry—I don't mean it so, it's just that—well, I'll come to that later. My darling, forgive me, but you know I've never stopped loving you, and now you're free, and I want to ask, I've got to ask—"

"*Conal!*" she exclaimed. "You cannot, you really cannot be saying what I think! It's quite disgraceful that you should behave so to me—this soon—only five months after! You know I can't listen to that, I must ask you to go if you are so lost to all—"

"Lauretta, please, my darling," he said desperately, and in that moment he was ready to compromise his opinions, he paid lip service to her orthodoxies anxiously, thoughtlessly. "I know it's disgraceful, I agree with you, I apologize, but don't you see, I've got to *know*. Please just listen, darling dear. I've only a few weeks here now, I'm due back in Lisbon at the end of next month, and that means I must leave England in the second week of November at least, and likely I'll be gone God knows how long. My service isn't up for fifteen months, it'd be that long at least. My dearest, I'm not asking you to marry me now, of course, I know that's unthinkable, I just want to know you will. Please, Lauretta—"

"Oh, no, Con, I can't listen to you, really," she protested faintly.

McDonagh was out of his chair before he knew he would move and bending over her, leaning on both arms of her chair, afraid to touch her but talking swift and urgent, trying to project his urgency to her. "Don't you see, Lauretta, it's just to know—my darling, you told me you loved me, once—remember, Lauretta? You said you loved me and you'd marry me if—but it all went wrong! I've never stopped loving you, and—you said you loved me then, and I've not changed—I'll make you love me again, my dearest. Even after you were engaged to him, you said you still loved me, remember? I caught you—and kissed you under the stairs, remember, dearest?—you were so sweet, so lovely—I loved you so! And you used to meet me in the park—Lauretta darling—"

"I had on a white gown," she said tremulously, "that first time. Yes, I remember. You startled me so, Con, it was very improper of you." She pressed back in the chair, turning from his leaning, hot urgency there so close. "Please, you're being so improper *now*, I—I can't know what to say to you now, you must see—" The words trailed off weakly.

"Oh, God, Lauretta," he said, and transferred his grasp to her shoulders. "Say yes to me again, my dearest, I'm not asking any more now, I know I can't—just to know you're mine for always. You loved me, you said so, I'll make you love me again, darling, please—"

"Let me go, Con, please," she whispered.

"Not until you say! Be kind to me, darling—please, just say—one day you will marry me—that's all I'm asking, Lauretta, say it to me—" He leaned close, tightening his grasp, shaking her gently.

"I—"

"Darling, say yes to me, Lauretta—"

She turned away blindly from his eyes. "Yes—all right, Con," she gasped. "Let me go now, go away." With sudden strength she evaded him and got up, pushing him away, crossing to the window to put the room between them. "No, you simply must not—not—approach me, Con, this is quite dreadful enough as it is! And, please, you must not—"

"All right, my dearest," he said; he sat on the arm of the chair, feeling suddenly weak, as if he had spent all the strength in him on persuading her. "It'll be just however you want, always. Just, now I know, oh, Lauretta, darling—I'll tell you what I thought, when my military service is up, I—"

"Listen to me, Con!" she said almost sharply. "I cannot hear anything like that either now. Oh, dear, you are so—so— Con, I *absolutely* forbid you to mention this to anyone, do you understand? I am going to send you away, you've been here far too long as it is, and—and I'm sorry, Con, but I must ask you not to call here alone again! Yes, yes, I know, my—my dear, you're not to be here long, and of course, you may come to say good-bye to me—"

"And I'll write you, Lauretta. All right, however you like, dearest, just so I know you are mine. I know you wouldn't consider—until a year at least, but that's next June, darling, and if somehow I can get back—"

"I will not discuss it now! Really this is disgraceful! Yes, very well, Con, I've said I will, it's all right, but please do leave now—" She was trembling and pale.

"Darling love, I never meant to upset you so," he said humbly, anxiously. "I'll go. You know you've made me so happy, Lauretta—always love you—" She had already pulled the bell for the maid; she was visibly collecting herself, to appear cool and correct before the servant.

He wasn't made the way he could do that, or care about it; he said a hasty, almost rude farewell when the maid came, and went out to the street hardly yet realizing that it was true—it would all come true, and she would be his wife. Not even allowed to kiss her, take her hand—his prim, conventional dear!—

but she had said yes, he had only to be patient and somehow get over the time between. Already it stretched before him like eternity, but it would pass. Try every way he could to get leave, be back in England sometime next year. A year might be the very minimum time before she'd consider, but it would be perfectly proper then by her lights, and if he could persuade her . . .

He walked down to Piccadilly entirely unaware of the pavement he trod, the people he passed. It all would come true, his heart's desire. It seemed suddenly to him that these last seven years—all the storms and stresses he had come through, the petty irritations and the dangers, the willful ruination he had brought on himself and the climb back from that to a personal security again, all the work of learning and experience—had been an interim of time between his first frustration to now, when he knew it would come right as he had always wanted it.

"You're merry as a grig tonight," said Meredith curiously. "And on two pints of ale! Come into a fortune?"

McDonagh laughed. "Something very much like that, Rob. But it's a secret, I've promised not to tell, not a living soul."

But he broke that promise, without meaning to. He went out that next morning to collect his watch. It was going to be difficult, in a sense, to pass this time in London after all—not allowed even to go and see her!—but now he could appreciate a civilized city again, take some casual pleasure in that.

He had picked up his watch and was sauntering down Piccadilly, taking simple enjoyment in the clean coldness of the air and the shops he passed, when his name was called sharply, and he looked around to see Fleur emerging from a mantua maker's.

"Conal, how pleasant to see you! You are back in London for good?"

"On leave only," he said. He was not, right now, too pleased to meet her. It was nothing so—orthodox—as a reluctance to be reminded of liaisons with her kind of woman, when he had his own true love pledged to him. That would be senseless; he'd always enjoy looking back to the women he had known, the complacent women who had given him much pleasure. He wasn't sure why he was not pleased to meet Fleur; it was just a feeling in him, and it didn't matter. He told her she was looking well; she was—suave and elegant in cream and gold, with a rather outrageous hat.

"Oh, I am always well. This is well met. I shall allow you to give me a cup of chocolate and some pastries, for a little luncheon. I wish to speak with you—"

"I'm sorry, I don't think—"

"Nonsense, you do not escape me! I extend my sympathy to you if ever you marry a wife, Conal, for you are an extremely bad liar, any woman knows at once when you are lying! If you tell me you have an engagement of the most urgent, I do not believe you, so do not trouble to say it. Let us go around the corner to the Chanson, we are early and it will not be crowded."

Unwillingly he went with her; when they came into the restaurant, he knew suddenly why he had not wanted to come, had not been pleased to see her. This was the place they had come that night for that damned *bal masqué*—Madeleine in a daffodil yellow gown, and Dunstan. He had felt ... As if it had been yesterday, he remembered the violence of emotion shaking him, the furious jealousy that that posturing fop should enjoy her first, and that had not happened, no. Fleur reminded him of Madeleine, that was it, and why in hell's name should he mind that? Only another woman—no, a bit different from that—was it that he had, after all, never quite got over the guilt for that, even though—

"What is it the English say, a penny for your thoughts, Conal?" she asked pleasantly.

"Not worth it," said McDonagh brusquely. They had been seated at one of the little tables; he ordered her chocolate and pastries and coffee for himself. "How are you situated these days, Fleur?"

"Me? Oh, I am"— she laughed— "almost retired! The truth is, Saul and I find we suit each other very well, and perhaps in the end, who knows, we will marry. He is lonely, he has only nephews, and he comes and finds comfort in complaining to me how they do not listen to him about the business and are altogether impertinent. He is a wealthy man, you know, and very kind to me. But I did not wish to talk to you of myself." She studied him, head on one side. "You are looking older, Conal. And yet in much you are still the young man who"— she smiled—"rescued me at the theater that evening! What a drollery that was, eh! Yes, you were never very young, were you, Conal?"

"Let's say, never very callow," he amended, smiling back. Now that he had identified the reason for his reluctance, he could push it to the back of his mind, because it was so utterly reasonless. He looked at her, thinking of something else rather odd. He'd enjoyed himself with Fleur all that time ago, but that feeling for her was quite dead in him now. She was no less attractive, nor was he lacking in passion for women in general because he was committed to one woman legally, or would be; unfortunately for all the orthodox precepts, perhaps, men weren't made so. It was just dead. He liked Fleur, he always had; something to her that was like something in himself. But it was a friendly feeling, nothing more.

"What," she asked him, stirring her chocolate, "happened between you and Maddi, Conal?"

"What the hell's that got to do with you? Nothing, of course—beyond all that damn fool play acting! What d'you mean?" At once he was in turmoil; he said furiously, "For God's sake! It's all finished, all that business, she's off your hands and I suppose leading a lively life with her latest protector!" Who had her now, yes, who? One of those wealthy gentleman fops like Dunstan—she had mentioned a name, he couldn't remember it—and it was all no matter to him anyway.

"You sound upset," said Fleur softly. "But you are not going to tell me, I see, when you are so vehement. If there was anything indeed. It was only to satisfy my curiosity. I do not know that it was anything to do with you at all, for she is very obstinate and would say nothing, she does not confide. I only wondered—ah, well, it is done."

"What?" asked McDonagh. "What's done?"

"I do wonder," said Fleur amusedly, "since you are so disturbed!"

"Damn it, I'm not disturbed, as you put it! The damned female's nothing to me, I only— I know you thought I was a damned fool, trying to—to—to reform her, but it's a thing any man— And in any case, my God, it's years ago! Doesn't matter, but when you're so mysterious, dropping hints—I was only being curious too, damn it."

"Very well, so that was it." Fleur's little smile vanished, and for a moment she looked angry. "I was exceedingly furious at Maddi. I still do not understand it at all, though it is also funny, a little. Conceive to yourself, I took time and trouble with her, as you know—a young, ignorant, raw girl from the provinces! I teach her everything, but everything!—though you will agree, I think, that there was somewhat to build on there, a capacity for elegance and an unusual type of charm. Still, when she frankly asks, and is so determined to make this career for herself, I was pleased to help her. I have family feeling, as I have said, and I grew very fond of Maddi. Everything I did for her—oh, I admit to you it was all businesslike, she returned me every pound!—the coiffure, the wardrobe, the cosmetics, the poise, the manner, the nuances, besides, of course, a great deal of equally practicable knowledge! I was quite enchanted at the result. It was not *le type*, but something different, unusual, a personality."

"Yes, very well, what of it?" he asked roughly, and scalded his tongue on the hot coffee.

Fleur laughed and shrugged; there was both amusement and a remnant of anger in her eyes. "It is nothing to do with me, any more than with you now. But I still am a little astonished at it. Figure to yourself, I quite thought she had the flair, and she was so anxious, so amenable. She is with Dunstan some time, and then she went to a Mr. Harry Bourdon—"

That had been the name she had said, yes.

"Who is a very pleasant young man, what I hear of him—but very shortly, perhaps she finds they do not suit some way together, I hear she is about to transfer herself to a Mr. Fabian Archbold. Him I did not know, I asked Saul—for if you will believe it, Maddi was never coming to see me, to tell me this herself, and we had been friends, or so I thought. Saul says this Archbold is most personable, not exactly young but an attractive man, a city merchant of much wealth. And well, I am pleased that Maddi does so well for herself, but I was concerned, as you may imagine, to know if I had offended her some way, that she never comes to see me and talk a little, you know?"

"Yes. So?"

"So," said Fleur, "I am very devious, I make inquiries here and there and learn the address where this Bourdon has been keeping her, and it is Burkhampstead Street, number nine. And I go to see if she is still there, to call on her. This is more than three years ago, if you will believe it. She was only a short time with Bourdon, you see—it is really very curious. Well, it is in the morning when I call, and when Maddi lets me in—and a most pleasant little suite it was, too, in excellent taste, no one could ask better—here are all her bandboxes standing about, ready to be moved. She was, I deduced, about to move elsewhere."

"Yes. And?" Another man—count them. What did Bourdon and Archbold look like? What kind of men—

"So of course, I ask. And you will never guess what Maddi says to me. She says there is nothing in the Archbold story. Quite calmly she says she has decided this is not the sort of life she can live, she is not suited to it at all, she dislikes feeling so unsettled, and she has been very fortunate to obtain a *position*—now I ask you!—a *position*, as she calls it, as a governess! You are too astonished to laugh, I comprehend. So was I then. It is the most ridiculous thing I have ever heard, which I was frank to say to her. Conceive it, she is given by any respectable protector worth the capturing five, six hundred pounds the year—and a suite of rooms, all furnished, at a good address. She need not do any labor, she is at no one's beck and call—beyond, naturally, exerting herself to please the man, that is understood—it is an easy, enjoyable livelihood. And she says to me that she is fortunate to obtain this respectable position—shepherding some family's horrid little children about and teaching them lessons in history and drawing!—at the magnificent wage of twenty pounds the year! It is quite mad, and when I had recovered a little from my astonishment—and my anger to see her tossing away an excellent career in such a fashion—I told her so."

"And what did she say?" asked McDonagh. He noticed absently that his hand was shaking slightly on the spoon stirring his coffee.

"What she had said before—she was not suited to the life! Oh, I was angry—such an absurd thing, meaningless! Of course, me,

I have the temperament," said Fleur frankly. "Possibly Maddi has not. But to be so determined, to take such trouble over preparing herself—a thing not always possible—and then on a whim to throw it all away! It is not as if she were a silly little miss without experience, then. True, some men are more attractive than others, and occasionally one must put up with an unattractive man for the financial benefit, but generally speaking, one may pick and choose, especially a girl like Maddi." She set down her cup with a little clatter. "To go and live in a little cell of one bedchamber, likely on the attic floor, in the house of people named Tenpence or something equally impossible in Woolhampton Street! It is beyond everything senseless."

"Yes," said McDonagh mechanically. "Isn't it, indeed." The waiter came up and looked at them pointedly. McDonagh fumbled in his pocket for money, sent the man away.

"Of course, it may please you to know, Conal, that your moral lecture to her bore fruit—if somewhat late! Yes, you know, I did just wonder—if it had been something to do with you. Curious as it may seem, for she had not seen you then for some time, had she? You were out of London, were you not—or were you?"

"Yes, damn it, I was. It wasn't anything—couldn't have been—damnedest silly idea you ever had, Fleur! I—"

"Very well, so it was. Are you pleased about it, Conal?"

"It doesn't matter one good damn to me either way," he said. "I suppose you were angry. Damned amusing. Yes, I wonder why she did. Well, it's been very good to see you again, Fleur, but I'm afraid I really do have an urgent engagement, you'll have to excuse me. Good luck to you with Isaacs, he seemed a nice chap."

"And pleasant to see you, Conal. I thought you would be interested, about Maddi! Must you really go? Well, I will not delay you longer if you must. No, you need not find me a hack, I think I shall sit on here a little and have another cup of chocolate."

He left her there, awaiting her fresh chocolate and observing the other patrons with her quick, curious, shrewd glances, and he walked blindly out into the street with indefinable but upsetting emotion seething in him.

21

The news hawker regarded Mc-
Donagh with lively, amused interest. "That do be a rum 'un,"
he said. "Certing I know this street, same as I know lots—reg'lar
delivery I got 's well as odd sales, see. It wouldn't be old Mr.
Farthing y'mean, at number six?"

"No, I don't think so."

"Come ter think, there do be some rum nymes abaht. I
knowed a fella named Catchpenny onct, but that weren't in this
'ere street, o' course. And there used t' be a ol' chap dahn in
Cheapside when I were a young 'un, by the nyme o' Gotobed.
Bloody good nyme for 'im, too, sixteen in the fambly 'e 'ad. And
another time—"

"This street," said McDonagh through his teeth.

"Ow, yers, to be sure." The news hawker took off his woolen
cap and scratched his head. "Well—*Tenpence*, I mean ter
say!—There's a nouse in the square, end o' the street, what's
called Groats. . . . An' there's Mr. Schilling at number twelve.
German 'e is, 'e come over a long while back with 'Is Majesty's
German sodgers, an orfcer 'e were. An' then"— he bright-

318

ened—"there's the Gascoynes at number twenty-two. Come ter think, it's comic, what you can myke of a nyme, amn't it? *Tenpence.* O' course, there's Mrs. Bobbs, housekeeper hat number fourteen."

"You evidently have a taste for wordplay," said McDonagh grimly. "Go on."

"Well, it's dahnright comic, amn't it, mester? *Tenpence,* naow. Wunnerful 'ow windy-minded folk can get, tryin' remember nymes. It wouldn't be the Truepennys, would it? Number nineteen."

"Very likely—yes, it might easily be. Thanks very much." He gave the man tuppence and turned away with the news hawker's snuffling laugh still sounding.

He didn't know what the hell he was doing here. He had no reason to be here, damn it. Taking this much trouble over it, asking the way, going out of his own road in life to come to Woolhampton Street out toward Kensington, stuffy, respectable neighborhood, tall, grim-looking houses.

He walked up to number nineteen, which was even taller and chillier-looking than its neighbors, and wielded the knocker. He had no idea what he was going to say to the servant who opened the door. Something outside himself was leading him on, in some way, for some reason. He wasn't even thinking much about that; he just stood there waiting, not trying to formulate words.

A plump little butler opened the door to him and wished him a polite good afternoon. And it was exactly like that night at the Portsmouth hospital when he'd walked in on a murderer and his unsuspecting victim, and in his fright and indecision somehow found his body acting and talking for him without conscious direction. He smiled easily at the man and said, "Could you tell me if Mr. Truepenny employs a Miss Olivier as governess?"

The butler's careful expression-for-gentlemen-callers relaxed a trifle, and a dubious look came into his eyes. "Why, yes, sir, Miss Olivier is hemployed here, sir."

"Then I've come to the right place." If he'd been acting without this automatic direction, he might at that point have produced a shilling, but intuitively he knew that would be an insult to this dignified personage. "I'd like to speak with Miss Olivier for a moment, if I may. Would that be possible?"

"I'm afraid, sir, I could not take it upon myself—there's no followers hallowed, though I do not mean to hinclude the lady governess with the help, sir, but still, a rule's a rule. Miss Olivier has Saturday hafternoons, sir, if you would care to leave a note . . ."

McDonagh shook his head. "I really would like to see her now. If your mistress is in, perhaps you'd ask. You see, I'm Miss Olivier's cousin, and I have some—er—family news for her. I'm sure there could be no objection to my seeing her for a few moments privately?"

"Oh, I see, sir. Well, the mistress and master is both hout, but I'm bound to say it seem reasonable enough. Won't you come in, sir? The young gentlemen haven't any lessons in the hafternoon I make sure Miss Olivier'll be able to slip down for just a bit, sir. A very nice young lady, sir, I hunderstand she comes of one of these emmy-gray families, but raised in England, down in Tunbridge Wells. Hat least, I mind the master saying as that's where her references come from, Miss Olivier wanting to live in London awhile. Hexcuse me, sir, might you be just up from there?"

"No. No, I live here."

"I'm sure I beg your pardon, sir, I only mentioned it because my sister, she lives in Tunbridge, and I was—but of course, your family wouldn't be knowing her. If you'd like to wait here, sir, I'll see can Miss Olivier come down. What name should I say, sir?"

"Oh, don't bother," said McDonagh. "Just say her cousin—she's only one I know of." It was a small morning room he was left in; not proper, of course, to show a governess's callers into the parlor. He looked around this strangers' room vaguely, wondering how he'd come here, why he'd come here. Why the hell? Most ridiculous damned thing that had ever happened to him.

He hadn't anything to say to her. It was finished, a closed episode. When she came, if she came, he had nothing at all he wanted to say to her. All this trouble and search, to look at her—just that—and she would think it either impossibly odd of him, or even that he meant righteously to give her away to her employers. His mind seemed numb; he could think of nothing whatever to have ready to say to her.

He thought it would be a very sensible move to go away quickly, out of the house, before she came. Just leave it. Most senseless goddamned thing ever happened to him. He remembered saying to her once, *Devil sitting on my shoulder*. It was like that.

Better go—at once, before—

And then it was too late. She came into the room and saw him. She stepped over the threshold, with the butler's fatherly beam behind her as he shut the door discreetly. Astonishment came into her eyes, and then something he couldn't identify, and then anger. McDonagh just stood and looked at her.

She hadn't changed at all. It was nearly six years since he had first met Madeleine, but she looked much the same as then, and exactly as he'd last seen her. Except that she hadn't put any color, even faint, on her cheeks and lips, and she was wearing a rather drab earth-colored gown that made her mat white skin look even paler. And her voice was just the same, too deep for a woman's and faintly husky.

"Haven't you plagued me enough, Conal McDonagh?" she asked rigidly. "How did you ever find me here? I could not imagine—"

"It doesn't matter," said McDonagh absently.

"What do you want? And I'll ask you to keep your voice down, if you mean to lose your temper at me as you usually do. I have a respectable position in this household, and while I don't think Rowland or the other servants listen at doors, one never knows. What do you want now?"

"I don't know," said McDonagh. And it was a lie. He wanted Madeleine. Still, the same way: something about this damned female made him want her harder than any other complacent woman he'd ever known. A jumble of thoughts and feelings in him about it. She wasn't an easy woman any longer. Could a woman ever stop being, once she had been—the other side of the line? Faint shame for it—Lauretta—but damn, as he'd thought an hour ago, another place the orthodox notions didn't jibe with human nature; a man didn't stop noticing other women, having random lascivious thoughts about them, because he was in love with one woman. Alchemical properties, yes, undoubtedly. And any man might be forgiven, with Madeleine. Only, an ugly gown; she ought not to wear such a drab gown. "I don't know why I came," he said. "I—was surprised—Fleur said— Madeleine, why—why did you? It—" Abruptly he tried to pull himself together, make more sense. Sounded as maundering as that idiot Ringwood. "Damn it, it's senseless! To think you could—"

"Yes, to think I could. Please come to the window, away from the door, and keep your voice down. You are given to shouting at people, aren't you?"

"I wasn't shouting at you."

"Not yet perhaps." She faced him erectly. "*To think I could!* But I have, you see. Possibly you wonder how. I asked a woman I had known in Tunbridge to write me a reference, it was really laughably simple. I have a decent position here, I would scarcely care to have it endangered, and when I leave, I shall have a good reference to show. It's not a difficult job, you know—"

"Or a very well-paid one."

"Oh, no. But it seems to be all I can get, and at least my free time is my own. Why did you come here? Haven't you plagued me enough? Damn you, Conal, coming here when I have been—settled—looking at me like that—why?"

"Have I plagued you, Madeleine? I—it didn't seem—"

"Oh, God," she said suddenly. She turned half away from him. "If you didn't come here—for any particular reason—I wish you'd go."

"Maybe I was just curious," he said hardly. "Like Fleur. You once thought a good deal of a luxurious income."

Slowly she turned back to him. She had smoothed her expression to hardness matching his. "So I did, Conal, so I did. I still do. Only, you see, I was a failure at the career I had chosen."

"Oh, that's a damned lie," he said.

"Of course, you know, don't you? But you aren't the best judge by any means. I had to pretend—all of it, all the while— and I was simply not very clever at pretending. Men don't mind that with street harlots, do they, but after all, when they have come to an arrangement with an exclusive, shall we use the current term, *Fashionable Impure?*—at five hundred pounds a year, they expect something more for their money, it's only reasonable. And they did not get it from me, because I wasn't nearly clever enough to pretend. Almerick was stupid, he never knew. He was a little annoyed at thinking I'd deceived him all along, to make him think I was an innocent. But about the other, he didn't really know—that it was pretense, because he was stupid. Harry knew. And it is very irritating to a man, you know—or perhaps you don't know, Conal!—because it implies that he's a poor lover and incompetent. Harry was rather insulting, if he pretended to be amused. He said, My dear, if I want that sort of thing, I can pick it up in any alley off Covent Garden for five shillings an entry! You see? So it appeared I was an abject failure at my work, and since, as I once told you, I certainly don't mean to end on the streets, I cast around and went to a little trouble to become respectable again, to earn my living this way instead."

"Why?" he asked. "I don't understand—Madeleine—"

"Don't you?" She smiled at him, but the smile did not touch her pewter-colored eyes. "That's very funny. I don't say this is a good living, but it's a living. My work isn't very hard, I'm fed and sheltered, and I'm paid twenty pounds a year. You stole the rest, Conal. At a conservative estimate, four hundred and eighty pounds a year you stole. Because I have not, as Fleur puts it, the temperament—by nature—and I always knew I would earn hardly what money I was given by lovers. But I thought I'd be better at pretending than I possibly could be, after you. You want to know why? It was because neither of them was Conal McDonagh, that was why! And you were halfway drunk, too, weren't you? It's really very funny and ironic."

"That's the damnedest silliest thing I ever—I don't—"

"Oh, do you think so?" Her smile was bright and artificial. "You always had a cynical turn of mind. Don't you believe in romantic love? No, no, I should say, in foolish women imagining it in themselves for a little while—"

"Well, it—yes, but—"

"But not, of course, for women the other side of that line, I see—no, obviously not. We are immune from such absurd things. Which is just as well, for in the unthinkable event—well, you would not be too good a prospect for a husband, I shouldn't think."

"What in God's name are you talking about, all this natter, natter? Said something like that to me before, and it was nonsense then, too. As far as that goes—"

"Oh, yes, undoubtedly nonsense," said Madeleine. "Women are all foolish, imaginative creatures, good or bad."

"I think," said McDonagh, "I do know why I came." That had, in fact, been occupying his mind as she talked, and he had heard her absently. Such a damned silly thing, not just that he wanted to look at her again. (Yes, *something unusual—a personality*. No figure, she was too tall and thin, but that fluid grace—even when she was angry. Angry at him again, she was—why?) It was an excuse he had to find for acting irrationally, for the real reason was just that: to see her. And the desire for her rising like a tide—the real reason—always had been the reason with her, the fury of frustration that she was an easy woman, but not for him, he couldn't buy her. Everything else went out of his mind, the half-heard things she'd said, what he had started to say, where they were and what she was here, now. He covered the distance between in a stride and seized hold of her roughly, and his mind was quite blank until awhile later it told him she was straining up to him, holding him desperately, meeting his mouth with eager hunger. And just as suddenly she pulled free, thrusting him away violently, and turned her back and put half the room between them.

"Don't ever—do that to me again, Conal. Not ever. The way—you would take hold—of a woman for sale, never mind if the price is five shillings or five hundred pounds. I'm not that kind of woman now."

"Damn it, damn it," he said; it was not swearing at her, but himself. No, it was nothing to do with Lauretta, this kind of thing; all the same, something to be vaguely ashamed of. Damn alchemical properties or whatever it was! In a moment he said, "I'm sorry, I didn't mean to do that. What I wanted to say—" What had been in his mind? An excuse, yes, must be what he'd really felt, the reason he had come. "Madeleine, I—maybe, I don't know, I've kept on feeling guilty about you, all this time. I know it's damned silly, but I—"

"You apologized to me," she said, back still turned. "Are you intending to make it an annual affair, to ease what passes for a guilty conscience with you? Because I don't think I could bear that, Conal."

"Yes—no, of course not. The thing is"—and he laughed—"damn it, I should be embarrassed to confess it—whatever else I am, I've never been accused of sentimentality!—but the truth is, maybe I'm feeling sentimental, some queer way, lately. I'm engaged to be married, next year, I hope, and, well—" He stopped; promised not to tell anyone, but Madeleine didn't matter, of course; she didn't know—and he needn't say a name.

Madeleine turned and looked at him. After a moment she said expressionlessly, "Oh, are you? Fleur said once—you had told her—that you were most romantically in love with a girl who'd married someone else by arrangement. Dear me, I'd forgotten that, or I shouldn't have asked you if you believed in romantic love!" And he had forgotten telling that to Fleur, all those years ago, in a moment of sentimental aberration. "Is this by any chance your original true love, or have you found another?"

"I—not that it's any of your business, but yes—she has been left a widow, I—"

"How very convenient!" said Madeleine. "Did you come here to tell me that, Conal?—to boast of your good fortune?" She came toward him slowly, and her voice went down a register, the way he remembered it did on her anger. Her eyes were bright as diamonds on him. "A virtuous widow!—and still, no doubt, young and lovely! And perhaps with a little property left by her husband? I congratulate you, Conal!" Suddenly, viciously, she struck him hard, twice, across the face with her open hand. "Go and marry your virtuous lady, damn you, and leave me alone! I wish you much joy of your chaste, stupid, namby-pamby, mealymouthed, submissive little widow, Conal—I'm certain that's what she's like, the sort of silly creature you big, forceful, masterful men always choose! You'll be bored to death with her in a month, and you'll play her false with twenty or fifty women like Fleur—and lower—and if she learns it, she'll put up with it meek and mild as a lap spaniel with beating—women like that always do. I should kill you myself, I should want to kill you. But women like me—reformed or not—we're not supposed to have emotions, are we?"

"Madeleine, I don't—I didn't mean to offend—"

"Oh, for God's sake, go away!" she said. "I tell myself I'm recovered from you, from such childish sentimental feelings, and the minute I see you again—! And you're not worth it, stupid as you are. I never want to see you again in my life, for the love of God go away and leave me in peace! Go back to your—your damned widow, and leave me alone!" She whirled and walked out of the room, erect and stiff, and left the door wide behind her.

When he came out to the hall, she had vanished; the corridor was empty of any servant. McDonagh went down to the front door and let himself out of the house.

He was a little distance away before a random curious thought struck him. He had not been at all angry with Madeleine this time; he'd had no small impulse to lose his temper at her. Not for her strange fury at him, anything she had said or done, or for no reason at all that he knew, as it had happened before. For the first time since she'd walked into Fleur's parlor that night six years ago, and he had first laid eyes on her and begun to feel anger and pity for her, for the first time he felt at peace with Madeleine.

The time in London, after all, passed quickly. With the settled knowledge that Lauretta was his, somehow he did not too much mind not seeing her; it was a comfortable awareness in him that she was there and that the time would pass. It was just a period to get through, and all the urgency and impatience in him seemed to have died for the fact that she was promised to him. He could look with equanimity on a return to Portugal and the rest of his service there, for at the end of it were Lauretta and a new beginning.

He went to the theater; he spent evenings with Rob; he wrote a long, jubilant letter to Matt, for that couldn't matter, Matt being so far away and not in touch with anyone else in England.

He didn't think a great deal about that last scene with Madeleine, for two reasons. Nothing, however absurd, was deviling him about Madeleine anymore; the thought of her did not irritate him or worry him or raise guilt in him. He put that down, belatedly, to his certainty of Lauretta's love; the one had nothing to do with the other, of course, but his shame—on account of Lauretta—for that repeated violence of desire for an easy woman had, maybe, killed the thing dead right there. As for what she had said to him, women talked a good deal of nonsense, and the truth probably was that she simply hadn't the temperament, as Fleur put it; she'd been reared respectably and perhaps had not been able in the end to get past that after all. Odd, when—but women were changeable—and in any case he was at last finished with Madeleine Olivier, with all the irrational thoughts and feelings she had ever roused in him.

Even though it meant the end of his leave, he looked forward to the day he could call on Lauretta again. And it came; he had written her a note asking to come in the afternoon, and had a prim little note in reply asking him to tea.

When the maid showed him in, Lauretta gave him her hand, and he kissed it before letting it go. "Oh, Con, please! She might have seen. I do hope you're going to behave."

"You make it very hard, my darling, when you look so lovely."

"Now sit down there, please," she said. She sat a little way off and looked at him candidly. "You know, you upset me so that day—which was very foolish of me in a way, for I should know how you are, you are always doing something outrageous!—that I may have been more sharp with you than I meant. I'm sorry, but really, you must see how disgraceful it is."

"Even to talk about alone, dearest?" he asked gently. "It's all right, Lauretta, now I know for certain. I won't worry you. I won't try to talk about what plans I've thought of, or——but I can write them to you, can't I? Or is there anything impossibly improper about that?"

"You will jest so, and I'm never sure whether you are jesting or not! You may write me, yes, I'll look forward to your letters, but please, Con, no oftener than once a month, that will give the servants enough to speculate about! When do you leave?"

"I'm off to Portsmouth tomorrow, going back on the *Quintus*, sail next Monday or Tuesday. I've fifteen months of service yet, but I'll try my damnedest to get posted back, or get leave, next summer, Lauretta. I—" He hesitated, remembering something else that had occurred to him, and scowled. "There's only one thing I am worried about, love—can't be helped, I suppose, but I expect some people are going to say I'm marrying you for what property FitzEustace left you."

Lauretta smiled gently. "I don't think anyone who knows you would say that, Con. It isn't very important to you, is it? I daresay some people will."

"Damn," he said, "of course they will! I don't want anything to do with it, Lauretta. I don't want any damned part of it, don't want to know how much it is! I'd ask you to deed it away to charity or something, but that wouldn't be fair to you, surgeons never earn fortunes after all, and you're accustomed to the hell of a lot better things than I could ever—"

"Dear Con," she murmured, "could you possibly manage to talk without cursing so much? I know you don't mean anything by it, you always did, but it isn't considered quite the thing before ladies, you know."

He laughed; he'd got up and been walking the room, and now paused beside her to drop a light kiss on her cheek. "Darling love, will you ever manage to civilize me? I'm sorry, I didn't realize. But it galls me to think—"

"Well, as to that, Con, I'm afraid there's nothing you can do about it. All of what I own will pass to you legally when we are married, you know. And of course, as to giving it away, well, there is my darling boy to think of, you know."

"Yes," said McDonagh. "Of course. I've said I wouldn't, Lauretta. It will—come to me? Yes, I suppose so." Vaguely he had realized how the law read, but for the first time it came to him how unequivocal it was, titles, deeds, cash, everything, to be transferred to her husband. . . . God, how furious FitzEustace would have been! He laughed at that thought, but angrily, he didn't want it, he loathed the idea.

"There is tenant farm property, I think, somewhere near

Dublin," she was saying, "and this house, and other property in Wexford—I'm not exactly sure. The gentleman at the bank, Mr. Forsythe-Smith, looks after it and brings me the money for the servants and so on. He could explain it to you—but afterward, Con, of course!"

"I don't want to know about it, damn it! I suppose I'll have to, but it will be yours, Lauretta, you know that. Let's not talk about it, for God's sake—oh, I'm sorry."

Yes, he had faults; greed wasn't one of them; but aside from that—

"Oh, love, I'd put up with more annoyance than that to have you—my lovely Lauretta!"

"No—don't kiss me again, you really are dreadful! Go and sit down politely! Con, I hope—it's hard to say what I feel exactly, but my dear, we're neither of us the people we were, eight years ago—perhaps I'm not quite the same girl you fell in love with. I hope—you won't be sorry, Con."

"Sorry!" Regardless of her protests, he sat on the arm of her chair, an arm around her, and kissed her, but gently not to offend her. "My dearest love, sorry to have the only girl I ever fell in love with? Silly little thing you are!"

"Now do go over there and sit down and behave properly! You are always so—so violent a person— No, I'm not angry with you, of course, but I think we had better have our tea."

And after tea, inevitably, she sent for the boy. "Of course there is no time now for you to grow acquainted, but you will. I—I am so happy that he will have you, Con. A boy needs a father in growing up, and I do hope so very much that you will be—will be affectionate with him." Her gaze was a little anxious. "Don't be offended, but please be gentle with him, Con, he's rather shy and easily frightened, and you don't mean it, I know, but you have a rather abrupt manner sometimes."

McDonagh looked at the boy, feeling a little helpless and irritated. He didn't (for whatever reason) feel any jealousy of the child, either for Lauretta's affection or because another man had sired him; it wasn't anything like that bringing this dim impersonal impatience into him. He liked children and usually got along with them; he'd rather enjoyed the work he'd done on occasion, at Queens' and St. Luke's, with the cheeky, ragamuffin-thin street children brought in from minor road accidents and the like. The feeling he had for this child was . . . just nothing. Little white rat of a thing. Damn, he thought suddenly, he's just exactly what Bates must have been at that age!

"Say how do you do nicely, darling."

The boy whispered and retreated to her skirts. Well, women were apt to be too soft, overindulgent with only boys, pampering them, and the child hadn't been strong evidently. Maybe, as he got older, if he were talked to sensibly, encouraged to stand on his own feet—

She didn't send the boy away, and McDonagh couldn't, in view of everything, even kiss her cheek when he left. He held her hand at the door; he kissed that quickly and said, "Please write to me, Lauretta. Every month—promise?"

"Yes, I will, Con." She prompted the child to offer his hand, and it was like a frail claw in McDonagh's.

"Well, then this is good-bye for—for such a long while, my darling. You know I'll be counting the days. Please keep well, Lauretta, and—and think of me often, won't you, love?"

"Yes, of course, Con," she said sedately with a glance at the child.

"And thank you again—for making me so happy." He took her hand and kissed it again, and then the prim maid came and politely offered his hat and coat, and he was out of the house, with a faint feeling of dissatisfaction at the back of his mind. . . . But damn it, it was an unconventional situation, you couldn't expect her— And never mind, next time he saw her it would be different, it could all be made open, and she wouldn't be so concerned for the conventions. She was promised to him; he had her safe now; it would all come right for them at last.

Such an eternity to get through first, but it would pass. . . .

If only that youngster didn't remind him so damned much of Bates. . . .

And in one way—just one way—he would be rather glad to get back to work again. Even in Libson. It was only for another fifteen months, less perhaps with luck; he could get through that. And then, a new beginning to life.

22

McDonagh swore as his pen dropped a blot for his involuntary start at the loud crack of thunder. He blotted it carefully with a scrap of paper and finished the sentence. "And so we have not been too busy here, with major military action halted. There are always skirmishes going on, of course, as the French are still threatening the frontier forts, though there are practically no enemy forces left actually in Portugal. There is some rumor that the commanding general has a plan to blockade and storm Badajoz, and in that event we can expect an influx of new casualties. Only last week (on the twentieth of April) the Portuguese volunteer troops first reoccupied the positions they had lost two years ago, so you see the war seems to be approaching a conclusion here."

He laid down the pen and regarded this effusion with exasperation. A very damned loverly letter, this sounded! He started to tear it up and shrugged; it served to fill up the page, and he'd do better in the next paragraph.

"I say, 've you any ink?" asked Robinson, barging in cheerfully. "How I loathe writing letters, don't you? Phew, that one was close!" Another peal of thunder. "Hottish, in between showers, ain't it? Oh, you're *using* your ink. Well, that's all right, old man, perfectly all right, wouldn't have asked if I'd known. Don't know what the hell I did with mine. You go right on, I'll wait and get it when you've finished, or tomorrow."

McDonagh looked at his quill and made a few silent remarks to himself. He thrust the quill and the unfinished letter to Lauretta into the drawer of the rickety little table and said, "No, you take it along. I'll finish this another time." Anything to get rid of Robinson.

There were now between thirty-five and forty thousand British troops in Portugal, and along with the military reinforcements last year and in the first months of this a number of men had been added to the medical staff in the Lisbon depot hospital. When McDonagh arrived back from England on the first of December five months ago, he had found his second room preempted by Robinson, under a new ruling of allotting quarters. ("I'm sure you don't mind, Mr. McDonagh"—the senior clerk in the chief medical officer's office looked at him severely—"it's desirable for as many of the staff as possible to be resident in the building, and after all, it is a very large building, provided some of the staff do not occupy quarters suitable for several men. For one thing, the chief officer has found that some staff members quartering themselves among the townspeople have formed immoral relationships with—er—the native women, which is deplorable, I'm sure you'll agree.")

George Sidney Robinson was just a piece of bad luck for McDonagh; almost any other surgeon on the staff he could have tolerated easier. Robinson was a big, beefy, clumsy young man, overfriendly in a manner given to shoulder patting and bluff masculine embraces to show goodwill; he had the sense of humor of a schoolboy of seven, and took simple pleasure in retelling elementary jests, repeating the point several times to make sure it got across. He was rather clumsy as a surgeon, too, from what McDonagh had seen of him at work.

"Oh, I didn't mean to interrupt you, old man," said Robinson, whacking him on the shoulder for no apparent reason and picking up the ink bottle. "You're sure? Oh, well, then, I suppose I'd better get on with it." He went off to his own bedchamber a little disconsolately; probably he had hoped to settle down for the evening. McDonagh stretched out on his bed, lit a cigarillo, listened to the thunder and occasional spatter of rain, and thought vaguely about what else he would put in his letter to Lauretta; his mind wandered in dim discontent over that and other matters.

Never good at letter writing anyway, and her letters were so short and full of correct phrases, somehow they didn't give him anything to get hold of, to prompt a feeling of wanting to answer. Letters never very satisfactory anyway. June . . . but it didn't seem at all likely that he would be able to get back to England until much later, maybe until his service was up. If the war was still on then, he'd be pressed hard to stay, to sign on for another four years of crown service. Well, he wouldn't do that.

Steadier, she had said. Settled. Try to plan for the future, a permanent place—one of the London hospitals—and private practice on the side, yes . . . Wouldn't want to live in the Queen Square house, probably too expensive for him to keep up anyway, and be damned if he'd let her use her money.

If only he could feel he had a firm hold on the situation, somehow; damned ridiculous way to put it even to himself, that was, but expressed how he felt. The colorless, conventional letters in her schoolgirl hand . . . just, neither of them very good at writing letters.

And the damned property.

All right, so that was it—pull it into the open and look at it, he thought angrily. That if you liked was about the most damned irrational feeling he'd ever had. No, he didn't like the idea of legally coming into the property FitzEustace had left Lauretta, but he could have put up with it if it had been property in England—or Afghanistan, or the moon. The house didn't matter. But the land in Meath and Wexford—tenant land—and maybe some of the land that had been fought on, where the blood had run fresh into the earth . . .

Could have put up with it. He'd damned well have to put up with it. Not a lot of land, it wouldn't be, a great land fortune, like that of the Wesley-Wellesleys—modest holdings only. But land, like that of that great Anglophile family's, cut up into tenant farms, with the poor devils of farmers going hungry and cold to meet the rent, times.

Not a foot of land in Ireland, he thought, I can't.

Confiscated the single modest house his father owned in Belfast, they had. That would have been his. Any man might own a house.

Tenant farms: ten pounds a year, twelve, for little cut-up acreage administered by a factor, the owner living in England and never knowing the names of his tenants. Ten pounds a year for an acre or two. In Wexford. County Wexford, which held Enniscorthy and Vinegar Hill and the town of Wexford.

The land factors and the landowners, they were fond of saying, lazy Irish, feckless farmers, ignorant of how to get the most out of the land. Maybe they were, maybe they were bad farmers, but by the living God, they had proved they were good fighters. Come out with scythes and clubs and carpenters' mauls and met the straight lines of regular uniformed troops and beat them. But the French support came too late. . . .

McDonagh got off the bed in one angry motion and began to walk the floor of the little bare room. Why the hell was he emoting like this, like a damned melodramatic actor delivering asides to an audience? Been the hell of a long time since he'd been such a sentimental, childish, callow fool to give himself up to black-and-white patriotism, up the United Irishmen and hang all the bloody Sassenachs. It didn't matter one damn; that was how things were, and it behooved a sensible man to look after himself first the best way, and let other men do the same. Ideals came a long way behind and had damn little to do with realities.

As the legal owner of that modest parcel of land Conal McDonagh would scarcely compare to the arrogant Wellesleys.

"Oh, hell and damnation!" he said aloud, furiously, at his own irrationality.

" 'S matter, old man?" asked Robinson instantly, helpfully, from the other room.

It would indeed be a sensible thing to do, go in and hit Robinson. Good and hard. Sensual, satisfying impact of fist on Robinson's jaw. McDonagh very nearly did; a blind rage at Robinson possessed him. Then he drew a breath, controlling himself with a struggle. He said curtly, "Nothing—it's all right," and went out of the room to the corridor, just managing not to bang the door after him.

He stood there in the dark corridor for a moment; there was no place it led to save the privy room at the end, and a few other rooms occupied by staff men. Maybe some casual talk with Tebbs or Adams would settle him down a bit.

Ten in the evening of a lowering, humid-growing, wet May night in Lisbon; he would be on duty at six; he ought to go to bed. But so damned restless he'd been this while since he was back—no reason or a lot of little reasons—it was the waiting, he told himself, this dreary time to be got through here.

He lifted his head then sharply, and everything in his mind retreated a way. There it was again. The harp music—faint, but clear.

He had heard it twice, since that first time last summer. Thought he was hearing things that couldn't be, that the intolerable heat and his state of mind had sent him a little queer. But it was real; it couldn't be, but it was. He had heard it twice since, in the corridors, at night. It seemed to come from the other wing of this top floor.

There was, of course, an explanation. Amateur musician among the resident physicians over in that wing, and apparently an Irishman. That was all. Nothing uncanny about it. But for some reason McDonagh felt a deep reluctance to investigate; he was curious and yet something warned him, Leave it alone.

There was a children's tale about the great hero Fionn mac Cumhal and how he had once done battle with a demon who came playing the harp so sweetly that all the fighting strength died in the king's champions.

McDonagh went down to the end of this corridor and turned into the long cross hall that led to the north wing of this building. The medical wards were on the ground and second floors, and the resident physicians had quarters on the top floor—probably more spacious, since there weren't so many of them. As he passed through the arch that gave to the corridor there, the harp music, which had been no more than an occasional note struck louder, in the distance, grew in volume. It was not loud, but it was somewhere here. He walked slowly up the corridor.

Somewhere at the end of this hall. The wall was staggered out here, making a little inadvertent alcove, and the last door in this hallway was set in the staggered-out wall. McDonagh stood by the little alcove, in the dim light, listening.

The harpist was in there. He was playing and singing very softly to himself, the same song McDonagh had heard that summer night last year. Too softly now for McDonagh to hear all the words, but he found they had stayed in his mind: *That I were now in Ireland . . . Or if I might stand looking out over the Lough of Belfast . . . That I might lie again with my darling, the pulse of my heart.*

It was like all the Gaelic music, sorrowful and gay at once; like all the Gaelic poetry, saying two things at once. Like all the Gaels, the lighthearted friendly men who had such black deeps inside them.

He heard a step, and quickly, involuntarily, he pressed back into the alcove. Not so much that he had no business here as that he did not want to have to explain, to be pushed into talking about the harp music.

A man came down the corridor from the head of the stairway at the other end. As he passed by the single wall sconce of four tallow candles, halfway along the corridor, McDonagh saw him clearly. He was a middle-sized man about McDonagh's age, with a pleasant-looking face, long inquisitive nose, blue eyes, a firm mouth, waving light brown hair, and he walked quickly and lightly like an active, busy man. He did not see McDonagh pressed against the wall; he opened the door and went in, shut it behind him.

The harping stopped, and there was a low murmur of voices, too low to say on what language. McDonagh turned and went back quietly to his own place.

"My God in heaven," said Tebbs, "if this keeps up, we'll have to ask an armistice with the French to get the whole army back on its feet again!"

McDonagh agreed wearily. "Turning us all into physicians. It's this damned climate—hot and wet."

"Been wet enough this year anyway." The spring rains had been torrential, most roads were impassable, and the spirits of the British army had dropped low for the enforced halting of military action, for renewed criticism at home of their commander's policies. Between the downpours the atmosphere was humid, thundery even on days when it did not rain. The great majority of the army was bivouacked in and about Lisbon, and whether it was overcrowding, bad water, or the effects of the weather, the Guadiana fever was rife, hundreds of men down with it to jam the medical wards. A couple of surgical wards had been requisitioned for the overflow, and though the staff physicians were technically in charge of all fever patients, the surgeons helped as they could. The only treatment was chinchona and opium, and time; it was a particularly virulent form of ague.

"You feeling all right? You don't look quite the thing."

"I'm all right," said McDonagh. "Didn't sleep much last night, that's all—headache—I've taken some laudanum." It had not helped much, his head felt thick and heavy. He looked without appetite at the plate the *cantina* girl slapped down before him—damned Portuguese messes—vegetables, a few pieces of mutton or goat in a watery gravy, and probably lukewarm. He ate some of it without enthusiasm. Robinson came blundering into the *cantina*, loud and cheerful as always, and made a beeline for them.

"You're not looking quite the thing, old chap," he said, hitting McDonagh playfully on the arm and straddling the other chair at the table. "Noticed it this morning. I say, don't you come down with this damned thing—I don't want to have to sit up nursing you! Medical men the worst patients of any, they say. Dr. Gale's down with it—Adams was telling me just now—got him over in the fourth med ward, and they say he's being more trouble than any other dozen patients. Are you feeling all right, old man? See you're not eating—won't do, got to keep your strength up, y'know! Be a good boy and clean your plate for nursie, eh?"

"I am perfectly all right," said McDonagh distinctly, repressing the impulse to empty his plate over Robinson's head.

Tebbs grinned. "Don't tease the captive animals, George."

"Oh, I say, no offense, no offense! All working hard, cross-grained, I understand, old boy." He patted McDonagh's arm. "Isn't this the damnedest plague! But y'know, I must say—you may think it mean of me—I can't help bein' damned amused at what some o' these chaps come out with when they're delirious. Funny as be damned. Love affairs and I don't know what all—never know what you're going to hear next! Fellow in one o' my wards this morning, all on a sudden he began yelling, 'All right, I killed her—I killed her, I did it, I killed her!' Just fancy! Wonder if his officer'll question him about it when he's rational—after all, if he was confessing to a murder—"

"Wouldn't be legal, would it?" asked Tebbs doubtfully. "Confession while of unsound mind or something—"

"Oh, I really couldn't say. I say, old chap, if you aren't going to eat that, just pass over the meat, would you? They never put enough in these damned messes—I'm starving, must keep up my strength, eh?—thanks very much, old man—"

"Will you kindly keep your hands off me, Robinson?" said McDonagh irritably. "My God, anyone'd think you were a Miss Nancy, pawing at—"

"Here, I say, that's not funny," said Robinson, looking hurt.

"Peace, children," said Tebbs. "You aren't looking awfully up to the mark, Con. Maybe you'd better take the rest of the day off."

"Damn it, I've just got a head, that's all—nothing to fuss over—this damned heat. I'm not hungry, I'll go on back, want some cigarillos anyway." He escaped from the *cantina*, which seemed to have shrunk for containing Robinson's loud yokelish laugh. It was close and breathless outside, and the laudanum certainly had not helped his head much as yet; he'd take a bit more in an hour or so.

When he came into the hospital entry hall, one of the senior physicians, Dr. Howard, greeted him with relief. "Have you had a little spell off, Mr. McDonagh? Do something for me, would you? There's a couple of new ones just come in, would you shepherd 'em into bed somewhere for me? I'm dead on my feet, I want to snatch a meal and sit down for a quarter hour."

"Certainly, Doctor." McDonagh glanced casually at the two stretchers lying against the wall. "Matter where they go?"

"Well, all the wards we've stolen from you are full. Take 'em t'other side, but not the first or fourth wards—better make it the third, not that they're any less busy—yes, that'll do. Thanks very much."

McDonagh sent out a call for some bearers and strolled over toward the new patients. The clerk on duty said chattily, "Taken bad on review parade, I understand—some o' these latest arrived troops, they're not used to the climate yet."

"Are any of us?" said McDonagh. He went on to the patients.

Newly arrived troops, and they'd been taken bad on parade. They were both still in uniform, scarlet coats, white trousers—a British Hessian regiment.

One of them grinned feebly up at him. "This d-damned ague mortal, be it, Doctor?" He was shaking in cold sweat but probably running a fever already as well.

"No," said McDonagh. His own teeth seemed to be chattering, and he felt sweat break out cold on his own face. It was very damned silly, because probably he'd tended other men from the Hessian regiments before and hadn't known or noticed because they weren't, of course, in uniform. "You'll be all right," he managed to say.

"You don't—look so damned—all right yerself, Doctor. Shakin' as bad as me, eh?"

No, of course he wasn't, it was just that— He thought suddenly, panicky, he had better look under the blanket—to make sure there was no bayonet. Did they parade on review with fixed bayonets? He tried to pull himself together, couldn't think straight with his head so thick.

It would be all right once the uniforms had been taken off them. Just other men then.

Which was ridiculous.

The bearers came, and he followed the two stretchers over to the medical side, asked for the third ward. A couple of new pallet beds had to be fetched, and room made along one wall; the regular beds were all full long ago. He set a couple of orderlies to undressing the patients, went down to the unfamiliar pharmacy room and found the chinchona-bark solution, mixed up two doses of it. His hands were shaking, and he spilled some, and swore.

A quiet voice said behind him, "You don't look as if you should be out of bed, sir."

"All right, I'm all right," he muttered. He turned, and it was the man he had seen on the top floor that night—the man who belonged where the harp music came from. One of the physicians, evidently. "Sorry—invade your domain," said McDonagh. "Dr. Howard asked me to see two new patients in for him. I'm from surgery side—"

"That's quite all right. I'll take a look at them. I also think I'd better have a look at you." The other man smiled. "It's outrageous that it should be so, but physicians and surgeons are also subject to falling ill, much as we hate to admit it."

"I've got a headache," said McDonagh. "That's all, just a thick head." He picked up the two glasses carefully and went back to the patients.

The men were stripped to their smallclothes now, lying on the pallets; it made very little difference, for he knew who they were. But no bayonets—that was good. A hand took one of the glasses from him. "If you would administer that?—thank you." Slowly, reluctantly, McDonagh knelt down and held out the glass. The man was shaking and weak, and needed help to drink.

"Thanks—Doctor," he mumbled. "Certingly 'ope that 'ere do s-some good—do it? Damned country—never see such—dust, mud, rain, can't breathe—the damned air. Been stationed in Ireland we 'ave, an' I—damn well 'd like be back there—even that's better—"

McDonagh got up to his feet, steadying himself on the wall. He dropped the empty glass and it shattered with a noise like a musket going off.

Oh, my God, yes, yes, they had been in Ireland.

There was summer undergrowth, bracken and gorse, thick on the hill, and he pulled Matt up the slope, Matt swearing and gasping with pain, dragging his wounded leg. Cover up beyond—trees—but they must get clear away, for it had been a rout at the last, and the English would search, they would chase—

Got Sullivan they had, blown open right through the middle, his blood and mangled guts and flesh all over McDonagh closest there to him. A damned rout—too many of them—coming like that, a tide of blood in their scarlet coats, and the sun blinding on their bayonets.

"Hold up a minute, Con—let me breathe—" Under the tall bracken, lying panting, hearing other men scrambling frantically up this hill.

"I've lost my knife, Matt," he said. "That last bastard I got—buried in him, I couldn't—"

Must get away clear, much farther away. Never thought they'd make the top of the slope—trees—and tearing his shirt, bandage Matt's leg. Lay and looked down through cover to that bloody field. Tide of blood. The fight was over, but the sun still blinding bright on the Hessian bayonets down there—they were hacking their way across the field among the wounded, they were blood-mad, gone berserk, laughing and yelling, in their scarlet coats, stripping off clothes from wounded and dead men, disemboweling and castrating them, throat cutting—wounded men screaming, trying to get up and run.

"Get off—farther, Con, they'll be quartering like hounds, for everyone got away. I can't make it with this leg—"

"You'll make it, Matt—Come on, damn you! Look down there—and get up on your feet, you coward! They'll be coming up here in ten minutes—"

"Who—the hell—you calling a coward? All right, damn you—"

And all the way to the first temporary shelter they found, hidden under the farmer's new hay crop in the shed, he was looking behind for them—bearing Matt's weight, swearing at him, encouraging him, no breath or heart left, but by God they would make it—all the while, looking behind for a big laughing man in a scarlet coat, coming at a run with bayonet fixed and dripping with blood off Enniscorthy field.

He opened his eyes and looked at a dirty stone ceiling a long way above. Sounds, muttering and people walking, about. Lying here on something he was. Suddenly frightened, he made an effort and raised up on one elbow.

The same ward he'd been in a bit ago, wasn't it? Pallet bed. He had the damned fever, been suspecting it all day, have to admit it. He was ice cold inside, burning hot out, and he felt alarmingly weak. Just have to run its course. No, damn it, he wouldn't have it, he couldn't have it—never ill, he was—be damned if he would be now—

"Well, you're awake, are you," said a quiet pleasant voice. "You'd better have some of this. Let me help you."

"I haven't got the damned fever," said McDonagh. "Why've you got me laid out here? I'm never ill, I've only got—bit of a headache, that's all."

"All the same, I believe you'd better have this." It was the same physician he had seen in the pharmacy room. He was half lifted up, an arm around him, and a glass held to his mouth.

"Ridiculous," he said. "I won't have it." He was frightened to find how weak he was.

"It's a bit late to say that," said the physician amusedly. "You've got up quite a little fever already. I suppose"—that seemed to be to himself—"I'd better report you, they'll be wondering. Can you tell me your name? Your name, sir?"

McDonagh heard him and knew he ought to answer, but the effort was for the moment beyond him. He lay quite still, recruiting all his strength to answer that ordinary question. The man was quite right; he ought to be reported as a patient. Properly on records somewhere. All right, he had the damned thing, couldn't deny it. Just lie here a day or so, soon get on top of it, never ill he was; it wouldn't keep him down so long or bad as other men, of course. Meanwhile, they wanted to know his name.

He turned his head a little on the husk-filled pillow, and saw one of the British Hessian soldiers on the next pallet, not two feet away.

He hadn't thought he could move, but in a flash he had scrambled over the pallet to get his back to the wall, never taking his eyes off the man. But he couldn't find his knife—lost his knife—

"Here, where'd d'you think you're going? What's the trouble? Come back here and lie down to rest, now—don't fight me, man, no one's trying to harm you—"

McDonagh's mind cleared a little. He said, "Not here. Not—no." He never moved his eyes from the soldier. Just lying there, not looking dangerous, but you couldn't take a chance. Blanket over him. Might have the bayonet hidden under that.

"What? That chap's not going to trouble you any, he's as bad off as you, or nearly. Don't you worry. Try to tell me your name, and then we'll get a little opium down you."

"No, no, no—*not,*" he said frantically, clutching at the hands on him, trying to pull away, "not—any opium, please. Drug —couldn't defend myself—wouldn't do that to a man, but I lost my knife, that last English bastard I took—buried in him—please get me another knife, not fair if he has his bayonet hid—"

"Well, my God," said the soft voice, half-amused, "you've worked up a fever indeed. Easy now—you going to be one of those we have to tie down in delirium? What a nuisance—and such a big bruiser to manage, too—why do I always get 'em? Have to send for somebody over in surgery, tell us who you are. Come on now, down you go—"

McDonagh suddenly put one hand over his mouth and bit it hard. His mind was struggling to tell him something urgent, across the vague gray fog between him and it. Delirium. Fever. Men talked in fever. Often quite plain—shouted. All the queer things from the bottoms of their minds. Mustn't talk, mustn't go delirious. There was something—something—not very long ago, either—damned yokel Robinson, Tebbs—*Funny as be damned . . . what some o' these chaps come out with . . . If he was confessing to a murder . . . Confession while of unsound mind.*

My God, my God, he thought, panic clearing his mind in little flashes. Mustn't talk. Mustn't let myself. Dangerous. Don't know how the law reads, but— Know what I'd come out with—No amnesty ever for traitors—traitors . . . an old United man—ten, eleven, twelve, thirteen years, but no amnesty—take him out and hang him along with all the rest. Childish, idealistic patriot—*say damn fool*—give away his life if he talked.

"D'you feel sick now?"

He moved his head from side to side. He whispered, "Doctor —you?"

"Yes, I'm one of the doctors—Justin Devlin. Can you tell me who you are? I see your mind's cleared a little."

His mind was, that moment, frighteningly and coldly clear. He lay and looked up into the face bent over him. A good face, pale clear skin, blue eyes blistered round the edges with tiredness but kind and smiling, a firm mouth. "I've got this damned fever," he told it.

"So you have. But don't fret over it, just take it easy, it's not fatal, you know. Your name?"

"Doctor," he said, "Doctor—mustn't talk. Don't listen—what I say—if delirious."

The eyes smiled. "Oh, I'm far too busy to listen to delirious patients."

But that was senseless. Only one man. All the other men. So many English. And that man in the next bed. "Not here—not here, please. Oh, God, I mustn't—don't want to be hanged—" He bit his lip hard and tasted blood. Already, already babbling.

"Now you take it easy, I'm going to get some opium down you, you won't be delirious for an hour or so after that, anyway."

McDonagh raised a shaking hand and put it on his mouth and turned to watch the soldier. Just lying there, but he could swear he saw the shape of the bayonet there beside him under the blanket. He kept his eyes on it, ready for any move.

Voices spoke over him again. Voice he knew. His mind connected it with a name after struggle. Shotworth. "Why, it's Mr. McDonagh. Yes, one of our surgeons—I'll report it if you like, and keep in touch to see how he does. I thought he wasn't looking any too grand when we met yesterday in the theater. Yes, indeed. You look to him, Dr. Devlin, we'll need every surgeon we've got here when the action gets under way again."

Devlin was an Irish name. But you never knew—you never knew friend from foe.

An arm about his shoulders again. "Can you drink this?"

He pushed away the hand with the glass. "No—mustn't. Devlin? Devlin? But—you never know. Sometimes—trust an Englishman—and not an Irishman. Never know. Depends."

"That's so," said the physician. "However, you can trust me."

McDonagh tried to focus on the blue eyes so near his own. Trust—yes—thought so, had to take a chance. "Be careful," he whispered. "Take care. Next bed—the Hessian. A bayonet he has—you don't know—what they do with bayonets. Listen, please—for God's sake, get me out of the ward—mustn't be heard—won't know what I'm saying—and I don't want—to hang. Have to trust you—for God's sake, please promise me—"

Devlin looked at the next bed and back to McDonagh; sudden sharp enlightenment showed in his eyes, and the hand laid on McDonagh's shoulder was firm and gentle.

"Be easy now. Try to help yourself and get this down."

"Careful—take care of the Hessian," he repeated anxiously.

"Yes, we'll do that. Just drink this."

McDonagh swallowed the draft and lay down again. Wrong to trust? He'd gone away. Opium—and no one on guard to watch for the quick move with the bayonet. Devlin not to be trusted—mistake? Mustn't let out anything dangerous—*I don't want to hang*, he thought painfully. Mustn't get into the danger of being hanged, because there was something he had to do, something important. Of course, he had to get back to England and marry Lauretta.

Satisfied with this achievement of memory, he let the opium take him.

When his mind came back to him again, it was clear. It felt like a long time later. He lay for a while with eyes shut, not wanting to move or know anything except that he was back to himself. He remembered the ward and his panic in beginning fever, and a little dim alarm rose in him lest he had somehow given himself away to someone. He put off moving because he knew, in an equally dim way, that he was still very weak, and that was alarming—dangerous. He wasn't over the damned fever yet. But after a while the message got through to him that the bed under him was softer than the pallet bed on the ward floor and that sounds about were different.

Someone was near him, but only one man. Otherwise quiet.

Still he lay motionless, trying to summon any strength left to him. He heard soft steps on a stone floor, and then the creak of a chair. Then, in a moment, the harp spoke, very soft, from a little distance off, as if the harpist spent a few leisure moments amusing himself without any intent to disturb others nearby. Slowly, note by note, the melody fell thin and sweet into being, and because it was one he knew, the words came automatically into his mind with it. An old, old tune it was, but the words he knew were the new words men had made for it only a little while ago:

> I'll sit me down on Vinegar Hill,
> And there alone I'll cry my fill,
> Till every tear does turn a mill—
> For Johnny is gone for a soldier.
>
> SHULE, SHULE, SHULE, AGRAH—
> Only death can ease my woe
> Since the lad of my heart from me did go—
> For Johnny is gone for a soldier.
>
> I sold my rock, I sold my reel,
> When my flax was spun I sold my wheel,
> To buy my love a sword of steel—

He moved, made some sound, for it was an unbearable pain in his chest, sharp as a knife, heavy as death on him, and with noticed but unfelt shame at the back of his mind he found the tears hot on his face. The slow sad music stopped, and then someone was bending over him.

He tried to lift a hand to wipe his face. The absurd, childish words came out of him in a gasp, like another man's voice heard. "I want to go home—I want to go home," he heard himself whisper.

A light hand was laid on his shoulder, and a firm resonant voice spoke to him very quietly. "To be sure, McDonagh, that is what we are all wanting, every man in this world. And sometimes it's a long, weary way to go, for not every man knows where his home is that he needs to find. But the lucky ones and the brave ones, they find out the direction to go, and reach it they will in the end. You will be coming home, McDonagh, and a welcome waiting for you there."

Instant peace fell over him for the reassurance, and he smiled and opened his eyes.

23

────────●────────

　　　　　　　　　　 When Devlin came in, past six, several days later, McDonagh was dressed for the first time and sitting up to the table. "Well, you're making an excellent recovery. My prize patient."

　　"I ought to be, all the special attention I've had. Now I'm taking notice again, I'm ashamed, Devlin—you taking me into your private quarters like this. I just need a week's rest now, I'll get back to my own—"

　　"McDonagh will stay another day," said Neil O'Derrica. He rose lithely from squatting beside the brazier in a corner of the room and came to set a plate before Devlin. "Devlin has had a good day, I hope? He looks tired and will want his meal."

　　"Well, I do," said Devlin. He smiled at McDonagh. "The voice of authority speaks—you stay another day. Nonsense, you don't put me out. As you see, I'm fortunate to have two good-sized rooms."

　　"And I wish to God I had," said McDonagh. He was still weak, but gaining in strength this last day since he'd been eating well. He looked from one of them to the other; these two days

since he had been free of fever, he was increasingly curious about his host and nurse. "But it's damned good of you, looking after me like this—can't imagine why you bothered—"

O'Derrica said, "Is McDonagh a stray dog that he finds a friendly hand and a gift astonishing?"

"You've been very good." McDonagh's tongue stumbled a little on the Gaelic, always what O'Derrica used; he had not spoken it for long, and hesitated for words.

"It is always a duty to honor brave men," said O'Derrica. "And also to protect them. There are never too many of the breed. The men who went out thirteen years back were brave men."

McDonagh said bitterly, "They were damned fools, as idealistic patriots always are." He got up from the table, feeling the need of a solider chair under him, and O'Derrica went to support him. Without fuss he got McDonagh settled on the couch which was his bed, thrust pillows behind him, and lit his cigarillo with a spill from the brazier.

"That is a sideroad, not the highway," he said. McDonagh looked up at him. O'Derrica was ageless; he might have been thirty or sixty. He was a broad man, not overly tall but solid-looking, with a ruddy complexion, light hazel eyes, a broad, smooth brow, a standing crest of fair hair. He was not a canny man; there was a strangeness about him, an obliqueness. He was an excellent servant, in the old true Gael sense, not holding himself inferior or obsequious, but with the stately formality that used the third person to the master even while he took the real authority.

He turned now and said courteously, "If Devlin will excuse it, I will go out for two hours."

"Devlin grants you leave, you old poseur," said Devlin.

"He will leave the plates and cups," said O'Derrica firmly, and went out, shutting the door noiselessly.

McDonagh said abruptly in English, "Well, I understand I must have done some talking—just as I feared."

Devlin looked amused. "That you did indeed. You in such mortal terror of that Hessian, I could guess where you'd been and what you'd seen, and a bit later I realized you'd been talking

sound sense, begging to get out of the ward." He rubbed his jaw thoughtfully. "We had some convalescent men in, and apart from anything else, I thought it might send their temperatures up to listen to your extensive vocabulary turned loose on the British army."

"Biting the hand that feeds me," said McDonagh with a short laugh.

"Oh, I'm not intending to blackmail you," said Devlin. He finished his meal, carried the used dishes to the table beside the brazier, and came to occupy the chair near the couch, got out his pipe, and began to fill it. "They say the young and the old are the true fanatics. Trouble is, some men never quite grow up, and some are never quite young. Thirteen years back— 'ninety-eight. I was eighteen, in my first year of training at Edinburgh, or I might have been out alongside you, McDonagh. You must have been about the same age."

"Sixteen. You were a wise man to stay where you were. What did I—did I—"

"Don't fret about it," said Devlin, striking a light for his pipe. "I didn't know what else to do with you, to be frank, so I fetched you up here to Neil. Hope you don't mind—I had to tell the orderlies you were a personal friend and so on, as an excuse. Neil's the one heard most of it, and you needn't worry about him. He never gets drunk, for one thing—I don't think he can—and he has, very likely, much higher standards of conduct than I have."

"Where on earth did you pick him up, and who is he?" asked McDonagh. "He's unbelievable. I thought they all died out three centuries ago."

Devlin laughed. "So they did. I believe he's a reincarnation, McDonagh. I don't know how old he is, but he was always about my father's house—ran the place, I think. My father was superstitious about him, and so am I. He's born out of his time, whatever else he is. Should have been one of the old chiefs' bards—you've heard him, of course—"

"I heard him before. I thought it was an illusion, whatever you call it—hearing things. A very old song I didn't know—"

Devlin hummed a few bars. "Oh, yes—that one? One of his.

After the old Gaelic style. Yes. He's a magnificent musician, of course, but not everyone appreciates that kind of thing. However, there's something else about him, McDonagh, and since I gather that he has a feeling about you, I'll warn you. He's second-sighted."

"For God's sake, don't tell me you believe in—"

"Well, I don't say I do," said Devlin seriously. "But I believe in Neil O'Derrica. He's told me too many damned queer things. Picked my wife for me, for one. It's a fact. There I was, gay young blade, thinking no more about marrying than going to the moon—you know?—and a patient comes into my consulting room with his daughter. Neil was acting sort of general orderly for me those days—he can turn his hand to everything, you know—and when they'd gone, he looked at me square and said, 'That young lady is the young lady Devlin will wed in a twelve-month.' And damned if I didn't." He grinned at McDonagh. "You're a skeptic, maybe you'll take a bet he's wrong about the twins. Not until August—I was home on leave last year. When I told Peggy what he'd said, she was delighted and started to make a list of names, but we know him."

"I take back what I said about your being a wise man. This is 1811, Dr. Devlin, and scientifically speaking—"

"Oh, science be damned,"said Devlin mildly. "I know Neil. Do as you please, but if he says anything to you, I'd think about it if I were you, that's all."

"Well, anyway, I'm damned grateful to you for doing this— I'll take myself off your hands tomorrow."

"Pleasure," said Devlin. "Least one Irishman can do for another. Where's your home, by the way? I'm a Dubliner myself. We must get together on leave or when we're both out—my time's up in January, thank God."

"I don't live in Ireland, I'll never go back, I've no desire to set foot in the country again. No money to be made there, in my job at least, and—oh, personal reasons—I don't know." McDonagh put out his cigarillo rather violently. "I'm going to be married— whenever I can get back to England—my service is up in February, and I'll not rejoin. Try to get a place in one of the big London hospitals."

Devlin was smoking quietly, watching him. "I see. Yes, I expect you'd have a better chance of private practice there too."

"Damned right. Have to think about a decent living—when you have a wife." And family. Little bleached rat of a thing—just like Bates. Poor little devil, not his fault. And the damned property—the property in Wexford. He scowled down at his clasped hands.

"I think you've sat up talking long enough," said Devlin. "You're only two days out of bed after the best part of a week in fever, you know. Here, I'll help you. As your physician, sir, you mind what I say, see?—you still need rest."

"All right, Doctor." He wasn't really reluctant; the effort of dressing and talking had tired him. "But I will get off your hands tomorrow now I'm sensible again."

He stayed another day, whatever his intentions; O'Derrica simply did not hear him when he said he would remove to his own quarters. When he did go back, the day after that, O'Derrica walked across to the other wing with him and made up his bed fresh. "Thank you," said McDonagh, feeling awkward, feeling—as you did with O'Derrica—that he should be addressed in statelier language than that of these modern days. "I do appreciate very much what you've done, for a stranger, too—thank you."

"McDonagh is not a stranger, he is one of our own."

"I'll get on fine now—bribe one of the orderlies to fetch up my meals for a few days—bit of a rest and I'll be quite all right again."

"Yes, McDonagh will be in health of the body very well soon." O'Derrica paused and looked at him, where he had settled McDonagh on his bed, propped up on pillows with a book to hand and a dish for his cigarillo. "I would say a thing to McDonagh."

"Yes?"

"I have, sometimes, the sight, McDonagh. A thing will come to me. And also, I am not a fool for reading men in the ways they may be read, as they reveal themselves. There is a saying from our old literature—*Three keys that unlock thoughts, drunkenness, trustfulness, love.* There is another key, kin to the first, and that is illness. I know a thing about McDonagh, I would say and have him listen."

"Yes, all right." Somehow it was impossible to laugh at this sort of nonsense when the man was there looking at you.

"There are two great troubles on McDonagh, and there is a link between them. McDonagh says to himself he is a man who looks at life ruthless and honest, there is in him no sentimentality or prejudice. But the trouble has fallen on him because for some matters in his life, this is a lie, and he sees a wrong image through a clouded pane. He must look longer from another place to see truth, and then the trouble will be lifted from him."

"There's no trouble on me," said McDonagh sharply. "Not now I'm well again."

"It is on McDonagh," said O'Derrica simply. "It is a weight in his mind and heart, but perhaps he is denying it is there—it is a thing men will do. It has sent him down the wrong road. McDonagh, there were times this year, and once in the last summer, as I had my hands on my harp, I had a feeling on me that one was listening who needed to hear me. Perhaps it was McDonagh, I do not know. But I know there is this trouble on him, like a raven sitting on his shoulder talking of death. I would say to him that he must not listen, he must use his courage, he must look hard and plain on his trouble, and see it clear."

"Oh, yes, very likely," said McDonagh. "I always try to look at things plain, without prejudice. Thank you, O'Derrica, I'll do that."

O'Derrica hesitated and then went to the door. "McDonagh will come to visit Devlin," he said firmly. "They are alike men, it will be good for them to sit and talk. He will come to dinner on Friday evening."

"Thanks very much, all right."

O'Derrica nodded courteously and took himself out. McDonagh laughed quietly to himself, taking up his book. Not quite a poseur perhaps—the old devil believed himself—but, in this day and age! Should stick to his harping—an accomplished musician he was.

But he did, as O'Derrica bade him, go across to see Devlin, and not only the once; they liked each other's talk, and the rest of that long, hot, dreary summer was made more tolerable for both of them by the friendship.

"O'Derrica says we're alike men," said McDonagh amusedly. "It's a black lie. You must be half an Englishman, the way you never get excited over anything." Devlin, in fact, grew calmer and milder as men about him waxed hot in any emotion; it should have been an infuriating quality, but McDonagh found it rather comic. "So much for your tame seer!"

Devlin grunted and asked if O'Derrica had ever said anything to McDonagh about himself. McDonagh told him what O'Derrica had said. "Oh, quite meaningless, of course—unless I'm harboring worries I know nothing about!"

Devlin grunted again and changed the subject.

McDonagh mended back to full health again and resumed work in his wards; he was considerably startled when Devlin strolled over to the surgical wing one morning to inform him that he'd been officially reported dead. "The usual official muddle, and you can blame me if you like for taking you out of the ward. You were right next to that Hessian private, and he came down with pneumonia and passed out a week later. I don't know exactly how it happened, but one of the orderlies must have got the beds mixed. Anyway, nobody caught it as it went through, and there it is. You'd better go and get it into the records you're still alive, and write your fiancée."

"Well, I will be damned," said McDonagh indignantly. "You might be a little less careless over in medical! You know what you've done, don't you, damn it? All my pay withheld from the date in question, and I'll have to write seventeen letters to the War Office and make out affidavits and God knows what to get back on the list! Damn you, Justin, talk about wanton malice—"

"Good God, I never thought of that, so you will. I am sorry, man, but it was a muddle. First thing that occurred to me was your girl in England, you'd better get a letter off at once, she'll see it in the papers even if you didn't request formal notification. The *Times* prints casualty lists every week, you know."

"My God, yes, that's so. I'd better." It was a nuisance, but he was more concerned about the War Office side of it than

Lauretta; the papers did not receive casualty lists to print until official notification had been made, and that took time. He could get a letter to her before that happened, and did so.

And had another of her colorless, prim letters in reply. Both of them so bad at writing letters ... Rereading it, sitting chewing his quill trying to answer it, all that insidious, reluctant feeling about the property took possession of his mind again, and he swore to himself. He must force himself to be reasonable about this, it was childish—and even, perhaps, a little sentimental.

He grimaced and laughed at that thought and began to write again, and Robinson barged in, having to pass through this room to reach his own, made a few loud jovial remarks, and started to undress with the door open, whistling shrilly to himself. McDonagh said, "Oh, hell," silently, put his letter away, and went across to spend the rest of the evening with Devlin.

In the midst of some casual talk about the slackening of the fever plague, which seemed to have run its course by now, he suddenly swore again and announced that he was a damned fool. All that business still insistently at the front of his mind, he couldn't get clear of it.

"I have long suspected it," said Devlin, "but what brought it home to you?"

"Oh, my God," said McDonagh, and got up to pace the room, frowning. "It's the damnedest silliest thing, Justin—" he told Devlin about it, rather disjointedly, and broke off to laugh and add, "Maybe this is the trouble O'Derrica saw on me! I know it's a childish, superstitious thing, but I can't seem to get past feeling like this. And I'll be caught with it—legal owner technically—because morally it's Lauretta's and the boy's, damn it, and I can't ask her to give it up—and there's no reason to get rid of it for another investment."

"Every reason not to," said Devlin softly. "Capital in Irish tenant land pays about the highest percentage of any investment you can make. ... Yes, maybe that's your trouble, Con. Do you mind if I say something?" he added abruptly. "O'Derrica said—*raven sitting on your shoulder*. I think there is, and—to continue the fanciful metaphor—it's a raven off Enniscorthy field, isn't it? I don't suppose, if there is any right age for seeing a bloody war, sixteen's the best age for it. You lost something at Enniscorthy, Con."

McDonagh sat down again and poured himself another glass of the thin, bitter wine of Portugal. "Yes, I lost my knife," he said dully. "It was a damned good knife, too, with a double edge."

"Maybe it had three edges," said Devlin. "You lost something else—or you thought you did—your belief in ideals."

"Yes, by God, that I did," said McDonagh. "The damn fool storybook ideals that make damn fools out of men, in the name of patriotism. Patriotism! An excuse for violence—for arrogance—as ideals always are an excuse for something, whether it's bad manners or brutality to inferiors or irresponsibility or murder and rape and sudden death. Yes, I'll never be caught in that trap again, it's all a jape and a lie, the ones on top victimizing the ones underneath with all the fine words, *love of country, freedom, faith, liberty, justice!*—to go out and be killed, a thousand messy ways, for the fine words—that never come true. Say patriot, say damn fool. Or any other kind of idealist. Whether anything comes of it or not—all the glorious victories and glorious defeats—they never get anything out of it themselves, of the ideals that sent them out. Worse off than before, times. No, I'll never be seduced by ideals again, Justin, you're very damned right there."

Devlin was slowly, carefully digging out the bowl of his pipe with his pocketknife. "Well, you know," he said ruminatively, "that's just one edge of the knife, Con. Something there, yes. But the words mean something, or they wouldn't be in the language. Great ideals haven't a lot to do with realities in life, no, they haven't indeed, and maybe it's just as well—but it's a damned funny thing, you know—in the end the world most often gets kicked on another few steps toward realizing the ideals by the idealists, not by the cynics, those fellows who see the truth hard and clear and know it just can't be done. It's the ones who haven't an ounce of healthy cynicism in 'em, the ones who really believe in all the fine words, and believe they can come true, that sometimes—surprisingly often—do start to make 'em come true."

"All right, so they do," said McDonagh. "Me, I'm not a reformer or a fanatic or a patriot or any other damned kind of idealist. They can get on with it, and the hell with them. I've a living to earn and a life to live, and that means dealing in realities."

"And so it does," said Devlin. He blew down the stem of his pipe, examined it critically, and began to fill the bowl. "It's like," he added unexpectedly, "the difference between having a harlot and a woman you really love, romantic and other ways, for herself. Cut whiskey. You get a little temporary pleasure out of it, but it's a long way from the real thing. Ideals—oh, they're just fantasies, impossible of realization—to any sensible man with his feet on the ground—but they're like love and whiskey, Con—provide all the stimulant to life, they do."

McDonagh laughed and said he preferred the first two.

Devlin put his pipe in his mouth and lit it. " 'Ninety-eight," he said, and emitted a blue cloud of smoke, and sighed. " 'Ninety-eight, and how many thousand dead—in the name of burning patriotism? I'll tell you something that always struck me queer about that war. Nobody seemed really to understand what began it. I was seeing the English papers at the time, of course. Wild rebel outlaws they talked about, restless element in the population, wanton stirring up of violence. Never pointed out it was—even by the handful of radical Englishmen who applauded him—that Harry McCracken wasn't a rebel outlaw chief out o' the mountains. He was a cotton manufacturer." That was said sadly. "He owned a cotton-processing manufactory in Belfast. And Harry Munroe, and most of the other men who joined the Cavehill Pact—Cavehill Conspiracy, English translation—they were businessmen. And most of the other leaders under 'em priests and Protestant landholders."

McDonagh swirled the drop of wine in his glass. "Yes, that's so, of course."

"It wasn't so much ideals that brought out the patriots in 'ninety-eight as it was hard cash profits. Or the lack of them. A very amusing game, the one England's been playing on Ireland the last hundred years, about those. Cat and mouse, you might say. Ireland sets to work, practical hardheaded businessmen, building up a trade—as it was the cotton processing, in the eighties—and presently she's exporting enough of that particular thing to England that it's hurting English business in the same line. So Parliament passes a law against importing that kind of Irish goods—and so the Irish businessmen commence to sell to the Continent and America, and presently they're taking business away from English firms. So Parliament passes a law forbidding Ireland to export those goods anywhere, and the business is killed and the factories shut down. So the Irish set to work again—" Devlin took his pipe out of his mouth and looked at it wryly. "They did it with the lace trade, and with raw wool and woolen yardage, and with the cotton, and they did it with Ulster sheep, and with live cattle, and with slaughtered beef, and they did it with horses for the army, and with the hay and barley, and with the fisheries. Twenty times we built up commerce, and money began to come into the country, and in time it'd have got spread around—the ordinary folk living better, wages higher, more of everything to be had, better standards of health and diet, money for schools and medical services— and then it stopped, because England's commerce mustn't be interfered with. And then they look at us, over the channel there, and they say, Feckless Irish, no ambition, ignorant peasantry."

"And just why the hell are you making a speech about it to me? I know all that as well as you do!" said McDonagh violently. "Why the hell d'you think I got out?"

"But that wasn't why you went out with the United army in 'ninety-eight," said Devlin.

"No, it wasn't. Nor nine-tenths of any of the rest of us. I went out in 'ninety-eight because I was filled up with a lot of nonsense about Irish independence, throwing off the tyrant's yoke, and equality before the law for all men, and freedom of the individual."

Devlin looked at him sidewise. "And that isn't what you lost at Enniscorthy. Are you going to tell me you don't still believe in all that? That's what 'ninety-eight was all about."

"Oh, don't devil me, Justin—don't sit there picking fiddling little subtleties out of words! As abstract principles, yes, damn it, certainly. But I'm done thinking about abstract principles before thinking of Con McDonagh."

"Ah," said Devlin, "and that is what you lost at Enniscorthy, Con. The faith to sacrifice for an ideal. Or rather, you tried your damnedest to lose it—ever since, you've been talking loud and long about how you lost it, and were glad to lose it—and all the time you knew it was sitting snug there inside you just where it'd always been, only you couldn't admit it to yourself. For thirteen years you've been running away from Enniscorthy field—and never getting clear of it."

O'Derrica had come quietly in several minutes before, and his grave eyes fastened on McDonagh now. "Devlin says one true thing there. It is one of the troubles on McDonagh. But it is a very simple trouble, more than Devlin says it with his long English words."

"What words does O'Derrica have?" asked Devlin, smiling.

O'Derrica came and touched McDonagh's shoulder once, lightly. "All men have a love for the land they spring from and an eagerness to defend that land against any comer. McDonagh has denied this to himself, and so there is a weight of guilt on him."

"Well," said Devlin thoughtfully. "Yes, that, too."

"Now you can draw out my horoscope," said McDonagh, "and weave spells over the caldron, and consult the Gypsy's crystal! You're making Con McDonagh out the hell of a lot deeper character than I ever thought he was."

Devlin laughed, if without much humor, but O'Derrica touched McDonagh's shoulder again. "I will put it a way McDonagh will understand. The patient is bleeding to death, and McDonagh has gone out to attend the theater, saying to himself, Another surgeon may take the responsibility. But all the while he is looking at the play there is black guilt on him that he left the patient in such case." He went on into the next room silently.

After a moment McDonagh said, "Hell," and stood up. "And I thought a nice quiet evening of talk with you would put me in better spirits! You're as bad as O'Derrica. Good night, you damned patriot—and I hope I don't have the nightmare for all these somber metaphors!"

August came, and with it a letter notifying Devlin of his twin sons. "And what price O'Derrica now, you skeptic?"

September came and began to grow toward October, and the

fall rains came to break the heat. The year was turning, and McDonagh was constantly reckoning the weeks now before he would be free. Yet the thought of getting back to England, of beginning his new cycle of life with Lauretta, was darkened by his feeling about the property; that was all it was, surely, this vague dissatisfaction surrounding the thought of that, like a nimbus of fog. It would be quite different when he saw her again and, now the conventions were satisfied, could hold her in his arms and kiss her—and maybe try to explain.

Then, early in October, a solution was offered him, and he was excited about it; his mind seized on it eagerly. He hadn't got around to telling anyone about it, or writing Lauretta, when the chief medical officer called him in and, as he had fully expected, probed at him about his term of service. Mr. McDonagh was aware that there was still need for surgeons, a recommendation could be put through for a rise of ten pounds a year—

McDonagh repeated several times that he'd decided against signing on for another tour of military service. He was to be married and would prefer a permanent appointment somewhere. The chief officer sighed, shrugged, and smiled. "Well, Mr. McDonagh, we can't force you! Your service is up early in February. I will try to arrange that you be assigned to take charge of some shipload of disabled men being sent home at the end of the year. You may then report to the War Office, but in view of the fact that you have, let me see, a fortnight of leave due you, I should expect that you'd receive no posting for such a short remaining period. I needn't say I'm sorry to see you leave us. It is a secure and useful career for a medical man."

"But their wives don't find it so, sir," said McDonagh with a grin.

The chief officer smiled. "No, I daresay not. Well, I will arrange that for you as I said, so long as your mind is definitely made up."

"Thank you, sir."

He went across that evening to discuss his new solution with Devlin, but before he had opened his mouth about it, Devlin said he wanted to talk to him. "I was going to send Neil over for you, matter of fact. I've been thinking about this, Con, and while

I was of two minds about approaching you, I want to—I want to lay it in front of you anyway. I just want you to think about it. I daresay you're going to call me seven kinds of a fool and say, No, damn it, right off. But I'm going to ask you nevertheless."

O'Derrica came in with coffee. God knew where he got it, but he always had some; McDonagh suspected black magic. "Well, all right, say your piece, whatever it is, and·I'll listen, but not for long. I've something to tell you, too."

Devlin cast him an oblique look. "Involves lecturing you again. Ever wonder why I signed up with the army?—me, a quiet decent family man? I'll tell you. Because you can save more money from wages, a living being provided. I haven't enjoyed it much. But there's something· I want to do. . . . You know, I've always felt that it's a mistake to keep our different branches of one profession so far apart. After all, quite a good many sort of cases—overlap, so to speak. If we each knew a bit more about all the job, and worked together, I believe we'd both be better at our jobs, and find out things, maybe, we don't know now—and cure more patients. I could cite a hundred instances, but you know the sort of thing I mean. Questions of diagnosis and treatment both. Things you'd recognize that I wouldn't, and vice versa. The poor devil of a patient picks a surgeon to go to, times, when he needs a physician—all doctors to him, though the degree doesn't dignify you men with the title!—you know? As it is, we have a few years' more training than you, but only a very hasty course in practical anatomy, none at all in dissection—while you aren't required to know a damned thing about properties of drugs, chemical reactions, or physical illnesses in general where it doesn't involve any cutting."

McDonagh was interested, momentarily diverted. "That's so. I expect we both pick up a little with experience—random information—but not the hell of a lot."

"And neither of us is required to know anything about midwifery, unless we're one of those queer perverted fellows that want to be men midwives—about one midwife out of a hundred is a man, and you know as well as me what most other medical men think of 'em! Damn it, Con, there's nothing sensible about the situation, it seems to me. A good many physicians look down on surgeons as mere skilled mechanical tradesmen—and because they don't have as long a training. Wouldn't dream of consulting a surgeon about a patient. And the surgeons, because they haven't—you must agree—training in recognizing nonsurgical illness, all too often they make a wrong diagnosis and cut where it isn't needful. And you may think me radical, but I do believe that if more women were delivered by surgeons with sound grounding in anatomy, we'd have fewer childbed deaths—most midwives are an ignorant lot, and there's no training legally required for them at all."

"I don't think you're radical, I agree with you. God knows enough physicians have looked down their noses at me, and I must admit I've looked down mine at the surgeons who went into specializing midwifery! But you're right, of course. In my hospital days I've seen patients who'd wasted time going to a physician for symptoms neither the patient nor the doctor knew called for surgery. Daresay you've seen some the other way round. If you men knew enough to say to the patient, This is a stone in the kidney, This is a hernia—and send him to us! But no, you deal with materia medica, and it's the first thing you think of, stir up a dose. And—"

"Yes, and if you knew enough to say, this is consumption, and send him to me! Accepted curricula being what it is, it's just in the nature of things. But you know, I'd like to try. . . . I've been in private practice in Dublin—I inherited my father's practice, luckily for me—until I signed into military service. When I get out and go home, I'd like to go into joint practice with a surgeon, a man who'd cooperate with me, get along, exchange ideas, teach each other all the things we should know about the other job. You see? And—another reason, too—" Devlin was silent, looking down at his pipe, and then said, "Oh, Lord, I said I meant to tell you the whole thing, all my—call 'em grandiose plans. I'll be rude, Con. There are too many Irishmen like you. Looking around them, saying, Nothing here for me—no money to be made, no opportunity—and going off. To England, America, the Continent, where they can—just maybe—do better for themselves. For two hundred years they've been going out of the country—two, three, four hundred thousand of them by now—scattering all over Europe, America."

McDonagh said, "Improved all the foreign bloodlines, they have." He was trying to think who had said something like that to him before. *The best ones, the ones with the guts and the brains and the ambition.*

"It's a bad thing for the country," said Devlin quietly. "Enough of the best of our young men are dead in rebellions. You know, Con, it seems to me there are different kinds of patriotism. War's a bad thing, but there are times and places a man—or a nation—has to fight in the open, violence meeting violence, for life itself. That's one kind, the kind of patriotism the men had who went out in 'ninety-eight. But more often a country needs the men who will help her build. Do you know those lines from Isaiah? *The bricks are fallen down, but we will build with hewn stones—the sycamores are cut down, but we will change them into cedars.* There's such the hell of a lot of work to be done, there at home. . . . You know how most of the people live. There isn't a hospital in the country outside of five or six of the bigger towns, and not one person in a thousand could afford medical fees anyway. Appalling ignorance, in the more isolated districts—my God, sometimes you see whole villages down with scurvy, and we've known the remedy for that for two hundred years! But I believe—I've got to believe, we've all got to believe—that there are signs of better times coming. There's agitation for Ireland to have her own Parliament established again—"

"And what the hell good would that do when all the seats were for sale at such prices that only Anglophile landholders could buy them, and Catholics still excluded? Oh, they made a damned great show, talking proud about reform, when they gave the franchise to the papists at last! Result was, being no different from men anywhere, the papists had to think about their skins first, and when the factor told 'em to vote for Lord Thus-and-Such, they did. They did—or got driven off their farms or had their crops burned and their stock killed!"

"It might be different next time," said Devlin. "Freer—it's got to be! And there's agitation for reform in a lot of ways, things will get better gradually. I know this present Parliament's dead against full Catholic emancipation, but we've got most of the worst of the Penal Laws, if not off the lawbooks, at least no longer enforced. Men aren't hanged now for teaching Catholics to read and write—there are schools being established. Not many, but some—and in the more isolated districts, too. Some church schools, but some charity-sponsored by Protestants too. And towns are growing. I tell you, it will be better if we all pull together and make it so—in spite of all the discrimination. Well, I'm delivering a lecture, but it's that kind of thing in my mind, Con—"

"Yes, you needn't have said all that to tell me you're an idealist."

"What I'd like to do," said Devlin, "is to start the nucleus of a small hospital myself. Probably just me and a surgeon, to begin with. If I can get the right man to come in with me. Not call it a hospital, or we'd never get gentry patients, of course—the ones who can pay! But with the Dublin practice I have—I've a young Englishman holding it for me—and the hope of a good private practice on the surgery side, we could manage. Give one day a week to charity patients—I've thought about this, got all sorts of schemes!—get the word spread about of free treatment, so they'd come in. We've never used the house my father left me— just outside Dublin, out toward Dunboyne—it's rather a barracks of a place, I've got it leased, but the lease is up next June. Just a good distance, not too far to ride into the city to patients, but we'd draw from the countryside, too, you see. My service is up this January, as I said, and I'll have somewhere around four hundred pounds to put into equipment and so on. And to carry us until we're fairly started. And as time goes on—this is all just a dream, but they do sometimes come true!—I've thought we might somehow qualify as a regular established hospital and get an allotment of public funds, maybe even start a small medical school in conjunction, and if we could, if we did, somehow arrange to carry at least one or two poor students free of tuition— there must be hundreds who never could afford to study. And—" Devlin was becoming quite excited for him, riding his hobbyhorse—"Peggy has a scheme for starting a school for the tenants' children—no tuition, you know, nothing much more than reading and writing, but it'd be a start, you see? She says she could teach classes, and if whatever man goes in with me is married, maybe his wife could help, too. It's the hell of a big house, room for almost anything, and grounds, too, with out-houses. Ideal for the purpose. Oh, I know,"—he laughed—"it sounds like a tall order and a lot of damned hard work, but it's worth doing! Well, you know what I'm putting to you. I'd like you to think about it. I've not met another man in your line of the job I thought might take it on—and I'd like you in with me, I think we'd work well together."

"You can stop talking, boy," said McDonagh. "Didn't I tell you I'm a servant of Mammon? It's one hell of an interesting idea, I wish it luck and you with it, I'd be interested to know how it turns out. But you don't catch me, Justin—I don't want to go back to Ireland, no, thank you, not ever in this world, please-God-amen! As a matter of fact, I think I'm going to New York."

24

———————•———————

The letter from Matt had been nearly three months on the way, what with going to England first. It seemed to McDonagh that destiny was manipulating a situation for him again, as he read it. Matt had written this in reply to McDonagh's letter telling of his engagement, and if his suggestion was staggering at first, it deserved thought. In a new young country with an expanding population, there was room and work for professional men and money to be made. Matt talked casually of fifteen, eighteen hundred dollars a year; that was more than three hundred pounds. "Just give it some thought, Con—be a fresh start for both of you, and probably a better opportunity, certainly the possibility of more money, than you'd have in England."

That sounded very good indeed, but what came into McDonagh's mind almost at once was that if he and Lauretta emigrated to America, the English investments would sensibly have to be sold and the capital reinvested in America somewhere; at least that would be the most reasonable thing.

Devlin listened to the letter and McDonagh's vague plans, and finally he said in a heavy tone, "Well, it sounds a good prospect, all right. I hope you'll find it—as represented. And that your fiancée will be willing."

"Damn, Lauretta must see it's a wise move—not as if she was a society figure, to think anywhere but London's the wilderness. Besides, New York's quite a decent-sized town, I believe."

"Yes. Well, you know I wish you good luck. I'm sorry I can't persuade you to come in with me, but—maybe it isn't meant. Things have a way of working themselves out."

"So they have," said McDonagh cheerfully, and went off to write a long and rather incoherent letter to Lauretta about New York. Fortunately he hadn't finished it when the chief officer sent for him and told him that he was assigned to take charge of thirty disabled convalescent men going back to England in the *Quintus*, sailing on the thirteenth of December. McDonagh added that information to his letter. "So this will be my last letter, my dearest, and you'll not have time to get another to me. I hope you are counting the days as I am."

He sent that off, and went about the business of getting through the next six weeks as patiently as possible. There weren't many casualties in, action being slack, and he had not a great deal to do. And a few days after he had sent that letter, he reread Matt's letter again, and it came into his mind that he had been acting a lie to himself.

How did he really feel about emigrating to New York? Not very enthusiastic. He had seized on the idea for just one reason: as an excuse to get rid of the property. All right, be honest and look at it—plain, as O'Derrica advised him. Now he did, he couldn't maintain that he wanted to go. And he couldn't make himself believe that Lauretta would want to go.

She was such a, well, rather timid and prim little thing.

—*Much joy of your chaste, stupid, namby-pamby, mealy-mouthed, submissive little widow....* He heard her saying it to him, sudden and clear, like a slap across the face, like the blow she had struck him. Madeleine. Damn Madeleine. Finished and done. Other things to think about, new sort of life to live, with Lauretta.

McDonagh realized something else, slowly, still looking at

Matt's letter, his mind wandering, worrying at this. He couldn't clearly visualize that new life to begin so soon; he couldn't see himself living with Lauretta, sharing a home with her, playing stepfather to that child, established in that routine. . . . It had been an unconventional situation, that was probably the reason—not able (for her notions about orthodoxies) to feel she was really his, at last safely his. It would be different, better, when he was with her again this time.

He hadn't written Matt, and he wouldn't now, until he'd thought it over carefully and was sure.

The night before he was to sail, he dined by invitation with Devlin. And Devlin said shrewdly, "You've not quite made up your mind about New York, have you?"

"No, damn it, I can't seem to. Maybe—maybe it's best to talk it over with Lauretta anyway."

"I won't press you anymore, Con, but—you know how I'd like you to decide. In any case, I'll be in England soon after you—I'm sailing myself next week, you know. Usually stay at the Berwick Hotel, you might drop round if you like. I'll have to be in London a few days, for official resignation."

"Certainly I'd like. Introduce you to Lauretta, make you envy me."

Devlin looked at him, started to speak, and then closed his mouth. "I'll look forward to seeing you there then," he said politely.

As McDonagh was enjoying the little surge of excitement a leave-taking always put in him, coming onto the wharf that morning with his baggage, he felt a touch on his arm and turned to see Neil O'Derrica beside him. "I have come to say a last word to McDonagh."

"Oh, that's—very good of you," he said, constrained as always with this grave man out of another time.

"McDonagh," said O'Derrica slowly and carefully, "is on a wrong road, that leads nowhere for him. He is running away, he is still running away. I have received a thing to say to McDonagh. I do not know what it means, but perhaps he will know."

"Yes?"

"I am to say this to McDonagh. The strong feeling, the feeling of violence, it is the true feeling. It has two edges, and they look in opposite directions. Life is change and interplay, and the small rules men make for it are nothing real to do with life. If McDonagh will look with open eyes and use honesty with himself, he will come to the truth."

"You said something like that to me before, O'Derrica," said McDonagh with a smile. "I am not a good liar, to myself or anyone else."

O'Derrica touched his arm. "All men lie to themselves easier than to other men. McDonagh said to me, he wants to go home. Let him go, then. Let him find the right road—with the help of God—and go to his home." He turned without other farewell and walked off among the crowd on the dock.

McDonagh laughed after him and called a lounger nearby to carry his bags up the plank.

On the fourteenth day of the new year he stood—for the second time since his return—in Lauretta's little parlor, and faced the stark ruination of all he had felt, and thought, and planned.

"Do you think you will receive the appointment to the staff of the London Hospital, Con? So convenient."

"I don't know," said McDonagh. "Yes, wouldn't it be? I'm to see someone on the committee tomorrow afternoon, but there may be no definite decision at once, I don't know."

"You do understand how I felt about New York?" As he turned from the window, Lauretta smiled fleetingly, pleadingly and made one of her unfinished, vague gestures. "To go so far from home—I—I would, Con, if it were absolutely necessary for you in your work, but it's really not, is it? That is, you have this application in at the London Hospital, and—of course, I know nothing about such things, but after all, the—the prospects in America all sounded rather vague, didn't they?"

"Yes, eminently," said McDonagh, looking at her.

It was nothing to do with what that old poseur O'Derrica had said to him; it had just happened. Walking in here, day before yesterday, to see her after absence. Out of full mourning she was—in a prim, plain lavender gown. Feeling slight and soft against him, protesting against his hard embrace, and her mouth prim, too, just accepting his kisses; and suddenly, frighteningly, McDonagh felt that he was perverted, to use passion with a child, to expect an ignorant child to meet and return passion.

He looked at Lauretta, and saw that she was a pretty young woman, no pretense to beauty, or charm, or much intelligence; she hadn't been raised to be intelligent, she'd never needed to be. A gentle, pretty woman, growing a bit plump and soft, who had always had someone to tell her what to do, how to behave, and who had never dreamed of rebelling against authority. A woman who, true to her type and breeding, was all surface— very little real at all under her correct lip service to convention.

He had gone to a dance at the Amisons' Dublin house, with Matt, and she had been wearing a white gown, smiling and greeting guests in her soft voice. He had been twenty, and he had fallen a little in love with her. Ten years, or nearly—it was a long time, but maybe the ten years between twenty and thirty was a longer time than it was on the calendar. No stranger to women he'd been, but he was twenty, and tell himself as he had that he was a cynic, still, he had automatically set the kind of woman Lauretta was a distance off from the other kind he'd known. Didn't connect Lauretta with the crudities, the realities, but had vague romantic-colored fancies about her.

"Yes, darling, what is it? Oh, what a lovely picture! Is it a lady?—of course it is, and I expect she's all elegantly dressed, so, for church on Sunday morning!" She smiled fondly down at the boy, who was carefully turning the pages of a ladies' magazine. It was suddenly borne in on McDonagh, looking at them, that the boy looked like her, not FitzEustace. The same small plump chin, and Lauretta's was growing a little roll underneath already—the same soft features and pale blue eyes under almost colorless brows.

Quite irrelevantly he was trying to remember how many times he had kissed her. They had used to meet in the park. . . .

She didn't intend to remove from this house, he could tell that by the little discussion they'd had about it. Quite reasonable, of course, when she had the house and was comfortable here, and he could not afford anything half so spacious. She was entirely docile about it, as she would be about most things, but there was a soft, woolly obstinacy there, too. Never quarrel, she would, but simply get her own way in the end—because it would be too damned much trouble to try to drive any understanding into her head of someone else's point of view.

"You aren't really disappointed about it, Con? You seemed to think it a good idea, but—"

"No, I'm not at all," he said. "On second thoughts I didn't really—I agree with you. Lauretta, when would you like to be married? It's eighteen months now, a perfectly proper period of time."

She looked up doubtfully from her sewing. "Are you teasing me again? Oh, well, two years is more proper, of course. I—I hadn't really thought of a time. Do you think June? It would really be better."

By some quirk of memory he recalled the date FitzEustace had died, the twenty-ninth of May, and he very nearly suggested that they be married on the anniversary.

No, she hadn't thought. If she could ever be got to admit the truth, if she knew the truth about herself, she did not much care for being married to any man. There was no capacity for passion in her at all; it was all the surface look to her, about everything: the display of sentiment, of romance, but no remote understanding of anything deeper to express it. All the correct feelings as exemplified in the best romantic novels written by other ladies, but no glimmer of knowledge of what lay beneath and behind.

She was a nice child, of good nature and pretty ways, and she always would be. Never knew when he was jesting, she said helplessly. Such a violent person, Con.

Ten years ago, with two calendar years between them, maybe he had been ten years older than she, in himself. Now he felt half a lifetime older.

She hadn't anything at all to give him; she was nothing at all to him. For ten years he had preserved the mummified figure of an anemic, barely begun adolescent romance, cherishing it to him, like a small boy with an insignificant treasure, and suddenly, on exposure to the air, the mummy had crumbled into dust and vanished. It was just nothing.

"I am going to send you away very soon." She smiled at him, with a glance at the clock. "I have this frivolous female party this evening, and I must dress and dine early, to be ready."

"Yes, certainly," he returned absently. "I have an engagement with a friend for dinner anyway."

Female parties, innocent small gatherings for gentle gossip and penny-point cardplaying, she would give, and a great fuss over the preparations. She would know and care nothing whatever about his work, and when he made little satiric jests, she would look at him bewildered, doubtful. There was no core to Lauretta; she was soft all the way through—like a child's rag mommet made out of sewing scraps. And just about as stimulating to make love to or to live with.

"I'll go and leave you to it," said McDonagh, still absently. She folded her sewing and went with him to the door.

"Do come to tea tomorrow, Con, or next day, and let me know what results from your interview at the hospital. It's so lovely for you to have this month free, on account of the leave owing to you. You must be horridly in need of rest after all that time abroad!" She lifted her face obediently for his kiss. "Good-bye, my dear."

Her mind, most of it, was on her party.

McDonagh brushed her cheek with his mouth and went out into a drifting, thin January fog. He was to meet Rob at the Fallow Deer; he fastened up his coat against the beginning damp chill of evening and plodded east across the city.

O'Derrica had said to him, See it plain and honest. He hadn't tried; it had just happened. And now, because of his own willful blind folly in trying to preserve intact a random, immature emotion—which would have been fleeting but for his obstinacy (like pumping a cadaver full of air and dyed liquid wax, to give it the semblance of life)—he was trapped, he was shackled to her. She would never know, and that was possibly the worst part of it, she would never know that anything was lacking between them. A very stupid woman, when it came to emotions.

He got to the Deer before Rob, and started to order a whiskey; and then he thought, a little sardonic, a little grim, that his dreary time in Portsmouth that had sent him on the drink was nothing like the lifetime he would spend with Lauretta, and that if he were to salvage anything out of the wreck of his personal life, he had better begin now. He ordered an ale and sat down at a table to wait for Rob.

That had been the first shock awaiting him in London; that Gillespie was dead. He hadn't realized how fond of the old man he'd been, how he had looked forward to having a place of his own to invite Gillespie and Rob, to the good desultory talk they had enjoyed together.

"I remember he wasn't looking well," he'd said numbly.

"He hadn't been, I don't think, the last six months or so. But the once I suggested it, of course, he absolutely refused to see a doctor or let me look at him." Meredith smiled faintly. " 'Nonsense, Robin, do you think I've been treating patients for forty years and don't know how to treat maself? Feeling my years a bit, that's all that's wrong with me, and verra natural, too.' But it was a good way he went, Con—I suppose it was his heart. He was in the theater, just preparing to do a hernia. It was in a rather awkward spot and looked like being a longish job, so I'd come up to assist. He'd just said to the orderly, 'Verra well, you may strap the patient down,' when he looked a bit surprised, and raised a hand to his chest, and . . . just fell. I'm glad it was that way for him, he'd have fretted and fumed under a long illness."

"Yes—a good way to go. But damn, I'll miss—feeling he's there, somehow."

"Not the same place without him," agreed Meredith. "I didn't write you, then, because I thought you were dead too, you know. I'd seen your name on a casualty list in the *Times*. Biggest shock in my life when you walked into the hospital today." And after a silence, "I've put in for promotion to his place. Feel it's very brash of me, but the appropriation for St. Luke's isn't awfully big, you know, they don't pay as high as other hospitals, and they can't afford a chief surgeon of dignified age and experience to start with. Matter of fact, Gillespie being as good as he was, I think he stuck there so long out of sheer absentmindedness about money—he never gave a damn about money or prestige, you know."

"No. I hope you get it, Rob. But—"

"Oh, you needn't tell me I'm not the old man! I'm to hear definitely on Wednesday. Meet me for dinner, and I'll tell you how it goes."

When Rob came into the Deer tonight, McDonagh knew at once by his expression that he had got the place. Rob lifted a hand to him and made a detour to the bar, came up with two glasses of whiskey. "Celebration. Yes, I've got the appointment."

"Congratulations. But only one," said McDonagh to the whiskey. "You once told me you wouldn't lay a wager the second time round, on the odds against me."

Meredith swallowed whiskey and looked at him. "You starting down the course the second time, Con?"

"No, and I don't mean to." He turned his attention to the waiter and ordered their dinner.

When the man had gone, Meredith said, "Something deviling you, boy? You don't look too uplifted in soul."

"Deviling me?" said McDonagh. "What would be deviling me? Every reason I've got to be—uplifted in soul—haven't I? Engaged to be married—going to settle down permanent to my career—good chance of getting on at the London, I think. Why, I'm merry as a grig, Rob."

And Meredith asked bluntly, "D'you want to get out of it?"

"Oh, *Christ!*" said McDonagh, and set down his glass so violently that it shattered and cut his hand. He got out his handkerchief and wound it around the cut, and noticed that his hands were shaking. The waiter hurried over to clear away the broken glass. "Oh, God," said McDonagh in a lower voice, "if I've got a soul, I'd sell it—to get out of it. . . . What makes a man such a goddamned fool as I've been? Hanging on to a callow, adolescent, so-called romance—as if, God knows, I hadn't stopped believing in all the fairy-tale romance years ago!—keeping myself persuaded into feeling that was never very strong, building it up—oh, damn!" He unwound the handkerchief and licked the cut; it had almost stopped bleeding. "Did you ever, suddenly, get a totally different look at something you'd—been taking for granted? Like—like a hundred candles lit all at once, so you saw everything clear, in one flash? Very damned frightening thing it is. Just never thought about it—only felt—and not that either, because you never do think about things you feel strong, just believing I felt, and never stopping to ask myself, Do I really? Oh, hell and damnation—I was almost better off that time I cried mercy of you five years back—at least I had a chance to pull myself out of that and get free!" He passed a hand across his face. "Now tell me I'm no gentleman, haven't any decent instincts, to blow off about it so frank to you. But then, everybody knows no Irishman is ever quite a gentleman anyway."

Meredith finished his drink and sat staring down into the glass for a moment. "Man's got to blow off at someone once in a while," he said absently. "If you feel like that, Con, you'll have to get out of it, and damn all the conventions."

"And how the hell am I going to do that?"

"Doesn't matter how," said Meredith. "This way or that way, you're bound to come in for recriminations and tears and all sorts of silly accusations. One of those things that just isn't done. But you'd come in for a lot worse things—and I daresay so would she—if you don't cut yourself clear."

"Thanks very much for the helpful advice," said McDonagh morosely. "Oh, how the hell can a man be such a fool?"

"Academic question," said Meredith. "When you're dangling in a noose, not much use to review how you happened to get your neck caught in it."

"And all my own doing, damn it—if I hadn't—if I only had—" He broke off as the waiter came with their plates.

"Oh, for God's sake, don't waste time and energy on that either. Just gird up your loins like a man, and go and get yourself out of it. Knowing you, I won't say I think you'll make a very tactful job of it, but that's really immaterial so long as you get clear. Did you ever stop to think maybe she'd be just as pleased to have an excuse to be out of it too?" Meredith grinned. "Widows proverbially give a bit more thought to economics in a second marriage. You may be a good prospect in certain other ways, but as far as money goes, she may be having second thoughts too."

McDonagh looked up slowly. "I—hadn't thought, no. . . . Let's talk about something else, for God's sake!"

"All right," said Meredith amiably. "We'll talk shop. You think you've a good chance of getting on at London? Well, I can't offer you anything to compete with that. But if you don't, there's a job open for you with me at St. Luke's. I've been carrying on alone, this six months since the old man's been gone, because we haven't found any qualified surgeon who wants the job. Not much pay, but you could take private practice, too, of course. Just keep it in mind, Con, if you need it."

McDonagh said he would. And he knew Rob was right when he said it was senseless to worry over the how of the way you got into bad situations, water under the bridge, but he couldn't help it, his mind kept going over it, ferreting around for the key to the how and why of his being such a damned fool.

They sat leisurely over coffee, not talking much, and then Rob apologized for having to get back. "Like to come along? I can show you a rather interesting concussion."

"No, thanks," said McDonagh. "No, I—feel I've got to—to think this out somehow."

"You do that. Look at it square, Con, and you'll see I'm right." They came out into the moving thin wisps of fog, and Meredith put a hand on McDonagh's shoulder in farewell. "Just look at it plain, and don't be a coward for any damned fool nice conventions. Come down to it, they haven't much reality behind them, you know."

"No," said McDonagh. "I know. Thanks, Rob, good night— I'll drop round one day this week and let you know how things turn out." He turned in the opposite direction and walked slowly down toward Aldergate.

The times he had walked about London at random, that time five years back when he was getting off the drink. Should know his way around any part of it by now, but he wasn't exactly sure where he'd got to, in this thin fog. Senselessly his mind kept shying off any decision, away from any firm coming-to-grips with himself, for worrying around it—how had he been such a fool?

And it didn't matter where he was, but he stopped the next man he met and asked. He was in Lombard Street.

Been in Lombard Street before. A tavern somewhere along here, and a mellow Colonel Devesey singing Irish songs. Ridiculous scene, that fight. McDonagh laughed aloud in the dark street. . . . Lauretta wouldn't see anything funny in that scene at all. A drunken brawl. But then gentlemen were always such violent persons.

Lured in by an old ballad he remembered his father singing, so he'd been. Funny how things happened in life. Led to his signing up for army service—going to Portugal—seeing Fitz-Eustace die—meeting Devlin and O'Derrica.

The staff position at London Hospital would pay ninety pounds to start, but he would—in a way—rather be back at St. Luke's. Queer too, how he'd come to be at St. Luke's in the first place. Come to England with twenty-two pounds on him, make a better opportunity for himself, nine years ago—

Suddenly he stopped in the middle of the pavement. He thought, So that was why. Oh, yes. Saw it now—just now—clear and plain. That was why he'd been such a damned fool.

He had fallen a little in love with her, romantic, romanticizing it to himself, because he was twenty. And Amison had very sensibly rejected his suit for her. Amison didn't want his daughter to wed an impecunious Irish surgeon just qualified. No, McDonagh had known bitterly, he'd have a respectable English name for his daughter, more of a gentleman. Amison hadn't said that—*a respectable English gentleman preferred*—but that was what he had meant, and McDonagh had known it. So all these years he had cherished emotion, thinking it was one thing when it was something utterly different. The black resentment that he had been discriminated against because of his name and nationality. So Amison (convention, society) had balked him of a thing he wanted on that account?—by God, he would never forget an insult like that, and when it came about that, after all, he could take what he wanted, it was that he sought vindication for—not for love, not anything near romantic love!

He had resented losing Lauretta—Lauretta he had wanted, vague and romantic, for a little while—because of why he had lost her. It was not love for Lauretta he had been nourishing like a secret in his heart all these years, but his dark pride of nationalism that had made a small incident take on gigantic proportions in his mind. *A raven sitting on his shoulder.* A raven off Enniscorthy field, where he had lost—where he had lost—

She had never been a woman to him, but a symbol—the symbol of a very different kind of love. Because, somehow, if in the end he could achieve Lauretta—who had been denied to him (or he thought she had) because he was an Irishman—it would not be a victory so much for Con McDonagh, as for his country and people. A vindication, if a small and unworthy one, a vindication for the patriots who had died in 'ninety-eight.

That was the truth, seen hard and clear and plain. Muddled and human as it was. *The Saxon lion's paw.* Reaching out, cat with mouse, to play lazy and cruel with the lives of a whole nation . . . A tall spare man with cold eyes ogling a Portugese servant girl, and—the last insult—the arrogance quite unconscious, arrogance unaware that it was arrogance.

Oh, no, see it clear and admit it firm, he had lost nothing at all at Enniscorthy, no, by God.

McDonagh leaned on the house wall there, feeling curiously weak, but something, some warm moving thing, stirred deep in him from a stillness of fourteen years, and it was a thing he had not been whole without. A thing no man could lack and be whole.

And the troubles are linked. Oh, yes. He had been running away from Enniscorthy for fourteen years, but in the end he had come to the same place, he had run profitless in a circle, and nothing—nothing at all he had lost at Enniscorthy. The blood had run over it and submerged it for a while, but it was still there.

"Be you a' right, mester?"

McDonagh straightened slowly, still leaning on the wall. Vague form peering at him out of the fog, charitable passing stranger. "I'm—all right, thanks, yes. Just stopped—to get my bearings—in the fog."

"Ow, jest thort I'd ask."

McDonagh has said he wants to go home. Let him go then— let him find the right road—with the help of God—and go to his home.

"Nasty, it's getting. Better get 'ome and bide, all on us had, night like this."

"Yes," said McDonagh. "Yes, we had indeed. Thanks—good night."

"Good night, mester."

Not ever Ireland again please-God-amen. The gray country washed over with tragedy and violence. *Little difference to the lone keening in my heart these many long days and nights, that I might again* . . .

Without shame, without guilt, he felt the moving tears on his cheeks. He leaned on the wall, and he said soundlessly against the rough bricks, I want to go home.

Such the hell of a lot to be done, there at home, for the people. Living for a country instead of dying for a country. *The bricks are fallen down, but we will build with hewn stones.*

Oh, after all he owed something to her. In the end she had been the means of telling him the truth. A trouble on him, yes, a dissatisfaction. Working its way to the surface ever since he had been away—that Con McDonagh was not in a place he belonged to be, not doing what he should be doing, not traveling a road in the right direction. Been here and there, and met these people and that, and all the while running away.

The sycamores are cut down, but we will change them into cedars.

And he had not wanted to go to New York, he had not wanted to stay in crown service, and the London Hospital job would be a good one, and he liked Rob Meredith and he could work well and contented enough at St. Luke's, but all those places were other wrong places for Con McDonagh.

For Con McDonagh, who was, at the end and beginning of everything, a man out of the country of Ireland, with an abiding love and concern for his own place and his own people. That was a thing no man could ever run away from, however far or fast or deep or high he might go.

In the end she had showed him the truth. And where did it come in Scripture, somewhere, and it was true, oh, yes—*The truth shall set ye free.*

He stood against the wall, drawing deep breaths of freedom.

He felt taller and broader and easier inside himself than ever before in his life. He thought, Between Dublin and Dunboyne.

He started down Lombard Street, back toward Cheapside. As he went, he walked faster and faster until, when he turned into Cheapside, he was nearly running. Where Paternoster Row opened off, just by St. Paul's, a black shape loomed up at him, and he smelled horse, and a voice called hoarsely, " 'Ack, mester?"

"Yes—" He stumbled over the wet cobbles to it, wrenched the door open. "Take me to the Berwick Hotel in Berwick Street."

"Ryechar, sir."

What a hell of a fool a man could be. Running away from himself. He felt very tired suddenly, and leaned back in the seat and shut his eyes. A right to be tired, he thought dimly. Been running so fast and so long, to get away from a thing inside him all the while. He was finished trying to run away from Con McDonagh; he was on the road home, and that was where he wanted to go. A deep peace enveloped him like a private warm fog, and when the jolting stopped and the door was pulled open it was a moment before he realized it.

"Sixpence, sir."

"Will you wait for me?" He fumbled in his pocket and gave the man a coin. "I won't be long." He went into the tavern and asked the clerk on duty for Dr. Devlin.

"I b'lieve I know that name, sir—oh, yes, we're holdin' two rooms for a Dr. Devlin, he's expected on the fifteenth, tomorrow, sir."

"Yes. Will you give him a message?—no, I won't trouble to leave a note—just tell him that Mr. McDonagh is at the Leicester Arms and wants to see him—very urgently. Thanks." He gave the man a groat and went out to the waiting hack.

In the little bedchamber upstairs at the inn, he flung up the window and stood by it staring unseeingly out to a black moonless night. The swirls of fog and icy night air came in around him, and he never felt it, his mind at once numb and yet concentrated despairingly on more blinding revelation. For there was something more to the stupid, stupid business of Lauretta, and indeed how stupid could a man be? For, set free from bondage to that monstrous irrationality, his whole being was flooded with another sword-sharp simple truth. And in fury, in frustration, in abject self-contempt, he thought—Justin's word for it as good as any—it had been the last raven off Enniscorthy field.

25

"Oh," said Lauretta, and her mouth dropped a little open in surprise. "Well, really, this must be a very sudden decision, Con, isn't it? What of the position at the London Hospital?"

"No, I don't know that it is. I haven't gone to see about that job, I won't bother."

"Well, I must say it seems sudden to me! You are rather given to sudden enthusiasms, you know. And to come in and announce it so abruptly—"

"Damn it, I've been trying to get in to talk to you all day! If you've taken offense, I'm sorry, Lauretta, but ever since eleven o'clock I've been trying to see you, and your damned maid saying you weren't to be seen—and it's now nearly six! Not as if I was any casual caller, or is it?"

"Oh, I am sorry, Con," she said contritely. "But my party was quite late, and I had rather a headache this morning, so I did not get up until afternoon, and then the seamstress came for a fitting. I promise you the girl never said who it was, she is rather stupid, you know. I had thought you might come to tea, as I asked, but when she never brought up your name—If I had known, I should certainly have come to you! But my dear, you mustn't take offense for so little a thing! You burst in here like a—like a ravening wolf and by way of greeting announce to me that you are going back to Ireland to live, and I am expected to—"

McDonagh stood over her chair; she tilted her head back to look up at him. "You don't care for the idea, do you?" he asked. Such a foolish, little, soft mouth she had.

"I—well, my dear, I should certainly prefer to live in England. But if it's necessary—"

"Necessary," he repeated. "Yes. I'm an Irishman, any reason I shouldn't want to live in my own country?"

"Oh, no, Con, of course not. You are strange today, is anything troubling you?"

He laughed and turned away. Strange. He felt rather strange. Seeing everything right way up for the first time. But—but— "Lauretta, for God's sake, be honest with me, will you? Please, just be honest and tell me what you really feel!"

"I've just told you," she returned gently. "If you feel—this is what you want to do, then, well, I've promised to be your wife, and—"

"And you must put up with it!" He had been walking the room; he came back to her, bent over her chair urgently. "Lauretta—oh, God help me, how can I say it?—I don't want to hurt you, Lauretta—" He felt the sweat break on his forehead. "Please, if you never forgot convention in your life, forget it now and be honest with me! Do you want to marry me, Lauretta?"

She shrank back a little from him, so close there. "Why, I don't understand you. I've promised—"

"No, for the love of God, I don't want to hear all the orthodox phrases, damn it! Do you, really, in yourself, Lauretta? Do you want to go to bed with me and share passion—and live together all your life with me—and maybe—"

"Really, you needn't be so crude—we are not—"

"Married yet. No. Do you?"

"Please, don't stand so close," she said faintly. "You look as if you were about to hit me—"

McDonagh turned and walked across the room. He found that he was trembling slightly. "Please answer me, Lauretta."

383

She got up from the chair suddenly and stood behind it, holding its upholstered back tightly as if for support. "I—I—oh, Con, I'm s-sorry, but I *don't!* I'll try to be honest about it—if you will have it, I n-never did! I can't get used—you're so big and always saying things I—and doing odd things—and so—and so—v-violent. I think, well, all that time ago, it was just a silly little romance—wasn't it?—the sort most people have before—anything real. And then you came—last year, and you simply browbeat me into it, Con, you know you did—I c-can't help it, I'm always just a bit frightened of—you kept saying things like making love, but you looked so angry! And you held me so hard you bruised my arms—and I couldn't get away any way but to say yes! And then—and then—I'd promised, and I meant to, Con—I meant to try, but if you will have it—"

"Don't cry," he whispered. "Don't cry, Lauretta. It's all right, my dear. You were frightened of me—don't be, please."

"Oh, I know you don't m-mean it," she sobbed, "it's just how you are, but I don't want to, Con. I—I don't think I want to marry anybody—"

"I don't think you do either, my dear," he said. He felt a kind of hollow weakness inside, a kind of curiously humble gratefulness to her. "You don't have to. It's all right, Lauretta." He went over to her and kissed her cheek gently. "Thank you—so much, for being honest—once, anyway." She didn't know what he meant.

She didn't know, she would never know, what she had done for him. He left her there with her face still wet with tears, her mouth a little open foolishly, and he went out into the dusk that was almost deepened to night. And oh, God, all this time wasted, he had to hurry—

He picked up a hack at the mouth of the square, by the grace of God. "As fast as your nag will go—nineteen Woolhampton Street, out toward Kensington way—lay it on!"

From the first minute he saw her, he thought agonizingly. And didn't know what it was. Finding all sorts of other names for it, excuses—because of a damned aberration about another female, and because she was the other side of that line. That line of orthodox thinking, neatly dividing the sex into two portions.

She'd walked into Fleur's parlor and instantly he'd got into a turmoil about her. Called it pity, anger, comic impulse to reform her. Just a tall, thin girl looking at him with gray eyes, and something in her that was like something in himself. He had known then, some part of him knowing, and not able to admit it to himself. Being a damned fool, such a goddamned fool as he had been.

So angry with her. He could have killed her, that time, hearing the talk about Dunstan. It had flared up between them like wildfire, lightning striking dry bracken—instant they saw each other that time. Strangers did not lash out at each other like that. Fleur saw—Fleur guessed. He could have taken Madeleine's slim white throat in his hands and— Because she belonged to Conal McDonagh, and she meant to give herself to another man.

She knew, too, please, God, she knew it, too, but obstinate, damned, wrongheaded little fool—

And Christ, he could have killed Dunstan that night—the red storm of fury on him. Such a Christ-damned fool, call it another name because of a convention. Him, McDonagh, accepting a convention as a piece of truth!

Every time he saw her, all that turmoil of desire and fury in him, and still he was blind to the truth! Even after he'd cheated Dustan, after he had known her passion . . .

That I might lie again with my darling, the pulse of my heart.

He put his head out the window and called desperately, "Can't you make a better pace? I said lay it on!"

"I ain't off to kill me horse, mester."

Every time he had seen her, except the last time. She had said—she had— And he had come away at peace with Madeleine—the first time since that night nearly seven years before when she had walked into Fleur's parlor. Because for the first time (oh, look at the truth clear!) he didn't have to think of Madeleine with another man; he knew she lay alone, and he was at peace.

Awhile ago he had been thinking Lauretta stupid about emotions. God, God . . . He shut his eyes and clenched his fists against the intolerable slow pace across London.

"Eleven pence, mester." The door jerked open.

McDonagh half fell out over the high iron step, flung the man a shilling and ran up the walk to the house. He hammered the knocker on the door and went on banging it until the latch was turned and the plump dignified butler opened to him. McDonagh pushed past him into the entrance hall. "I want Miss Olivier—go and fetch her at once! Where is she?"

The butler, and he even remembered the man's name, Rowland, remembered everything so sharp and hurtful about that day, the butler gaped at him. "Here, sir, you can't come pushing into a gentleman's house like that there—"

"Miss Olivier—go and fetch her down, hear me? I must see her at once—damn you, go and tell her—"

"Well, that I can't do," said the butler angrily, "on account Miss Olivier, she's not hemployed here any longer, and I'll ask you to leave, if you please—"

"*Where's she gone? Where—*"

"That I could not say, but doubtless the master knows, having provided a reference, naturally, and hif so be has you'd call hat a proper hour, sir, and hask him in a gentlemanlike way, he would give you the hinformation. But—"

"Where is he? Is he in? I must find out—"

"I could not take it upon myself to disturb the master at his dinner, sir," said the butler, shocked. McDonagh shouldered him aside and went hunting for the dining room, with the butler in agitated pursuit. He found it beyond the third door he tried: small, stuffy room hung with green plush, loaded table, loud Turkey carpet, red-faced man in tight knee breeches and fancy waistcoat, staring over a lifted fork.

"*Sir*, I beg parding, but he just pushed past me—I'll call the watch, sir—not my fault, do hassure you—"

"I beg your pardon, too, Mr.—Mr."—damn it—"Mr. Truepenny, isn't it? I'm very sorry to disturb you at such an unconventional hour, but it's very urgent that I find Miss Madeleine Olivier, whom you recently employed—I understand she has left. Please, can you tell me where she went, sir?"

Slowly the loaded fork descended. "Gobbless me soul," said Mr. Truepenny.

"If you'd just tell me the address, sir—"

"Left last February," said Mr. Truepenny. "Daresay a very satisfactory governess—don't trouble about domestic details meself—but m' wife had no complaints. Boys old enough for regular school, y'see."

"Yes—where did she go, did you write her a reference—did anyone ask about it? Where—"

"*Sir*, I do think has I'd best call the watch—barging in here at such a time without a by-your-leave—"

"Man says it's urgent, Rowland. No matter. Thinking," said Mr. Truepenny, nodding at McDonagh. "Have it in a minute. Ah. The Bryson Kents. South Audley Street. Knew it was a feller I know. Number seven."

"Thanks very much, sir!" McDonagh ran for the door.

He had let the hack go, damn, damn—he ran up Woolhampton Street, looking frantically for another. He didn't find one for nearly a quarter mile, and shouted the address at the man and tumbled into it breathless. A year, fourteen months—he had to hurry. All this time wasted because he was a fool . . .

Every time since that first minute he had laid eyes on her, every time he saw her or thought about her, turmoil inside him. Any man but the fool of the world would have known.

Should have taken firm hold of her that first time and said, You belong to McDonagh. Any time after, should have kept hold of her, never let her go. That night, that night. Not only a fool, a stupid lout. Not understanding either of them . . .

Last year—in that house back there. McDonagh put a hand to his face as if just now he felt her hard blow, heard again her anguished, angry voice. Oh, God, she knew, too; not such a fool, she knew before. The others had never reached her, in herself, because she belonged to Conal McDonagh and no one else. But had he lost her, for his crass, stupid, willful blindness—after all? Could he ever say, make her believe—

The hack jolted to a stop, and he got out. Quiet street with the few oil-lamp standards trying vainly to pierce the fog. He paid the driver and told him to wait and went up the steps and banged on the door. Madeleine, Madeleine.

Unhurriedly, after a while, the door opened. This butler was tall and thin. "Good evening, sir—" He gasped indignantly as McDonagh shouldered in.

"I want Miss Olivier, I believe she's employed here. I want to see her at once, please."

The butler recovered himself. "I'm afraid I must ask you to leave, sir," he said with awful dignity. "There's no followers allowed, as is the usual rule. The master and mistress is both hout, and I could not take the responsibility—"

"Oh, no," said McDonagh. "Don't try to put me off, man, I warn you, I warn you. Is she here?" The man took slow breath for some new pompous utterance, and McDonagh suddenly seized hold of him and shook him hard. "*Is she here?* Tell me, you thickheaded bastard!"

"James," quavered the butler, wrenching free and retreating back into the hall. "James! Run for the watch—this chap's broke in—" A young weedy footman, must be a wealthy household to keep one of those, appeared from the nearest door and stared.

"Oh, for God's sake!" said McDonagh. He threw off the butler's feebly plucking hand and plunged past him up the wide stair. He met a middle-aged maidservant at the landing and nearly upset her; she let out a frightened squeal. He heard the two men come pounding after him, and two more maids peered out of a door halfway down the corridor. "Madeleine!" he shouted. "Madeleine, come here to me!"

The footman pulled him around by one arm, announcing absurdly, "Have to hask yer to leave, sir—nobody in, there ain't— you go peaceable, now, and we won't call the watch—"

McDonagh hit him very satisfactorily hard under the jaw, and he fell against the banister and rolled a few steps down the stair. "Madeleine!" Governess wouldn't be on this floor—top floor among the servants—He took the second flight three treads at a time and came out on a bare-floored top landing, narrower corridor, doors about—"Madeleine!"

The second door down the corridor opened slowly, and she stood there, leaning on it. All these damned people crowding up the stair after him, butler squeaking agitatedly, maids flocking behind, *Killed James 'e 'as—well, 'e looked dead! —Aggie's run out for the watch—Ooh, whatever'll master say!*—She just stood there, sagging against the door, looking at him, her eyes wide and darkening and hazed on him, looking blind. Another drab dark gown, oughtn't to wear such clothes. She looked at him, and her lips moved, but soundless. Madeleine, Madeleine, Madeleine.

"Well, for the love of God!" he said. "You never did have much figure, but what've you been doing to yourself?—you're thin as a rail! Don't they feed you here, for God's sake?"

Her lips moved again to form his name. All these damned people. Couldn't touch her. "Madeleine," he said, sharp and rough, "you hear me? You're going to marry me tomorrow, and damn the six pounds for a special license! Understand? You go in there now and pack up all your gear, you're coming with me now, understand?"

She put out a wavering hand toward him. "You're—dead," she said, very low. "You're dead—I saw your name—on that list. Conal—Conal—have you come for me?"

"I just said so, damn it! Hurry, for God's sake, I don't want to hang about here half the night waiting!" Oh, God, all the time before he had her to himself, all these prying eyes, my darling, my darling, thou pulse of my heart. Pound of feet on the stairs behind.

"Nah then, what's agoin' on 'ere?" He didn't turn to look, knew it was the usual watchman, old, shaky, fit only to carry a lantern and call the hours.

Her eyes were enormous and drowned-looking on him. "Did they let you come for me, Conal? Because I wanted you so? But I don't remember dying—"

"You're not dead and neither am I, damn it!" he said. He took one step toward her. "You obstinate little fool—you knew too, from the first minute—something in both of us knew—but you were stubborn and I was the biggest goddamned fool on the face of the earth for it. Even we are, for both making damned senseless mistakes, but doesn't mean we can't start over, Madeleine. That's what we're going to do—and never ever hurt each other again, my darling heart. If you can forgive—my being such a fool, Madeleine—"

She said suddenly in her old full husky voice, "I forgave you for everything—when I saw your name there, that you were dead. Conal—Conal? Do you know about it now? Want me—like that—for always? Not for sale?"

He said, "You were never bought and sold because you were never on the market—you belonged to me from the first time we laid eyes on each other. But I will be goddamned if I try to make love to you with a crowd of damned English servants gawking at us. Didn't you hear me? Go and pack up your gear, everything you've got here, you're not going out of my sight until I've got you tied to me by law, you understand? You're going to marry me tomorrow. And to hell with whatever they owe you here or the brats you're in charge of. I'll give you fifteen minutes to pack. And if you've any other damned dowdy gowns like that one, you can leave 'em here, I won't have you seen in such clothes. Now make it quick!"

"Marry you tomorrow," she said, her eyes fascinated on him. And then she started to laugh, and the laugh turned into a little sob. "Yes, Conal. Ordering me about—swearing at me and never meaning anything by it at all, don't I know you—and I'll never get over—being a damned fool for you—"

"Both of us," he said. "Both of us. For the love of Christ go and pack up your belongings!"

"Yes," said Madeleine. She turned and went back into the room. He leaned on the doorpost with his hands clenched in his pockets and watched her moving about, putting things in bandboxes. The servants whispered and squeaked excitedly behind him, and the watchman said aggrievedly that he didn't understand any of what was going on here.

"Miss," protested the butler feebly as she came out to the hall, "you can't just go—Miss, what'll the master say—you'll lose all your wages, just awalking out when they're away—"

She went by him as if she had not heard. McDonagh picked up the three bandboxes and followed.

"Miss, you can't—you really can't just go off—"

"Get to hell out of the way!" said McDonagh. She went down the stair ahead of him, past the first landing, where the footman was shakily sitting up fingering his jaw, her back slim and stiff as always. The hackman was stamping his feet and blowing on his hands against the cold, and a few snowflakes were beginning to drift down lazily. He opened the door, took the boxes from McDonagh to stow inside, and helped her into the hack. "The Leicester Arms," said McDonagh, and then he could follow her, and shut the door on them, and begin to try to tell her, all the ways there were that he knew, all that was in him for his heart's desire.

McDonagh walked into the private dining chamber of the Leicester Arms and glanced about. He saw Justin Devlin sitting at a table by the hearth and went over to him. "See you got my message."

Devlin started at the hand on his shoulder. "Might warn a man, you've made me spill my drink. Yes, I just asked for you, they said you were out. Frankly, the *urgent* sounded as if you wanted to make a touch. Don't tell me your past has caught up with you and somebody's blackmailing you at last."

McDonagh laughed. "Boy, we're neither of us going to be in a situation to lend anybody any money—both being damned fool idealistic patriots! I'm coming home with you to Ireland, Justin—I'm coming in on your harebrained schemes. And if you've found another surgeon to throw in, you can just damn well get rid of him, because it's my job."

Devlin reached out and gripped his arm. "I don't have to say how glad I am to hear that, man. You know it."

"Ask you a little favor right now. Come out this afternoon and witness my wedding. I've just got rid of all my spare cash on a special license and a new gown for the bride, on account I refused to marry her in any she had."

"Why"—Devlin looked a little puzzled, smiling—"I'll be happy to do that, Con. Sudden impatience?"

"Yes—and no," said McDonagh, smiling back. "I'll tell you about some of it later." He looked across to the door and saw Madeleine come in, tall and elegant and lovely in the new blue gown, and he straightened and started across the room to her. She did not see him for a moment in the little crowd, and he could look at her unawares. And as he threaded his way among the tables toward her, he thought vaguely, strangely, that he was safe, after all the tempests and turbulence. He had found his way home, and he was forever safe. Whatever new ventures carried him again into storm and stress, they were both forever safe, together.

Then she turned her head and saw him, and smiled, and came forward to meet him.